"The most moving, monumental love story ever written about gay life . . . This book makes *Catcher in the Rye, Lord of the Flies* and *A Separate Peace* look like *Mary Poppins* . . . How a woman was able to capture so beautifully, tenderly and accurately the mature adult gay psyche is also overwhelming . . . The most emotionally charged and romantic novel I've read in years should be on your bestseller list."   —*The New York Times*

"This is, literally, a homosexual love story in which the emotions, aspirations and way of life of the gay people are recounted with poignancy and conviction . . . The story is played out against the background of long-distance running and training for the Olympics."   — *Publisher's Weekly*

"[We] correctly predicted that 'this could be the first significantly popular gay love story'—it has sold ten million copies."   — *Library Journal*

"Amazing that a woman could have gotten so deeply, so strongly, so movingly into the gay male psyche."
                    — *In Touch Magazine*

"*The Front Runner* first made gay history by cracking *The New York Times* bestseller list."   — *The Advocate*

"Patricia Nell Warren was one of the first authors writing fiction with openly gay and lesbian characters for a mainstream publisher in the days just following Stonewall, when most queer fiction was published independently."
                    — *Lambda Book Report*

"The author is a keen observer of the gay community. She tells it like it is."
—*Post Intelligencer*, Alexander Hamilton Veterans Services

"A barn-burner from the moment coach Harlan Brown locks on to runner Billy Sive's 'extraordinary blue-gray eyes'."   — *New York Newsday*

"One of the most moving and involving love stories ever written. There is little question that it will be read and discussed and taken to heart all over the world . . . Warren has written a novel of love and of sports that captures in true and telling detail the struggles and the pain and the triumphs and the losses that are inevitable in each. Her book cannot fail but to involve all readers in its magnificent, compelling story."   — William Morrow & Co.

"This book must be read and reread by everyone who considers himself or herself to be aware . . . an enlightening experience in learning the meaning that love is good."
                              — *Mattachine Times*

"The atmosphere of track meets and Olympic competition has been faithfully captured, and the shocking jolts at the end will knock some readers off balance. Don't deny yourself the joy of one of the finest novels published in the last ten years."   — *Vector*

"The most popular gay-themed novel of the '70s . . . this book captured the hearts of a generation of gay people (of both genders) just beginning to be comfortable with their sexual identities in the heady aftermath of the Stonewall Riots."   — *Gay & Lesbian Times*

"This is the author who wrote what is thought by some to be the most important piece of literature of the Post-Stonewall Era, *The Front Runner*."   — *Update*

"A trail-blazing novel about gays in professional athletics."
                              — *B'nai B'rith*

"It's been 20 years since Patricia Nell Warren busted the chops of macho American athletes with her novel, *The Front Runner*. Warren's tale of love between an Olympic runner, Billy Sive, and his coach, Harlan Brown, opened the closet door for queer athletes." — *Bay Area Reporter*

Chapter 18 of *The Front Runner* was selected as one of the great sports stories of all time by Brandt Aymar in his 1994 anthology, *Men in Sports* (Crown Publishers).

The
Front Runner

PATRICIA NELL WARREN

Wildcat Press
Beverly Hills

Copyright © 1974 by Patricia Nell Warren

Jacket design:
Barbara Brown, Jay Fraley, Tyler St. Mark and Patricia Nell Warren

Jacket art, photographs and half-tone illustrations:
Jay Fraley

Book design:
Barbara Brown Desktop Publishing and Patricia Nell Warren

Typesetting:
Barbara Brown Desktop Publishing

First printing: June 1996

10 9 8

PRINTED IN THE UNITED STATES OF AMERICA

Library of Congress Catalog Card Number 95-60336

ISBN: 0-9641099-6-4

Dedicated to all the athletes who
have fought for human rights in sports,
and to the young gay runner I met at a party,
who gave me the idea for this book.

P.N.W.

PRINT HISTORY OF *THE FRONT RUNNER*

1974 William Morrow & Co. (U.S. hardcover edition)

1975 Bantam Books, Inc. (U.S. mass-market paperback edition)

1975 Bantam Books, Inc. (UK paperback edition)

1975 Revolt (Swedish first serial)

1975 Esprit (Canadian second serial)

1976 Rippun Shobo (first Japanese edition)

1979 Tiebosch (Dutch edition)

1981 Presses de la Renaissance (French edition)

1985 Rhodos (Danish edition)

1987 Droemer Knaur (German edition)

1987 Plume/Penguin USA (trade paperback edition)

1990 Daisan Shokan (second Japanese edition)

1990 Gay Men's Press (UK paperback edition)

1995 Wildcat Press (20th anniversary edition hardcover)

1996 Wildcat Press (20th anniversary trade paperback edition)

1999 Atēnas Klubs (Latvian edition)

1999 Imaju-club (Japanese serial)

2001 Book of the Month Club & Triangle Classics

2001 Editorial Egales (Spanish edition)

2001 Bruno Gmünder Verlag (second German edition)

OTHER NOVELS BY PATRICIA NELL WARREN

HARLAN'S RACE (Wildcat Press, 1994)

ONE IS THE SUN (Ballantine, 1991)

THE BEAUTY QUEEN (William Morrow, 1978)

THE FANCY DANCER (William Morrow, 1976)

THE LAST CENTENNIAL (Dial Press, 1971)

POETRY BY PATRICIA NELL WARREN

HORSE WITH A GREEN VINYL MANE (Novi Poezii, 1970)

ROSE-HUED CITIES (Novi Poezii, 1966)

LEGENDS AND DREAMS (Novi Poezii, 1962)

A TRAGEDY OF BEES (Novi Poezii, 1959)

ABOUT THE AUTHOR

Patricia Nell Warren was born in 1936. She grew up on a Montana cattle ranch, and worked as a Reader's Digest editor for 22 years. Three of her novels were bestsellers. She has won numerous awards, including the 1978 Walt Whitman Award for Gay Literature and a 1982 Western Heritage Award from the National Cowboy Hall of Fame. She lives in California today.

An Introduction

Patricia Nell Warren, who now celebrates twenty million readers, may need no introduction. But for those who have come upon the gay community long after her landmark novel was first published, a footnote or two might be helpful . . .

Twenty years ago, when I read *The Front Runner* at the age of 20, I had no reason to believe that one day the author and I would partner in a publishing enterprise. That she would awaken my personal awareness of Mother Earth and arouse my outrage at the mistreatment of women in our society and also within our gay community. That she would become my guide and mentor into the arduous and challenging adventure that is the literary world.

Twenty years ago, like Harlan Brown, I was a conservative, homophobic coach with a deep secret. And just like countless other young gay men groping in the dark for the pull cord which might bring light into the closet, I read her novel about true love between a gay track coach and his Olympic-bound runner with awed fascination. And I wept. Not for the tragedy which befell these gay literary icons, but for the ideals and principles they represented. Ideals which to this day are denied to gay men and women by our society—and by ourselves.

Twenty years ago, *The Front Runner* became an internationally acclaimed bestseller, received the highest critical praise, and won a prestigious gay literary award. It also captured the hearts of grateful gay men and women across the world.

Recently, I spent an entire weekend reading hundreds of letters she had received over the years from her readers, notes of love and appreciation for her courage to write what had not then been revealed about the gay condition. She wrote that we are worthy. We are loving. We are proud. Scrupulously filed by month and year, noted with the date of her reply — every letter had been kept.

When I accompany PNW on her rare book tours, I hear many equally heartfelt testimonials from her readers. "I know you've heard this story a thousand times," they often say to her in tears, "but your book changed my life."

"I have not heard *your* story," PNW will answer earnestly. "Please tell me."

Each experience is uniquely individual and deeply personal, but the common thread throughout her intricate tapestry of readers is spun from fear and prejudice. The fabric is woven out of torment and loneliness. Yet through the illumination of her books, the outcome is always a design of distinct beauty and lasting endurance.

Twenty years later, *The Front Runner* has been reprinted in numerous editions, sold an estimated ten million copies, and been translated into seven languages. It has the dubious distinction of being perhaps the most famous unmade film of all time. A stage production is now in preparation.

Twenty years later, this early miler into the mainstream consciousness continues to be one of the top selling gay novels, and is thought by many to be the most celebrated novel about gay love ever written.

Twenty years later, some of these earliest readers have gone on to become gay and lesbian heroes in their own right. We encounter them in our promotional travels. It still stirs me intensely to see a pillar of the gay community, a prominent literary colleague, or a well-known activist, part of the crowd, grasp the hand of PNW, and proclaim in that familiar, fervent tone, "Your book changed my life."

Twenty years later, *The Front Runner* is more than just a landmark novel and a milestone in the long and winding road of progress for gay men and women. It has become a symbol of our individual and collective ability to uplift our community, and to conquer our ignorant and evil adversaries.

Twenty years later, there are new enemies to replace those we have defeated. Fresh detractors who are determined to force us back into the closet of oppression.

But there is also *The Front Runner* and a new generation of readers who find the same strength and courage in its classic story that I and so many others have done.

Patricia Nell Warren has written the most inspiring gay love story of all time. She also has brought light into the lives of millions of gays and lesbians who were made to believe that they were unworthy to love themselves or each other. She has helped us believe we could pass our opponents in the race of intolerance and embrace them heartily at the finish line. That each of us can be a front-runner in our struggle for social equality, and a winner in the great human Olympics.

Congratulations my dear friend and, on behalf of the millions of your readers all over the world, thank you for your remarkable literary works and, in particular, for this timeless book. With the 20th Anniversary of *The Front Runner*, the torch of acceptance and understanding is passed from our brothers and sisters who have fallen to those who will carry it into the new century, and hopefully, into a more enlightened world.

— Tyler St. Mark
Wildcat Press

Author's Foreword

By the spring of 1994, my friend Gene had been fighting active symptoms of AIDS since he was 30. He was 38 now, and suddenly he just got tired of being sick.

We "did lunch" for the last time, driving out in his battered sky-blue Cadillac convertible, and sitting for hours in his favorite Sunset Boulevard café. From there we progressed to sitting on his hospital bed, with me massaging his feet or helping him keep the drip-lines untangled. Finally he was home again, wanting to die there, drawing friends around him for the last afternoons of laughter and talk. His bedroom was almost bare, possessions given away — nothing left but sunshine, and music from his tape-deck, and his spirit, ever more powerful as his body waned.

He was thinking deeply about his life, weighing it as we see it weighed in ancient Egyptian tomb art — the human heart resting in those awesome scales held by the Goddess Ma-at, balanced against Her single feather, symbol of the laws of Life.

Gene had a last few things to say about reading my novel *The Front Runner*.

He'd already told me he was 17 years old when he first read it, and saw his own nature mirrored in my story of two men who struggled to find the highest nobility in their love for each other. Halfway through the book, the night came when Gene acted on his new vision for the first time. When it was over, he felt that he'd been treated offhandedly. A disillusioned teenager cried half the night, alone in a motel room. Between bouts of tears, Gene finished reading the book. When morning came, he pulled himself together, and walked out of the motel determined to fight for his vision.

As I listened to this friend, I found myself looking deep into a karma with my readers.

In our electronic age, when ink printing is supposedly obsolete, a simple novel can still have a tremendous impact.

In the 20 years that the book has been in print, millions of people speaking 7 different languages have now read *The Front Runner*. Gay men and lesbians tell me in person, or in letters, of how the novel helped them to accept their gay nature.

Gene had become an internationally celebrated model—an athletic six-footer who was so handsome that he caused roomfuls of men to go hushed with awe when he walked in. But Gene was no fluffhead clone. He was a queer theorist, and a writer with a file box of poems and essays still unpublished.

Now, in his gaunt face, his deep-sunk eyes, with their long eyelashes, were still mysteriously beautiful. He was the poster boy for Death. He was also my karmic son, come home to tell me of his long journey and die in my arms. But in no way was he self-pitying. Those final sunny afternoons were spent sharing the last of his thoughts. He gave me his unpublished writings, and asked to be remembered in my work, especially to the young.

I began to see how his life touched into my own personal weighing-in with the Goddess Ma-at—my responsibility towards him, towards all humans, towards the planet where I live.

It is one of the scariest questions — this question of how we all affect one another. Sometimes we do this in unforeseen ways. A hiker lights a fire to keep warm, and the flames blow into a brushfire that destroys half a township and half a hundred homes. But often our actions are more deliberate. A fundamentalist preacher makes a fiery sermon, and two or three falling dominoes down the line, he knows that a gay boy or a lesbian girl will be bashed in a school hallway.

There is a delicate line between responsibility and guilt, and our culture lives on the guilt side of the line. The social life of our nation is often described by observers as a vast, trembling spider-web of intersecting guilts. "The devil made me do it," is the way some people express their guilt. Other people phrase it as, "It's all my parents' fault." Or, "Why doesn't the government do more?"

Still others consider that a simple self-chosen destiny is more dignified than being programmed by the devil. They prefer to be directly responsible for their lives. I'm one of those latter . . . I'd rather be responsible, not guilty, for what's in my world.

Responsibility holds a springtime power of change and healing, while guilt is a frozen graveyard—what's done is done. My decision to wear a cotton shirt could make me feel intense guilt, because of how cotton is farmed by agribusiness, complete with workers getting sick in fields drenched with pesticides. In the 1990s, there is virtually nothing I could wear that is non-polluting, except possibly a grass skirt. Yet paradoxically, while wearing that cotton shirt, I can make myself responsible. I can fight for a cleaner Earth. Somehow, in those scales held high by Ma-at, my fight will find a balance with Her feather.

A writer's decision to publish a book about gay life weaves a vast, living web of responsibilities through all that writer's readership. Readers tell me that they met lovers, lost lovers, found and lost careers, lost and found families, because of me. Neither I, nor any other gay writer of the '70s, could know that so many people were about to experience mass death from a disease that came to be known as AIDS in English, *la SIDA* in Spanish, "slim" in Nigeria. But we had to know that our readers might leap into other experiences of an equally intense and extreme kind. After all, gay men and women had already experienced extremes like prison, forced institutionalizing, shock treatment, loss of child custody, social ostracism, attempted suicide, alcoholism, broken hearts.

The question is a delicate one. Caught between those concepts of the devil and destiny, our culture agonizes helplessly. Does the producer of a violent film "make" people murder one another? Does the writer of gay fiction or liberal straight fiction "make" people get AIDS? As

American lawmakers wrestle with these questions—some of them wanting to ban violent films, others wanting to put HIV-positives in jail—we writers go on writing books, as we have for centuries. A book can move a person to sink as low as humans can sink. The very same book can inspire the highest kind of destiny.

So it's one of the laws of Life, that people's lives are touched and changed by books, by paintings, by music and film. I know this is true, because of the writings that affected me profoundly when I was a teenager in the 1950s. Did those books turn an innocent cowgirl into a dyke? No. What they did was help me recognize my own nature . . . help me find my own North Star in the night sky of destiny. The point is—nobody piloted my ship but me.

In short, we creative people have an enormous reach, and a enormous responsibility, for the symbols that we cast in print and paint and CDI and videotape.

A few months after Gene's death, the day came when his sister felt it was time to scatter his ashes.

Late in the afternoon, high above the ocean, there was a last glow of day on the ridge where I stood, with songbirds singing in the sun-warmed chaparral. I lifted the first handful of ashes into the air. It felt clean to my fingers, like desert gravel and dust. A few bone fragments rained down the slope, into patches of blooming sage. But a creamy dust still hung in the air. The body of a six-foot man was now light as Ma-at's feather.

Even now, from wherever his spirit moved among the stars, or from what might be his newest life on Earth — a helpless babe growing into new challenges, perhaps to finish the book that he left undone, a book that might be a life raft for me next time around — this dear friend managed a last kiss, as his dust drifted to touch my cheek.

— Patricia Nell Warren
February, 1995

The
Front Runner

ONE

I can be precise about the day it began. It was December 10, 1974. That was the day I met Billy Sive, and he asked me to coach him.

The night before, a heavy snowfall had blanketed New York State. Around eight that morning, I ate breakfast as usual in the college dining room. Then, whistling cheerfully, I walked over to the athletic building. The sun had already come out, and the white landscape of the campus was blinding. I stepped past the students shoveling snow.

"Hi," I said to them. I smiled. I had no idea how my life was about to change.

"Hi, Mr. Brown," they said. They smiled back.

When I got to my office, I found the president and founder of Prescott College, Joseph A. Prescott, waiting for me by the locked door. He was wearing a sheepskin jacket, carrying his usual briefcase fat with papers, plus two steaming cups, one coffee, one tea.

When Joe comes around early in the morning like that, I always know something is up.

"Here's something to thaw you out," he said, giving me the tea.

We went into the office. Joe hauled off his sheepskin and settled his lanky brown-suited frame into the battered oak armchair by my desk. I settled my lanky parka-ed form into the creaky swivel desk-chair. On the desk, everything was neat, but very piled: students' papers, entry

1

blanks for meets, track and field publications. On the raw concrete wall, the big bulletin board displayed schedules. Some framed photographs: myself in Marine dress uniform twenty years ago, myself as a Villanova miler, other runners I'd trained. A big bookshelf was stuffed with books on sports.

"What's up, Joe?" I said, sipping my tea.

Joe lit a cigarette, boldly facing down my frown. "Harlan," he said, "you know those three boys that were suspended from Oregon?"

I nodded. The track press had been full of it. Boys often get suspended from school teams these days. The youth revolution has hit track, and disciplinarian coaches have endless squabbles with their runners about late hours, hair styles, sex, drugs, etc. I had had a few of those squabbles myself. But the University of Oregon, the Jerusalem of U.S. track, had just unloaded three of its best senior-year runners. That was something else again. "Disciplinary reasons," head coach Gus Lindquist had said. But he hadn't been specific. Everybody had been mystified by the biblical heat of Lindquist's wrath.

"What do you know about the boys?" Joe asked.

"Not much, Joe," I said. "I've never even seen them run."

Joe's eyes sparkled wickedly. "Supposing I told you that they want to transfer here?"

I slowly put down my cup of tea. I couldn't believe my ears. For a moment I couldn't speak. I hadn't coached big burners like those three since I'd been fired from my coaching job at Penn State six years ago. What I had on this campus was a nice group of kids coming along, but definitely the ruck of Eastern college runners. The big burners wouldn't be caught dead at a school like Prescott. They all wanted to run for Oregon, Villanova, UCLA.

"Well," I said, "I'm not sure I want to have Lindquist's headaches."

"The boys say they were unfairly treated. They say no one ever listened to their side of the story. They want to talk to you about it. They and I agree that the decision will be up to you."

"You mean they're *here*?"

Joe was doing the smoker's comedy act: he hunted automatically for an ashtray, didn't find one, tipped his ashes into the palm of his hand, finally put them in the empty wastebasket.

"They showed up in the snowstorm late last night and knocked on my door," he said. "Marian put them up in the den. They hitchhiked all the way from Oregon. They ate everything in the house."

I was beginning to be more puzzled. Their action sounded desperate. I could see the three of them half-frozen by the highway in the Dakotas somewhere, with their thumbs out and a hand-lettered sign reading NEW YORK.

"But why here? I mean, there are big-time teams with permissive coaches who would snap them up."

"Prescott has you, doesn't it?"

"But I've been out of sight for years. Those kids wouldn't even know who I am."

"I'm sure they'll tell you all about it," said Joe, getting up.

"All right," I said. "I have classes at nine and ten, but I'm free between eleven and lunch. Why don't you send them over at eleven?"

After Joe left, I sat a minute before I went to nine o'clock track practice. To have runners like those three on my little team had been the hurting dream ever since I'd left Penn State. I felt overcome by memories and pain.

The moment I first saw the Oregon three, I felt a vague unease. They sat, or sprawled, in my office. I had shut the door and hung out my COACH IN CONFERENCE DO NOT DISTURB sign. They gazed at me in silence. I gazed back. I knew their faces well from all the photos I'd seen in *Track & Field News, Runner's World* and *Sports Illustrated*.

They looked like three travel-stained rock musicians who'd been busted flat in Memphis. They had hollowed eyes and beards. I thought with a twinge of nostalgia of the 1950s, when every runner had a crewcut and a clean shave. Even I didn't insist on crewcuts any more.

The superstar of the three was miler Vince Matti. He was also the best-looking. He was twenty-two, from Los Angeles, tall and rangy, as a miler should be. He had wavy coal-black hair down to his collar, insolent brown eyes, and a little scar under his right eye. He wore faded Levi's, a torn Air Force jacket and mountain boots. He owned a 3:52.19, the third-fastest U.S. mile in history. He also owned a pair of injury-prone legs that kept him from running like that about half the time. He was, I knew, very free with his elbows in a race and very hot-tempered.

My eyes moved on to Jacques LaFont. He was twenty-one, from Canton, Illinois. He wasn't in Vince's class, but he was a top miler and half-miler. The track magazines characterized him as a screwball and a cutup, and also as sensitive and highstrung. He was a shade more muscular than Vince, as a half-miler might be. He had exuberant frizzy auburn hair and beard, and wore a plaid headband and a motorcycle jacket. His bright blue eyes wavered between lively and anxious.

My eyes came to rest on Billy Sive. He was twenty-two, from San Francisco. He had been one of those spectacular California high-school distance runners. When he got to Oregon, he ran a 28:49 10,000 meter, but he seemed to have stopped improving. I wondered why he had not fulfilled that early promise. Maybe he had burned himself out.

Billy sat easily in the oak armchair where Joe had sat earlier. He looked calmly back at me through his gold-rimmed glasses. Behind those glasses were the most beautiful eyes I had ever seen in a man. They were a clear blue-gray. But they were beautiful because of their proud, spookily candid expression.

Vince Matti was snapping his gum in a way that already irritated me.

I pointed out the wastebasket. "Your gum in there," I said.

Vince hesitated. Then, possibly because he felt that the main thing at the moment was getting on my team, he obeyed.

My eyes went back to Billy Sive.

He sat there looking straight through me. He was wearing a faded, tattered blue-quilted Mao jacket. His brown leather pants must have been expensive—they were bagged and worn now, but they still displayed his long racehorse legs. My coach's eye measured his slender body at five-foot-eleven and weighed him at around 138 pounds. On his feet he had worn-out blue Tiger racing flats. I thought of him standing beside the icy highway in those thin-soled shoes.

"Well," I said to them, "Lindquist canned your asses for 'disciplinary reasons.' What am I supposed to do with you? If you know anything about me, you know that I'm just as authoritarian as Lindquist."

"Yeah sure, the press said disciplinary," said Sive. Quiet as he was, he seemed to be their spokesman. "Lindquist was afraid to tell the truth to the press."

"So?" I said.

"So we'll tell you the truth," said Sive. "Then you can issue us tracksuits if you want, or tell us to split if you want."

"Okay," I said. "What's the big dramatic truth?"

The two others looked down, a little uncomfortable. But Sive's extraordinary blue-gray eyes never left mine. I had the spooky feeling that the kid knew everything about my life. (As it turned out, this feeling was correct.) His face, I thought, was young American Gothic. It was pleasantly handsome, fine-cut, with high cheekbones, a high forehead, a blunt nose, a good mouth. His mop of light brown curls looked like it had been through a wind tunnel.

"We're gay," he said to me.

I felt as if somebody had hit me in the stomach with the thirty-five-pound shot. After a moment, a prickling sweat of panic broke out all over my body.

Outside, my girls' freshman track team was going off for practice. The hallway echoed with girls' shrieks, laughs and giggles as they trooped past.

Sive was still talking. He pointed at Vince and Jacques.

"Lindquist caught those two fooling around in the locker room one evening," he said. "They were being very sexy, and Vince was taking off Jacques' belt. And old Lindquist just caught them cold. They sassed him, and said that gay lib had come to Oregon U and a lot of other crap."

Now all three of them were talking heatedly, leaning forward. "Lindquist was fucking *livid*, man," said Vince. "He put Jacques on the rack and Billy's name came out. And Lindquist is a big straight fascist, so there went our scholarships."

Jacques was now doing an imitation of a Lindquist tirade, complete with Swedish accent, that I would have found very funny at any other time.

"Enemies uff sport, dot is vot you are," Jacques said. "Away wid you, to de fire. Der vill be no Sodom und Gomorrah on my skvad."

Billy and Vince were laughing, choking, till the tears came. Possibly they were a little hysterical from pressure and fatigue.

I just sat there looking at them, unsmiling, unable to say a word.

Finally they quieted down and looked at me expectantly.

"How come he didn't have you busted?" I finally said. "It's illegal in Oregon, isn't it?"

"He didn't want it all over the papers that he had three queers on his team," said Billy. "You know, people would start wondering about the rest, about him . . . I mean, he was just shitting in his pants, he was so afraid of what the papers would say."

"Does that mean nobody knows but you three and him?"
I asked.

"No," said Vince bluntly. "He yelled enough behind
closed doors that some of the team and the administration
know. Word'll get around, all right."

I went silent again, staring at my desk. I found that
I was shaking slightly.

Billy started talking again, slowly and softly. "We have
to finish school. And we figured that we might get the
same hassle everywhere else. So we came straight here."
Out of the corner of my eye, I could glimpse his eyes
searching me.

"We have a right to run," he said. "We weren't bothering anybody. There's nothing in the AAU rules or
the NCAA rules about the sex of the person you sleep
with."

I looked over into his eyes again, fighting to control
myself. An ex-Marine ought to have better self-control than
that. But I had been caught off-guard. I had been naive
enough to think that, after four years' seclusion at this
little college, the subject would never be brought up again,
and I could lead a normal life. But *three* of them. Macho
gays, all of them. I should have recognized those leather
pants of Billy's. I was ready to get mad at them for breaking
into my peaceful exile.

I made one last attempt to put up a front. "What makes
you think I'll understand? What makes you think I won't
give you a big lecture on the morality and purity of the
American boy?"

"My father said you might understand," said Billy.

"Who's your father?"

"John Sive."

I shook my head. "Sorry, don't know the name."

"He's a gay activist lawyer," said Billy implacably. "He's
working on the Supreme Court case that challenges the
sodomy laws. We told him what happened and that we
might not be able to make a team anywhere, and he said
to try Harlan Brown at Prescott."

There was nothing diplomatic about the way Billy put this. He backed me right into the corner. I was shortly to learn that this was—always—his way. Billy lived for the pitiless truth because it was the only way he'd been able to survive.

"If you don't want us, we'll understand," said Jacques, a little forlornly.

I didn't know what to say. It was a big decision to make so suddenly. I knew that it would affect me, them, the school and—perhaps—track itself. If I took them on the team, people would talk about it.

To buy a little time, I said, "Tell you what. I'll show you around the campus first. Prescott isn't like most schools. You ought to know what you're getting into."

T he four of us walked all over the campus.

The sidewalks were scraped clean now. The snow was melting already, and falling from the trees into the snow below with little whumps! everywhere. Students bundled in polo coats, Mexican sweaters, sheepskins, army surplus crisscrossed the campus with their briefcases.

"Prescott is an experiment," I told them. "About ten years ago, Joe Prescott decided that America was going to the dogs, and that American education was going to the dogs. He decided that what we needed was more human people, better able to survive, and cheaper, more practical education. So he turned his computer software company over to his board of directors, and out of his profits he built this school. This campus used to be his estate."

"He's some kind of straight liberal, huh?" said Jacques.

We walked and walked. I pointed out everything to them. "There are no regular courses. Each student chooses his area of interest, and fills a portfolio full of projects. If you want to learn carpentry, we have a damn good vocational department. If you want to learn political or environmental activism, you go out and do it. A faculty advisor keeps track of your portfolio of projects, and it's graded pass or fail."

"Sounds easy," said Vince cheerfully.

"It isn't," I said. "That's what I thought when I came here. No sir. Students without self-discipline wash out pretty fast."

All the time I was trying not to look at them too hard. Three class runners. And beautiful. Especially Billy Sive.

I showed them the plush athletic facilities.

"Joe's a big nut on fitness," I said. "He thinks the American body is going to the dogs too. I happen to agree with that. Physical education is the only required course here. We've got a broad fitness program. It's all aerobic sports. No ping-pong or golf. Only handicapped students are excused."

We were walking along the trail toward the track, our breath blowing white on the sunny air.

"Then, on a level above the fitness program, we have a few competitive sports," I said. "Swimming, field hockey, cycling. But the big emphasis is on track."

We stood looking across the quarter-mile cinder track. It lay in a great open field surrounded by woods. The school's little snowplow had almost finished clearing the track, though the bleachers along it remained buried. The girls' team, about twenty-five of them, were all over the track, striding, doing bursts.

"I've made track a big thing at this school," I said. My heart pained me at the thought of the four happy years I'd spent here, and how these three boys were maybe going to mess it up. "We have the same kind of enthusiasm for track that you had at Oregon, only on a smaller scale. The students and the faculty really get worked up about track. They run, or they jog, and they go to meets. Last year I even fielded that girls' team." I pointed at the girls. "The girls *demanded* it. They gave me a lot of crap about women's equal rights in sports, so I had to."

The boys all laughed.

"Foxes," said Billy, "will be foxes."

"Of course," I said, "we aren't big-time here. We don't have athletic scholarships. But even if we did, I couldn't go out and sign burners like you guys, because you all want to run for Oregon. We think more in terms of fitness and having a good time. We go to the local meets, and we do very well, and that's about it."

"What you're saying is," said Vince, "if you take us, it'll be a whole new ball game here."

"It will be," I said. "But it's no problem . . . we have the facilities, and the money, as you can see. We don't have an indoor track, but we're breaking ground for one this spring. And we're also going to install a Tartan track." The old-time cinder tracks are not as fast as the new synthetic tracks.

All three were looking hungrily at the track. Probably they hadn't had a good workout for several days, and they were feeling withdrawal symptoms. Vince had his arm over Jacques' shoulders. They were being quite natural around me—what could Billy's father have told them?

Billy couldn't stand it. He took off and ran gently around the track alone. He passed the chugging snowplow in the turn. He passed among the girl runners like a thoroughbred among a lot of ponies. He loped easily along, with perfect form. I noticed some of the girls turn to look at him, but he ignored them.

Perhaps it was the sight of his lonely, graceful figure among the girls, against the snowy landscape, that decided me. They were like three young birds driven away from the flock. Four years ago, Joe Prescott had sheltered me, an older storm-driven bird. It would be a sin not to pass on his Christian kindness.

Billy rounded the turn and came back to us, breathing easily, grinning.

"Ready to go, huh?" I said, smiling myself for the first time.

"Yeah," he said.

"All right, you're on," I said. "Go register, and get your rooms assigned. You'll probably lose a semester's credit, but we can work something out. Then report back to me, and I'll issue you your gear."

They all grinned happily, and Vince slapped Billy gently on the back.

"We really appreciate it, Harlan," said Billy.

"It's Mr. Brown," I said.

Their faces fell a little. Billy looked at me strangely.

"Okay, Mr. Brown," he said.

TWO

All my life, I have been haunted by the ghost of a runner.

I was born in Philadelphia on August 14, 1935. My father was a track nut, and among my earliest memories is being taken to meets. He'd hold me up so I could see over the crowd at the distant, flitting figures of men in shorts and singlets. "Look there," he'd say, "look how fine they are, my boy."

My father, Michael Brown, was a big, strapping man, half-English, half-Scot, who owned a small printing plant there in Philadelphia. From 1941 to 1945 he was off in the Pacific fighting with the Marines. He helped take Guadalcanal, and he came home with a slight limp and a Purple Heart.

He was a strict man, but also warm and merry, and I adored him. My mother was less close to me—she was a devoted, dutiful Black Irish woman, but a little cold and always nervous. He and my mother were both staunch Protestants, and they gave me the upbringing that one would expect. No smoking, no drinking, no dancing, church every Sunday, pledge allegiance to the flag.

And running. For my father, running was almost part of his religion. "Runners," he used to say to me, "those are the real men. Baseball is for babies, and football is a brainless business. Running takes more effort and more discipline than any other sport."

Ironically, then, it was my fine, big, straight father who taught me to worship at the altar of manhood. Whereas if stereotype had its way, I should have had a milquetoast father, a fierce and castrating mother, and grown up disturbed and shy with girls. That was not the case at all. My father, at odd variance with his puritanism in other areas, had no objection to girls. He said it was part of being a real man. Already in grade school, I discovered that the sexual part of my nature was powerful and insistent.

When I got to Fairview High School, the main thing on my mind was getting onto its famous track team. I wasn't much of a student. But I worked at it, because if I got poor grades, my father scolded me and asked what I was doing with the school taxes he paid so painfully.

I loved competition, and pitting myself against the other boys. But running was also good for its own sake— the discipline and the joy of motion. And physically, running made me different from boys (especially the fat, pampered ones, whom I despised) who didn't engage in high-stress sports. Very early, I got to thinking of myself, and of all runners, as a separate and superior species of human being.

In the summers, we always vacationed in the Poconos. My mother had asthma and said the city air was bad for her, and my father loved to fish. So we had a tiny cabin in a remote area of the mountains. My father would drive up to be with us on weekends. I was alone there all week long with my mother, and missed him very much. So I hunted up any boys I could find in the area, and spent the days roaming with them.

The summer between my junior and senior year in high school, I met a boy whom I'll call Chris Shelbourne. His family had just bought a summer cabin nearby. He was blond, with calm, blue eyes, very quiet, lean and sun-browned. It turned out he was a runner. We were delighted to discover this common passion, and we quickly became close friends.

In fact, my feelings for him became so strong that I wonder now why I didn't understand them correctly. Perhaps it was because I was so poorly educated about these things. My father had told me what he thought I needed to know about girls. But he had never told me such feelings could exist between two males. As far as I knew, there was no name for what I felt. But instinctively I realized that these feelings were something to be hidden from everyone, even from Chris, even from myself.

Chris, possibly, felt the same confusion. He feverishly sought every opportunity to be with me that summer, but he never discussed his feelings.

An hour passed without Chris was an eternal loss. We fished, hiked, or just lay in the sun and talked about track. We daydreamed out loud to each other about being top college runners, then of going to the Olympic Games.

Every day we took long runs together through the woods, following the many lonely trails for eight or ten miles. We jumped the streams and ran brushing through the mountain laurel. The laurel was all in bloom shortly after we met, heavy and fragrant with pink and white blossoms. We tore up hills and ran sliding down them, running free like two deer. We dashed through the dappled sunlight under the great trees. We were hyperoxidated and deliriously happy. The act of running was all tied up in my mind with the feelings I had when he was near me.

Miles off in the woods, there was a small, lonely, clear lake. We would always strip there and go swimming. I had seen hundreds of boys naked in the locker rooms at school. But when I saw this adored friend of mine naked, my feelings turned to sexual desire. In confusion and distress, trying to be casual, I always smothered this feeling. Chris apparently did the same.

So we squandered the summer of '52 that way.

At the end of our last run, as we were nearing the edge of the woods but still out of sight from our cabins, Chris suddenly stopped and said, "I want to say good-bye here."

He put his arms around me. But panic equaled affection, so we did no more than embrace each other awkwardly with our panting sweaty bodies brushing together. He touched his lips to my cheek, near my mouth, and after a moment's shaky hesitation I did the same to him. We swore that we would write to each other, and that we'd see each other next summer.

The next day his family closed up their cabin and returned to New Jersey. I ran alone in the woods that day. I would have cried bitterly, but my father had taught me that real men don't cry.

I didn't have the courage or the verbal ability to put my feelings on paper, so I never wrote to Chris. He never wrote to me either. The next year we heard that the Shelbourne cottage had been sold to somebody else. I never saw Chris again.

My senior year in high school, I went through two or three casual girlfriends, searching in vain for that feeling that Chris had stirred up in me. Part of the problem seemed to be that their intensity about sex did not match my own. That year, too, I won the mile run at the Penn Relays. My dad was tremendously proud, and kept those first newspaper clippings framed on the living-room wall till they yellowed.

After graduation in 1953, I was a little torn. I wanted to go straight to college and run, but the Korean War was still on, and I was itching to go over there and collect a belt-full of gook scalps. So my parents let me enlist in the Marines. But I had scarcely finished boot training when the truce was signed.

This was a big disappointment, but I thrilled at being a Marine anyway. They promoted me to lieutenant, put me on the Marine track team and let me compete as much as duty would permit. I trained hard, and my personal best in the mile was a 4:04.3, which was considered very good in those days—Roger Bannister had broken four minutes in 1954. I began to hope I could make the Olympic team in 1956.

But when my four-year hitch ended early in 1956, my dad's business was in trouble. Instead of training, I had to help him out, and to take a job as copyreader at a newspaper. Bitterly I sat in the noisy city room and proofread the results of the Olympic trials.

That fall I went to Villanova on an athletic scholarship, majoring in journalism and minoring in phys ed. But I was still working nights and my training suffered. When I made the varsity track team, my running went nowhere near as well as in the Marines.

To make things worse, in 1959, my senior year, I was dating a girl named Mary Ellen Rache. While looking for the Chris feeling, I managed to get her in trouble. Of course it was my duty to marry her, and I did. Neither of our families was happy with the event. It was a bad way to start a marriage.

Out of college in 1960, the next Olympic year, I had to face it, With two family responsibilities weighing on me, there was no place in my life for amateur track competition.

But I could stay close to the sport by choosing a profession connected with it. I still didn't have the graduate credits for teaching physical education, so it had to be newspaper work. I went to work for the Philadelphia *Eagle* as a trackwriter, and went to school nights. By getting up early every morning and running a few miles, I managed to stay in minimal shape.

The work was exciting and paid pretty well. I could travel to all the big meets, which got me away from the uneasy situation with Mary Ellen. I could chum with the big-time runners, share vicariously in their griefs and glories. I was the classic sock-sniffer.

Only now was I beginning to admit to myself how dangerously deep my feelings about all this went. In the Marines, the discipline and hard work had helped me suppress it, but now it was boiling up again. On the excuse that we weren't getting along, I stopped having relations with Mary Ellen, and used prostitutes and pickups while traveling.

I went to meets with a throbbing excitement that devoured me. Outdoors under the sky, or indoors in the smoky arenas, I devoured the sight of those other fine-looking young men. They were stretched out in full flight, gleaming with sweat, as their muscles and tendons strained toward the unattainable. Now and then I'd see someone whom I found so attractive that he gave me that hurting, wanting feeling that Chris had.

I quickly got discontented with reporting because it didn't get me really inside the sport. In 1961 I heard about a coaching job open in a Philadelphia high school, St. Anthony's, applied and got it. It paid less, but it opened up a whole world to me. That very first year, I fielded a crack little team that burned up the Penn Relays and attracted a lot of attention.

The drawback was that I didn't like high-school students. They were noisy little animals. The next year, my beloved Villanova offered me a post as assistant track coach, and I fell over my own feet accepting. College boys were more comfortable to be with, because they already had a sense of self.

In fact, I felt too comfortable with them. It was in 1962, that first year of coaching at Villanova, that I finally had to confess to myself that my feelings had a name: homosexuality.

It's hard to convey the intensity of the suffering I felt. Everything in my upbringing made me see myself in the worst possible light. Runners are men, my father had said. A Marine is a man, the armed forces had said. A coach is a man. For chrissake, even reporters were men. The reporters I knew were a raunchy, whoring bunch.

What puzzled me most was that I couldn't see in myself the mannerisms that society said were the mark of homosexuals. I knew all about "queers," or thought I did. Queers were ballet dancers, interior decorators and actors. They were effeminate, pretty, fluttered their hands, wiggled their rears and talked in high, breathless voices.

Every day I was in the locker room with those beautiful naked bodies, close enough to touch.

Those Villanova runners used to do some pretty wild horsing around. Supposedly it was all just manly fun and games to grab at somebody else's goodies in the shower. But now and then I'd divine some real feeling there. You can't bring together a bunch of high-spirited young men full of all the urges, and teach them the cult of the body, and throw them together nude in a locker room, in such a physical sport, and not have a few random feelings happening.

Runners are the most highly conditioned and shamelessly physical of athletes. They have a love affair going with their bodies: how the body responds to training, how it doesn't respond. Runners talk obsessively, like little old ladies, about their injuries and illnesses and bowel movements and mineral deficiencies. They are more avid about physiology than sex researchers. Runners even swear that they make better lovers than other men because they have stronger hip muscles. They are so addicted physiologically to running that if you take it away from them, they climb the walls like junkies. Their very hormones are intimate in the gush of power they put out: male hormones with strength, female hormones with endurance.

A man's body is good to look at only when he is conditioned, because of the muscling. So it follows, as the night the day, that sports harbor as much homosexuality as anywhere else in American society—possibly more. But everybody goes on pretending that sports are the bunting-draped sanctuary of the straight American he-man. Once in a while somebody is brave enough to hint at the truth, as Jim Bouton did in *Ball Four*, and he quickly gets shouted down as an enemy of sport. Homosexuality is the great skeleton in the closet of American athletics.

So there I was in the Villanova locker rooms with all those fine-looking male bodies.

Now and then I saw a boy who—I sensed—might respond if I chose to start something. In fact I knew two at Villanova who were carrying on, because I caught them at it, just as Gus Lindquist would. By threatening to reveal their activities to the head coach, I could have blackmailed them into bed with me. But I let them off with a Marine-type lecture about moral purity. Unfortunately, they were both so frightened that they dropped off the team.

I was close enough to touch—but I didn't.

Religion, discipline, military experience, upbringing and just plain fear gave me the strength. Every day I used to pray to God to give me strength, just for that day, to keep my hands off my boys. I felt I had a sacred trust in not fouling their lives with what I then regarded as my monstrous feelings. And it also occurred to me that I couldn't indulge these feelings without risking being caught at it myself.

It helped to keep up my Marine facade. I was pokerfaced, harsh, hair cut close to my skull, conservatively dressed, barking at my athletes as if they were recruits on Parris Island. Running helped me too. More accurately, the fatigue from running helped blot my suffering and need from my mind. That year at Villanova, I started training seriously again. Not to compete (I couldn't anyway, since I was now a pro), but to survive. Every morning I got up extra early, put in ten miles on the road at a fast pace, even did some speed work on the track if I had time.

I was curious to know what my father's attitude toward homosexuality would be. He was still getting around the shop in Philadelphia, his big hands black with ink. But he was a little creaky and bent with arthritis these days. Casually I mentioned one day that I had seen a queer at Villanova.

He was very reluctant to admit that such people existed. But finally he said, "Well, Harlan, they're few. Very few. Thank God, for they are sick twisted people. The Lord will cast them into the eternal fire."

Insane? Was I insane? I knew one thing. Maybe I wasn't insane now, but I would be shortly, if I kept repressing these feelings.

So in 1963, while still at Villanova, I started making little forays into a tiny, underground corner of American society where, I had learned, these needs would be met. And I learned a few things right away. The right word for my feelings was not "queer," but "gay." And the right word for me, with my natural male mannerisms and my desire for other such men, was "macho gay."

I told myself: You have to try it just once. Maybe you won't even like it, and you can go back to women and relax.

There were gay bars in Philadelphia, but I couldn't risk going there because it was too close to home. So now and then, on weekends when there weren't any meets, or on holidays, or during the summer, I managed to slip away to New York.

There, wearing the most extreme disguise I could think of—hippie clothes, sunglasses and a hairy wig—I started exploring the gay turf downtown with that familiar feeling of throbbing excitement.

That first weekend I just cruised around the bars and porno stores. A few guys tried to pick me up, but I wasn't ready for it yet. I sat there sipping Cokes, amazed at the feverish crush of young men. Few, my father had said?

No virgin where blue movies and dirty pictures were concerned, I was still overwhelmed by all-male pornography. After looking at some for the first time, I was like a drunk. The sight of men making love to each other seemed so shockingly beautiful, so right.

I found one under-the-counter book with high-quality color photos that showed two runners of twenty or so. I knew at a glance that they were conditioned athletes. I wondered who the models were, and what kind of money need had driven them to do it. Would the AAU consider that they'd jeopardized their amateur status, since they had profited from their sport by fornicating in their track clothes?

The photographs showed them starting off on a run through the woods together. Then they stopped to fall on each other's necks and strip each other. Picture after picture, they rolled on the leaves in the most abandoned fashion, their fine, lean bodies gleaming with sweat. With a terrible pang, I remembered Chris. What a fool I'd been, what a coward.

Before I left New York that Sunday afternoon, I carefully destroyed the book and dropped it in a trash can, like a spy destroying his code book. But those powerful images stayed with me.

It was several weeks before I got back to New York again. On that second weekend, I was doing what everybody else was doing. I was cruising the bars and streets around Sheridan Square, looking for a quickie and hoping I didn't pick up a "cot," one of those plainclothes policemen who hung around trying to nab gays.

Of course, you could buy somebody for far less walking. You ask, "How much?" and he says, "Seven inches, twenty-five dollars," or whatever. But for my first time I didn't want a hustler. So I wandered around half the weekend, till I was half-deaf from the jukeboxes in the bars, rating faces and bodies. I was looking for that particular physiognomy, that hint of my ghost, that would strike the deep erotic response in me.

About one o'clock Sunday afternoon, I was about to give up when I went into the Loews-Sheridan theater, notorious as a place where gays could have sexual encounters. Several dozen men were there. Two couples were already twined together, and the others sat alone here and there. One of them had shaggy, bright blond hair that looked almost silver in the light from the screen.

Needing a closer look, I walked slowly, nervously down the aisle. He was sitting slouched a little, with his thighs spread, wearing a red leather jacket and tight, striped, bellbottom slacks. A little too well dressed to be a hippie, but obviously not an establishment type either. (I, the ex-Marine, already talking about the establishment.) He was younger than I, maybe twenty-one or twenty-two, very lean and hard-looking. The changing light from the screen lit up his thoroughbred profile in the smoky dark.

I hesitated only a moment, wondering if he were a plainclothes policeman. Then I did what I'd seen had to be done. I went into the row, along the seats, and sat down by him. My heart was pounding like I'd just run the mile. Feigning indifference, I looked straight ahead at the screen. But out of the corner of my eye, I saw him turn his head. Was he rating me or just getting ready to arrest me? If he was rating me and didn't like what he saw, I'd have to keep walking.

What happened next is still burned in my memory after all these years.

He moved his thigh over and touched his knee to mine. I turned my head a little. His thighs were long and slender, their corded muscles visible through the thin, tight pants. A runner? Who knows? He was certainly athletic-looking. The open jacket displayed his narrow hips and his full crotch, with the cock bulging in the left pants-leg. Even his hands, on the armrests, were attractive, tan, strong-looking, with long fingers.

I returned the pressure of his knee, then shakily laid my hand on his nearest thigh. Its hardness and heat hit my fingers like a shock. He laid his hand over mine tenderly. I had not expected tenderness. My hand was startled into turning over so that our moist hot palms touched and our fingers twined.

As we held hands, I finally dared to let my eyes slide up to his face. He was looking at me unsmiling, that provocative witchy look with which the gay in rut rivets his peer. This was no cot. His sex seemed suffused into his features like a bright light. His eyes seemed to say, I can make your fantasy real.

Then, with his free hand, he reached inside his jacket and drew out a shiny metal thing like a lipstick tube, and held it over to me. It was the rite of the offering of amyl nitrite. I relaxed just a little. Trying to look as expert as possible, I put the inhaler to one nostril as I'd seen others do. Breathing deeply and slowly, I wondered what it would do to me. After a moment, a burning delicious rush flashed through my body, exploding in my genitals.

Neither of us spoke. He was already caressing my thigh. I gave him back the amyl nitrite and he inhaled it himself. On the screen, to the accompaniment of tender violins, a couple of young heterosexual lovers were kissing frantically. But the man beside me was unhurried, and drew me into his own rhythm.

His hand had already slid down to his fly and was slowly undoing the half-dozen small buttons there. His hips were grinding and thrusting up slowly in the seat, and he looked as if he were in an ecstatic trance. His eyes were half-closed, his lips parted, and a couple of locks of hair stuck to his iridescent cheek. For a moment I panicked a little, realizing that he was going to precipitate me into it without any foreplay.

But after another drag on the inhaler, I had my hand on the bulge in his pants-leg, rubbing it tenderly. He caressed my hand, pressing it there while he kept unbuttoning with the other. He wore no underwear, and the opening fly bared his lean sucked-in abdomen, then the light bronze pubic hair and the hip bones moving sweetly under the skin.

My whole body was vibrating with excitement—no woman had ever made me feel like this. I put my hand on his abdomen, feeling the muscles ripple in it, and slid my arm around his shoulders. Rapt and terrified, I watched as he raised his body a little and pushed his slacks down to his knees. The long, rose-dark cock was swelling between his parted thighs; that thing that society most severely forbade me, and that I wanted most. I had my face buried in his hot neck, running my hand up and down his bare thighs, and he was tenderly rubbing my fly, then unzipping it.

Finally I had the courage to touch his genitals, and he lifted his hips and pressed them into my hand. He groaned, a barely audible sound that seemed to come up from his pelvis, and slid his hand in along my bare flank. Never till

24

that moment did I realize how many nerve endings there were in that sensitive skin. My own eyes closed, my own mouth opened, and I was ready to give all my hoarded passion and tenderness to this stranger, as he was willing to give it to me.

About half an hour later, I was in the grimy little lavatory in the theater basement, washing myself and shaking violently. When I went back upstairs, I glanced back in the theater. He was still laying in his seat with his head hanging back, shirt open, exactly as I'd left him. Probably his pants were still down around his ankles. In the light from the screen, a few splashes of my semen glistened on his face.

I fled out of the theater, blinking in the cruel daylight, and walked shakily down the street. Coming to a bench, I sank down on it. I couldn't stop shaking, and my skin was burning under my clothes. I had hoped for some excitement from the first go at oral sex with a male. What I had not expected was to be so totally and agreeably shattered. For the first time in my life, another human being had made me lose control of myself—and all in silence, without a word spoken. I had always thought of the male's erotic sensations being centered at the groin. But I could still feel the ghosts of his hands and his mouth on my body, touching me about the neck, the nipples, the sides, the flanks, the buttocks—as much of me as he could reach in the seat.

I looked back at the Loews-Sheridan entrance for a while. He didn't come out. I wanted to go back in there and find out his name and address. But I didn't dare. Like a spy, I could leave no traces. There would be no seeing him again. But I knew I would never forget him as long as I lived.

Finally I got up and walked shakily to the subway station at Sheridan Square and Christopher Street. My objective attained, I might as well go back uptown to the Port Authority and catch the next bus south.

On the bus, roaring along the parkway, I sat motionless

in my regular clothes, with sunglasses still on, still
shattered. But there was also a gloating maniac elation at
having tasted what my nature had craved so long! I was
surprised to find that I did not feel in the least guilty and
soiled. I was sure I was not insane. It might be possible
to feel good about being gay—as long as I could keep it
hidden from the rest of the world.

But back at Villanova, amid the cold reality of Ace
bandages and stopwatches, my elation vanished. If it could
be so good with a pickup, then it must be even better with
a man you loved. Yet my own peculiar sexual logic told me
that I could love only an athlete. And that was impossible.

I sneaked back to New York a few more times, and it
became obvious that I'd had dumb luck at the Loews-
Sheridan. Not until years later did I find anyone quite so
satisfying as the kid in the red leather jacket. Maybe it
was because of the amyl nitrite, and its being the first
time.

I had a horror of the screaming queens and the TV's
(transvestites). Nothing that smelled of women was
acceptable. What I wanted was an athletic-looking guy in
his late teens or early twenties. And there were plenty of
them. If the athlete is at the heart of the straight man's
vision, it is at the heart of the gay vision also. For the gay,
looking athletic is as important as being well hung.

The sad thing was, as I usually found when I got their
clothes off, that so few of my bed partners were real
athletes. You know at a glance when somebody has been
working hard: the fined-down look, the big veins. Most of
my lovers were lean, but limp—as much a facade as my
tough Marine act. So there I was, searching pathetically
for the image of my Villanova milers, and of Chris, in the
bodies of those soft kids. I'd end up getting it over with
fast. Wham, bam, pay them if they were hustlers, back on
the street in twenty minutes, catch the next bus. I learned
fast not to waste my tenderness on them. Often I'd wonder
if I'd run into the youth in the red leather jacket. But he
never crossed my path again.

Once in a while, a man offered me money. A hand would be laid on my arm, a voice would say, "How much?" After all, I really was an athlete. I was only twenty-eight, and looked younger, and didn't weigh an ounce more than in my miling days. I even fluttered the heart of more than one queen. "Darling, how divine you look." But the idea of selling my body didn't appeal.

Sometimes my nameless lovers asked me how I kept in shape. They recognized that I was the real thing. I'd lie like mad, tell them I was a rower, a long-distance cyclist, anything but the truth: that I was assistant coach for one of America's plushest track teams. I was so mortally afraid of being recognized that I never took my dark glasses off, even in bed. When we were at meets with the team, I'd manage to avoid having my picture taken, for fear somebody who'd chewed my cock in some tenement stairway might read *Track & Field News*.

Those were dangerous weekends. I always felt like a spy going behind the Iron Curtain on some nerve-wracking mission. One misstep and I'd be dead. It wasn't the gays that I feared, though a hustler did steal my wallet once. It was the straight homophobes who preyed on gays that I feared. Fascist male hets sometimes roamed the streets downtown and beat up gays for fun. On two occasions I set some kind of new world record out the back door of a gay bar when the police bust came in the front. On another occasion I went straight through the bathroom window into a back alley, amid shattering glass, and had to go bleeding to a hospital emergency room for stitches. There were always the plainclothesmen lurking in the parks and the public toilets. And there was jail if you were caught in the only act of love that made sense to you.

It wasn't long before I felt that bewilderment, that choking rage, that the gay feels. We were hunted animals. We were huddled underground in the dark, like the Christians in the catacombs, sheltering the tiny flame of our sexual faith. What just emperor would declare the edict that would let us out into the light? What harm did we do? Murderers and thieves harmed others, but we harmed no one except possibly—in our confusion and unresolved guilts—ourselves.

I could never relax until I was on that bus back to Pennsylvania. It was always with a feeling of unreality that I came home to my comfortable suburban house just off the Villanova campus. I would sit in front of the TV with a Coke, with my two little sons (little Mark had been born two years after Kevin). They would be rough-and-tumbling around me on the living-room rug, and I would be haunted by the memory of some strange man's body. The dishwasher would be noising in the kitchen, and I would still be vibrating with the fear of the police bust I'd just escaped.

"Daddy, Kevin took my airplane," little Mark would yell, and come weeping to me.

"Kevin," I'd say in my Parris Island tone, "give that airplane back right now." And before my eyes, like a hallucination, would be an erect penis pumping its milky life out over the lean, male hand holding it.

"Have a good time with your newspaper chums?" my wife would ask sarcastically.

"Oh, we had a great time," I'd say. "Dinner at Mamma Leone's and a burlesque show downtown."

"You're disgusting," she'd say. "And you never take me out."

"Who'd want to take a sourpuss like you out?" I'd say. "If you want to go out that bad, find someone."

Paradoxically, I tried to cover up by seeing that she had every comfort. My two little sons were growing up, and I found that I loved them more and more as my fear of being exposed grew stronger. Someday they'd find out about me. That would be a hard moment.

After two years at Villanova, the U of Iowa offered me the job of head track coach. But I turned it down. Out there in the cornfields there was no gay underground for me to lose myself in.

A year later, my frenzied patience paid off. Penn State offered me a contract as head track coach. It was heady stuff for a man only thirty-one years old, and $30,000 a year was more money than I'd ever had in my life. The team had had a slump under the previous coach, who was a soft, permissive guy. The administration and the alumni hoped I would whip things into shape.

And I did. I was Mr. Parris Island of track. I was Mr. Drill Instructor of distance running. I was the toughest, barkingest coach in the U.S. at that time.

The reason that my boys didn't hate my guts was that I made them respect me. I was not one of your coaches with a bowler belly and a big cigar, who tells a boy to bust fifteen 63-second quarters while he goes off and has four beers. I went out running with my boys, and they knew I could do much of what they did. They knew that I cared deeply about the sport, and about what happened to them. I made them want to meet my challenge. I made them reach down and discover themselves. I would have run through fire for them, and the ones that survived the first few weeks on my team ended up running through fire for me.

By then it was the Aquarius generation coming onto the campus, and we were having battles with the boys over sex, drinking, long hair and the rest. I am a Leo myself, so I didn't have any truck with that Aquarius crap. I won every one of those battles. I was adamant about crewcuts and pre-meet chastity. If a boy didn't conform, he was dropped from the team.

Needless to say, I knew I was a hypocrite. I shut them away from their girlfriends because I wanted them myself. I made them cut their hair because I went into New York and ran my fingers through the shaggy locks of twenty-five-dollar fantasies.

Along about 1968, the pressures of being head coach on a big-time team, and the terror of being discovered, were finally starting to get me. I didn't have much time to go to New York any more. That year, my team was sweeping college titles everywhere, and I was about ready for a strait jacket.

It was in 1968—March 1968 to be exact—that the atom bomb fell on my world.

Early that spring, a sophomore half-miler, Denny Falks, nineteen years old, started flirting with me. That's the only way I can describe his behavior. He was open about it, though he was careful to do it only when we were alone. Of all the runners who'd gone through my life by then, only Denny had divined what was going on in my mind.

He was always coming around to my office for solo chats about pretended problems. Denny, it seemed, had more family problems, and more aches and pains, and more psych problems about running, than anyone else on the team.

Since I had never before been cruised by a runner, it scared hell out of me.

Out of self-defense, I was extra hard on him. But he saw through my Marine act too. Once during a workout, he actually faked a groin injury so that he could bare that part of his body to me in the locker room. I sensed he was malingering, and I had the doctor deal with him.

Denny was attractive too. He would have caused a riot on Sheridan Square, even though I had forced him to cut off his long blond hair. I kept chewing him out and running him into the ground and trying to break his spirit. Then I'd have to get up at 4:30 a.m. and run fifteen miles to kill the thought of him.

For two months, Denny tried every way he could think of to get my hand inside his jock strap. Then he did what so many piqued lovers do: he took revenge.

He cheerfully and casually told a couple of his teammates, "Hey, you know, I think the coach is a queer."

"No kidding," they said, quite amazed.

"Yeah," said Denny breezily, "he kinda flirts with me when I'm in his office to talk."

The rumor went like wildfire, and wasn't long in

reaching the ears of the dean, Marvin Federman. Federman called me in and told me about the rumor.

I was simply stunned.

Federman was cold and brusque. "The boy says that you have shown sexual interest in him."

I was seared with shock and panic, but I managed to keep a calm exterior. "That's simply not true."

"The rumor has reached a few of the trustees and alumni," said Federman. "There is heavy pressure on me. We can't have that kind of scandal. I'm sure you'll understand my position."

"But this is ridiculous," I said.

"Are you prepared to contest his statements legally?" said Federman.

How could I contest them? I was afraid they would find out the truth about me. I was silent.

"The best thing for you to do would be to resign. I've noticed that you look tired and strained lately. You can say that it's for reasons of health."

With that rumor, and that brief chilling conversation with the dean, my coaching career at Penn State ended. I submitted my resignation that day.

As I left my office for the last time, I saw Denny, beautiful Denny, walking out the building in his sweats. He was going to the track to work out, whistling.

But the rumor stayed around, and continued to poison my life. It reached my wife. She had been looking for an excuse to divorce me, and now she had one. She put on a big act of self-righteous anger, got the divorce, and the house, and the children, and a really punitive alimony and child-support settlement of $12,000 a year. She told the rumor to my mother and the rest of my family, and they turned their backs on me and froze me out. (At least I didn't have to bear my father's disapproval—he had died the year before.)

There were no headlines, except PENN STATE TRACK COACH RESIGNS FOR REASONS OF HEALTH, and a casual quote from me that I was thinking of going back to newspaper work. But the rumor washed gently through the track world and died out. A number of people said they didn't believe it. "After all, he was married, and he acted so masculine." But the thought stayed there, in the back of people's minds.

Shattered and angry, I fled to New York and took a small apartment downtown in the gay ghetto. My savings went to pay my lawyer and the initial alimony payments, and then I was faced with finding money or going to jail for nonsupport. "The first check you miss," my wife had sworn, "I'm having you arrested."

Bruce Cayton, an old buddy from the New York *Post*, offered to help me find a newspaper job in town. But I was all panicky, sure that everybody in the world now knew the rumor, and that I would be turned down because I was a homosexual. Besides, the last thing I wanted at the moment was to be part of a big institution again, where I could be scrutinized and pressured. The best thing would be self-employment, that would let me drop out of sight and sneak over into the gay world sometimes for relief.

So I told Bruce thanks, and I forged off on my own.

There wasn't much skill I had, to start earning immediate money on my own. I tried freelance writing, but the market had become very difficult to break into. I ran an ad offering to work as a freelance copyreader and editor, but it paid pitifully little—four or five dollars an hour; and even this market was tightening up due to the recession. Coaching had taught me how to give rubdowns, so I tried to set myself up as a licensed masseur. My ad, a typical one, ran in the *Village Voice* and other papers: "Rubdowns by Chris, athletic masseur." (I didn't want to use my real name.) But New York was full of masseurs who went out at all hours of the day and night to rub down sleepless middle-aged ladies. The customers came in slowly.

So I tried some modeling. My ad read: "Handsome ex-Marine, athlete, miler's build, 6' 1", 159 pounds, 25-inch waist, 42-inch chest." I did get some calls, but it wasn't totaling more than the $200 a week I had to send my ex-wife.

There were just a few weeks to make up my mind what I was going to do, and I did it.

In a bar one evening, I had met a personable gay named Steve Goodnight, a struggling serious writer who kept himself alive by doing pornographic books. Steve and I became friends, not lovers. Through him I met a number of other gays in a kind of inner artistic circle and hidden high society. To these people I revealed my true identity, and found that the Penn State dismissal made me something of a martyr/celebrity in a small way. So it happened one night that a well-to-do and lascivious gay acquainted with this circle thought I should go to bed with him, and I was needing money and I said, "I think that's going to cost you $200."

That was how I became a hustler.

I was a very expensive, very exclusive hustler. None of your twenty-five-dollar sodomies in hotel rooms, none of your selling your meat on the street. I couldn't risk it. Nobody got to me except through a blind of telephone calls. I usually charged $200-250, and sometimes went higher. I was worth every penny of it, and pretty soon had more business than I could handle, but I didn't have to exert myself. At $200 a trick, twice a week was enough to satisfy the divorce court and to pay my living expenses.

They tell you a hustler's career is over at thirty, when his youth starts to fade. I started mine at thirty-four and found that there was a small but solid market for meat like mine. My numbers didn't want faun-like boys. They wanted a hard, angry, bitter, mature beauty. Sometimes they wanted a whipping too. I am not a sadist at heart, but I was angry enough to pass for one—I gave a damn good whipping for $200. It was clear profit, because I wasn't working for a pimp.

There was something about the harshness of hustling that reminded me I was surviving, that the straights would not crush me. There was something of raising the flag on Iwo Jima in the way I said, "Eight inches." It was, in a way, my first gesture of gay pride. One of the reasons I stayed off the street was that it was more dangerous than ever now, and I wasn't looking to go to jail. On June 28, 1969, just after I arrived in the city, the New York City police started their now-famous crackdown on the gay bars. The first to be blitzed was the Stonewall. During the next twelve months, they raided and closed the Zoo, the Zodiac and about twenty others, mostly on Barrow Street. It was the watershed in gay history, and—in a way—it was my watershed too.

The night the Stonewall was busted, I was in the neighborhood on business. Someone called my client and told him what was happening, and we got out of bed and ran over there to see, because we hadn't been able to believe our ears.

The street was full of cops and flashing red lights. But what was more amazing, the street was full of hundreds of gays, and they were fighting the cops. For years they had run, let themselves be shoved to the wall, submitted to harassments and arrest, because they felt in their hearts that it was their fate. But the night of the Stonewall, they made the instant visceral decision that they had had enough. They were throwing rocks and bottles, your "powderpuff pansies" were. They were fighting New York's Finest with their bare hands. They were daring the nightsticks to crunch on their bodies.

I watched with growing anger and sorrow. I didn't drink, but those bars were about the only public places where gays could be themselves. No straight could understand how precious they were to us. I had always believed in law and order, supported the police. But those cops were busting me, busting my entire lifetime of anguish. They were riding over me with their big horses, and shoving me into vans handcuffed.

Then an amazing thing happened. I had a rock in my hand, and I threw it with all the deadly accuracy of a

Marine throwing a grenade. Me, Harlan Brown, the pride of the Marines, I threw a rock at the cops. I punched a cop. I completely forgot that I might wind up in jail. I found myself against a wall, being beaten by two big cops. Then I was on the ground in the crush, being kicked and stomped. Somebody rode a horse over me.

Somehow, in the confusion, I managed to get away, bleeding and battered, with three cracked ribs and a broken nose and a few hoofprints on me.

Something cracked in my head that night, and in the heads of the gays. That night saw the coming out of the militant gay. After that they were fighting everybody in sight, demanding human rights and fairer laws. I was not exactly ready for radical activism. But it had dawned on me that I was now a citizen of a nation where straight Americans did not permit the flag to fly.

So I stuck to my hustling. It might be felt that if I'd really wanted to spare myself the degradation, I could have. Surely I could have found honest work. Or I could have done what some upright men do: starve first.

The answer was that I didn't see it as degradation. Venal, perhaps. But I was earning my living like everybody else. The Protestant work ethic never shone forth in my life so clearly. Hustling, I could earn far more money than I had at Penn State. My ex-wife never failed to get the biweekly check. I even paid my income taxes down to the last cent. Most prostitutes don't, but I wasn't looking for trouble with the IRS. My earnings were on record through my ex-wife, and I was still patriotic enough to think it was my duty to pay.

In fact, in my pain and anger, I was wallowing in my gayness a little, trying to get to the very bottom of it. There was the period when I liked parading around in macho paraphernalia. But sometimes I'd get a glimpse of myself in a mirror, in that black leather harness with gold studs and chains on it, and a cock-ring on, and that long whip in my hand, flailing hell out of some quivering delighted score, and something inside me would cry out:

"This isn't me. I'm really a peaceful man." And I'd long for the simple eroticism of the jock strap.

One of the gay celebrities I met through Steve Goodnight was filmmaker Gil Harkness. His name isn't a household word to most Americans, but to the gays he is an Ingmar Bergman or a John Ford. He made one of the first gay art films, *The Double Cross*, that broke away from the la-de-da pornography of the little nine-to-midnight all-male theaters. If you ever catch this sadomasochistic classic (it sometimes makes a second run in uptown art theaters now), note the Roman officer who whips the sexy Jesus. That's me. My anonymity was preserved by a shiny helmet, and a pseudonym appeared in the credits.

Hustling being the job it is, I quickly learned to hoard my feelings for off-hours. There were several men—two my age, the rest younger—that I became fond of. It was with them that I was first able to explore the gentler and more passionate side of my sexuality. But I continued to live alone, and I never fell in love. In fact, I found myself always holding back, as if in waiting for something better to come. None of them was that ghost of Chris.

I kept in shape by running eight miles a day round and round Washington Square or down to Battery Park. Sometimes I did it in the afternoon, after being up all night doing my work. I felt a lonely figure in my gray sweats, striding along past the students, the junkies, the hippies and the derelicts that thronged the square. Sometimes I looked up at the statue of George Washington on top of the triumphal arch and thought, "You bastard, if you only knew where duty, honor and country lead some people."

Sometimes, to treat myself, I took the subway uptown and ran in Central Park, where the struggling trees and grass passed for woods. Or I went all the way up to Van Cortlandt Park in the Bronx, whose steep rocky wooded trails are the scene of so many metropolitan-area collegiate and open cross-country races. Always those trails were thronged with runners. I didn't go there often—I felt too alone there. How I longed, sometimes, for the freedom and innocence of those summer runs in the Poconos so long ago.

During those two years in Manhattan, I even managed to hang onto the shreds of my religion. Other gays felt the same outrage at being shut away from God for performing sexual acts which differed little from those that society sanctioned in holy matrimony. So the little gay churches were springing up in the metropolitan area, with a priest here and a minister there who were brave enough to care.

Every Sunday I went to the small Church of the Beloved Disciple on Fourteenth Street, and I played rather desperately. I did not pray to be miraculously changed back into a heterosexual. I prayed for knowledge to know myself and accept myself totally. Being gay, I now realized, was not merely a question of sex—it was a state of mind. Society had told me I was a disease, but I was convinced that I had come to homosexuality by natural inclination. I prayed for someone to love, and I prayed for a less venal way to make my living. The Gospel of St. John was comforting—he loved the Lord and laid his head on His breast. I could not believe that Jesus had less compassion for gays than for the thieves that He was so gentle with.

I also thought a lot about the hatred and intolerance that we were subjected to. I had lived on the butter-rich crest of America, on the star-spangled crest of the wave. I had been intolerant myself, though I had called it by other names, such as "tough-minded," "upright" and "clean-living." I had thought these were the qualities that made America great. For the first time in my life, I had been made a butt of these virtues. They had been poured over my bare body like acid.

Sometimes I wondered if that peculiar American hatred of homosexuality isn't a result of its being so rooted, so silent and unacknowledged, yet so pervasive, in our history. In school we are taught the Victorian proprieties of this history. Yet much of that early history is men alone with each other out on the reaches of the continent. Strong young men with all the urges, like my athletes horsing around in the shower rooms. Explorers, scouts, mountain men, trappers, Indian fighters, cowboys, prospectors, trailblazers. Men with their women left hundreds of miles behind, or men with no women at all.

They came to the frontier with that Western puritanism in their consciences, and there they were broken by sexual need, and forced to deny this puritanism and reach out to each other. Once need was satisfied, who knows how many male loves grew up there in the Kentucky wilderness, or out on the plains, or in the dry-baked desert canyons?

They were the vanguards of Columbia Gem of the Ocean, yet a glance at their circumstances and you know that many of them were gay. Sometimes I think that we reached from sea to shining sea over these young macho bodies in their buckskins and corduroys and khakis. There was no gay ghetto then—nowhere to take shelter if you were forced to come out. In those days, the penalties for being found out were far more crushing than they are even now.

In their fear and helpless guilt, they denied what they had felt, repressed it, called it by other names, such as having a partner or a sidekick. When they got to town, they wore out the whores, and they brought their docile perfumed wives out to the frontier as fast as they could. And we have gone on denying it to this day.

While I don't want to over-dramatize the thought processes of that period in New York, the whole experience did radically change my view of American society. Steve Goodnight made me realize how uneducated I was, and I started reading a lot. For the first time in my life, I was reading something besides *Track & Field News* with enthusiasm.

Most of all, I came to hate violence. While I was being violent myself, it was only because I was angry. I wondered how I could ever have thirsted to go to Korea and kill gooks. I even started to wonder about Vietnam. The thing that really depressed me the most was being away from track. When the big indoor meets came to Madison Square Garden, I yearned to go, but I didn't. My only touch with events was the sports magazines, and a few people I still saw. Bruce Cayton from the *Post* sometimes took me to lunch. Aldo Franconi was another, a Long Island coach and local AAU official who was a crusty liberal.

All anybody in the outside world knew about me was that I was a very respectable masseur, and sometimes appeared in men's fashion ads. Bruce and Aldo had their suspicions, but never mentioned them.

I didn't cry. Tears were not in my education.

If Joe Prescott had not come along with his incredible offer to go to Prescott, I suppose I would still be there in Manhattan. Sooner or later, my growing anger at the gay sufferings would have led me—unwillingly but inevitably— to violent gay activism. Possibly I would have ended up in jail. Who knows? In recent years a number of God-fearing men have ended up in jail. Look at the Berrigans.

So when Joe got in touch with me, it was—I assumed— God's answer to my prayer.

Joe was busy building Prescott. He had lost his athletic director. He wanted a high-quality replacement, but had been unable to pry the kind of man he wanted away from the big schools. He had remembered my case. He also loved to rescue people. He applied his Yankee thrift to people as well as money. "Waste people not, want people not," he used to say. His faculty was full of brilliant castoffs: ex-alcoholics, ex-convicts, ex-junkies, handicapped Vietnam veterans.

So he traced me through Bruce Cayton, and came to see me.

I'll never forget that evening. We sat in my small apartment on West Ninth Street. Joe made me his pitch. I vacillated. Joe kept talking.

I sat there looking at this tall, genial, old curmudgeon with his thatch of prematurely white hair and his baggy, gray suit. He was drinking a whiskey straight up, and I was drinking a glass of milk.

I thought about being back in the locker rooms with naked athletes again, and all the torments that would mean. I was now a battle-hardened gay veteran, used to indulging my sex, and I might lose control of myself with some really attractive runner.

"Look," I said, "I think I have to be honest with you. It's something you ought to find out now, rather than later. I was forced to resign at Penn State because a rumor went around that I was a homosexual."

"Yes, I heard the rumor," said Joe, "when I was trying to track you down."

"The kid started it himself. I didn't touch him, and that's a fact. He was gay, and he knew I was gay. I wasn't interested in him, so he started the rumor out of spite."

Joe sat thinking.

"Nobody knows it for sure outside," I said, my voice shaking a little. "But if it ever comes out, your school might be embarrassed. And your alumni, the parents . . ."

"My alumni are still mostly under thirty," said Joe. "And nobody pressures me."

He sat thinking a moment more.

"Well," he said, "I've already got a couple of gays on my faculty. They haven't given me any problems. I offer you the job with just one condition. If you feel like shacking up with one of the students or faculty, that's your business—as long as he's not a minor. I just don't want trouble with the law. Otherwise it's not my business, or the school's business, or society's business what you do. And frankly, nobody on campus would pay attention. It's a live and let live place, which is what I wanted."

By now I was so scarred and cautious that I could scarcely believe the incredible Christian kindness of this offer.

"I'm hard on kids," I said. "I'm not one of your mealy-mouthed permissive liberals." (This from a man who was having some second thoughts about conservatism.)

Joe looked reflective. "I've talked to some men who were on your team at Penn State. One of them expressed their sentiments pretty well. He said, 'Harlan Brown was a mean son of a bitch, but the runners that failed him went away knowing that they had failed personally. They were unable to blame it on his harshness.'"

He swallowed the rest of his scotch.

"A four-year contract, Harlan. Twenty thousand to start with. Board and keep on campus, so you'll be spared living expenses. Think about it. Let me know sometime during the next week."

I swallowed the rest of my milk. "I don't have to think about it," I said. "I'll take it."

At Prescott, I found—for the first time since my childhood—a home. Joe's wife Marian was as kind as he was. Both of them taught me the real meaning of liberalism—a tough-minded and virile liberalism. The two of them were patient with me during the first few months as I licked my wounds and healed myself.

Prescott was even structured like a family. It was, if you must, a kind of a commune, and it worked. Faculty and students lived mixed together, with no visible difference in status. The students ran the campus, worked in the administration and even shoveled snow. Joe was almost never to be found in his walnut-paneled office in the main building (which had once been his house), unless he actually had some work to do there. He was usually out on the campus with his clipboard, thinking, listening, talking. Or he was traveling to get new ideas and new people.

No attempt was made to regulate anybody's morals at Prescott. Students and faculty were free to set up their own living arrangements. The dorms were coed. I found a few other gays already on campus. There was a tiny gay-lib student group, about four or five, and there were the two male faculty members he'd mentioned, who were living together. Since both the faculty and the student body were already so full of colorful heterosexual eccentrics, nobody paid much attention to them.

Prescott was not a fancy place. The buildings were

strictly functional, and the equipment was simply what was needed. Joe wanted something that really worked, not a glittering showcase full of problems and high overhead. As a result, it was one of the few private schools in the U.S. that wasn't having money problems, and whose enrollment was growing. When I came there, the school had 1,500 students, about the size of Oberlin.

The reason that an ex-Marine officer could feel so comfortable at Prescott was that a lot of my ideas had changed. My hardshell conservatism had suffered a death blow. I was no longer able to judge people, or myself, by the same standards as before. I was still deeply patriotic, and loved the flag, and believed in America's mission. But my patriotism was now tinged by deep anxiety over the human flaws in my country, and I began to think that these flaws should be polished away.

I was more lenient with my athletes now. I still expected as much hard work and responsibility from them as before. But I stopped hassling them about their hair. It occurred to me that fights about hair were a big waste of time and energy. The kids ran with their legs, not their hair.

I stopped hassling them about chastity. I had learned the hard way that when an athlete bottles up sexual energy, it can create destructive tensions. Sex is nature's sleeping pill. If I had a kid who got jumpy the night before a meet, I'd prescribe a hot bath, something warm to drink and a tender half hour with his girlfriend, and he'd sleep like a baby.

I even relaxed a little on the issue of drinking. How can you tell a kid not to have a beer when he sees so many world-class athletes having a beer? "Frank Shorter had a beer the night before he won the marathon at Munich," they'd tell me. How can you argue? And beer replaces the salts after a long hard run, too.

There were a number of things that I stayed uptight about, because I knew they were harmful no matter how liberal we got. Like smoking, drugs, hard spirits, etc. But all in all, I was not the same man as before. Coach Brown was rapidly being humanized.

The campus stood in the middle of 900 acres of wooded hills and lakes, all Joe's property. It was magnificent for running. I laid out twenty-five miles of trails through them, and ran on them as much as my teams did, recovering a little of that summer joy of the Poconos.

As those four happy years passed at Prescott, even my powerful sexual cravings slacked off. "Getting old," I thought, "and maybe it's just as well." I was busy, committed to something outside myself, and had less time for futile fantasies. No one on campus but the Prescotts knew I was gay. I had no sexual relationships with the campus gays, and stuck to my hands-off rule regarding my team. When the spirit moved me, I drove the sixty miles to New York City and picked somebody up.

A few parents muttered, but by and large no fuss was made at my being at Prescott. No one outside the hard core of the gay community knew about me, and no one knew about my hustling save my ex-clients, who weren't likely to talk about it. As far as the world was concerned, I had just crawled out of sight for a couple of years.

When Billy Sive came to Prescott, I was just past thirty-nine years old, and beginning to think that my secret fantasy would die a quiet and decent death. But I found I was wrong.

In those very first winter days, he stirred up all the old feelings, to a pitch of intensity that I'd never felt before. He was not merely physically attractive, but an appealing human being as well. I was that lonely mature man, but I was also like an adolescent seething with longing. For the first time in my life, I was deeply in love.

And I knew I didn't dare lay a hand on him.

THREE

T he three celebrated runners' appearance on our track-mad campus caused quite a stir.

The campus paper, a mimeographed thing called *The Daily Mantra*, gave them smudged headlines. I was amused to overhear a radical student, whose ideology should have excluded this kind of feeling, say, "Now we're gonna rip Manhattan and Villanova."

My track team was simply agog. Their finest moment, so far, had been running in the NCAA eastern cross-country championship in Van Cortlandt Park in the Bronx. They had gotten spattered with mud from the spikes of Manhattan, Penn and Villanova runners, and had placed seventh in the team scoring.

So having super-burners like Vince Matti fall from heaven onto their team produced mixed feelings among the boys. At first they were elated. "Now we're gonna wipe out the whole country." Then they were intimidated. "The rest of us will be ignored."

The next morning I found my male freshmen standing in a little huddle by the track, wearing their sweats and watching the Oregon three work out. The snow was melting with a rush, and the cinder track lay bare and steaming fresh. The sun was hot and the temperature about fifty.

As the Oregon three tore past, their spikes gnashing in the wet cinders, my boys' mouths made small O's in their faces. Their eyes shifted to me.

"Geez," said one of them.

"Get your asses out there and work," I said, "and maybe you'll run like that too."

"Yessir, Mr. Brown, sir," they said with a little sarcasm. But they took the hint and all jogged off to warm up.

I stood in the sunshine, pushing back my parka hood and pulling out my stopwatch, and watched the three ex-Oregoners whipping along the backstretch. They had thrown their brand-new Prescott sweats on the bleachers and were running bare-legged, in singlets. They were pacing each other, running shoulder to shoulder, their hair lifting. I could see they were having a good time.

Now they rounded into the turn toward me, and I could begin to hear the gnash, gnash of their spikes. They floated along on their long legs like whippets. Now I could hear their breathing amid the crunch of spikes. Then they were flashing past me. For a moment I was able to forget about practical things like oxygen capacity of lungs and lactic acid build-up in muscles, and see them as pure myth.

A nervous contentment suffused me, warm and unstable as the winter sunshine. The hidden beauties of my subconscious had again risen into view, on this cinder track, in this sweet sunshine.

The three had finished their quarter-mile speed lap and were jogging to take the recovery interval and let their pulses drop. I looked at my watch. After just thirty seconds they were off again. This was typical of the high-power stuff that Lindquist had his runners do.

That first morning, I was content just to watch and see what they did. Even their styles were different. Vince Matti hurtled along, full of raw strength. Jacques LaFont punched his way along with a kind of controlled tension. Billy was a puller, light and effortless.

After a set of quarters, Vince and Jacques broke away to take a couple miles of gentle striding around the field. But Billy kept on alone, reeling out 60-second quarters with only a 30-second jogging rest between. I was impressed. He was really burning through them. You put together four 60's, and you have a four-minute mile.

Sitting down beside his carelessly tossed sweats, I clocked him with my Harper Split and noted the times. He did fifteen of those quarters, pacing himself with such spooky precision that he never varied more than a quarter- or half-second. He paid absolutely no attention to me. To judge from the abstracted expression on his face, I don't think he knew that I was there.

What impressed me most was the effortlessness. His long, floating stride had an eerie, slow-motion quality. He just ghosted along. And he had a very light, soft stride— now that he was alone, I could scarcely hear his spikes stir the cinders as he went past. He had the most beautiful natural form I had ever seen—no wasted effort anywhere. He was almost unreal. He was that idea of a runner that haunts the minds of track people.

Finally he finished. While I worked with the other boys, he did two miles at a crisp 5:15 pace to warm down. Even his warm-down was no fooling around.

Then he came jogging over to me. He smiled a little, still abstracted, but he now looked quite tired. I said nothing, just tossed him his towel, and stood pretending to study his times noted on my clipboard.

Up close, he was no idea. He was painfully real. He smelled of wet hair and wet cloth. The realness of him hit me like a blow. And he looked even more attractive than yesterday.

In the daylight, his face and limbs were faintly speckled all over like a bird's egg. He had gotten too much sun on his fair skin. Just looking at his skin gave me a tender, hurting feeling. I wanted to caress it, and knew I would never do it. His glasses were what gave his handsome face its chief charm—they made him look like a sexy, young professor.

Glancing covertly up from the clipboard as he busied himself with the towel, I noticed that on his right shoulder he had a tattoo. That surprised me. It looked like a sun sign—a woman's naked torso with a laurel wreath.

"What's that tattoo?" I asked.

"That's Virgo," he said. He grinned, a sensual, sunny grin, and jerked his thumb toward the other two, who were back running on the track. "They've got tattoos too. Vince is a Scorpio, and Jacques is a Cancer."

"The three of you are good friends, aren't you?" My heart was sinking. He was probably sleeping with one or both of them.

"Yeah, we are," he said. "You're a Leo, aren't you? I looked it up."

"I think astrology is a lot of crap," I said, looking back down at my clipboard.

He shrugged pleasantly, putting one spiked foot on the bleachers and toweling himself between the thighs. At that, I was practically getting a hard-on, and I turned away to look at the rest of the team, searching vainly for someone to yell at. One of them ran past carrying his arms too high, and I barked, "Get those arms down!"

I felt drenched by his physicalness. I tried hard to remember if I had ever had this feeling with a woman. Perhaps in college with a girlfriend or two, perhaps with Mary Ellen. The gay feels this same total eroticization toward the body, only it's the male body. It wasn't merely the fullness in the crotch of his shorts that made me want him. It was even the littlest things. His damp wind-tossed curls. The moist, brown stubble that he still hadn't bothered to shave off. His shoulders and thighs steaming in the sunshine. His brown nipples and his navel showing through the wet shirt. The way his faded blue shorts were slit up the side a little, baring the hip (the manufacturers do this for more leg freedom, but it is also very sexy). To me his long, finely muscled legs, laced with veins, were as evocative as Raquel Welch's legs would be to a heterosexual. His light, spiked shoes were more fatal than Cinderella's slippers.

I turned back to him as the poker-faced Marine, having

crushed my rush of feeling successfully. Then I saw something that made me forget about sex. He had fine muscle tremors in those beautiful thighs of his. He was really tired.

"You have trouble with cramps?" I asked.

"Sometimes." He was bending, busy, not looking at me.

"At night?"

"Yeah, sometimes at night too."

"You must not be getting enough calcium and magnesium," I said. I was liking less and less what I saw. That magnificent body of his was on the edge of exhaustion. "And you've had a lot of injuries."

"Stress fractures," he said. "I was red-shirted all last year. One in the shin, one in the metatarsals. I try to drink a lot of milk, but I seem to have these brittle bones." He was shivering, standing straight now, looking at me with something like an appeal in his eyes.

"Get those sweats on," I said.

"Yeah, right," he said, and pulled them on.

"Well," he said, "I don't know what you're going to think about my program. I was doing what Lindquist told me to. But obviously we were doing something wrong."

"Why?"

"Because I should be improving, and I'm not. I mean, I've been putting in a lot of work, and no results. My best events are the 5,000 and the 10,000. I know there's a sub-28-minute 10,000 inside of me there. But I can't get down to it."

I stood looking at him thoughtfully, sex forgotten now. This was naked ambition. Breaking 28 in the 10,000 meter is a big deal, like breaking 4 in the mile, and only about 15 runners had ever done it.

"Well, we'll study your program carefully," I said slowly.

"That's one major reason I came here. I feel I need a good coach. I suppose I could have tried to cut it alone, training myself. I could forget about collegiate running, I guess, and just go into open. But I don't know enough yet about training to find the right way. I feel totally confused and stymied. So maybe you can figure it out."

He was zipping up the jacket of his sweats. Then he was polishing his glasses, which had a little moisture condensed on them. For a moment those spooky, clear eyes of his met mine without the glasses in between, and I noted his thick, chestnut eyelashes.

"I'm thinking about the Olympics," he said.

I was dubious. Vince and Jacques were clear Olympic prospects, but I didn't want to get Billy's hopes up.

"I want to double in the 5,000 and 10,000 in Montréal," he said.

The 5,000 meter and the 10,000 meter are the classic long-distance runs on the track and are equivalent to nearly three and six miles.

"That's a big order," I said. "You'll have to be breaking 28 in the 10,000 and 13:35 in the 5,000 by next fall. To win, you'd probably have to run anywhere between 27:30 and 27:35 in the 10,000, and around 13:10 or 15 in the 5,000. You haven't had any international experience, so we'd have to get you out there a time or two beforehand. That's why Steve Prefontaine lost the 5,000 at Munich— he didn't know how tough those European babies are."

I didn't add that Americans had won only two Olympic 5,000s and one 10,000 in history, and that only now were American distance runners becoming a serious challenge to European power in these two great events. Billy knew that.

"I worry that maybe I'm too young for this Olympics," said Billy.

"It isn't how young you are. It's how good you are."

"Okay," Billy grinned, "I'll take your word for it."

"Get your ass into the shower," I said. "I want to see all three of you at my house tonight. Seven sharp. We have team open house there every Monday and Thursday. Training films, consciousness-raising, and stuff."

"Okay, *Mr*. Brown," he said.

"No sarcasm," I barked. "And I mean that."

He looked at me strangely. "Sure, Mr. Brown," he said in a low voice and walked off.

That evening at seven, my house slowly filled with runners. I lived in what had once been the head gardener's cottage. It was a pleasant rambling stucco place, with a wisteria-covered veranda in front. It stood on the warm south side of several big spruces and pines, near the greenhouses. (The greenhouses had once housed Joe's famed orchid collection—now they sheltered a clutter of exotic botany and ecological experiments.) From my front window, I could look across the field to the track and the bleachers. Joe Prescott must have known what balm that little house, and that view, would be to my wounded soul.

The runners came in tracking mud. The big living room had windowseats and windows on three sides. Now the red chintz curtains were pulled. The fire in the fieldstone fireplace threw a pleasant glow on the dark old board floor, on the threadbare Afghan rug before the hearth. I had bought the wing chairs and sofa and coffee table at the local thrift shop.

The decor fit my needs exactly. Nothing fancy, so the boys could flop all over it. Easy to clean, since my ex-wife was still soaking me and I couldn't afford a cleaning lady. On the pine-paneled walls, I had photos of runners and a few fly-spotted old sporting prints.

On either side of the fireplace were two doors. The one on the right led into a small sunny kitchen, with old-fashioned cupboards painted so many times you could hardly close the doors. I did as little cooking as possible, preferring to eat with the students in the college dining room.

The door on the left led into the paneled bedroom. The hideous burled-walnut Victorian bed and dresser had come from the local Salvation Army warehouse. The big windows looked out into the spruce trees, but now the curtains were pulled. By the bed, another creaky door led into an ice-cold old-fashioned tile bathroom with a rusty shower and a cranky old toilet.

Four of the cross-country team were already there. I had two of them bringing in more wood from the tarp-covered pile behind the house, and the other two in the kitchen slicing carrots to make carrot sticks.

The Oregon three came at five after seven, just to establish their independence. They shucked their jackets and looked around.

"Carrot sticks," said Vince with disgust, leaning in the kitchen doorway.

"No junk food served on this campus," I said. "No potato chips, no hot dogs, none of that crap. Runners are what they eat."

Jacques came into the kitchen and started cutting carrots with exquisite precision. He was a biology major and had probably gotten his skill dissecting specimens in the lab.

Shortly they were all there. Joe Prescott came too, and settled into a wing chair. (I had made a track nut out of him, and he came to the open house as often as he could.) After initial awkwardness, they were all talking nicely, and my team discovered that the three newcomers were human beings. I showed a film of the recent national cross-country championship. We had a discussion, and all munched carrot sticks and cracked nuts and drank tea.

It was a pleasant evening, and when the rest moved off at about 8:30, I motioned Joe and the Oregon three to stay.

The five of us sat on alone by the fire, Joe and I in the wing chairs and the three boys sitting on the rug. I said a few things that had been on my mind.

"You know," I said, "I took you guys on the team in a weak moment. I don't regret it. But the more I think about what's ahead, the more I realize what a hassle it's going to be."

They were all silent.

"First of all, we've got to keep your being gay under wraps for as long as possible. I don't want you coming out on campus, joining the gay lib group or anything like that. Sooner or later, the rumor is going to get around, and we'll deal with it when it does. But let's buy ourselves as much peace and quiet as possible, for now. Is that agreeable?"

They all nodded.

"Another problem. When that rumor gets around, invariably people are going to remember what happened to me at Penn State. Did Billy's father tell you about that?"

"Yeah, he told us the whole story," said Vince.

"Okay," I said. "So I never touched the kid. But the fact is, the suspicion was planted in people's minds. Now, because of John Sive, you kids have become privy to information about me that very few people have. On this campus, for instance, only Joe and Marian know that I'm gay. Not even the other gays know that I'm gay. So I'm going to keep your secret, and you're going to keep mine. Agreed?"

They nodded. "Agreed," said Jacques softly.

"Because when you kids get forced out in the open, in all likelihood I'm going to be forced out too. That's going to be a painful moment. It might mean the end of my career for good."

There was total comprehension in their young eyes. Joe was lighting a cigarette, and there was comprehension in his eyes too.

"And that's just the human angle of the problem," I said. "Second, we have the athletic angle. I'm sure you know by now that there are conservative people in track who hate runners and coaches that don't conform. It doesn't much matter *how* they don't conform. The littlest misstep, and whammo."

The boys' eyes met mine squarely as I looked at each of them in turn. They knew what I was talking about, but I knew more than they did.

In amateur athletics, officialdom has an almost medieval power over the athletes. By "officialdom" I mean the various bodies that govern U.S. athletics. My three boys were presently under control of the National Collegiate Athletic Association (NCAA), which runs college sports. When they graduated, they would pass to the control of the Amateur Athletic Union (AAU), which directs most noncollegiate competition. There are other, smaller bodies, but the AAU is the giant, and controls access to international competition. Finally, there is the 300-member U.S. Olympic Committee, which cooperates with the AAU in selecting and preparing the American Olympic team every four years. These three powerful organizations were going to be the focus of our struggle.

Officialdom does not hesitate to use its power if it feels that an athlete or a coach has stepped out of line. The all-time example is the way the AAU treated Jesse Owens after he won four gold medals for the U.S. in the 1936 Olympics. The AAU wanted to show Owens off in post-Olympic meets in Europe, but Owens said he wanted to go home and see his wife and children—he was overtrained and exhausted. The AAU's reaction to this human situation was to punish the great athlete by revoking his amateur status, thus barring him from all further competition.

Today, forty years after the Owens tragedy, the power of officialdom is still that strong. In recent years, amateur athletes have started to fight this power, and to talk a lot about what they call "athletes' rights." They feel that too many officials were too interested in controlling and punishing athletes, and not interested enough in benefiting them and in recognizing their real human needs. They are forcing officials to rethink old attitudes, to liberalize old and irksome rules.

As a former runner, and as a fledgling liberal, I was strongly inclined to side with the athletes. There are, of course, some fine fair-minded people in all three of these organizations, who give unstintingly of their time and energy for the sport, and who join with the athletes in fighting for change. But all three organizations still harbor too many fanatic and/or senile men and women who form a dangerous power bloc. As in Owens' day, they feel that athletes should be wind-up dolls who run record times and don't talk back, and they are fighting the athletes' rights movement every step of the way.

"For instance," I said, "when people hassled Marty Liquori because he partied and had a beer or two. It didn't matter to them that Marty could beat Jim Ryun every time the two of them met. They were ready to throw Marty's best performances in the garbage can because he didn't fit their old-fashioned idea of what a runner is."

The three boys were nodding.

"And as far as the personal morality of athletes goes," I said, "these old men, their idea of total degeneracy was when those two guys on the New York Yankees swapped wives."

We all laughed a little, grimly.

"So," I said, "now we're going to have a gay coach with three gay runners. We are going to be out in full view, with 'gay is beautiful' written across our foreheads in letters of fire. And the conservative element in track is not going to like that at all."

They were silent again. Joe was smoking a cigarette, gazing into the fire. Joe and I had already had this same discussion, and I knew he wasn't afraid.

My Irish setter, Jim, came wagging into the room and curled up among the three boys, licking Vince's hand.

"I also think that they will avoid talking about homosexuality, if possible," I said. "It just scares them too much. So what they will do is try to trip us up with the rule book. If you put an extra spike on your shoes, and they catch you, you're disqualified, whether you're gay or straight. Do you follow me?"

They were all nodding. I tossed them three copies of the AAU handbook.

"If you've read it before, read it again. Learn it by

heart. Some of the rules are good, and some of them are stupid, but this is what they'll hit us with, if they can."

They flipped through the books, very soberly.

I was talking bluntly now, jabbing the air with my finger. "At all times, we are going to conduct ourselves with dignity. We are not going to give them any *extra* grounds for criticism. Like, Vince, the time you got disqualified for warming up during the national anthem. I agree that it's stupid to make an athlete stand around and get cold during the anthem, but the fact is—they can use things like that to hurt you. Let's not have any irrelevant provocations."

"Yeah, right," said Vince in a low voice.

"I want no doping. No taking under-the-table money. If any of you are hard up for money, come to me and we'll find money. I want you clean on money, so they can't use that against you." I paused a moment. "Have any of you taken money?"

"I've been offered money, but I never took it," said Jacques. "I didn't need it, so why take it?"

"Nobody ever offered me any," said Billy. "Anyway, I wouldn't . . ."

"How about you, Vince?" I said.

He shrugged. "I've taken it. Always."

I sighed. "That's bad."

"Everybody was taking it," he said.

"I know," I said. "But the point is, they close their eyes to their favorites taking it. If you're blacklisted, suddenly they maybe discover that you've taken it, and whammo."

"Then I guess the kiss of death is on me," said Vince morosely.

"Well, we'll just have to be optimistic," I said. "At any rate, from now on, we have to think of every contingency. We have to figure out every strategy that they'll try beforehand, and block it if we can. Because at least one of you is going to Montréal, probably, and I wouldn't want you knocked off the Olympic team just because we messed up our tactics. Some people in track, and some people in the country as a whole, will be very unhappy if any of you represent the U.S. They're going to take it as an insult to our national masculinity. I have a feeling that these people won't stop at anything to keep you kids from setting foot on the Montréal track."

Their eyes were fixed on mine, full of naked seriousness.

"We don't know anything much about track politics," said Billy. "We'll mess up for sure."

"You leave the politics to me," I said. I smiled a little. "That's what I'm for. All you have to worry about is running. And when I figure out the politics, you do what I suggest. That's all."

"We may have to go to court before it's over," said Billy.

"We might," I said. "Your father may have to help us out."

"Shit," said Vince, "I'd love to see the AAU in court."

"It won't be fun," I said. "Before this whole thing is over, we may have moments when we wish we'd never been born."

"But it's worth doing," said Billy, softly.

"Yes, I said, "it is."

When they got up to leave, I pointed at the messy kitchen and said, "One of you stay for KP." I hoped Billy would volunteer. To my delight, he did.

In another minute we were alone, busily cleaning up the piles of carrot peelings and nutshells and washing teacups. I was feeling benevolent and able to control my feelings. And I was hungry to know more about him. So I said, "Tell me about your father."

"He's coming to visit me at Christmas," said Billy, "so you'll meet him. My dad is a great guy."

I was washing the teacups in the old-fashioned enamel sink, and Billy was drying them with one of my scroungy dishtowels.

"So your father is gay."

"My mother left him when I was about nine months

old. She abandoned me. He married a gay after that, and the two of them raised me."

"How did your father manage to hold onto his law career and live openly with a gay?" I asked.

"Well," said Billy, "my father goes for TV's. None of my father's business colleagues ever suspected Frances was a male. He looked like a very slender Marilyn Monroe. He had beautiful silver-blonde hair. My father would entertain, and Frances would float around, saying, 'Another cocktail, darling?' Visually, he was incredible."

"A hermaphrodite?" I asked.

Billy shook his head. "No, he had male organs. I know, because I stumbled in on him once when he was in the bathroom. He was very modest and he screamed. After that I took it for granted that everybody's mother had a cock." He laughed a little, very busy with the teacups. "You can imagine what a shock I got when I found out the truth. I was in seventh grade, and one day the kids were handing around some dirty pictures. I saw a cunt for the first time. It was all red and wet, like a wound."

He was putting the cups carefully back in the cupboard. "To me, the real trauma was learning about the heterosexual world. Know what I mean?"

"So you're the second generation of the nation of gays," I said softly.

"But Frances and my father broke up when I was twelve," said Billy sadly. "After that, he's had a whole raft of lovers, but nothing permanent."

"So you grew up knowing everything?"

"Shit," said Billy, "I was into junior high before it really sank into my head that I lived in a different world than the other kids. I mean, I grew up in the gay ghetto in San Francisco. It was all I knew."

As a veteran of secretiveness and agonizing, I was fascinated by the kid's openness and directness. I was shortly to learn that Billy didn't volunteer personal information unasked. But if you asked him something straight out, he would give you the cold answer, without dramatics and without hesitation, no matter how personal it was.

When we had cleaned up the kitchen, I motioned him to the fireplace and threw one more log on the fire. He sank down onto the rug, and the setter immediately came over and curled up against him blissfully. I sat down in the wing chair.

"Did your father actually take you around in the gay world?" I asked.

"Not right away," said Billy. "He was pretty careful about what he let me see when I was smaller. He let me find out about things little by little, as I was ready for them. You know, like straight parents do."

"The straights would say you've been brainwashed," I said.

"Maybe," he said. "On the other hand, they brainwash their kids too. Anyway, I might have grown up straight. My father didn't force it on me. I mean, I chose it freely."

I was curious to see just how far I could force my probing.

"The straights might wonder about the relationship between you and your father," I said.

Billy shook his head and smiled. "No way. He was always very concerned about that. He wanted our relationship to be as healthy as possible. He never fooled around with men in front of me. He and Frances were very modest. He knew it had to be that way if I was going to grow up with my head in one piece."

I was shaking my head slowly in disbelief. John Sive had to be some kind of gay Dr. Spock.

"When did you have your first lover?" I asked.

"When I was fifteen." Billy was gazing into the fire, stroking the dog slowly. "It was kind of an unhappy business. I mean, I was happy with it, but he wasn't. Ricky was a mess, he couldn't accept himself. We broke up. Later on I heard what happened to him. In college he got busted on drug possession, and sentenced to twenty years. In prison he got gang-raped and committed suicide."

For a minute I had a terrible image in my head of Billy being gang-raped by five or six macho convicts. "Anything like that ever happen to you?"

He shook his head. "I got beat up by straights a few times, that's all."

"I presume," I said, "that you don't mess around with drugs."

"No," he said, "I was never into dope. That's something my dad is pretty uptight about. I don't even use poppers. I've always been afraid they would take away my edge in a race or something."

"Who came after Ricky?"

"Three more. All unhappy. Like, I haven't had much luck. My father was always saying, 'I raised you to be such a well-adjusted boy, what's going wrong with you?'"

He was still gazing into the fire, and his hand had stopped stroking the dog. He looked sad, and somehow older. I got my first glimpse, at that moment, of a tremendous sense of loss that he lived with. He was only twenty-two, and two mothers and four serious lovers had already caved in under him.

"So you weren't open about being gay in school," I said.

"No, I wasn't," he said. "I kept very quiet about it. I didn't feel guilty or anything. But I felt very, you know, very intimidated by straight attitudes, the more I learned about them. I'm not really a very brave person, maybe. But when I felt troubled, I could always go and talk it out with my dad. By the time I got to my junior year at Oregon, I wasn't really worried about it. So when Lindquist blew my cover, I thought, what the hell, from now on I'm going to come out."

His casual low-key confession was giving me a lump in the throat. We sat listening for a few moments to the soft sighing of the log on the fire. It was getting late, but I couldn't resist prolonging the moment.

"Have you ever slept with a girl?" I asked in a half-teasing tone of voice.

He shook his head and laughed.

"Do you hate girls?" I asked.

He laughed again. "No. Why should I? They just don't interest me. I mean, I'm not totally indifferent. I can feel amiable toward a girl, and be friends. There was a girl at Oregon, Janet Huss, we were friends. A lot of people assumed we were serious. Once in a while I thought I'd tell her I was gay, but I didn't. Then she found out about it when Lindquist kicked me off the team." He paused a moment, gazing into the fire. "She was very ugly about it. I told her, 'It's your own ugliness, it's going to make you ugly.' But she didn't believe me."

"Well, now you know," I said. "Men give, and women take."

He looked at me questioningly, and didn't say more. I sensed that he wanted to question me about my life. Since it had always been my policy never to discuss my personal life with my athletes, I was not about to answer his questions.

"Well," I said, "it's nine-thirty, and you ought to be getting back to the dorm. Who are you rooming with?"

I got up, and he got up too.

"I asked for a room to myself. Vince and Jacques are rooming together."

"What are the relationships here? Just so I don't put my foot in it."

Billy was picking up his battered Mao jacket from the window seat.

"Vince and Jacques are the lovers. I'm alone."

"Tell me one more thing," I said. "I just can't believe three of you on that team. One, maybe, but *three* . . ."

Billy laughed, pulling on his jacket. "Why not? It's a big team, sixty guys. And a big school."

"How did the three of you end up there?"

"Oh, we sort of accumulated. I met Vince my senior year in high school, when we ran in the Golden West Invitational. That was some race, man. He sat on my neck, and then he tried to blast me. Lucky for me, it was just over his distance. I beat him to the tape by about three inches. After the race we got to talking, and we became friends right away."

"Lovers?"

"No," said Billy, leaning against the door, answering as if I had just asked him the time. "D'ya have to be lovers all the time? No, we're just best friends. That summer we went crazy running together. We went to every open race we could get to, and we had a great time. And we'd decided we wanted to be on the same college team, and Oregon wanted to sign us both, so that was that."

"Then you met Jacques at Oregon."

"Right. And Jacques was still straight, then, but he'd been having suspicions about himself. When he saw Vince, it was love at first sight. Poor Jacques, he really suffered. Both of us helped him. Jacques adores Vince, but he's awfully nervous about the whole thing. I'll never forget how he cried when Lindquist got done with him. Vince and I were ready to kill Lindquist just because of Jacques."

"I've noticed he's very protective about Jacques."

"Yeah. A lotta guys that don't know Vince, they think he's a bird of paradise, and very fickle. But he's more of a mother hen."

Billy was leaning against the door, looking so wise and so appealing that the old panic was rising in me.

"Well," I said, trying to sound hearty, "any time any of the three of you have something on your minds, feel free to make an appointment to see me in my office."

Billy was opening the door, and the fresh night air poured into the room. "We sure will, Mr. Brown. You've been great. Thanks a lot."

He went out into the snow and closed the door. I was left alone.

FOUR

T he three boys' coming to my team also caused quite
a little stir in the track world. When runners of
their caliber change teams, it always causes a stir. Usually,
however, such runners move to a team or school of equal
or higher status.

"Prescott?" everybody wanted to know. "Where's that?"

Right away we had some reporters nosing around the
campus. The three runners said glibly that they'd come to
Prescott because they liked my coaching methods, and
that they were tired of the impersonality of big schools.

As the December days passed, I was better able to
assess my three new team members.

Jacques' biggest problem, I could see, was his
nervousness. He was going to be one of those runners who
wind up with a shelf full of trophies and a bleeding ulcer.
He was not only nervous about being gay, but about
competition. He went through agonies before races,
shaking, throwing up.

He settled straight into his studies, spending long hours
in the biology lab. His main interest was ornithology. He
also played the alto recorder, and immediately joined the
campus's tiny pro musica. He made a few friends and
amused everyone no end, but mostly he stayed with the
team and me.

Vince's biggest problem was going to be those fragile
legs of his. He came to me broken down by Lindquist's

high-power training methods. It pained me, as I worked
over his tendinitis, to think that a little common sense
would have averted this. Slavedriver though I am, I think
that there is such a thing as enough stress, beyond which
a given athlete's system breaks down. I got hold of an
experimental drug, dimethyl sulphoxide, that had been
successful in reducing the pain and inflammation of
tendinitis, and started dosing him with it.

Despite all I'd heard of Vince's temper on the track, he
was very docile with me. I just told him what I thought he
should do, and he did it, and I checked in on him every
other day. Like Jacques, he was a good student, and he
went right to work. He was also cheerfully promiscuous—
while he didn't sleep around much, because he was too
busy, he would lay anything that interested him, even
girls. Jacques put up with this stoically.

Vince hadn't been at Prescott a week before he tried
to lay me. "How about it, Mr. Brown?"

Had this been Denny Falks six years ago, I would
have jumped right out the window. This time I took it
very casually.

"Listen, you little nymphomaniac," I said, "you're a
very attractive kid. But I have a rule about not going to
bed with my runners, and I never break it. It's the only
way I can keep a job and earn a living. You understand?"

"Shit," he said, disappointed. "I really wanted to find
out what you're like. We heard so many stories."

"Stories?" I said.

"John Sive told us you were one of the heaviest studs
in New York."

"Tell the others about my rule too, so they don't get
any ideas," I said crisply.

Billy Sive had three problems. Shortly he had me
tearing my hair out.

His first and biggest problem was that he always
overdid. He was the most strongly motivated and hardest-
working runner that I had ever known, but he had no
common sense at all. It was obvious to me that if I didn't

keep a tight rein on him, he would train himself and race himself to death.

Second, he was a front-runner.

You have two kinds of runners: kickers and front-runners. Vince and Jacques were both kickers. The kicker likes to dawdle in the rear of the pack, letting the others carry the burden of setting the pace. He saves himself for a last-lap sprint to the front. But the front-runner goes out in front right away, and tries to stay there and burn off the rest of the field. If he goes out too slow or makes a tactical mistake, he sets himself up for the kicker's killing rush. Many a front-runner has given a world record to a kicker.

Later on, the sports magazines were always comparing Billy to the great Australian front-runner, Ron Clarke. As a former trackwriter, I was always irritated by these facile comparisons. If I were to compare Billy to anybody, it would be to Emiel Puttemans.

Billy and Ron Clarke were different in two ways.

First, Clarke was a front-runner on principle. He thought it was immoral to noodle along in the rear. Billy was a front-runner because, simply, it panicked him out of his mind to run in the pack. "I choke back there," he told me, "with all those elbows and feet. I have to have open space in front of me. I have to run free." For him, a race usually resolved itself into an animal struggle to keep that freedom. But he still didn't have the strength, or the speed, or the grasp of tactics, or the strong finish, to burn off the biggest kickers. My job would be to give him what he lacked, if I could.

Second, Clarke was a nervous uncompetitive guy who often psyched himself out before big races. Billy never had this problem. He was at his coolest in a big race, and he was savagely competitive. He would, as I said, kill himself to stay in front. His desperate need to be himself, and to prove that he had some worth as a man and as a human being, showed very movingly on the track.

Billy's third problem was that he was stubborn. In the

first months, I had battle after battle with him. He felt he needed my direction, yet—for reasons that I'll go into shortly—he also felt he had to put me down.

Our first battle was about mileage. This was ironic: Billy came to me hoping I would tell him what he was doing wrong. When I told him, he refused to listen.

At Oregon, he had lived in a euphoria of testing himself, and had been stacking up close to 200 miles a week. Lindquist, who is very big on volume training, had encouraged this. I wondered if Billy's lack of improvement had been due to simple overload. His history of cramps and stress fractures was a dead giveaway. He was calcium deficient, but magnesium deficiency can also cause cramps—magnesium regulates the motor impulses to the muscles, and high mileage really drains the runner's system of this crucial electrolyte. Beyond that, I think that Billy was simply unable to handle such high mileage, and the lactic-acid accumulation in his muscles would complicate the magnesium deficiency. At any rate, I found that dosing him with Magnesium Plus didn't solve the cramp problem. As for the fractures, his bones were simply giving away under the overload.

So I tried to get him to drop his mileage and concentrate on speed and strength training. Runners like Puttemans have done beautifully on little more than 100 miles a week. But Billy wouldn't listen. He fretted and moaned, "I'm sure I'm not working hard enough." So in January, to his great surprise, he found himself going sour, getting the flu and another stress fracture in his right shin. He had to wear a leg cast for a month, and nearly went crazy from the inactivity.

I was furious, and really laid into him. "You want to go to Montréal," I said. "You won't even live that long."

The experience shook him. But his deep-seated reasons for battling me were still there. He would sneak out for clandestine extra workouts like a ten-year-old sneaking a cigarette behind the barn in the old days.

Another battle was over diet. I lost this one.

I am a firm believer in lean, red meat. So when I found out that Billy was a vegetarian, I got very upset. He said he was a Buddhist, and that he couldn't eat any creature that had been killed.

I got very uptight about this. I'd already seen several of my runners get malnutrition on fad macrobiotic diets. But Billy explained patiently that, no, he wasn't into macrobiotics. He was killing two birds with one stone by adopting a bizarre vegetarian diet used successfully in recent years by some European distance runners. He lived on sour milk, yogurt, fruit and raw vegetables, whole-grained cereals, nuts and potatoes. He fixed these meals himself in the dorm kitchenette, and he was—as far as boiling potatoes went—a fair cook.

My upset finally slacked off when I had the science department analyze what he ate. They soberly reported that it contained the amounts of high-quality protein, carbohydrate, potassium, etc. that I judged vital for his work load. And, since there was no budging him on this religious issue, I let him alone. I can't say exactly how much the diet contributed to his later success. But it did help keep him at about 5 percent body fat, so it contributed to his speed. There is a thing in running called the power-weight ratio, and most runners find that the less fat they carry, the better they perform. Bone and fat are dead weight in running. Light-boned, fatless, Billy had almost the ideal physique for distance running.

Luckily, Billy's religion forbade alcohol. So at least I didn't have that to worry about.

Away from the track, Billy had a curious aimlessness. He was supposedly studying political science. The three boys had lost their first senior semester's credits at Oregon, but they had agreed to undertake an intensive single-project portfolio at Prescott. If they completed it to the faculty's satisfaction, they could graduate on schedule. Billy chose a grandiose subject: an assessment of the effects of civil-rights legislation in American life. But he worked on it in fits and starts—except when he had the leg cast on, during which time he studied furiously. When his school records came to me, I saw his teachers remarking all the way back through junior high: "A bright student, but doesn't apply himself."

He was, as I've said, involved with Buddhism, and also with yoga. In this he was no different from many students. But he had his own peculiar approach to it. Billy was no mystic, either about running or about life. He was coldly practical. He simply tried to live the basic Buddhist ideals of peace, control and compassion for other beings, and was not interested in the higher levels of spiritual enlightenment.

Since I knew almost nothing about Buddhism, I had no way of knowing how thorough or authentic a Buddhist he was. But one thing was sure: he learned from transcendental meditation an extra measure of concentration, relaxation and control that he quite deliberately fed back into his running. He could study (when he chose to study) in a room where six other students were arguing radical politics at the top of their lungs. When people harassed him, he simply tuned them out.

Before a workout or a race, he retreated inward, into the alpha state of TM, and he didn't come out till he was in the shower. While running, he was plainly in a TM trance, thinking only of his body movements, rhythm, breathing, pace. He plunged forward through the barriers of pain and effort with a serene expression on his sweat-streaked face. His blank look in races frequently brought comments that he was doped.

Once, out of curiosity, I took him to the Bingham Center for Athletic Research down in New York. They had been doing some research on other athletes who were using TM. They put Billy on the treadmill, ran him to exhaustion and found that while in the alpha state, he exhibited the highest tolerance of lactic buildup of any champion athlete they'd tested, as well as increased blood flow to the muscles.

It's been said that Billy was a classic animal. "Animal" is the somewhat derogatory word for an athlete who feels

no pain. This was true. I don't think he felt pain much. If
he did, he accepted it as casually as eating and breathing.
By contrast, Vince Matti was a connoisseur of pain and
gloried in it. Jacques had trouble dealing with pain—it
was part of his nervousness.

Billy "The Animal" Sive, the sportswriters started
calling him. My feeling was that, if being an animal got
him to Montréal, I wasn't going to criticize. Watching him,
I used to get cold chills sometimes. I thought: if I can ever
get him to train right, and keep him injury-free, I might
really have something here.

I kidded him a little about it. "Are you in Nirvana out
there?"

"Oh no, Mr. Brown," he said. He didn't laugh at my
joke. Among other things, he had little sense of humor.
"I'm a very pragmatic Buddhist. I just need a good dharma
to run well."

Dharma, I knew, was the Buddhist's right way of living,
in which one had a state of inner balance. If you were in
control and peaceful, your dharma was good. If you were
racked by anxieties and cravings, your dharma was bad.
The idea was to rid the mind of all cravings, leaving only
peace and compassion. Obviously I had a very poor
dharma—my craving for Billy was stronger every day.

Right away Billy became enormously popular with the
students and faculty. His sunny candor disarmed everyone.
He hardly stirred anywhere without other boys and girls
trailing after him. He was the gay Pied Piper.

Soon half the girls on campus were madly in love with
him. Several always went to the track to watch him work
out. He was friendly, went with them to campus films,
even danced with them. But he mystified them by his
refusal to date and/or sleep with any of them.

"Billy, you've got a secret old lady," they insisted.

He just shrugged and smiled.

Vince and Billy both loved to dance, though Jacques
didn't. Evenings, in the faculty-student union, there was
a permanent floating canteen-discotheque, and the three

of them usually spent a while there. In my youth I had
thought rock music was sinful and un-American, in spite
of the fact that Elvis Presley was already on the scene
when I was at Villanova. But in recent years I had come
to tolerate rock because I associated it with New York,
gay bars, Prescott, peace of mind and—now—Billy. So
sometimes, in the evening, I took to drifting past the
canteen, hoping to glimpse him in action.

One evening just before Christmas, I was passing the
canteen after a faculty meeting and saw him. I looked in.
From the crowd in the place, it was obvious that something
unusual was going on. The driving beat filled the room,
and a black singer was shouting and screaming. The tables
were packed with students and teachers eating health-
burgers and drinking health drinks. More stood along the
walls, and more were coming in and craning their necks
to watch.

Vince, Billy and two girls were right in the middle of
the floor, and the other couples were stopping and
watching. The two girls were doing a rather abandoned
heterosexual version of the Flop. Vince and Billy were not.
They were doing the gay boogie. And they were doing it as
I had seen it done only in films and at parties in New
York.

The gay who is a good dancer can turn even the fox
trot into an uninhibited celebration of male sexuality. Billy
and Vince were doing the boogie about six feet from their
partners, not looking at them or at each other. They were
dancing like blacks. They were loose, cool, with all the
foot-stomping and finger-snapping that goes with it. Their
shoulders and torsos barely moved. All the action was in
the hip-jerking, the crotch-gyrating, the buttock-twitching
and the thigh-weaving.

Vince was aware of the crowd, grandstanding a little.
But Billy was a shade more restrained, inner-directed, as
if he were dancing to that fantasy-lover that every gay
sees in his mind.

I watched them through the door, simply stunned. For

the first time, it was visible to me how deeply sexual Billy was, and how deep his sense of loss went. He was dancing that sense of loss right there in front of me.

I decided that I had to see it from up closer. Walking in casually, I went over to one of the faculty sitting at a table and fabricated something very important to say to him. Then I spotted Jacques sitting in the front row of tables, and worked my way through the crowd toward him. Jacques was sitting engrossed, looking worshipfully at Vince. When I touched his arm, he jumped.

"Just wanted to say I might be a little late for track practice tomorrow," I lied. "If I am late, don't look for me."

"Oh sure, Mr. Brown." Jacques' eyes barely left Vince. He pulled me down in an empty chair, that had Billy's jacket hung over the back of it. "Hey, watch these guys, Mr. Brown. They're outrageous."

There I was, right at ringside. The boys were dancing about twelve feet from me. "This is the kind of thing," I said, "that I told them they shouldn't do."

"Oh, I think it's all right. Look at everybody. They just think it's very sexy heterosexual stuff. After all, the guys are dancing with girls . . ."

I looked around. Judging by the students' faces, they had never seen anything quite like this before. A few started clapping to the beat, and pretty soon the whole room was clapping and stomping. I could hardly hear myself think. I watched a little nervously. On occasion I had seen this dance progress to pants falling, the dancer dexterously flipping his goodies around and finally jerking off magnificently. I couldn't believe these two would do that, especially Billy. If they did, they would be off the team tomorrow.

They were really vibrating with the beat now. The students started shouting things at them.

"Move it, Billy!"

"Shake it, Vince!"

"Hey, Vince, is that what they do out at Oregon?"

"Naw," said Vince. "They do this in California."

"Watcha got, Vince?" someone else shouted.

"Eight inches," said Vince.

I kept a straight face, but inside I was dismayed.

The place erupted with whoops and wolf whistles. "Show it!" "Take it off!"

"Don't provoke me," said Vince.

Just at that moment, Billy saw me there. A blush actually went up through his speckled cheek. I communicated my disapproval with my eyes. Immediately, imperceptibly, the gay raunch went out of his movements, and he was doing a facsimile of straight boogie.

Then I tried to catch Vince's eye, but he was joyfully engrossed in his movements. The shrieks, taunts, dares went on. Suddenly Vince laid his hands on his flanks and ran them slowly down to his thighs. The spectators looked at each other gleefully, and punched each other, playfully.

Vince ran his hands up and down a few more times, then unbuttoned the metal button at the waist of his jeans. Everybody howled and jumped up and down. Vince's body was really moving now, snapping, whipping, his hair tossing wildly. Very slowly he started to unzip his fly. His jeans slid down a little around his hips, showing a strip of torso under the hem of his T-shirt. All the tendons and muscles in it were working like a belly dancer's.

I glanced at Jacques, who was now looking nervous too.

"Well, supposing he does it?" said Jacques in a soft voice. "I mean, have you ever been at a rock concert? The musicians sometimes get dared to expose themselves, and they do . . ."

"Billy!" they were now calling pleadingly.

Billy shook his head, and kept dancing mechanically.

Vince's zipper was now down far enough that we could see a little black pubic hair. Then, just as it looked like his pants were going to fall, he grinned and pulled them up again and zipped his fly. The whole room howled with disappointment.

Now they were after Billy. "Come on, Billy. Watcha got?"

Suddenly Billy smiled. "Ten thousand meters," he said.

Everybody groaned. "Goddam runners," said somebody behind me. "They're so fucking single-minded."

They begged and pleaded, but Billy was adamant. I thought more of him for it.

The record ended, and the band hit its last jarring, whanging chords and bashes of cymbals. Vince stopped dancing and was hanging onto his female partner, laughing giddily. She didn't know it, but she had been subjected to some classic gay teasing. Billy walked away from his partner, hesitated as he saw that he had to rescue his jacket from behind my shoulders, and finally came slowly over.

"You know," said Jacques, "I think that if Vince ever comes out, he's going to be capable of just about anything."

I looked at Billy, giving him a Parris Island chewing-out with my eyes.

He pulled his jacket out from behind me, and mumbled, "Sorry, Mr. Brown. I don't know what came over me."

He gathered up his books and, still flushing strangely, he left. I yearned to walk out of there with him, but I didn't.

Another record started, a schmaltzy slow one, and the floor filled up with touch dancers. Vince was holding the girl close, his cheek against hers, his eyes closed. If he had noticed me there, he was being defiant. Jacques watched the pair, mournful and silent.

I got up and left.

Walking down the corridor outside, I felt deeply depressed. Billy was alone and full of craving. The only feeling he had shown for me had been a hesitant amiability, and a willingness to quarrel about his training. But even if he had shown love for me, I could make no claim on him.

I didn't fear the girls who pined to creep into his dormitory bed. But I feared the next young stud who would provoke his interest. It could be anyone, any time. It could be Vince, even Jacques. In fact, I assumed that he had lied, that he had slept with Vince. Or if he hadn't, he would do it soon. He had said he was alone, implying he wasn't sleeping with anyone. Sooner or later, his natural urges would drive him to someone, if only for relief. Supposing Vince said, "How about it, Billy?" After four years of friendship, they would discover each other as lovers.

In my imagination, I saw them dancing the boogie, not with girls, but with each other. They embraced, panting and sweaty, and they kissed. They fell naked onto a bed somewhere and made love with feverish abandon.

The sensible thing to do was to cruise Billy while he was still available.

Feeling a terrible, unreasonable jealousy, I trudged on down the corridor with my briefcase and out into the snowy night. He was not mine, and never would be. I would lose him without ever having had him.

FIVE

During Christmas vacation, Billy's father came to visit. The case he was working on, which was aiming at a Supreme Court decision repealing all sodomy laws, brought him often to New York to do business there with the gay lib front and the American Civil Liberties Union.

When he came out to the campus, Billy showed his affection for him the way he showed everything. As John got out of the taxi, Billy came racing out of the dorm without his jacket and hugged him. John ruffled his hair and hugged him back.

"Hey, kid, I've really missed you," he said.

I was able to appreciate their spontaneity. My dad would have been boiled in oil before he'd have hugged me, and so would I.

I had an immediate liking for John Sive, and he shortly became one of the few real friends I ever had. There was much of Billy in his ease and candor, though physically they resembled each other little. John was shorter, darker, more muscular, with straight ebony hair (tinted, in that vain gay attempt to hold onto youth). Billy's mop of brown curls and his blue eyes must have come from that mother of his, Leida, about whom neither of them would speak.

For many years, John had had a distinguished career as a corporate attorney in San Francisco, without any public suspicion that he was gay. He admitted to me that it took some doing, and some wear and tear on his psyche. "There was always the chance that Frances would lose one of his falsies at a party," he said. Finally, with Billy safe in college, he decided that he would come out. He quit his job, but stayed solvent because he had a good income from investments. (Luckily the stock market doesn't consider investors' sex preferences when it goes up or down.) John switched to civil-rights law, and was now, at the age of 51, putting his long shrewd experience to work for the gay community.

Joe and Marian Prescott invited John to stay at the house a couple of days, and we all had Christmas dinner with them. It was a wonderful evening, with the smell of turkey and the Christmas tree, and nuts to crack by the big fireplace. It made me realize all over again how homeless I was, and how starved I was for some sense of family life. We sat close around the table, with candles and good talk. Billy was quiet and didn't say much, munching at the special salad Marian had made for him.

The campus was empty, and the weather had turned sharply cold. Nearly everybody had migrated off to see their families. Vince and Jacques had gone home, and planned to tell their families that they were gay.

Every morning John got up early to watch Billy work out. He sat shivering in his Cardin overcoat, a lone figure on the snowy bleachers, and his eyes never left Billy as the boy ripped off 57-second quarters.

"It takes a lot of will, doesn't it?" John asked me.

He had never run a step, but instinctively he understood.

"Will is the main thing," I said. "But it takes other things too. Hard work gets you nowhere if you aren't naturally gifted. The lung capacity, the ability to tolerate high stress, that is partly hereditary, we know. Billy has some good genes in there somewhere. I've put him through the lab tests and he definitely is international class, physically. Your genes, probably," I added jokingly.

"Who knows?" said John. "Maybe they're his mother's genes."

"I won't believe it," I said. "She crapped out."

John grinned. "Well, I'd like to think that they're my genes."

We both watched as Billy tore by again.

"Billy has it upstairs, all right," I said. "I wish every American father could teach his son that kind of mental toughness. My congratulations."

"Well, I taught him some of that," said John. "The rest he learned himself."

"How did he get started running?"

"Well, he was a weak kid. He was very small when he was born. He was sick a lot. I encouraged him to try sports because I hoped they would build him up a little. In grade school he played a lot of basketball, and he finally started to look healthy. Then in high-school they had one of those age-group cross-country programs. He tried it, and that was it. He never went near a basketball court again. He'd come home glowing and all excited, and I'd think, he's in love, but no he'd just had a good run."

We both laughed a little.

"Then I changed him to another school, because the coach was putting too much pressure on him, and he didn't know how to handle pressure yet. He'd bomb out in the third quarter of a race." John had never run a step, but he understood the third quarter. I really admired that. "So his junior year I got him to Lou Rambo, and Rambo just let him come along easy, and discover self-discipline for himself. That was the main reason he did such good running his senior year . . ."

We watched Billy's slender figure pass again and again, his Tiger flats making scarcely any noise on the frozen track.

"I want him to be happy," said John softly. "I don't want him to go through what I did."

"I know what you mean," I said.

"You know," said John musingly, "I was never much of a sports fan till Billy started running. But I find myself fantasizing about a gold medal in Montréal. Of course I realize all the political obstacles in the way of that. And you've been frank with me—you're not even sure he has the speed to compete internationally. But . . . supposing it happens? I can see him standing on the podium with that medal on his neck and the band playing 'Oh say can you see.' And you know, it's not the medal for its own sake, or just that I'm proud of Billy. I see it as propaganda too. It would be an incredible moral victory for us."

He was articulating something that I had already thought many times. I hadn't dared to express the thought to Billy, but I knew that it was on his mind. It, precisely, was what drove him to strive for the trip to Montréal.

I laughed a little. "The ironic thing is . . . to make boys like Billy, we have to fool around with women."

John laughed too, and lit a cigarette.

"I've got two boys down in Pennsylvania," I said. "One is fifteen now, the other is thirteen. I haven't seen them since my wife divorced me. I'm thinking that one of these days I ought to go to court and demand my right to see them. I tried to visit them at first, but she made things so unpleasant that I stopped going. But it's probably too late now. I'd be a stranger. And she's probably taught them to hate me."

John's smile vanished. He didn't look at me, but his eyes were squinting in the winter sunlight. They were full of pain as he watched Billy pass again.

"What I don't want to be, though," he said, "is the father who pushes his son to achieve things for his own ego's sake."

"Listen," I said, "you don't have to push this one to Montréal. I've got all I can do to hold him back. He's like a crazy young horse with the bit in his teeth. Do me a favor and tell him to be more obedient with his training program, or we're not going to get anywhere."

We spent a couple of nights down in New York City. I figured that being up late a night or two wouldn't hurt Billy (that's how much I was getting humanized). It was the quiet time of year, with cross-country over, and outdoor track two months away, and we weren't going to any indoor meets. And I couldn't deny John a good holiday time with his son.

The Saturday before New Year's, we ate dinner at a restaurant downtown whose name I won't mention because we don't want all the straight tourists piling in there. I can say only that it's on the second floor, is dim and comfortable, with old red velvet chairs and fakes of Old Masters in heavy gold frames, and big chandeliers, and waiters who are young studs dressed up in Renaissance tights and jerkins. They serve very good steaks and chops and Italian food. And since my idea of cuisine is a steak this thick, or lasagna at Mamma Leone's for a trackwriters' lunch, I really enjoyed this place.

John and I ate steaks, medium rare, and Billy ate a plate of baked potatoes and a salad. John got a little drunk on red wine, and Billy and I got drunk on milk. We laughed and kidded around. John had on a black Cardin suit and a wide brocade silk tie. I was wearing my very best gray suit bought on sale at Barney's, and a white shirt, and my best black tie. Billy, from somewhere in the depths of his dorm closet, had produced a brown velvet suit and a white silk ruffed shirt. He didn't look at all foppish. Somehow it accentuated his slender hardness and his maleness.

After dinner we caught a cab uptown to the Continental Baths on West Seventy-fourth Street, to catch the midnight holiday show. It was an all-star bill of gay favorites, Bette Midler and the Sequins, and the new rock singer Jess Collett, who was being called the gay Jimi Hendrix.

"No picking up anybody now," I teased Billy. "You're in training."

He looked just a little annoyed with me. "I don't cruise," he said.

I kept after him. "No middle-aged hustlers."

I hadn't been to the Continental Baths for years. In fact, this evening would be the first time in four years that I had appeared so openly in gay society, and I was just a little nervous about it.

I hardly recognized the place. The Baths I remembered had been a hard-core refuge for gays who wanted to cruise naked meat. (In bars, everybody has clothes on, which can be regarded as an inconvenience.) In my absence, the straight radical chic crowd had started going there to take in the entertainments. They did this, I suppose, to show how broad-minded they were, but I suspect that they were simply curious and out for kinky thrills. The entrance was so full of women and straight celebrities that we could hardly wrestle our way in. The prices had gone way up— seven dollars just to look around.

"I can't believe this," I said.

"Neither can I," said John, a little sorrowfully." It's really changed. Oh well, the Divine Miss M is always good."

But once we got downstairs, we saw plenty of gays. No doubt a lot of them were getting the thrill of making straights look at their bodies. Most were cruising nonchalantly around wearing the classic towel wrapped around their hips. A few reckless souls were lounging nude in the wicker chairs, among the palms. Or they were swimming nude in the big pool, and the straights were looking at them avidly. Back in the underground days, I had taken plenty of swims in that pool. For a moment I had an urge to defy the world and do it again, but I couldn't do it in front of Billy.

We hadn't been there five minutes before a famous TV came rushing up to John.

"*Chéri,*" he cried.

He threw his arms around John's neck and bussed him on the cheek. John hugged him and bussed him back. He was a slender black man in his early thirties. He was wearing a black seal maxi coat with rhinestone buttons and a white satin gown. His woolly hair was cut very short, and he had on cascading rhinestone earrings and carried a little rhinestone bag.

"*Chéri*, it's been ages," said the TV, squeezing John's hands.

"In town for a little business," said John warmly. "How's Irving?"

"Irving," said the TV pleasantly, "is *merde*. Is this your son? My god, *chéri*, how he's grown. *Comme il est belle*." He kissed Billy on the cheek. Billy laughed and pecked him back. "He's ravishing, John."

"You stay away from my boy now," grinned John. "He's in training."

The TV raised his eyebrows archly. "Yes, we know all about that. We read the papers too, you know. He's our divine athlete. When is the Olympics, *chéri*? I fully intend to go."

Billy and I were laughing now. "The kid hasn't even made the team yet," I said. "But you'd better make reservations now, because they'll be hard to get."

"This is my coach, Harlan Brown," Billy explained. "Mr. Brown, this is Delphine de Sevigny."

"Oooooo, *chéri*, I know who you are," he crooned. "I thought you looked familiar. You're the big bad Marine."

I actually flushed. I sensed that Billy was looking at me strangely. I had always presumed that Billy knew of my hustling career, but somehow I felt deeply embarrassed. I wanted my runner to forget that his coach had sold his meat for fifty dollars. I wanted to punch Delphine de Sevigny in the mouth.

"If you're alone, why don't you join us?" John was saying, taking his arm.

"*Chéri*, I'm always alone. *Toujours*. Take me where you will."

Arm in arm, they strolled on ahead of us, through the crowd.

Billy stood looking at me for a moment. His eyes were full of pain, full of questions. For a moment we seemed to be all alone, in the middle of that shoving, babbling, cruising, staring mob.

I shoved my hands in my pockets and turned away, unable to meet his eyes. Feeling poured over me like a tidal wave. I had always thought of myself—even in the gay world—as a breed apart. The sight of the transvestites had always depressed me beyond words, and I had avoided them. I had always told myself: At least I'm not a freak like that. It was occurring to me now that there was an incredible manly courage in the TV's effort to live as a woman, and that I was still full of straight thinking.

Billy stood there looking at me sorrowfully. His world was his kingdom, his birthright, and I was still a tourist in it.

I walked past him. "Let's go, or we'll lose them," I said roughly.

We sat jostled at a table near the stage. John drank scotch. Delphine drank a champagne cocktail. I drank a Coke. They didn't have any milk, so Billy drank a glass of water. We heard Bette Midler and the rest. John and Delphine talked, and Billy and I sat silent. When Jess Collett came on and the crowd erupted into frenzied dancing, I was sure Billy would jump up to join them, but he didn't.

After a while, a dance band came out and started playing vintage stuff: slow jazz and Glenn Miller. It was the kind of stuff that I would have danced to in my youth if I had been irreligious enough to dance. It brought back memories of dances that I didn't dance, loves that I didn't love. The lights dimmed, and the crowd quieted and danced slow. Everybody was plastered together. The straights were plastered to the straights, and the gays were plastered to the gays. John and Delphine got up to dance, and drifted off cheek to cheek, body to body.

I sat there feeling more and more depressed. I was thinking about my whole blitzed youth, my blitzed running career, my blitzed romance and marriage, my blitzed summer with Chris.

Billy sat looking down, playing with a paper napkin.

A toweled boy passed by me, talking in a high excited voice to a friend. He pressed his hip lightly but meaningfully to my shoulder. Out of the corner I could see his lean torso. His towel was draped so that one buttock was half-bare, in hopes I would make a pass. Billy raised his eyes and watched me. He knew about the rooms available upstairs.

"Get lost," I said hostilely to the boy.

The hustler looked at me, then at Billy, said, "Oh, dear, pardon *me*," and walked off with his friend.

Finally Billy said, "You going to make a wallflower out of me?"

I felt that blow in my stomach. He wanted to dance with me.

"I don't dance," I said. "You go ahead if you want."

"Come on, it's a slow one," he said.

I wanted to take his hand in my right hand, and put my left arm around him, and dance with him, and feel his ruffled breast pressing against my tie.

"All we need," I said harshly, "is a little social note in *Sports Illustrated* about how Prescott track coach Harlan Brown was seen dancing with Billy Sive at the Continental Baths."

Billy shrugged. A few minutes later, an older man bent beside him and asked him to dance, but he shook his head.

"You're a very virtuous kid," I said.

"I go to bed only with people I love," he said.

"That makes a lot of sense," I said. "I suppose your father taught you that."

"No," he said.

"You're too young to know what love is," I said.

"I know," he said. "I guess I'll fall hard one of these days."

"He'll be a lucky man," I said. I was talking as though I had drunk five scotches. "And I suppose you'll get married."

He shrugged again. "Those marriages don't last. Anyway, if you really love someone, you don't have to formalize it. And Buddhists are supposed to reject rituals."

I felt like my heart was laying there on the sawdust floor, being pushed around by thousands of dancing feet.

"Do you love someone, Mr. Brown?" Billy asked very cautiously, playing with my empty Coke bottle, turning it around and around.

"No," I said.

"But you must have, sometime."

"No."

"Not ever?" he persisted.

I drained the last of my Coke from the glass.

"But you have to love someone, sometime," he said.

"True," I said.

"Look," he said, "don't be embarrassed by what Delphine said. I knew all about you when I came to Prescott."

This embarrassed me even more.

Billy went on. "My father started hearing about you in New York. He even saw you around a few times." Billy smiled a little. "I understand you cost an arm and a leg."

"Listen," I said, "that's a very painful period of my life, and I don't like to discuss it."

"All right," he said. "But in return do me a favor."

"What?"

"I wish you would cut this Mr. Brown crap with me," he said.

I shook my head. "If I let you call me by my first name, then I have to let all the other students do it."

Billy sat looking very sad for a moment. He pushed the empty Coke bottle back toward me. Then he shook his head. "Mr. Brown," he said, "I wish you weren't so unhappy."

My hands were lying on the table, knotted into fists. He reached slowly over and laid one hand over mine. His hand was hot and a little moist. My stomach jerked. Was it possible that he liked me?

I had an image in my head of a ballroom filled with people. A glass ball was turning slowly overhead, making those spots of light swirling over everything. A thousand John Sives in black suits were dancing cheek to cheek with a thousand sequined Delphine de Sevignys. They waltzed gaily, thousands of them, like Fred Astaire and Ginger Rogers. The band instruments glittered and blared. John Sive and Delphine de Sevigny were tapdancing, looking at each other with eyes of love. Then off among the drifting thousands, I could glimpse Billy. He was walking slowly toward me, cutting through the dancers. He was wearing track shorts and singlet, and his Tigers with the blue nylon uppers, and a headband keeping his hair out of his eyes. The sweat glistened on his limbs as the spots swirled over him. His face was grave. He came slowly and held out his arms to me. We held each other tightly, and put our cheeks together, and danced slowly while the band played "Stardust."

I shook his hand off. "Don't do that," I said. "You never know who's watching. I don't need sympathy anyway. I'm just fine."

He drew his hand away as if he'd been burned.

On New Year's we didn't go to a party.

In the evening the four of us walked around in the streets looking at the lavish Christmas decorations all over midtown. It was very cold. We walked up Park Avenue a ways and looked at the trees trimmed with white lights. We bought roasted chestnuts from the vendors and ate them, burning our fingers. Billy allowed himself to eat some chestnuts. We stopped to listen to the Salvation Army carolers on Fifth Avenue. A few blocks farther we stopped to listen to a few shivering members of the Hare Krishna Society, as they sang and prayed half-frozen in their saffron robes.

John and Delphine walked ahead, arm in arm. Nobody on the crowded sidewalks noticed them. John and Delphine were having a sudden romance. Billy raised his eyebrows a little and said, "Dad's off and running again."

Billy and I walked behind them, not arm in arm. Since the night at the Baths, a tension had sprung up between us. I sensed that I had hurt him, and was sure now that his touching my hand had been friendship, nothing more.

But I didn't want to apologize, because the distance between us would help me control my feelings for him. At the same time, if anyone had tried to prevent me from walking the streets of New York with him that night, I would have fought with both fists.

We went to Rockefeller Center and watched the skaters circle the big rink, their breath blowing white in the air. We looked up dizzily at the giant Christmas tree by the rink.

Billy looked at me and said, with a certain peculiar belligerence, "I'd like to skate."

I said, "That's all we need is you should twist an ankle."

"Where do they rent the skates?" Billy asked Delphine. "I'm going to skate."

"They don't rent them, *chéri*," said Delphine, touching Billy's cheek. "You have to bring your own."

Delphine was madly in love with both Billy and John at once. Billy handled this with tact. He put him down gently by treating him as a potential mother. Billy had total respect and seriousness for all transvestites.

That evening I finally relaxed toward Delphine myself, and decided he was delightful. I had seen so many flamboyant gay foxes that Delphine's relative naturalness of dress and manner took some getting used to.

"I'm past high drag, *chéri*," he told me as we thawed out over something warm to drink in the Plaza Hotel. "I'm into couture."

To see him play with his drink and his cigarette holder, there among the potted palms and crystal chandeliers of the Plaza, you would never know that Delphine lived in a tiny apartment on 123rd Street with ten cats and rent owing. He bought his beautiful clothes at thrift shops, and learned his French from a Berlitz record. "My limousine awaits," he would say as John put him into a taxi. He was

Palm Beach, the Riviera, a box at the Metropolitan Opera.

"I warn you," he told Billy that night, "I plan to go to the track meets, and cheer you and Vince and Jacques onward. I may even throw flowers at you."

"I'll look for you," said Billy, smiling.

He smiled at Delphine more than he did at me that night. Gentle filial smiles, devoid of sex. I would have settled for even one of those.

Back in John's room at the Chelsea Hotel, we thawed out again and John ordered up a big ice bucket. Reposing in it were two bottles: one of French champagne, and one of sparkling mineral water, as a concession to Billy and me. Delphine turned on the color TV so we could watch the midnight doings over on Times Square. John popped the cork on the champagne. As he opened the bottle of mineral water, he made a loud popping noise with his mouth, and we all laughed a little. He filled the glasses.

"Oh, bubbly!" Delphine cried.

The television was playing "Auld Lang Syne." I felt as if my heart was going to break. It was 1975, and on August 18, 1975, I was going to be forty years old.

We all touched glasses. "Heart's desires for all of us," said John. "For Delphine, a millionaire. For Billy, a sub-28 10,000 meter. For Harlan, love." His eyes rested on mine briefly, and I wondered how much he had sensed.

"And for you, and for all of us," I said, "good luck with the Supreme Court."

Billy and John hugged and kissed each other, and Delphine hugged and kissed me. John hugged and kissed me, and Billy hugged and kissed Delphine. But neither Billy nor I made a move toward each other. He just smiled a little, touched my glass with his, and said in an even voice, "Cheers, Mr. Brown," and drained his mineral water with the air of a debauchee.

On the TV, everybody was kissing everybody else. I drank off my mineral water in one gulp too.

SIX

When the holidays ended, Vince and Jacques came back to Prescott with their news.

Jacques had died a thousand deaths before he finally told his family. A cultivated, sensitive family of musicians, they were distressed but trying to understand. I was glad that it had turned out this well. Jacques went back to his studies and training more relaxed than I had seen him.

But Vince had had a bad time. His father was a union official in Los Angeles. He and his son were on poor terms already. He was ambivalent: proud of Vince's track exploits, but unhappy that Vince did these things while wearing a beard. When he heard that his son the miler was also a "fag," he was first incredulous, then livid.

"He told me never to come home again," said Vince bitterly. "He talked about killing me. He even talked about going to court to make me return the money he spent on my education. Can you believe? Fuck him."

He bared his shoulder to us, and showed us a new tattoo. It was the Lambda, the symbol of gay activism. He'd had it done in a Los Angeles tattoo parlor before he flew back.

I was distressed. "That's just the kind of thing I think we *shouldn't* do," I said. "That thing is going to be visible at every meet you're in."

"Oh hell," said Vince, "the old farts at the meets aren't going to know what it stands for."

On February 17, 1975, something very important happened to us. By a seven-to-two vote, the Supreme Court made their now-famous ruling on sodomy. They struck down all laws regulating sexual activity by both straight and gay consenting adults, stating that they were an unconstitutional attempt to regulate bedroom matters. The decision also clarified homosexuals' protection under the antidiscrimination laws of 1964.

The gay people and their liberal supporters rejoiced. John Sive and his colleagues had prepared their case painstakingly, and the years of work paid off.

But the ruling jolted the country, and gays were suddenly feeling more pressure than before, instead of less. I'm not a sociologist, but I have my own visceral theory about why.

Unlike the abortion issue back in 1973, the sodomy issue was not bruited about in the media a lot beforehand. By the time the Court finally ruled on abortion, most Americans were pretty accurately informed on the pros and cons. But the sodomy issue was just one of 126 other matters on the Court docket that year, and it hit middle America straight out of the blue.

All that the average taxpayer in Peoria, Illinois, knew was that suddenly the Court was saying it was all right for his kids to be fairies, a thing he had been taught to fear and despise. His ideas about homosexuality stayed away from facts, in the medieval murk.

This deep irrational fear was at the bottom of the reaction, and behind the unsuccessful but fanatic organized groups who tried to get the Court to reverse the ruling. In all the furor that spring, most people seemed to forget that the ruling also covered lesbians and straights, and they shot their hostilities at gay men.

The psychotic fear of gay men shows how deeply the issue went. American men are insecure and on the defensive anyway, what with all the women's lib stuff. And despite all the women's lib activity, American society still tends to regard a man as having a higher responsibility than a woman. A man has his privileges, but he also carries his burden. So a man who refuses to impregnate Miss America, who wastes his semen between another man's thighs, is a sexual traitor who threatens the very future of a society.

In my opinion, no other big social change in recent years —such as integration, drug use and relaxed heterosexual morals—has provoked the degree of anger that the sodomy thing did. Maybe I am biased, because I felt that anger. But I always felt keenly that the biggest backlash came from men who were insecure of their own roles. They feared—secretly perhaps—that I was a bigger stud than they were. I might practice my prowess on their own sons, and thus cut off their lifeline to genealogical immortality.

As far as I and my three gay runners were concerned, the Court ruling meant that we were both better off and worse off than before.

I wouldn't have to worry any more about their getting busted in some state with strict laws, while traveling to meets. We now had solid legal backing in case they were hassled on their way to the Olympics.

On the other hand, with the whole country boiling on the issue, people might show us even more hostility than they would have otherwise. And, as everybody knows, it's one thing to get a fair civil-rights law passed, and another thing to get it enforced.

By April Billy was recovered from the stress fracture and making some progress, and his 5,000 and 10,000 times were dropping slowly toward the goals I'd set. But he wasn't making the progress he should, because he was fighting me tooth and nail about his program. I wanted him to train just once a day. He insisted on twice. Sometimes he'd give in, and then a couple of weeks later, he'd fall off the wagon. It was like trying to keep an alcoholic away from booze.

We had all three of the boys entered in the Drake Relays, which were to be held April 25 and 26. I was especially anxious that Billy be fresh for this important meet, as it would be a major test of his potential.

I was cold and correct with him, and he was cold and correct with me.

As my feelings for him tortured me more and more, I started training hard again, the way I had at Villanova. The coach was working fully as hard as his athletes. Every morning I got up just as it was getting light, and busted ten or fifteen miles over the trails in the woods. In the afternoons, I even managed to squeeze in some speed work on the track. I was pathetically pleased, in my old age, to see how quickly my body responded and came back to racing condition. I was running 4:20 miles in time trials that spring.

And so the weeks passed, I barking at Billy and he running silent and stubborn.

One day his faculty advisor came to me and shook his head about Billy's portfolio. "It hasn't gone anywhere since that spate of studying when he had the cast on his leg," he said. "I know Billy's serious about track, but if he wants to graduate . . ."

"Yeah, sure," I said, sounding like the detached concerned athletic director. "I'll talk to him about it."

On April 15, in the early evening, I was working in my office in the silent athletic building when I heard Billy call me sharply from the dressing room down the hall.

"Harlan!" There was a note of urgency in his voice.

I ran down the hall and into the dressing room. He was standing bent over strangely by one of the benches. He was nude except for his jock strap, and his damp running clothes were thrown over the bench. His face was white and his teeth gritted, and he was kneading his thigh desperately. He had a mammoth cramp in his leg.

I knew at once that he had been out for one of his clandestine workouts. With Billy, muscle tremors and cramps were always the result of magnesium loss and overwork.

"Harlan," he panted, "help me."

It had always been my policy to stay away from the locker rooms and leave any rubdowns to my assistant. But there was nobody else around, and a cramp like that can do real damage if it's not handled right.

So I kneeled on the concrete floor in front of him, and massaged the leg. He bent over me, his hands clenched in the back of my shirt. Finally the cramp started to ease. I made him lay down on the bench and kept working at the leg, from the calf to the hip.

We were alone. The building was silent. It was the first time I had seen him so close to naked, and I found myself wishing that he had gotten the jock strap off before the cramp hit.

His body lay on the bench as if offered to me. His right leg was in my hands, and the other had fallen aside, the bare foot braced on the floor. His crotch was exposed: the powerful hamstrings, the small buttocks with curls of dark wet hair between them. More curls framed the manhood tight and hidden in its supporter. The broad dingy elastic band across his lean abdomen contrasted curiously with his pale skin. He was not flaunting himself, as Denny Falks had done, and that made the sight of him all the more moving.

He lay breathing deeply, one arm over his face, fighting to concentrate, to use his yoga to relax the muscle. Since he wasn't looking at me, I dared to let my eyes run over his body. He was beautiful by no standards save those of distance running. His muscles were good, but too starved-looking. The legs were too long and thin, too veined, the muscles too cruelly defined, for most tastes. His curving thigh was scarcely thicker than his calf.

Finally his leg lay limp and supple in my hands. I could still feel a feeble muscle tremor in the thigh as I held it.

"How does it feel?" I said, still daring to hold his thigh a moment.

"Okay," he said in a low shaky voice, still not taking his arm away from his eyes. "It hurts a little. There's a tremor there."

Then I saw that the front of his jock strap was swelling a little. Now that our worry was over, it had occurred to him as well that we were in a sexual situation. Possibly he liked me. Possibly he was just hard up for sex. But in any case he wanted me to touch him. All I had to do was bend over him and put my face against his hot flank, and gently pull the damp jock strap down around his thighs.

Instead, I panicked, and with the panic came my anger. I let go of his thigh. "Serves you right," I said.

My voice cracked in the silence of the locker room. His body jerked as if I had lashed it with a whip.

"How far did you run?" I demanded.

He still had his arm over his face, and his pale skin had turned a mottled pink-blue covered with goosebumps. "Fifteen miles," he said.

"What pace?" I said.

"Five fifteen," he said.

"A week before the Drake," I said. "You're an irresponsible brat. Who the hell do you think you are, taking my time with your tantrums? If you can't settle down and do this right, then I invite you to find another coach."

He sat up, turning away from me. His back was straight, but I sensed how humiliated he was. The front of his jock strap went back to normal. I ached with regret at having hurt him, but I also felt safer now.

"And now you're chilled too," I said. "Get your ass under the hot water."

Silently he got up and fumbled in his open locker for his towel. I looked mournfully at his body, feeling as if I was saying good-bye to it.

"Have you been taking magnesium?" I asked.

"No," he said in a stifled voice. "Just eating spinach and stuff."

"Well, get on the Magnesium Plus then," I said. "If you're out, I'll give you a bottle." I pretended I only cared about that: my athlete's condition.

Without looking at me, he started toward the shower room.

"One more thing," I barked. "It's Mr. Brown. Don't forget it a second time."

But that night, lying awake in bed, the memory of his body came back to me like a hallucination. My imagination staged a hard-core encounter between us, right on that locker-room bench. We would both be half-mad with desire, like in all the gay skin flicks I'd seen. Our panting and gasping would echo in the silent locker room. It was amazing how many different ways I could think of for us to make love to each other without moving off that bench. I rehearsed it over and over, and had an ejaculation just thinking about it—I didn't even touch myself.

In my misery, I tried to pray. It didn't make much sense to pray after having indulged in erotic fantasies like that, but I did. "Out of the depths I cry unto thee, oh Lord . . ." But then all I could think of was the *Song of Songs*. ". . . That at night on my bed I sought him whom my soul loveth, I sought him but found him not. O that his left hand were under my head, and that his right hand embraced me. Refresh me with apples, for I am sick with love."

About 3:30, I decided that the only thing to do was put in a really long run. So I pulled on my running clothes and shoes and went out. It was still dark, but light was coming in the east and the first birds were already singing in the dark woods. It was the kind of spring morning that might have delighted me, but I found the bird songs sad and oppressive.

I ran for three hours, and covered about twenty-five miles. The run put me into the necessary trance, and emptied my mind. But the last six miles, I was nearly falling apart. My legs were hurting and dead. When I got back to the campus, I was exhausted, sick, shaky and more jumpy than ever. I was a fine one to criticize Billy— I was now physically over the edge too.

That afternoon I had the yoga class for the men's and women's teams. As usual, when the weather was warm, we had it on the grassy infield of the track.

Billy hadn't inspired this class—we'd started it the year before, when we noticed a few runners elsewhere adapting yoga into stretching exercises. Flexibility is crucial in running, especially for avoiding injury. My kids and I had been happy with the class—I was making them supple, and they could imagine themselves as Siddarthas in sweatsuits.

So I was walking up and down before the rows of kids. The girls were on the left, in their red gymsuits, and the boys were on the right, in their blues. Neat rows of supple young bodies, doing this yoga contortion, then that, at my order.

"Semi-plow," I said. They all bent slowly backward from a kneeling position and touched their heads to the grass.

All but Billy Sive. He was in the lotus position, in the second row of the male team. He was sitting a little slumped, slowly picking early dandelions out of the grass, and his face looked strangely vacant. Sure, I told myself, you refused him sexually and you humiliated him. He probably hates you now.

But the sight of him letting himself go like that infuriated me. I was exhausted and edgy, and I lost my temper completely.

"Billy Sive!" I barked.

He looked slowly up at me.

"Semi-plow, on the double!" I said.

He dropped his eyes and went on pulling dandelions, making a little bouquet. He put the bouquet to his mouth.

I walked between the lines. I never showed my three top runners any favoritism before the others, boy or girl, and this was going to be one of those moments.

"Billy Sive," I said, between my teeth, vibrating with anger. I was furious at him for the mess he was making of my peaceful life.

Instead of doing the semi-plow, he got up slowly and looked me right in the eye, with his candid, vacant gaze. His lips were yellow with pollen.

All the kids lost their meditative look, and their eyes moved to us. They waited, kneeling.

"You're the one who wants to go to Montréal," I said.

He dropped the dandelions, turned and walked off. There was something in his manner of the battle-shocked soldier. In my anger, I decided that a little military stuff would bring him around.

I followed him away from the row of kids. "Billy," I barked.

He turned. I slapped him hard across the face, being careful not to hit his glasses. It was a slap like that famous one Patton gave a soldier in the hospital, that was meant only to be therapeutic. Even Zen Buddhists use the slap. They say it causes "psychic shock," which opens the mind to revelation.

The crack of my hand against his face sounded like a shot across the quiet track. The kids all gasped.

Billy's face went white and twisted with anger. The next thing I knew, he had swung his arm and slapped me right back. It was a slap in the highest tradition of the U.S. armed forces, and of the Zen masters. I had been making him do weight training and he was now nearly as strong as I was.

My face and nose stung. Livid, I seized his arms and he seized me by the front of my jacket. His eyes were about six inches from mine, blazing with fury.

"You big, stupid Marine," he cried in a strange broken voice.

He twisted loose from me and walked off. Then he broke into a jog and went off across the wide lawn.

I turned back to the kids, my face hot with anger and

pain. By the expression in their eyes, I could see that I had plummeted in their estimation. Vince Matti was on his feet now, raging. By the expression in Vince's eyes, I could see he was going to kill me.

"What's the matter with Billy?" asked one of the girls piteously.

"He's getting his period," said one of the straights on the boys' team.

Everybody laughed. Instantly Vince Matti started toward his straight teammate to kill him. By the time I got the two of them apart, Billy had disappeared around the corner of the athletic building.

When the class broke up, Vince hung back, glaring at me. "Look, Mr. Brown," he said, "there's something you ought to know."

"Since when is it your business?" I said.

"Billy is acting so crazy because he's in love with you."

I felt that blow in my stomach, and a roaring in my ears.

"He knows what my rule is," I managed to say.

"It's that you're so harsh with him," said Vince, hardly able to control himself. "At first you were, like, kind to him sometimes. But now he's convinced that you've got some kind of grudge against him. He knows it's hopeless to want a relationship with you, man, but if you aren't a little more human with him, you're gonna lose him off the team."

I had to turn away. I wondered if Billy had told him of the scene in the locker room yesterday.

"Did he ask you to talk to me?" I said hoarsely.

"Christ, no. He'd kill me if he knew. His father knows too, and Billy's forbidden him to say anything."

I went through the rest of the day in a daze. I was shaking with exhaustion and emotion. The whole campus was talking about the way we'd hit each other in yoga class. Everybody seemed to agree that Coach Brown was a monster. All I could think was: He loves me. How had he managed to hide it so well?

That evening I went to his dorm. All three of them were sitting silently in his room. Jacques was sitting in the middle of Billy's unmade bed, playing a mournful tune on his recorder. Vince was sitting on the end of the bed, his elbows on his knees. Billy was sitting hunched at his desk in front of his typewriter.

When I appeared in the door, Vince and Jacques looked at me, then got up and walked out past me without saying a word.

I closed the door to shut out all the talking, laughing and rock music that echoed up and down the hall. I sat down on the end of his bed by the desk, where Vince had sat, and looked at him. His research papers were spread out everywhere, books, notes in his backhand script—he had been trying to work. He sat there with quiet wounded dignity, staring at the typewriter, one hand on the keys. The light of his study lamp picked out the gold in his curls and the gold rims on his glasses. *He loves me.*

It occurred to me, looking at his emotionless profile, that I had better straighten this out to both our satisfactions right now. Without, of course, breaking my rule.

"Billy, I apologize," I said.

"Why did you do it in front of the others?" he said, still not looking at me.

"It was inexcusable, and you gave me exactly what I deserved. I'll apologize to you before the class next time."

"I keep asking myself," he said, "what I've done to make you so . . . so hostile to me. I know I get you very pissed at me all the time, but somehow that doesn't explain . . ."

"The only way I can explain it," I said awkwardly, "is that I am under some pressures of my own. I've been taking them out on you."

"Why not on the others too?"

"Maybe because I expect more of you than the others."

For the first time he looked at me. His eyes were level, accusing, sad.

"This has been a lesson to me," I said. "From now on, I'm going to treat you right.'"

"You know," he said, unsmiling, "I began to think you hated my guts."

I shook my head. "No," I said, as softly as I dared. "How could I hate you?"

Billy's shoulders slumped a little. "All right," he said. "I believe you."

As I got up to leave, I allowed myself the liberty of ruffling his hair—in nothing more than a fatherly fashion. "Get some rest," I said.

After I left him, Vince and Jacques headed back to his room. I learned later that Billy told them, "So he doesn't hate me. Where does that leave me? He doesn't love me either. What the hell am I going to do? How did I ever get myself into this mess, anyway?"

SEVEN

We went to Des Moines, to the Drake Relays. Vince's knees were hurting him, and the best he could do in the mile was fourth. Jacques won the half-mile. Billy ran poorly, listless and distracted. Considering his condition, the fifth-place 28:35 he turned in in the 10,000 meter was a tremendous effort.

After the race he was out cold. He had the dry heaves, and didn't recover the way he should have. He complained that his right leg, the one the cramp had hit, was tight and sore. And he had muscle tremors.

A couple of spectators yelled, "Faggot!" as he walked off the track. Obviously word was finally getting around: a little gossip at a meet, a snicker or two at a trackwriters' lunch or an AAU meeting. But Billy was so exhausted that he gave no sign of having heard.

Billy's father had flown in to see him run, and was worried. "I've never seen him look so bad," he said.

When the meet ended that Sunday afternoon, we all flew back to New York. I went on up to Prescott with the rest of the team, and Billy stayed in New York with his father. Late the next afternoon, after classes and workouts, I drove down to have dinner with them.

At the Fifth Avenue Hotel, I found John talking business with a gay activist, George Rayburn, a dark, swarthy and politically vehement guy. Billy was in his father's bed, looking as bad as yesterday.

I sat down on the bed by him and felt his forehead. He was running a low-grade fever, a typical symptom of over-training.

"Did you get any rest?" I said.

He answered in a low voice, barely moving his lips. "No. I can't sleep at all."

"I can tell just by your face you've lost weight."

"I've dropped five pounds."

He looked strangely apathetic, laying there on his stomach, the blankets piled clear up over his shoulders, his face half-buried in the pillow. John and George were standing over by the window, each with a whiskey glass in his hand, talking gay politics.

I sat looking at Billy with a feeling of anguished helplessness. If I wasn't careful, I was going to have a sick runner on my hands. Colds, flu. Or maybe mononucleosis, which a runner takes months or even years to recover from. It occurred to me then that the only way Billy Sive was going to get to Montréal was through my bed. I had to release him from the pressure I was putting on him. As I sat there, my starved body begged me to lay down beside him and ease his starved body.

I put my hand on the back of his neck. He was vibrating with tension, and his skin was burning hot.

"A little relaxation will help," I said gently. "A good dinner, a movie."

He shook his head.

"Come on," I said, putting my hand on the back of his neck again, letting a little of my feelings show in my voice.

He looked at me guardedly for a moment. I tossed a newspaper onto the bed. "Pick what you want to see."

He sat up and listlessly flipped till he found the film ads. Then he said, "*Song of the Loon* is on." After a minute he said, "I love that silly old film. Let's go."

Billy pulled on jeans and a turtleneck sweater, and we caught a cab downtown.

The theater was a rundown little place a few blocks

east of Washington Square. The whole area looked bombed out. The streets were littered with garbage.

In the small musty lobby, John and Rayburn left us and went up to the balcony. Obviously they wanted to be alone together. That left me with Billy. We sat downstairs, in a side row. Many seats were empty, and the men sat alone or in pairs here and there. The place had that stale smell that tells you it's probably going to be bulldozed for urban renewal. The velvet seat-cushions were ripped, and there were butts and papers underfoot.

Song of the Loon will never be seen on the "Late Late Show." It is a classic old gay film, very amateurish, very erotic, very hard to forget.

So Billy and I sat side by side without speaking to each other. Now and then I stole a glance at him out of the corner of my eye. He was sitting slid down a little, his eyes fixed on the screen. He looked sad and depressed, and had his clenched hands against his mouth. I felt a depression of my own. On the screen, the two lovers were swimming in the lake and looking at each other's nudity, and I was forcibly reminded of Chris. When they started to make love on the grass, I noticed that Billy looked down. I turned my head and looked at him. He was sitting with eyes shut, his clenched hands pressed against his opened lips, gnawing on his knuckles. He shifted a little in the seat, his thighs apart.

I reached over and touched his clenched hands. I took them and drew them toward me. He looked at me a little dazedly, his lips still open, as if not believing that I had touched him.

"I have a lot of apologizing to do to you," I said softly. I was shaking all over. At last I was ready to let go of my self-control. Was there any real reason why I had to live my whole life without having loved a single human being?

"I've never meant to be cruel," I said. "Maybe you won't understand why I behaved the way I did."

He was staring at me in disbelief, his lips parted, his

eyes glittering with pain in the silvery light from the screen. A visible shudder of emotion went through his body.

"Then," he said in that strange broken voice, lowered to a hoarse whisper, "my father was right."

He pulled his hands away from mine. That was the most terrible single moment of my life. It was all the pain of Penn State telescoped into a single few minutes. I knew I'd lost him. I'd abused him and insulted him. He was a man, with a man's pride. What else could I expect? I thought, I'll walk out of this theater and I'll throw myself on the subway tracks in front of a train.

He sat staring straight forward at the screen, but unseeingly. His hands were clenched on his thighs. "My father was dead sure you wanted me. He was always taking your side. Even when you hit me! I just about got furious at him." He sat breathing deeply, unevenly, for a few minutes. "How long have you felt this way?"

I sat bowed and miserable. I was ready to make a total fool of myself to make him stop being angry. "Ever since you came," I said. We were still talking in hoarse whispers. He turned and fixed me with those terrible eyes. Now he gave me back the whiplash I'd given him in the locker room. "The things you've put me through . . . I never took from anybody what I've taken from you."

I closed my eyes. "All I can say is, I hurt myself every time I hurt you. So we're even."

His eyes narrowed. "What do you want from me? If you're interested in a matinee, forget it."

I met his eyes and shook my head slowly. I let him see all the feeling that was in me, in my eyes. He saw that feeling, and was still hesitating in anguished disbelief.

"Harlan," he said. He touched my hand, which was laying clenched on the musty armrest.

"I'm in love with you," I said. "Do you want it on the dotted line?" I turned my hand up, clenching his so hard that I thought both our fingers were going to crack.

We sat there wringing each other's fingers like a couple of uptight high-school students.

Suddenly, he reached out with his free hand, grasped me by the shoulder. He leaned toward me, drawing me toward him, and he kissed me on the mouth, hard, but only for a few moments. Our hands untangled ourselves. He drew away just a little—I could still feel his breath on my lips. My certainty that I'd lost him was still trying to change into joy. I touched his cheek, and slid my fingers disbelievingly into his hair. He touched my neck.

He spoke against my lips in such a low whisper that I barely heard him. "I love you, Harlan."

We slid our arms around each other, and he kissed me again. The frankness and strength of that kiss was devastating. He opened my lips with his own, licking them slowly. His eyes shut, he moved his lips gently back and forth between mine, and then he slipped his tongue into my mouth. We clenched each other as hard as the creaky armrest would permit, and I laved his mouth with my own tongue. His mouth was sweet and clean. We gnawed and bruised each other's lips. He loved the way he ran: hard, deliberate, trancelike.

Then, with a lithe twist of his body, he was over the armrest and into my arms, half-sitting between my thighs, twisted to press against me, his arms around my neck. We held each other with frantic tightness, as if to make up all at once for the five months of pain. We were almost one body just from sheer pressure, and our mouths stayed together in an unrestrained open kiss.

My hands moved down him slowly, feeling him rather than caressing him, almost as if to make sure he was really there. I felt the long lean back through his sweater, then his narrow waist, a burning bare strip of skin where the sweater was pulled up. He was trying to feel me too, which was more difficult, but finally he got one hand inside my suit jacket, and felt my chest and my side.

Now and then we looked at each other, as if in disbelief, our eyes black with emotion. I held his head and kissed his face and his eyes, and he kept turning his head to kiss my hands. He precipitated me back to that first time 11 years before, so forceful and tender that he made it all new, except that this time, instead of amyl nitrite, it was love that had me stinging.

But we didn't do anything more than that. There was a silent agreement that we weren't going to do it in the theater. His hips were clamped firmly between my thighs, but with an unmoving dreamlike pulsing heaviness. We were both trembling with exhaustion, and content to rest against each other, like two drowning men who had just hauled themselves up on some floating wreckage.

Finally I whispered, "When did you fall in love with me, you spoiled brat?"

"Right away," he said against my cheek. "But I hid it because you were so cold. I thought I was going to lose my marbles."

I ruffled his hair. We were calming down a little. "You understand the risks, don't you?" I asked.

"Yes."

"You may lose your chance at Montréal. I may lose my career. We may lose everything we have."

"If you're worried about it, then we can't be lovers. But I'll have to leave the school in that case. I can't be around you every day and be held off. You've taught me a few things—maybe I could get to Montréal alone."

I thought of seeing his face only in newspaper photographs in the future. I thought of him facing all that fury with his youth and inexperience. Running a 27:30 10,000 meter was one thing. Maybe he could do that. But in-fighting with the track politicos was something else. They would wipe him out.

"All right," I said. "But don't say I didn't warn you."

"Darlings," somebody said behind us, "you're better than the movie, but could you be a teensy bit quieter?"

"Let's get out of this cruddy place," said Billy.

We walked out into the lobby. My knees were actually shaking. In the lurid fluorescent light, amid the billboards and the dusty plastic potted plants, we looked at each other. Billy's face was a strange pale color. His eyes were dark and wild behind his glasses, and his lips were raw. I presumed I looked the same.

"What about your father?" I said.

"Oh, hell, he approves," said Billy. "He'll be delighted that I'm not gonna run up his phone bill any more. Calling him up, crying . . ."

"All right, wait here and I'll tell him."

I went up to the balcony. John and Rayburn were either finished, or not in the mood, as they were sitting there calmly viewing the film. I sat down by John for a moment.

"I'm going to take Billy back up to school. No alarm. He needs a good night's sleep. Why don't you come up tomorrow afternoon?"

John looked at me. He knew. He smiled a little. "Okay, see you then," he said. With those four words, he surrendered his only son to me.

Billy and I walked out onto the street. "We'll go get my car and go on up to the school."

Billy's face fell. "I thought we were going back to the hotel."

"I'm a romantic," I said. "I'm not going to make love to you the first time in a goddam hotel."

"But, at school, that's . . . coming out."

We were walking along the dark street, stepping over garbage and dog shit and broken boards. Since there were no cabs around, we headed for the 9th Street subway station.

"No," I said. "We'll have to be careful at school. I know Joe won't care, but I don't want to come out with it. What we'll do is, we'll get a good night's sleep first. We're both worn out. Then first thing in the morning we'll go for a little run in the woods. We'll find a nice spot up there somewhere."

Billy's eyes sparkled wickedly. "That's your fantasy, huh? In the grass, huh, like in the movie?"

"Yeah," I said, "what's yours?"

He laughed out loud and took my hand. "Oh, I have a lot of them," he said. "Making out in *Loon* with you, for one."

We had a dangerous drive back up to the college. I was so shaky that it was a wonder I didn't smash up the car. Billy lay with his head in my lap the whole way, and I kept running my fingers through his hair, and told him the whole story of my life. I had never told it to anyone.

I unloaded the whole thing on him. It should have given me some relief. But instead, the more I talked, the more nervous I got, the more flimsy my reasons seemed for giving in to my feelings. I kept looking down at his profile eerily lit by the dashboard lights, at his hand on my thigh. He still didn't seem real.

I thought to myself: You're out of your mind. You can still back out.

EIGHT

I'd given Billy this big lecture about how we both needed a good night's rest. But I didn't sleep at all that night.

I spent the whole night tossing around in that creaky Victorian bed, torturing myself with thoughts. I was going to do the wrong thing. I was going to destroy his running career just to satisfy my selfish feelings. If we became lovers, the fury would hit us. It would obliterate us. It might even destroy our feeling for each other. I wasn't so sure that love could survive something like that. Having had no experience with love, I had no data on which to base an opinion.

Finally it was just getting light, and the birds started to sing off in the nearby woods. They sang wildly, sharply, sweetly. I lay listening to them vibrating with nervousness.

Finally I got up and shaved. I had the shakes so bad I could hardly hold the shaver. I looked at myself in the rust-specked old bathroom mirror, and the great gay dread about aging hit me. There is no society, no law, no social convention to keep two gays together. Everything is based on feeling and on personal attractiveness. The moment you cease to be desirable to your partner, he decamps.

I ran my hands back over my close-barbered curls. My hair was still good, though its brunette color now had a gunmetal tint. But sooner or later I'd start to bald. My tanned face was still recognizable as the Villanova miler of twenty years ago, but sun and bitterness had cut hard lines in it. My body and skin were the best things I had, but for how much longer? I wondered if I'd ever get paranoid enough for cosmetics and hair transplants. I needed a love that I could lean on for the rest of my life, and that was too much to hope for. By the time Billy was my age, and still a healthy vigorous man, I would be nearly sixty. Sooner or later he might elbow me aside for someone younger, the way he might elbow some stranger in a race.

My heart almost stopped when I heard him knock on the door. I looked at my alarm clock. He was fifteen minutes early.

When I came out on the verandah, the sun was just showing through the trees. Billy was kicking around in the pine needles by the house. He was wearing a faded red long-sleeved T-shirt, his old blue shorts, his spiked cross-country shoes, no socks and his headband.

"Hi," he said cheerfully.

"Did you sleep?" I said as I shut the door.

"Some," he said, smiling a little. Now that the uncertainty of the past months was resolved he was his normal relaxed self. He wasn't nervous at all, I could see. He could hardly wait. Fifteen minutes early.

We set off across the field, and shortly we were in the woods. It was an unseasonably warm morning, and we started sweating right away.

"Stay at a seven-minute pace," I said. "This is going to be a rest day."

"Seven minutes?" said Billy. "Christ!" He was used to clipping along out there at a five-minute-mile pace. But he struck a seven and stayed on it with his usual uncanny precision.

At first I was so shaky that my legs felt bad. But after I warmed up, I felt a little lifted. The woods smelled fresh and spicy—there had been no rain for a week, and the leaves sent up their herby smell. The bird songs were everywhere, echoing through the groves and hollows. They stopped singing as we passed, then started up again, or flew off and started singing farther off. We could hear no other sounds but the steady crunch of our spikes along the soft trail, and our breathing.

Billy ran about ten feet ahead of me, not looking back. Even on his way to make love, he was businesslike about running. He seemed hardly to touch the ground—I had to look to see his spike marks to make sure. His elbows and buttocks moved a little—rather, the rhythm suffused his whole body. After a little while, his shirt was soaked through in back, and his shorts had that dark line between the buttocks. Without missing a stride, he pulled the shirt over his head and tied the sleeves around his waist. Now I could watch the subtle play of muscle, spine and shoulder blade in his back.

I kept my eyes on him so hard that, a couple of times, I nearly stumbled over rocks or roots. He was not real. He was just a photograph, just a flickering phantom in a film. When the reel ran out, he would disappear.

We ran softly for about three miles. We wended among the great silver beeches hazed with pink buds. Early violets and wood anemones poked up through the carpet of dead leaves. In the marshy spots, the skunk cabbages' bloom was long past and they were thrusting up their coarse green leaves. We leaped over logs fallen across the trail. We splashed over streams, where the witch hazel still bent its frail yellow sprays of bloom. We leaped up hills and floated down on the other side.

Only once did Billy turn to speak to me. "Seven minutes," he said over his shoulder, grinning a little. "You have to be some kind of masochist."

Then we came to a spot where a faint side trail forked off.

"Billy," I said. He looked back. My stomach plunged with nervousness. "This way," I said.

He fell in behind me this time. We followed the barely visible trail over a ridge and down along a slope through some stately, old, half-dead hemlocks, then up another slope and down along it into a little valley. The slope here was grown up with mountain laurel, shoulder high. At the bottom of the valley, a little stream noised along among the rocks. It slid in a shining sheet over a mossy rock shelf into a little pool, then wound on. I had slowed us down—we were barely more than jogging now. I wanted to warm us down as much as possible, and the trail was so rough here I didn't want Billy to trip and hurt himself.

I stopped in a little clearing in the mountain laurel, and looked around. I knew this place already. It faced south, the sun would hit it in a few minutes, and we'd be warm here. It was secluded—the teams never took that side trail during their woods workouts. Surely nobody would come, especially at this hour. And if they did, the gnarled trunks and green leaves of the laurel would screen us. The crunching of leaves would warn us.

I stood there, still breathing a little heavily. Billy was still coming down the slope through the mountain laurel. All around him, the laurel was putting out the buds that would bloom in June. His torso, arms and legs were laced with bright sweat. He looked at me questioningly. I couldn't speak. My eyes said that this was the place.

Slowly he came on toward me, his spiked shoes crunching softly on the carpet of tan beech leaves. His eyes had the same intent look as in the movie last night, but less tortured now. He was that image of myself, which had been torn from me in my teens and sent off on a long lonely trip. Now he was coming back, to join with his own flesh again, with that body that had been kept waiting for him like a house rented to many tenants, but now swept out for its returning owner.

He came up to me and laid his hand on my wet, hairy chest. I put my hand on his tattooed shoulder. It was that loaded gesture of two males touching each other. We destroyed the tabu in it, we made it clean.

We stood lightly pressed together, breathing now less from running than from excitement. Suddenly we were free to caress each other. To caress him—how unbelievable that was after twenty years of starvation and paid grapplings. Do people really understand what it means to caress someone? We kissed and touched everything we could reach, tasted the salt of each other's skin. His sweat was sweeter than mine because of the no-salt diet.

I buried my face in his damp hair and untied the sleeves of the red shirt from his waist, and it slipped to the leaves. Billy took off his glasses and let them lie on the sweatshirt. His hands were already sliding feverishly under the waistband of my shorts. There was no sound but the silence of the woods and the birds caroling senselessly, and the leaves, crackling under our spikes.

I went to my knees, sliding down against him and kissing his body all the way down. My hands shucked down his shorts and jock strap both at once. The harsh brown patch of pubic hair was startling on his pale, supple, veined loins, and the swollen cock between those runner's thighs. I had it in my mouth almost before I'd seen it. The only sound, in that silence, was Billy groaning softly as he fondled my head and thrust his hips slowly against my face. He was real.

D espite my wish to be frank, I can't describe everything we did.

There are several reasons why. I am better at hiding feelings than displaying them. I am not literary enough. I have to keep some memories for myself. I am not sure that I remember what we did in exact serial order. Besides, I think it is generally known by now what happens when two human bodies come together.

Maybe if I were the Jean Genet or the Steve Goodnight of the trackwriters, I could put on paper the peculiar intensity of that first sexual encounter.

The word "ecstasy" isn't quite right. We both rejected mysticism in favor of simple directness and rough tenderness. If Billy let himself go so far as to moan sometimes and close his eyes and toss his head around on the leaves, I was silent and open-eyed. I had to see in

order to believe. Even in his arms, I was the doubting
Thomas.

The lesbians tell us that only a woman knows how to
love a woman. The gays will answer that only a man
knows how to love a man. I had always found women
passive, devouring. They seemed to have no notion of how
important sex is to a man, and no willingness to learn.
Women had always robbed me of my sex for money—first
my wife, then the prostitutes. But Billy's male intensity
met me halfway. Instead of taking, he gave. Each of us
gave, and gave again, until we were drained and hurting.

That first time, we shied away from the ultimate act
of love and possession that the Supreme Court had declared
legal. In our macho pride, neither of us had ever permitted
another man to do that. For months yet, each of us would
still have a deep-rooted fear of offending precisely that
maleness that we loved in the other. In addition, I dreaded
the idea of hurting Billy physically, or of upsetting that
relentless psych that kept him in front on the track.

It would take far more trust and confidence than we
had on that April morning before each of us would not
only tolerate being taken, but actually wish for it as the
ultimate way of pleasing the other. In fact, I would be the
first to surrender—my fear of damaging Billy was so strong
that I would wind up hurting his feelings by at first
refusing his own surrender.

But for now, what we were able to give and receive
was more than enough.

W e lay finished.

I had expected to feel shattered after this intimacy
with my ghost. Instead I felt peaceful. It was warm there
on the dry leaves. The warming sun was shining right on
us, and I felt empty, almost weightless. I felt very clean,
as if the light were shining straight through me—as if the
forest air were moving through all the cells of my body.

His legs lay across my arm, and my head lay on his thighs. He still had his arms around my lower body, and his face pressed against my groin. In the silence, I could almost hear our hearts beat. They had the slow deep pulse of the distance runner—mine was about forty-eight and his was forty. I could see that pulse beating in his genitals—the penis, still swollen and moist, moved slowly as it lay across his thigh. My mouth tasted of his salt and his semen.

The leaves crackled a little under us. Nearby, the water gurgled as it slid over the rock. The birds had stopped their dawn caroling and were into the softer, more businesslike daytime notes. In the distance was the soft rumble of a jet plane.

I couldn't move. In my sweet inertia, I was like a rock. I would lay there till a glacier moved me.

Billy drew a long slow breath and ran his hand along my thigh one more time. My arm was going to sleep, so with deep regrets I pulled it slowly from under his thighs. It took an effort, but I raised myself up on my elbow. He stayed as he was, his face between my thighs, his hand stroking. My groin was spattered with a little glistening semen, and Billy started to lick it up slowly, first out of the pubic hair, then off my bare skin to the side. His eyes were closed.

It was dreamlike yet so real: the feel of his warm tongue on my body. He moved slowly, turning against me, kissing his way up along my torso. He was dry now, and warm, with a fine dust of salt on his skin. His tongue left a wet trail in my body hair. He reached my breast, kissed my nipples, nuzzled his face in my thick, chest hair. Something in this mute act of worship made me think that no other lovemaking had ever stirred him so deeply.

I lay back down, putting one arm around him, and he lay against me with his face buried in my neck, his fingers playing slowly in my chest hair.

"You're hairy," he said in that low voice I could barely catch. "I like hair." Suddenly he raised his head and smiled at me drowsily. "The first time I saw you in shorts, your hairy thighs really turned me on."

I stroked his head, picking the leaves out of his hair.

"Mr. Brown, you're very well hung."

I laughed a little. "You're good for my ego."

"Really. You have a great body. I hope I look like you when I'm your age. You look more like thirty-three, thirty-four."

He wasn't going to lie and tell me I looked like twenty-three. I couldn't have accepted that, and he knew it. Thirty-three I could accept. It made me feel relieved. I wondered how I could have panicked in front of the mirror earlier.

"How did you manage all these months?" I asked.

He laughed softly. "I got very depraved. My dharma was a mess."

"Now I suppose you'll tell me you slept with Vince or something."

"Christ, no," he said. "I just thought of you like mad and jerked off."

He sat up slowly, blinking in the bright light. We were both a sight. That book of photographs hadn't shown the cruel realities of screwing in the woods. Our sticky buttocks were stuck with bits of leaf and bark and moss. Our knees and elbows were black with dirt. The carpet of leaves was somewhat torn up. All around us, the silky fiddleheads of ferns were pushing up—we had rolled on some of them and crushed them. Our clothes lay in soggy disorder where they had fallen.

"You're jealous," said Billy.

"Sure," I answered. "Would you want me to be otherwise?"

"*I'm* jealous," said Billy. "I know Vince tried to cruise you when we came. And you told him he was a very attractive kid." He smiled blissfully, picked off a broken fiddlehead and threw it at me. "But there's no reason for either of us to be jealous."

I was gently, sleepily brushing the leaves off him. It was not a tense conversation—we were both too limp for that. But suddenly we were saying things we had to say. "Does that mean you won't get tired of me too soon?" I said, trying to say it as casually as possible.

He looked at me steadily. "Yeah," he said, "my dad is anxious like that. He puts up a good front, but . . . Anyway, you don't have to worry. I'll be loving you for the rest of my life."

"That's a long time," I said. I didn't want to remind him of his own observation that gay relationships seldom lasted that long.

He shook his head. "I never wanted to love anyone that long before." He laughed a little. "It's funny. You're the first thing that I can project into the future, after Montréal. The rest just goes up to Montréal and stops. Even running somehow . . . stops there. I don't mean that I'll stop running afterward. But . . . you know what I mean. Right now, I'm just running and loving you, and that's all I want to do with myself."

He lay down on the leaves again and stretched luxuriously beside me. I felt that same ease, that same slackening of the months of hurt and tension.

"I want to sleep," he said.

"Nothing doing," I said. "We both have classes. We have to get back."

We both got stiffly up. We moved so slowly that we might have been drugged. Suddenly Billy started laughing.

"What?" I said.

He pointed down at our feet. We were both still wearing our shoes.

We stood by the little waterfall and cleaned ourselves off. Then we pulled our clammy clothes back on. We were shivering a little, even in the warm sun.

"Speaking of Montréal," I said, "there's something we ought to agree on. For the moment, this has to take its place in what we're trying to do. If it interferes, it might cause you to fail. That might spoil our feeling for each other too."

"Yeah," said Billy. "I was thinking of that. Actually,

the pressure's off us now, so it'll be easier. We can both just relax and get on with it."

"The pressure is going to be coming from other people from now on," I said.

Suddenly I had more questions. I wanted to talk to him about being married and about living together. But he'd already said he disapproved of ceremonies, and anyway I knew it was not the moment to come out with our relationship. I wanted to keep it secret as long as I could.

I decided not to spoil that moment with any discussions of this sort, and just swallowed the questions.

Billy was laughing again. He was convulsed. He pointed at my stopwatch. "Mr. Brown, you even forgot to stop your watch before you grabbed me."

We both leaned against the rock, laughing, shivering in our wet clothes. "Mr. Brown," he said, "what was our pace per mile?"

"More like 3:50," I said.

We walked slowly back with our arms around each other, our sides pressed together. About a mile from the edge of the woods, we saw Vince and Jacques coming along the trail. I drew away from Billy nervously.

"Hell," said Billy, "we want them to know, don't we?"

So we kept walking like that, two lovers, with bits of leaf still in our hair. Vince and Jacques came loping up to us, grinning widely. They stopped just long enough to enable Jacques to caper around us. He was playing an invisible recorder and making noises that sounded like the Mendelssohn wedding march. Vince punched me gently, and punched Billy gently.

"Now maybe we'll have some peace and quiet," he said.

NINE

As graduation 1975 neared, every passing day told me how right I'd been not to say no to Billy. The decision had been right not only for me, but for him too.

Both of us relaxed. I stopped barking at him. He stopped fighting me about his training schedule. It was amazing how docile he suddenly was about cutting down his mileage. He was still a little addicted to it, and fidgeted like an ex-junkie sometimes. "I fought you because I resented your behavior to me," he said. "Now I'm going to be good."

For me, the relaxation was gradual, as the buried tensions and pains of years slowly dissolved. For Billy, the relaxation was immediate. From that first morning in the woods, he abandoned himself to love.

"I always fell in love with unhappy people," he said. "I was a sucker that way. I wanted to change their lives and make them happy. It never worked out. It was the same with you. You were the unhappiest guy I ever saw. But you're stronger than the others, and you really want to be happy. This time it's going to work."

The relaxation had a curious effect: for the first week or so, both of us wanted to sleep all the time. Billy nodded off in classes. In the afternoons he went back to his dorm and napped. I found myself falling asleep in my office with my head on the typewriter. I found my eyes falling shut as I stood by the track supposedly timing my runners.

We both found that we couldn't stay awake past nine p.m. We laughed about it.

But our happiness was far from complete. It was painful to continue on the same daily schedule as before. We saw each other only during workouts, classes and team open house. We snatched an hour of love every day or every other day, in the evenings at my house, or in the woods, or in my car somewhere. When Billy's father came to New York, we snatched a half hour in his hotel room when he was out. When night came, Billy always went back to his dorm to sleep.

Above all I hungered for him at night—not merely for his body, but for his presence. I thought: Have I waited twenty years for this, only to wake up in the morning and find myself in an empty bed?

We often called each other up on the phone. I'd be home about ten p.m. working out new training schedules for the teams, and the phone would ring. "Hi, Mr. Brown," he would say. "Hello, Mr. Sive," I would say. "Mr. Brown," he'd say, "I can't get any studying done because I'm thinking about your body." "You're not even supposed to be *up* at this hour," I'd say. "You're supposed to be asleep."

Though Joe Prescott had told me long ago it would be strictly my business, I felt obliged to tell him. He took the news with his usual equanimity. Vince and Jacques had not been able to resist telling a couple of friends among their straight teammates, who in turn couldn't resist telling a few other students and faculty. They observed that Billy did indeed sometimes go to my house alone in the evening, and that I wasn't yelling at him any more.

The reaction was: Ho hum, another picturesque pair. Unfortunately this knowledge eventually found its way off campus.

Billy started studying extra hard, trying to make up for lost time. When May came, all three boys' portfolios were graded "Pass" and they were able to graduate.

Whereupon Joe Prescott then hired Vince and Billy as teachers, with the idea that they would develop a gay studies program. Joe had gotten more and more interested in the whole question of gay rights, and thought Prescott could make a practical contribution that would be in keeping with the college's aim of "more human people."

He also took Jacques onto the faculty as a graduate assistant in the environmental activist course.

All three boys were delighted with this development, and so was I. It solved the problem of a base for their training until the Olympic Trials. Billy, of course, stayed on campus to be near me, and the other two stayed on to start working up their course material. It was making their gayness more public, but the rumors in the track world were now so insistent that we knew by next fall sometime their cover would be blown.

That summer I finally began to see Billy's true potential as a runner. For the first time I began to think that a medal in Montréal was not just a wet dream.

After the Drake Relays, his improvement had stopped, as his overstrained system slowly, secretly healed itself. I wasn't too worried—it was the familiar plateau in an athlete's development. By now I had him on the program I was sure was right for him. I'd run it through a computer and tinkered with it endlessly, studying the results. He was now weaned down to a mere 100 miles a week, and a single daily workout. But it was all quality and strength work.

Every day he ran thirty to eighty minutes in the woods, burning through it at a 5 or 5:15 mile pace. All the hills made it a beautiful brutal strength exercise. Then he went back to the track for speed laps. He would do, say ten quarters or twenty to twenty-five 110s at seventy-five percent effort. Before a major meet I would let him add some second daily workouts of five miles run at nearly race pace. He loved that second workout—he behaved like a child who'd been given a popsicle.

In July he suddenly started improving again. His three- and six-mile times started dropping so rapidly that I knew he would break twenty-eight minutes in the 10,000 meter any time now, and go 13:35 in the 5,000.

We kept strictly to our sparse meeting schedule, and did not parade our relationship on campus, because summer school was going on, and a good number of students and faculty were there. Nevertheless, we were met with a growing number of hostile remarks when we traveled to meets that summer.

I found it more and more unbelievable that spectators and officials could deride those three handsome manly dignified young men. I found it particularly curious that they could deride Billy, when he looked more and more like the only serious threat to European domination in the 5,000 and 10,000 that America had so far had. But the deriders wanted to have their cake and eat it too. They wanted medals hung only on clean-cut heterosexuals.

Thus, a paunchy track nut sitting in the first row, with his well-thumbed program and his cigar would yell at Billy, "Hey, lover boy, whose girlfriend are you?"

If Billy came in second, some wit would be sure to yell, "Nice gays never win."

Vince and Billy were not disturbed by the remarks. Vince might throw the guy a bird or yell back something smart- ass. Billy simply ignored them. But Jacques shrank from them. "I don't know how long I can take this," he said. His performances that summer really dropped off. He was so nervous that his legs were dead by the time he got to the starting line.

We got to one meet in July and they told us the boys couldn't compete. They were very sorry. They said that our entries hadn't been received before the closing date. They were polite, but firm. They didn't say anything about the boys being gay. They just said they couldn't run.

I had anticipated this kind of trick. I pulled out a signed certified-mail return receipt with the meet secretary's signature on it. I always sent the boys' entries by certified mail now. Since I'd sent them in weeks before, the meet people had forgotten somebody had signed. They had to let the three run.

At another meet, Vince was barred from the track at the last moment. The officials insisted that his new AAU registration was not valid. Vince fumed and cursed, and got out his AAU card. The officials insisted that the matter would have to be looked into, and meantime he couldn't compete. They practically shoved him off the track. We had the matter investigated immediately, and of course his card was okay.

They picked on Vince a lot because they disliked his impudence. At still another meet they wouldn't let him run until he'd paid an extra fifty cents of entry fee to make up for an official's mistake. Vince was scrounging madly for two quarters at trackside, and barely got to his marks on time.

In late July a more serious matter came up. I wanted to take all three of them to Europe for a month, to get the international experience they needed so badly. We planned to go to a number of big meets, including Helsinki. But when we applied to the AAU for the routine travel permits, the AAU would not give them to us.

It may seem strange that in this day and age of total freedom, when Americans travel freely everywhere, even to Red China, an amateur athlete does not enjoy quite the same freedom of travel. But the matter of who goes on European tours is a big point of politics with the AAU. They reserve the right to arrange for travel, whether or not it is in accord with the athlete's wishes and needs, and they reserve the right to give or deny permission to go. They insist that foreign meet promoters contact them and not the individual athletes that the promoters might like.

Recently athletes have been quarreling bitterly with the AAU over travel, especially in view of AAU abuses. Say a Belgian promoter contacts AAU executive director Mel Steinbock and says, "Could I have miler John Doe in my meet?" and the executive director might reply cavalierly, "Sorry, buddy, the meet schedule here conflicts—

we need John Doe." John Doe is furious because (1) the meet schedule doesn't conflict and he would have been free to go, and (2) he feels that he should have been consulted about this important decision.

It reached the point where foreign promoters were as pissed at the AAU as American runners were, and finally the AAU was starting to be more careful.

That summer, the AAU organized a European tour for a number of athletes as part of the Olympic development program. Some of the athletes' expenses would be paid by the AAU, some by the European promoters. Naturally, though their status clearly warranted it, Billy, Vince and Jacques were not invited on the tour.

I had known that they wouldn't be. So well in advance I had surreptitiously contacted the European promoters myself, saying we planned to come abroad and asking if they were interested. Quite a few were. Knowing the AAU's strange ways, they kept me surreptitiously informed while they made the formal request to the AAU.

The AAU was panicked and embarrassed at the thought of their three rumored homosexuals touring Europe. But they didn't say the word "homosexual" out loud once. To the promoter they said, "Oh, we're awfully sorry, we want those three boys for the U.S.-Soviet invitational in Los Angeles in mid-August."

When the foreign promoters relayed this information to us, we told Steinbock that the boys did not plan to go to Los Angeles, and that they damn well wanted their travel permits. Steinbock got furious and said he wasn't issuing them any permits.

Then I got furious and called Steinbock up. "You've got a choice," I said. "You can issue these permits and the whole thing will blow over. Or you can deny them, and we'll go anyway."

"If you do that, I'll suspend all three boys," said Steinbock crisply.

"Then you're going to buy yourself a lot of trouble," I said. "I'll get a court injunction preventing you from punishing them pending a hearing. Do you want a hearing? What's the big deal? They don't plan to run at the Soviet meet, so why not let them go? What have you got against them?"

We packed our bags, and John Sive prepared to get the injunction. But at the last minute, following the AAU's new policy of caution, Steinbock backed down and issued the permits.

B illy Sive arrived in Europe unknown to track fans there. But he wasn't an unknown long. In Helsinki, right on schedule, he broke twenty-eight in the 10,000 meter, which was already then—and would be—his best race. By doing so he joined the select club of fifteen world-class runners who had run under twenty-eight in this event, and was now in fifth place on the world list. But he had a long way to go before be could beat the world-record holders like Lasse Viren and Armas Sepponan, who held the current record of 27:36.11 in the 10,000.

Sepponan, in fact, was sure to be Billy's biggest worry in Montréal—if he got to Montréal at all. Sepponan had a crushing kick, and blew the front-runners right off the track. Two other big kickers were in that Helsinki race— Australia's Jim Felts and Spain's Roberto Gil—and both of them had run well under 28. So, that day in Helsinki, I wasn't really thinking of Billy winning.

Still, I was nervous as I watched the men line up at the start. The big stadium hushed a little. The Europeans really idolize distance runners, in a way that Americans are only now learning. For them, this was a big moment.

The gun fired and they rolled off the line.

The pace dragged a little. Nobody wanted to lead. The kickers were noodling in the rear. Sepponan was running easily in last place. Billy, unusual for him, was running in third place. He told me later that he had felt suddenly intimidated by the thought of all those big guns behind him. Then he thought, what the heck, what was he worried about, and he was worried somebody would elbow him.

So he moved to the front, and picked up the pace sharply. I was relieved to see him do that. The rest had their choice: hang back or go with him. So they all picked up, and three others stayed close to the front with him.

Billy was running easily, beautifully, his shaggy curls lifting, his glasses glinting as the sun caught them. He might have been a perfect machine, except that he was so real, flesh and blood turned to an ultrasonic pitch of rhythm and control. His spiked shoes seemed scarcely to strike the track. He kept pulling the other front-runners farther ahead, sticking to the pace he'd struck.

With a half-mile left to go, Billy suddenly picked up the pace sharply again. This was his long drive, running flat out to the finish, the tactic that was supposed to burn off the kickers. The other front-runners immediately lost contact with him, and he sped on alone. The crowd started to scream, because now Seponnan, Felts and Gil were moving up fast, hauling Billy down.

With one lap to go, Sepponan and Felts were coming up for the kill. The crowd was screaming. They were mostly Finns, so they wanted to see Sepponan kill off the presumptuous young American that nobody had heard of.

Billy didn't turn his head to look, but he heard them coming. And then I saw a glimpse of what he was capable of. He accelerated too, ghosting along with those great soft strides, his face impassive.

The crowd was going wild. As the four men rounded the last turn, we all knew that three, possibly four of them would go under 28. They had left the pack laboring far behind. They tore out of the turn in a tight little bunch, Billy still ahead, Sepponan at his shoulder, Felts and Gil behind.

I knew in my heart that he didn't have the stamina yet to hold them off.

Almost at the moment I thought it, Billy seemed to falter a little. Sepponan burst past him. The four were sprinting down the straight to the tape. In a last heart-breaking effort, Billy stayed even with Felts until just ten yards from the tape. Then he cracked. He had nothing left. He crossed the line staggering in third place, just barely shading out Gil.

The Finns were going wild, and Armas Sepponan was taking a victory lap. Nobody paid much attention to Billy as he circled shakily back.

I went out to him. He bent over, his hair hanging, his hands braced on his knees. Then, as always when he'd really extended himself, his streaming sides contracted with the dry heaves. I threw a towel over his shoulders, wiped his face with a wet rag. Then I showed him my stopwatch. He smiled faintly, nodded—he'd already known—but didn't speak.

The times were already going up in lights on the big scoreboard. SEPPONAN 27:47. FELTS 27:49.05. SIVE 27:50.2. GIL 27:50.7.

The two other American runners in the race, Bob Dellinger and Mike Stella, placed ninth and fifteenth with a 28:15 and a 28:25.3. They had the AAU's blessing.

Sepponan finished his victory lap, came up to Billy and put his hand on Billy's shoulders. Billy, recovered now, palmed him back.

Sepponan was a plain skinny man of 27 with close-cut blond hair and high Asiatic cheekbones. "You make me work very hard," he said in accented English.

"Yeah, you made me work hard too," said Billy.

That night, Billy, Sepponan, Felts and a few other European runners sat down together and talked. They all had beers. Billy had milk. They managed to talk, in their limited common languages, of running, and laughed a lot. Sepponan was straight as a yardstick, but his friendship and respect for Billy endured all the uproar that came later. "He has *sisu*," he said bluntly, using the Finnish word for guts and pride.

John Sive and I let the runners have their fun, and we went off somewhere else to sit and talk.

"You know," I said, "I think when Billy gets another year under his belt, he's going to be giving us some surprises. I think there's a reservoir of strength and speed that we're just now beginning to tap."

John was so proud of Billy's run that he got pretty drunk that night.

Those three weeks in Europe were the only length of time that Billy and I were able to spend together during the whole 1975-76 school year.

Of course, with Vince and Jacques along, we weren't precisely on a honeymoon for two. But at least we could be natural with each other in front of them. Little by little, I was getting over my fear of showing my feelings for Billy in front of other people.

Much was rumored about that trip. The gossips talked about little orgies for four. I am sorry to disappoint them, but it was a pretty innocent and proper affair.

The Europeans hadn't heard the rumors yet. Or else they were that much more broadminded. Or perhaps it was just because we couldn't understand any of what spectators shouted from the stands. But we didn't hear the word "fairy" once while we were over there. Jacques was delighted by this, and his performance improved in direct ratio to the absence of hassles.

The four of us traveled on the cheap, lost among the mass of young Americans who invade Europe in the summer.

We had come over on a charter flight. The boys' student ID cards got them a further fare reduction. We carried nothing but one suitcase each, with our athletic gear and one or two changes of good clothes. In front of the American Express in Helsinki, we bought a third-hand Renault for $250, and drove from meet to meet.

From Helsinki we went to a meet in Oslo, and saw some of Finland and Norway in the process. Then we took a ferry across to the Continent, the salt breeze blowing in our faces. Then we were driving again, through Germany, Belgium and France. The Europeans, who subsidize amateur athletes, kept asking us how the U.S. could allow athletes of the three boys' caliber to go on a European tour under such humble conditions. We were really pinching pennies. But we didn't mind—we had a wonderful time.

For the first time, I was as much a friend as a coach to Vince and Jacques. Finally I let them call me Harlan. How can you make a guy call you Mr. Brown after you borrow his tube of Tinactin to put on your case of jock itch?

We lived a warm footloose life. I had never felt so young and at ease—I was recapturing something of that summer with Chris. I don't think I was trying to lower myself to their age bracket on a false basis. It was just that my anxieties about getting old were finally falling away.

At any rate, my fortieth birthday fell during that trip, and I observed it without any heartbreak.

We celebrated it sitting in the sun by a canal in Bruges, eating some crusty bread and cheese. The boys gave me goofy presents. Jacques gave me a bottle of cheap wine. Vince gave me one of those weird European supporters with buttons (they don't have jock straps over there). Billy presented me with a little American flag, which I sewed on my knapsack.

Vince and Jacques drank a little of the wine, and then we poured the rest ceremoniously out as an offering to the earth.

The boys gave me a terrible razzing about being forty, and I loved it, because it was the kind of razzing they would give each other.

"Now you *are* a dirty old man," said Vince.

"Well, what was I before?" I asked.

"Just a dirty man," said Jacques.

"But I take a shower twice a day," I said.

We laughed until we were dizzy. Billy nearly choked on the fruit he was eating. Finally we calmed down.

"Someday we'll be forty," said Vince.

"It's not so bad," I said. "If you take care of your body, and have the right attitudes, and have someone you can count on, it's all right." Billy caught my eye and smiled.

We sat thoughtfully, gazing at the still canal. All around us were the mossy old stone houses, and the gabled roofs, and the church spires of Bruges. A pair of the city's famous swans swam slowly past us, with three half-grown cygnets paddling between them. Jacques pointed at them.

"There we go," he said. "Subtract the female, and you have us."

"What do you mean, Professor Audubon?" asked Vince.

"Well, the cob—the father swan—he swims behind, so he can look out for the little ones. He'll kill anything that goes near them. He's ferocious, really protective." He looked at me and grinned.

Jacques was right.

Day after day we fought our way through the summer traffic jams of little European cars. We were so bathed in fumes that I wondered what was happening to my runners' lungs. In Europe in summer, everybody is migrating somewhere else. The Germans go to Spain, and the Spanish go to Germany. The Swedes go to France, and the French go to Sweden. The main roads are lined with litter, and the smell of shit hangs over the roadside grass and bushes, in the hot air. We learned fast, and kept mostly to the byroads. There it was cleaner, the countryside less spoiled, the towns less crowded. With Jacques' French and Vince's limping Italian, we had few language problems.

The three of them taught me the sensuous joys of traveling. I had been on European tours with athletes before, but always as the ill-at-ease Yankee yearning for apple pie. They taught me how to fall in with people, how to react viscerally to every sight and sound. We picked up hitch-hikers, often other athletes going to meets.

We got drunk on the air and silence of the northern forests. We sniffed the flowers in the flower market of

Brussels, though we were too broke to buy any. We ran very early in the morning in the Bois de Boulogne in Paris, and saw the whores going home to call it a night. In Paris the three of them marched me into a tattoo parlor and made me get a lion put on my right shoulder. "You have to join the club," they said. In the Rhine valley, we filched ripening grapes from the roadside vineyards.

I have one haunting memory of stopping somewhere on the plains of northern France, at Billy's request. We parked on the side of the road in the silence, while he went along a wheat field picking a fistful of the little red poppies that grow wild in Europe.

When he put them in my hand, they were already wilting. "The Leo flower," he said.

"I hope I stay up better than that," I said. But we put them in a paper cup of water, and propped them between two suitcases, where they flopped and shortly died.

At night we settled in some cheap hotel in a small town. Hotels were one small luxury I insisted on—the boys had to get proper rest to do international-class running. No flopping somewhere on the ground in sleeping bags, or sleeping in the car. A runner can go short of sleep one night, but not two nights, or his performance suffers.

We ate dinner in small restaurants or cafés, and other meals out of grocery stores. That was another area where I didn't skimp—they had to eat right. Luckily one can eat very well in places like that in Europe (though sometimes I had to holler if grease was put in the food—neither Vince nor Billy could tolerate grease in their systems).

Sometimes we ate, talked, laughed with other athletes if we had them along. But usually we ate alone. By ten we were usually in bed. Billy and I could sometimes hear the mattress squeaking next door as Vince and Jacques made love, and no doubt they could hear our mattress.

A couple of times on the road, we had to share one

large room with two beds. Those were nights that we did without. Vince and I were shameless enough for it, but neither Billy nor Jacques would have tolerated it.

But, relaxed as we were, we didn't forget for a moment why we were over there.

The boys were scrupulous about training, working out wherever they could scrounge a track or a city park. I can still see Billy pacing off a quarter-mile along a lonely country road in Belgium, so that he could do his ten quarters for the day. We made sure we showed up for meets in plenty of time to settle in, case the scene. In between, we talked tirelessly, analyzing their performances and their European opponents, some of whom they might be meeting in Montréal. I could see them picking up the rough European track tactics, and knew the trip would not be wasted.

We were careful about the water, sticking to bottled stuff, but we all got tourist diarrhea anyway. Billy got it so bad in Oslo that, after the 10,000 meter, he ran straight off the track to the bathroom.

We showed up at the meets travel-stained, but rested and ready to kill. The officials looked at me and the expressions in their eyes said: This is the coach? A couple of times I was taken for an uninvited runner. While I wasn't dressed exactly like a hippie, I did wear faded stovepipe jeans, hiking boots and a lumberjack shirt, and had let my hair grow a shade—it was now maybe two inches long. But when they saw my kids run, they stopped smiling. They knew I was dangerous.

After the meet, there was the pleasant socializing. The awards banquet, maybe a dance, young athletes arguing about training methods in six languages, girls hanging around. I was always proud of the three of them— handsome in their good suits, ties, dress shirts, showered and combed and glowing, each poised in his way. They danced straight-facedly with girls, and if they boogied, it was never gay.

Vince and Jacques were both unfaithful to each other—

Jacques for the first time—and tasted the joys of European females. But Billy was—as usual—impervious.

"Hey, Harlan," said Vince, "these European foxes, they don't work as hard as American foxes at being sexy."

The morning after the meet, we loaded up our car and were on our way again.

Never again were the four of us so close in feeling and purpose. We were two couples in love. We were friends that would do anything for each other. We were a motherless clan, a gay commune, a little band of guerrillas living off the land. All three boys were in top form, injury-free, pitting themselves against some of the world's best, racing flat-out every few days, running well, placing if not winning.

I was engrossed in taking care of them. There was always something I could do. Vince bruised his left foot badly, and I crafted a marvelous emergency insert for his shoe that would be springy enough but legal. Just toward the end, Billy started losing his edge a little and having muscle tremors, and I had to feed him magnesium and massage his legs. Jacques was having insomnia, partly from the usual nervousness about racing, partly from euphoria.

Vince would get the hotel kitchen to heat milk for him while I rubbed him down, and usually we managed to get him off to sleep.

They looked after me too. When I stupidly injured my knee running in the Bois in Paris (it ended my running for the rest of the trip), they were all icing the knee and winding the Ace bandage around it. When I got laid low by stomach flu, they ransacked the drugstores for something powerful to kill it.

We left a trail of victories and surprises across the Continent.

Jacques had the first stretch of consistent running since he'd left Oregon. He ran mostly the 800 meter, his best event, and he was beaten only once, by Willi Kruse in Stuttgart. All my work on Vince's knees was finally showing—he was having one of his rare stretches of injury-free competition, and he was unbeaten in the 1,500.

Billy didn't win a single race, but his explosive appearance on the international scene was causing a lot of talk. He was usually second, or third.

The feeling of a couple of European track experts was that, if I brought the three of them to Montréal like that or better, we would collect enough gold to balance the U.S. foreign debt.

I wasn't so sure, though. Jacques' euphoria would wilt once he was back in the U.S. having "fag" yelled at him. Vince was clearly one of the top 1,500-meter men in the world at that moment, but I didn't know if I could keep his legs in one piece for another year. Billy was still, as he had always been, a question mark.

But we decided to leave these matters to the analysts, and live for the moment.

In Amsterdam there was a rock concert, and the boys begged to go. I agreed, providing they would depart at a decent hour. We went and I sat getting my eardrums bent while the three of them whooped and shrieked with the other 20,000 young souls crowded into the park. When I said, "Let's go," they left, looking back lingeringly.

In London, Billy reached the other wayside marker on his road to Montréal. He ran third in the 5,000 meter and broke 13:35 for the first time, turning in a 13:26 with an impressive effort. The 5,000 was definitely his second-best race.

When the month ended, none of us wanted to go home. I told myself I was unpatriotic.

"Happiness," said Vince, "is bumming around over here, running like a dream."

Sadly we sold our car for $200 in front of the London American Express and took our plane back to New York.

When we arrived, we found that the boys' fine European showing had gotten the press coverage one would expect. Track people maybe didn't approve of them, but they couldn't ignore them either. Special note was taken of Billy's lightning appearance as an international threat in the 5,000-10,000 double.

In fact, the discussions about the boys' being gay—rumors, arguments, were they, weren't they, how could they be if they were so masculine, etc.—were going on so openly at trackside that we realized public disclosure was near.

Possibly we were all wanting to get it over with, and tired of pretending.

At any rate, when we were back in New York, we started to get a little careless, and went about more openly in gay society.

The gay community wanted to lionize the three of them. Jacques refused to go to the parties, mostly because big parties made him nervous. But Vince and Billy went with John and me. We went to a big party at Steve Goodnight's and a few other parties. Billy and Vince didn't stay up too late, and they didn't drink anything, and they managed to handle all the intense interest in their persons graciously. They had become the reigning sex gods.

The gays threw themselves on their necks. People who had never looked at the sports page were subscribing to *Track & Field News* and *Runner's World*. Delphine de Sevigny and a number of others announced their intention of going to every eastern meet where the boys would be running. In his old age, Delphine had become a track nut.

A number of men made some heavy passes at Billy. It enraged me. Several were far younger and (I thought) far more attractive than I was. Had Billy shown a flicker of interest in any of them, I think I might have been capable of killing him. But he looked at them pleasantly through his glasses and said, "You'll have to ask my coach."

To even things up, a number of men made heavy passes at me. Billy didn't like it any better. His eyes were on me, clear, trustful—but also level and watchful. I never knew if, despite all Buddhist nonviolence, he thought of killing me.

We didn't exactly send out press releases about those parties we went to. But one of them got into the news. In a way, it helped precipitate all the trouble that came that fall.

Steve Goodnight was suddenly a celebrity. His book *The Rape of the Angel Gabriel* had emerged as the great break-through gay novel. All the straights were reading it, and some were saying, How shocking, and others were saying, How moving. So his big party got written up on the "People" page in *Time*. My name, Billy's, Vince's and John's were listed among the people present. There was a photograph of Billy and me, he in his velvet suit and ruffles, both of us holding glasses of what looked like gin on the rocks (it was mineral water) and looking social and happy.

The track conservatives all over the country read this, and they shuddered. Billy's and my publicly associating with a man famous for his novels about gay sex was just too much for them.

Meanwhile, the four of us sadly went back to Prescott to start the school year. Billy and I returned to our life of seeing each other only a few hours a day.

TEN

That fall, several class high-school runners came to Prescott for the express purpose of being coached by me. Not one of them was gay. They had been reading about me in the papers, and thought also that Prescott sounded like a school worth attending. Also on the strength of the European publicity, five top college runners had transferred to Prescott. Of these, three were straight and two were gay. The gays came for shelter.

It all meant that, for the first time, my track team was going to have some real depth. And when the cross-country season started, we went to that NCAA regional championship in Van Cortlandt, and we wiped out Penn and Manhattan and a few other fine teams, and came in second in the team ranking.

If Billy and I had been living together, my happiness would have known no bounds. For the first time I was really enjoying everything I did, and feeling that what I did meant something. The humanization of Coach Brown was finally complete. If I barked now, it was a joke. The kids laughed—and they obeyed me instantly. I became something that I'd never wanted to be or planned to be—a popular teacher.

But Billy was a more popular teacher than I was. I can still see him bicycling across the campus, with his briefcase full of the brand-new gay studies program. I can still see the warm autumn sun shining on his windblown curls (now that he was a prof, they were as uncombed as they'd been while he was a student). As he pedaled past the track, he'd always wave at me if I was out there yelling "Get those knees up" at the girls' team.

With Vince and Billy working on it, the gay studies program grew into a counseling service that was the first of its kind on an American campus. Back in 1971 and 1972, a few tiny programs like this had sprung up at big universities, as well as administration-condoned "gay lounges" where the gay kids could meet, talk and be themselves. But our program at Prescott was something unique, and it grew out of athletics.

The two new gay runners were very gifted and very messed up mentally. One of them was UCLA two-miler Tom Harrigan, and the other I can't name because he never came out. We had a really difficult time with those two boys.

I was always mortally afraid of the track team split ting up into the "gay squad" and the "straight squad," with no communication or cooperation between the two. This would happen, I knew, if we started paying too much attention to the gay thing in front of the straight boys. They would start feeling crowded psychologically, feeling put on. They would start grumbling that the gays were taking over, and that all this had nothing to do with running.

So we solved this problem by establishing a rule that sex preferences were not to be mentioned at track practice, in the dressing room or anywhere else where the team was as a group. Only in my house on Mondays and Thursdays did we mention these things. And we mentioned them only in a bigger context that could be called "The Athlete and Society."

As the boys sat in front of my fire munching carrot sticks, we had open forum on feelings and hang-ups—any that were related to running and society. We spent a lot of time discussing the whole masculine mystique of the athlete. So timewise, we probably talked about gay problems only thirty percent of the time. The straight boys slowly learned to understand and respect the gay view of the world, and to understand the gay anguish. My heart used to hurt for Tom as he sat there struggling to come out with his feelings, fearful that he would be judged and punished. But when he finally did, he learned that the straights weren't always as smug as they seemed.

Vince and Billy were always at these open forums, sitting in, and Jacques came whenever he could. Vince was the great talker, and good at helping me direct the discussion. Jacques was a genius of the mind-provoking gag. Billy was less of a manipulator, but it was always to him that the boys turned when they had something to confide that they hesitated to tell me because I was older.

We finally decided that, one night a week, we would throw this forum open to the girls' team, and to anyone else on campus who wanted to attend. Quite a number of people did. It got so you couldn't shoehorn another person into my house on Thursday nights, and I thanked God that the head gardener had opted for a big living room. I needed a whole crew for KP afterwards.

One of the most startling newcomers to the forum was a little half-miler from the girls' team, Betsy Heden. She was about five foot two, with short, wavy hair and big astonished long-lashed eyes à la Bette Midler, and she was the only militant lesbian on campus. She started coming, I think, to stir up conflicts, and she and Vince would sit there and smart-ass each other till the rest of us had to quiet them down.

But Billy took her on. There were evenings when the whole crowded living room would be silent and rapt as the two of them went at it. Betsy was the demagogue, waving her fist, jabbing her finger. Billy countered her with Buddhist nonviolence, putting out his simple observations in his quiet way, unruffled, sunny, always compassionate to her point of view. They fought their way through the whole verbal battle of male-female hostilities.

One night he finally forced her to admit, "It's true. I don't want you. But I feel that you reject me."

Everybody laughed. The whole room just broke up.

She and Billy ended by becoming close friends.

Vince would kid me, "Harlan, aren't you *worried* about this?" He would see Betsy hitching a ride across campus on Billy's bike, or Billy dropping by girls' track practice to give her a few pointers on half-miling that he'd picked up from Jacques. They could even be seen dancing together in the canteen. "Harlan, aren't you *jealous?*"

I used to laugh at Vince. Those two kids would no more investigate each other's bodies than they would put their hands in a fire.

But I found myself jealous of Tom Harrigan. The minute he landed on campus, he made a heavy cruise in Billy's direction, just to see if it would succeed. Billy rejected him, but Tom seemed to stay interested.

The gay program and open forum ended up growing into a counseling service available to students from any other campus. Joe Prescott brought in a top young psychotherapist, David Silver, whose aim was to help gay students adjust rather than attempt forcible "cures." We advertised in campus publications across the country.

In particular, athletes were welcome to our service. Here we were open not only to students, but to men and women in amateur open and pro competition. The strictest confidentiality was maintained. And gay athletes did come to us, nearly all of them in the dark of the night. If I could name names, I would include a list here that would not be very long, but would astound for the range of ages and sports that it covered.

We also had a gay switchboard. It was open from six p.m. to midnight and two of the boys were always on phone duty.

I can still hear Billy picking up the phone in his dorm room and saying "Gay Prescott." At first he was a little nervous, dealing anonymously in this way with strangers' problems. But with some pointers from Silver, he finally relaxed, and was able to pour his compassion into the telephone.

On October 7, I went into New York for the Monday trackwriters' lunch at Mamma Leone's. I hadn't been to one of these lunches since before leaving Penn State. Even after coming to Prescott, even after starting to coach my three star runners, I had stayed away, because I didn't feel confident enough. But this fall, I felt mentally ready for it. I had a whole bunch of good runners to do PR for, and I wanted to announce that Prescott would be holding its own first college cross-country meet on campus in late October. What could be more simple?

Mamma Leone's looks a little like the Baths of Caracalla, with gloomy arches and Roman busts everywhere, offset by the many tables with red-checked tablecloths.

About fifty people were there, mostly coaches and reporters, and they were putting away lasagna and spaghetti with clam sauce and many martinis and beers. They were all listening to coach after coach get up to the microphone and give news about his team or his upcoming meet and try to make it sound so compelling that the newspapers would write it up. The air was so full of cigarette smoke that my eyes watered, and the reporters were scribbling notes and asking questions. Only a single woman was present, a reporter. It was a very male, very conservative, very businesslike atmosphere.

I was sitting at a side table with Bruce Cayton, who had left the *Post* and was now freelancing, and with Aldo Franconi. Aldo was an old friend, one of the few who stayed on speaking terms with me during the dark days after Penn. He was coach of a Long Island team, head of the Metropolitan AAU track and field committee, and one of twenty-five members of the executive committee of the U.S. Olympic Committee. Aldo was one of those gruff, paunchy guys who is the salt of the earth of track, and devotes his entire life to it.

Both of these old friends of mine were curiously subdued. I did my best to make conversation. As we were waiting for my time at the mike, I said, "I notice a *few* more people are speaking to me these days. Just a few."

Aldo looked at me strangely for a moment. "They're jealous," he finally said. "None of them have gold-medal prospects like Matti or Sive on their teams."

I tried hard with Bruce. "Bruce," I said, "you didn't have much effect at the *Post*. They don't run any more track news than they used to."

"The *Post* is interested only in four-legged runners," said Bruce, swallowing a martini whole.

When I went up to the mike, I suddenly felt nervous. I was going into battle and they were going to shoot real bullets at me. I was a Marine making my first landing. The fifty faces, in the blue air, amid the glowering arches and the Roman busts, seemed hostile. I told myself I was imagining things.

I managed to give them my little spiel. I told them about my influx of class runners. I told them that Prescott would be a team to watch that year, that we were very strong on paper and that we planned to go to all the NCAA meets and burn everybody. I told them about our upcoming cross-country meet and urged the reporters to turn out in full force to cover it.

A last-minute rush of nervousness overcame me, and I didn't say anything specific about my three gay superstars and how their training was coming along.

The restaurant was silent.

"Any questions?" I asked.

Another silence. Finally one coach said, "You say you're going to have a girls' event at this meet?"

"That's right. A two-miler. We've got a strong girls' team now, and we're willing to put them up against anybody."

"You going in for women's lib?" somebody else cracked in a gravelly voice.

Everybody howled with laughter. There was, or so I thought, an undertone of malice in this laughter. I told myself that I was becoming a paranoid, and that this wouldn't do.

When the laughter died, I smiled my best, small, Parris Island smile and said, "I'm for equal rights for everybody. Any other questions?"

A silence that got longer and longer. Smoke curled up from cigarettes held in strong, thick fingers.

Finally, from the back of the room, the reporter from the *Daily News* said, "What about Billy Sive?"

The silence again. Heads turned toward the reporter, then back to me. Somehow, the way the question was phrased, it could mean anything. I knew he'd done it deliberately. Under ordinary circumstances, a good reporter doesn't ask such a goddamn vague question.

"What do you want to know?" I said.

"Well, what about his progress?"

"Billy's coming along fine." It took all my self-control to keep my voice steady. "He's on the same type of program that he's been on since he came to Prescott. I thought this high-mileage stuff was crazy for him, and I've got him doing 100-110 miles a week, with emphasis on quality and strength-building. This program was what gave him all his success in Europe. If he continues to develop the way he has, we're hopeful that he'll make the Olympic team."

Another voice chimed in. "What about Vince Matti and Jacques LaFont?" Was this a conspiracy?

"Both of them have had setbacks," I said. "Vince, as you know, is very injury-prone. He injured his knee again about a week ago. Jacques is having some hamstring problems. If I can keep Vince in one piece till the Olympics, then we're going to have a very strong contender in the 1,500. The same goes for Jacques in the 800 meter."

When I sat down again, I actually felt a little weak in the legs.

Men were leaving already. Empty tables were littered with cigarette ashes, mimeographed literature, dishes with tomato sauce on them, glasses with melting ice cubes in them, half-full coffee cups. Bruce and Aldo looked very gloomy.

I sipped at the last of my 7-Up, which had gone warm and flat while I was up at the mike. "They were kinda hostile," I said.

Bruce and Aldo looked at each other. Finally Aldo said, "Look, Harlan, are you a total innocent or what?"

"Huh?" I said.

"Listen," said Aldo, "I know you're a brave guy, and it took guts to get up there and face them. But you oughta know there's only so far you can go."

I was getting a little irritated. "I don't know what the hell you're talking about. Sooner or later I have to be able to lead a normal life. If I can't get up there and talk about my team, I might as well chuck it all and go live on a desert island."

"You must be completely naive," said Aldo. "Do you want me to fill you in? Can I be totally frank?"

"Sure," I said.

"If you go to that desert island," said Aldo, looking me straight in the eyes, "you'll be taking Billy Sive with you. Won't you?"

He put it just like that, brutally. Bruce heaved a heavy, gloomy sigh.

For a moment I thought I was going to lose my temper and break one of those marble busts in half over Aldo's bald head.

"What if I did?" I said. "I don't think it's anybody's business."

"You're wrong," said Aldo. "It's everybody's business, whether you like it or not. They're *making* it their business, is why. I can't think of anything in track right now that would get people more stirred up. The very idea touches a big, fat, throbbing nerve."

"All right, it's their business. So what? What does it have to do with running?"

"It has everything to do with that," said Aldo

vehemently. "Harlan, you and Billy are damn fools. I'm sorry to put it that way, but it's the truth. I admire you both, so you've got to know the truth. You've destroyed Billy's chances of going to Montréal." He made an Italian-type cutting gesture with his hands. *Finito*."

"Who's going to stop him?" I said.

"At the last USOC executive meeting, that was all they talked about. The Billy Sive case, they call it. At the last Met AAU meeting, ditto. I heard certain people say it with my own ears. There's no way that boy is going to Montréal. There's no way Matti or LaFont are going either. These guys are going to do everything they can to stop them."

"They're so greedy for medals," I said. "They'd pimp their own grandmother for gold medals."

"Not where something like this is concerned. They're perfectly willing to cut off their noses to spite their faces."

We sat silent. Bruce was morosely playing with pieces of drying-up Italian bread on the tablecloth. Nearly everybody had left, and the waiters were taking down the mike. At the bar outside, a few lingered—we could hear them laughing uproariously.

"Harlan," said Aldo, "I don't like to ask you, but is it true, about you and Billy?"

"Of course it's true." I was so mad that I could say it, finally.

Bruce and Aldo both studied my face. "You must be out of your mind," said Aldo softly.

"I was, for a while there. I fought my feelings for him for four months. It wasn't doing either of us any good. I finally decided that society has no right to deny me a mate. They all have mates. You guys have mates. Animals have mates. Even the goddamn bacteria have mates. Why should I be alone?"

"Has either of you ever thought of seeing a psychiatrist?" asked Bruce.

"You guys don't read the papers. The psychiatrists are starting to come around. A lot of them don't think it's a mental illness any longer. They look at it as an alternative."

Aldo snorted. "Go tell that to Mr. Track Fan. He pays his five bucks to see the pure red-blooded American boy run the mile. He doesn't pay it to see no fairies."

"Have you had any reaction from Billy's parents?" asked Bruce. "They must be furious."

"The kid's father is gay," Aldo said. "They all know that too."

"Jesus," muttered Bruce. The idea of a gay father was totally new to him.

"And Billy's father approves, if you want to know," I said.

They were silent for a moment. Then Aldo said, "Then the thing at Penn State . . . you gotta pardon me for bringing it up . . . but you must have been guilty."

"No, I wasn't," I said.

"Well, they don't know that." Aldo waved his hand at the empty restaurant, conjuring up the men who'd just left. "Their imaginations are just running *wild*. They're wondering how many teams you've slept your way through."

"The only athlete I ever slept with is Billy. But I suppose they won't believe that either."

Was it possible that I was saying these things? Right over this restaurant table? Was it possible that strangers would dare to sermonize to me about my right to love someone?

"No, they certainly won't," said Aldo. "For instance . . ." He started getting all steamed up again. "What really set everybody off was the four of you traveling around Europe together. They just assume that you're carrying on with all three of them."

"Did it ever occur to them that maybe Billy and I don't merely go to bed together? That we love each other?" I was really getting mad now. "That neither of us wants anybody else? Do they know so little about human nature?"

"You're the one's a dummy about human nature," said Aldo. "They want to think the worst. And then when you got back, that thing in *Time* about that party you were at. To them that was the last straw. They all know about Steve Goodnight, and that he writes dirty books about boys. The fact that you and Billy had the *chutzpah* to appear in public in this guy's company, it was just too much."

"There were a whole lot of straight celebrities at that party, and a lot of society people."

"That's not the point, and you know it."

"Steve's book isn't dirty. It's a work of art."

"What do you know about art?" said Aldo. "You don't know the Mona Lisa from a Marlboro ad."

"I don't know about art. But I know about love. Steve is writing about love in that book."

Aldo shook his head uncomprehendingly. "Harlan, you're beyond me. You're really a changed man."

"I am," I said. "And I'll tell you something else. And you can take it back and tell them. They are not going to stop Billy and Vince and Jacques from going to Montréal. In particular, they are not going to stop Billy. I will fight them every step of the way. The kid's father is one of the best civil-rights lawyers in the country. That means that if we have to fight them right up to the Supreme Court or something, we'll do that."

We were now alone in the restaurant. The waiters were clearing up, rattling dishes, looking at us, wishing we'd leave.

Aldo was looking at me searchingly. "Harlan, you're a brave, beautiful, Irish fool. You'll be all over the newspapers. You'll be roasted alive."

"I mean it," I said. "Billy and I are fighting for our lives. Nobody is going to take him away from me. He's all I have, Aldo."

"Christ," said Aldo, looking away. The heat of my feeling was beginning to impress him.

"Look," I said, "are they all enemies on the USOC?"

"No," said Aldo. "Not all of them. *Most* of them are. There's a few, like me, like most of the seven athletes' representatives, who feel that an athlete's private life is not the business of the AAU and the USOC. And I do believe that, Harlan."

"All I can promise you," I said, "is that Billy and I are going to conduct ourselves with dignity. If anybody makes fools of themselves, it's going to be those senile old fanatics."

"Look," said Bruce, "I'm sitting here thinking. There's a story here on the whole question of . . . of this kind of thing in sports. If I can find just the right handle on the story, and if I can find somebody to publish it, I'd like to try a piece. Would Billy let me interview him?"

"Sure," I said. "He's a beautiful interview. His head is an open book."

"All right," said Bruce, "I'll get in touch with you when I've worked things out."

"If you do a story," said Aldo viciously, "find some kinda way to dispel all the *other* rumors too."

"What other rumors?" I said.

"You really want to know?" Aldo asked. He was furiously tearing up a piece of bread.

He started to tell me. When he'd finished, I'd had one more sociological revelation. Society had tried to teach me that the gay mind was an open sewer. Now I knew, beyond any doubt, that it was the straight mind that was the sewer.

B illy was silent as I repeated to him what Aldo had told me.

"That I have orgies with some of my freshmen that I've seduced," I said. "That you and I go down to New York and pick up chickens. That students disappear off the campus because I take them down to New York drugged and tied up and sell them to pimps."

It was that evening, and we were laying in my big, hideous, Victorian bed made out of Caucasian walnut. Rain rattled against the windows. It was cold already, and the furnace in the little old house wasn't working very well, so we had the quilt pulled up over us. Making love had not had its usual therapeutic effect.

"And of course that I have orgies with all three of you. But what's worse, that you and your father and I . . . and that you and your father always . . ."

Billy sighed and shook his head. "Wow. I could tell you were upset when you came back from the city."

"Chickens," I said bitterly. "I can't even stand kids that age. And all the grief I had all those years precisely because I was prissy about sleeping with runners, and they've got me balling my whole goddamn team."

"And that one about the pimps," said Billy. "That's a classic. That's straight out of the Saturday-night horror flick. And the crap about me and my father . . . poor Dad, when I think how careful he always was. There's just no pleasing some people, is there?"

He was propped on his elbow by me, and his warm body was stretched out easily against mine. He tried to comfort me, caressing my side. But I could tell he wasn't all that upset about what I'd told him, and this irritated me. I wasn't comforted by his stroking.

"Well, what're you going to do?" said Billy. "We knew that people would react this way, didn't we?"

"They really believe these things," I said.

"Just don't think about them," said Billy. "Rumors like that just dry up and disappear."

"And another one," I said, "that you're two-timing me all the time with Vince and Jacques. That really hurt."

"Why did it hurt?" said Billy. After a minute, he said, "You don't trust me."

"I don't worry a minute about Jacques. But you and Vince are very close. Vince sleeps around. How do I know he's not going to sleep with you?"

"Look," said Billy, annoyed, sitting up, "when will you learn that I never lie? I've told you before that there's never been anything between Vince and me."

"All right," I said. "I'm just a jealous old man."

"Well, don't be," he said. He sat with his knees drawn

up against his chest and stared at the foot of the bed. Then he added, "Part of your problem is, you still haven't totally accepted the fact that you're gay. You still want to have things their way."

"I'm aware of that," I said, a little sarcastically.

"You won't be happy until you put your head in order. We won't be happy."

"Aren't you happy with us?"

"Don't put words in my mouth," said Billy. "I just meant that your straight hang-ups are gonna get in our way if you don't work them out."

"Are you that tired of me already? Are you about ready to move on?"

Billy got out of bed. "Look," he said, "I know you had a rough time at Mamma Leone's, but this is too much. I'm going back to the dorm."

I lay there under the quilt, watching him pull his clothes on. His face was expressionless, and his movements were deft and precise. He tied the laces of his worn-out Tigers, and pulled on his light red rain parka with a swish of nylon.

"See you tomorrow," he said in a toneless voice and walked out. I heard the front door slam and lock.

I lay there for about fifteen minutes, feeling helpless and desolate. The rain ticked on the windows, and the wind soughed in the spruce boughs outside. The clock ticked loudly by the bed. Automatically I reached out and set it for 5:30 a.m. I was just about to turn out the bedside light when I heard his key in the door again.

He came into the room swiftly, lay down on the quilt by me without even taking off his parka and pressed his face blindly against my chest. The parka was wet, and his hair smelled of rain and autumn leaves.

"Harlan, they want us to fight," he said.

He started to cry with strange, creaking sobs, clenching the quilt. He kicked off his Tigers and got under the quilt, pressing his body against me, holding me frantically. His damp clothes made me shiver. I held him as hard as he held me.

"What is really the matter with you?" he said.

"We're sneaking around snatching twenty minutes here and there in the dark. Our lives are passing like that."

"My God, if that's all that's bothering you, I'll move in with you tonight."

"No, it isn't all. Nothing ties us together. There's nothing to guarantee that we'll stay together a year, five years. You have to understand my jealousy. It isn't as simple as sexual jealousy. I'm terrified of losing you."

"Guarantees are for new cars," Billy said with his face still buried in the hair on my chest.

"Look, I'm going to ask you again. I want us to marry."

He lay beside me, quiet now. After a minute, he said, "I'll do anything you ask but that. Does it occur to you that I'm pretty terrified of losing you? Maybe I worry about you cruising off after some other young studhorse, huh? You've been around a lot more than me, how do I know you aren't totally fickle, huh?"

I sighed and nodded slowly. Billy was, in his way, superstitious. He was afraid of tempting fate by tying himself to me formally. He had never seen such a marriage last. At the age of twelve, he had seen his father and Frances break up.

"And another thing," said Billy. "Are you really ready to come out with this? You're so upset about all these rumors. Are you really ready to face the uproar if we married?"

"No, I'm not ready," I said.

"Look, I'll move in here tonight."

"I don't want to live with you without that declaration. I don't want to feel like I'm just shacking up with someone."

"Well, I don't know what we're going to do, then," said Billy.

I stroked his head. "I know one thing. It's stupid of us to fight."

"Maybe we just need more time together," he said. "Maybe once in a while I should spend the night."

"Anything is better than fighting," I said.

"Like tonight, maybe," he said, smiling a little.

He got out from under the quilt, kicked his Tigers over under the chair, and started undressing.

"Just once more," I said. "You've got to get your sleep."

ELEVEN

W e all tried hard to ignore the rumors.

But a number of parents started trying to pressure Joe Prescott. Two forced their straight boys to drop off the team, although the boys and Joe tried to show them that they were seeing ghosts under the bed.

Then the NCAA started making noises at Joe that either I should be dropped as coach or the NCAA would drop the school from membership. The rest of the team were indignant on Billy's and my behalf, and they wrote a letter to the NCAA that they all signed. Joe took a very strong stand, saying that the NCAA had better come up with solid proof of the rumors and reminding them of the Supreme Court decision. The NCAA finally decided that they were on uneasy legal ground, and they shelved the matter. But they then took a few cheap shots, hurting me by hurting my innocent team—they withheld the travel expenses that they might have paid us to NCAA meets. Joe covered the expenses himself.

Our little cross-country meet at Prescott was fairly successful, though fewer teams came than I'd hoped for, and it got about one inch of newspaper space.

Then, just a week after our meet, Billy's and my cover got blown in spectacular and painful fashion.

It happened when we took Billy to New York to run in the national Road Runners Club 15-kilometer cross-

country championship. It was being held on the famous
course in Van Cortlandt Park, known affectionately to
eastern runners as the "Vannie." I'd planned the race as
a little change for Billy—he'd been doing all that hard
track running in Europe, the distance was a good one for
him, and not many other top runners made the effort to
get to an odd-distance race like that, so he could just relax
and enjoy himself.

Vince and Jacques didn't run that day, as neither of
them was avid for cross-country, but they went to watch,
as did Betsy Heden.

Three hundred fifty-five runners gathered on the great
lawn at the edge of the park, where the start was to be.
Everybody was milling around doing stretching exercises
and warming up. There were sweatsuits and headbands and
shoes of every color. Runners' families and runners' children
were underfoot. The officials were cheerfully disorganized.

It was perfect weather, rainy and cool. All in all, it
was one of those big, informal, long-distance races, and
the five of us relaxed and were having a good time.

Finally they all massed at the start, with Billy one of
those seeded in the long front line. At the gun, a
multicolored sea of people poured off across the grass.
Everybody was running balls-out to be as far up front as
possible when the field funneled into the trail that led
into the woods.

While the race was in progress, Vince, Jacques and I
stood around chatting pleasantly with Aldo and a couple
other officials and the meet director. As usual, we felt that
odd, questioning atmosphere around us. We were waiting
for the field to finish the first of the three loops they'd
have to make, up through the hills.

When the leaders appeared far off, pouring down out
of the hills onto the lawn again, Billy was with them,
running in his usual just-in-front spot. As he went past,
I shouted his split time at him. He was running easily,
spattered with mud, and from the look on his face, he was
enjoying himself.

What seemed like an unusual number of reporters were present, plus an NBC-TV camera crew. Ordinarily the metropolitan media don't get very excited over these odd-distance open cross-country races up in the Vannie, so I could only conclude that they were there because of Billy. They had all approached him before the race, but he wouldn't talk because he was psyching himself, so they were waiting till afterward.

When the leaders streamed in a second time, Billy was still in front. He had opened his lead to about twenty yards. He came hurtling along the cinder path across the lawn, with the spectators cheering him pleasantly from both sides. He was more spattered with mud than ever, his legs black with it. His hair was sopping wet. A swift, soft gnashing of spikes, and he was past us. He made the rest of us seem so stationary and earthbound.

Then the long long line of the field started to pass us—the runners were all strung out now. I watched Billy's figure disappearing off across the lawn, starting the third and last loop.

"He looks like a racehorse," a guy behind me said.

"Jeez," said another guy, "the horse would die of embarrassment."

Vince and Jacques and I exchanged a glance.

We waited a little longer. A fine drizzle was coming down now, and the spectators and officials were all huddled under umbrellas. The officials' timesheets were so damp they were having a hard time writing on them.

Finally, off across the lawn, you could see a lone white figure springing down out of the woods. The words of the *Song of Solomon* came to my mind: "Behold, he comes bounding over the hills—my beloved is like a young stag." Billy had really pulled away, increasing his lead to several hundred yards.

As he came flashing down the cinder path toward the tape, the crowd along it cheered and applauded. Photographers jumped out and squatted for photos as he bore down on them.

He breasted the tape with a little smile on his face. Everybody crowded around him to pat him on the back and shake his hand. He was covered with mud from head to foot, and still looked fresh. It was one of his easiest victories.

Billy still left the reporters hanging. He did his usual careful warmdown, striding and jogging in his warmups, and then he slipped away to the locker room at the nearby athletic field to get under the shower and scrape off the mud.

Everybody started drifting off to the awards ceremony. Originally they'd planned to hold it right there on the lawn. But because of the rain, the officials adjourned it to a nearby bar on Broadway.

So everybody packed into the bar. The runners were dry and clean and bundled into sweats or regular clothes, their hair wet, their faces glowing. Hot coffee and tea were being served by the race committee. There were a couple of cardboard boxes of ham and bologna sandwiches, and the runners were all fishing into them hungrily. Everybody was relaxed, laughing, talking about their injuries and illnesses and how out of shape they were, and the usual bunch of lies.

Finally Billy came in, in his usual floppy bellbottoms and his Prescott blazer, his hair clean and wet and somewhat combed. The reporters wouldn't even let him get close to the tea urn—they backed him into a corner and asked him their questions, and he was very affable and relaxed with them.

Finally the race director got up, the talking shushed, and the director made a pleasant little speech. The first three finishers came up, and he handed them the trophies, and everybody clapped. Billy was given a big, handsome, sterling silver bowl, while flash cameras went off, and the other two guys got smaller bowls. Billy came back to us lugging it, stopping to talk to a couple of people. The soft glowing expression on his face told me that he'd had a good time that afternoon, which was just what I'd wanted.

Jacques clapped him on the shoulder, and Vince inspected the bowl. "Silver . . . they must have known you'd win," Vince said. Silver is for Virgos. We all laughed.

The metropolitan media left, but there were still quite a number of people around us, when another reporter stepped up, followed by his photographer. "I'm Ken McGill of the *National Intelligencer*," he said pleasantly. "Could I ask you a few questions?"

"Sure," said Billy. He was squatting on the floor, trying to fit the trophy into his gear bag, but it was too big. A little warning buzzer at the back of my mind sounded. The *Intelligencer* was a tabloid, and not overly interested in sports.

"There's been a lot of rumors going around about you," said McGill.

"Oh yeah?" said Billy, still holding the bowl. He must have picked up my thought, because he suddenly looked watchful.

"You have a reputation for answering questions very frankly," said McGill.

Billy now knew what was coming, and so did I. Out of the corner of my eye, I saw that Jacques' and Vince's smiles had disappeared.

"Like . . . what do you want to know?" said Billy.

"The rumor mill says you're a queer," said McGill.

The group around us went dead silent. Elsewhere in the bar, the talking and laughing and milling around seemed suddenly loud by contrast. A number of runners were still bent around the officials, getting their official times off the long long list of damp sheets.

Billy straightened up slowly, his face suddenly cold and set and defiant. He had gone white around the nostrils.

He looked down at five-foot-seven McGill from his five-foot-eleven with his terrible clear eyes for several long moments. McGill met his gaze boldly, earnestly.

In all fairness to McGill, he was not obnoxious. He had been sent to get a story, and he was getting it.

"The right word is gay," said Billy.

"Let's compromise and call it homosexual," said McGill.

I felt a slow, sad sinking of my stomach. A fine tremor started to spread along my arms and legs.

Billy smiled a little. "I think you're funny," he said. "I really haven't made any secret about being gay. What's the big deal?"

McGill looked at Vince and Jacques. "I understand you two are homosexuals also. Is that true?"

"That's right," said Vince. Jacques nodded his head slowly, looking down.

The group around us were frozen, mouths open. More and more people were getting up and coming over. Then McGill's eyes came to rest on me.

"Harlan," he said, "the rumor mill says . . ."

In my anger and my pain at the way he'd questioned the boys, I cut him off short. The words came so easily that I hardly thought about them.

"Save your fucking breath," I said. "I'm as gay as they are."

Betsy thrust forward, her chin out. "You forgot me," she blazed at McGill. "I'm a gay woman."

Aldo pushed through the group, and was about to grab the reporter by the lapel. "It's none of your goddamn business," he said. Vince was also moving toward McGill in a very threatening manner.

I grabbed both Vince's and Aldo's arms. "Leave him alone," I said. "He's just trying to do his job." I looked at McGill. "Maybe you've got some more questions," I said in my best Parris Island voice.

"Yes, I do, as a matter of fact," said McGill. "The rumor mill says that you and Billy are having a sexual relationship. Is that true?"

A number of people gasped softly around us. By now nearly everybody in the bar was packed around us. Even the officials got up from their rain-soaked time list to take in the spectacle.

Billy seemed to get even whiter around the nostrils, and his eyes narrowed. As for me, I was doing a job on my face, hoping that it showed nothing of my feelings.

"Hey, uh, your thing about the rumor mill is kind of tiresome," said Billy.

"Is it true?" asked McGill.

"I don't like that phrase 'sexual relationship,'" I said. "Why don't you say that Billy and I are in love? You can quote me on that."

McGill was writing it all down. You could have heard a pin drop in that bar. "How long has this relationship been going on?"

Billy stood at bay, the animal against the wall, the silver bowl held forgotten in the crook of his arm. He smiled a little. "Since April. Right after the Drake Relays. April 27, if you want the date."

McGill was really warming up now. He looked at me.

"How do you feel about the fact that many people feel you, as the coach, are doing a very improper thing by having a sexual relationship with the boy?"

"What's so improper about it?" I said. "I can name you half a dozen straight coaches who are married or engaged to their female runners. I could also name you another half a dozen who are just sleeping with their female runners."

"Don't you think this is different?" said McGill.

"I'm sorry," I said, "it's my gay point of view. But I don't see it as different at all."

"The rumor mill says that you seduced him," said McGill. "Is that true?"

"I don't think you've been listening to the rumor mill very carefully," said Billy. "What it really said was that all three of us were gay when we were at Oregon. That was why Gus Lindquist kicked us off the team. And I had four other lovers before Harlan, so nobody was doing any seducing."

McGill was still looking at me. No, he really wasn't obnoxious. The whole group around us was beginning to stir with comments and rustlings. People were nudging, looking at each other saying this is incredible, etc.

"Would you care to comment on your dismissal from Penn State in view of all this?"

"Yes, I will comment on that. I was innocent at Penn State. The kid was gay, and he sensed I was gay. He wanted to sleep with me, and I didn't want to sleep with him. I'm a discriminating guy, McGill, I don't screw just anybody. The kid made the charges out of pique, that's all."

"Have you been in the habit of sleeping with athletes through the years?"

Was it really possible that they were doing this to me? Was it really possible, right at this race, after the good run and the softly falling rain and that sea of runners on the wide lawn?

"No," I said. "I made it a habit of separating my love life and my profession, so to speak."

"Could you tell me how many?"

Billy was white with fury, his lips twitching.

"Only Billy," I said. "But I'm sure you don't believe me."

Jacques had turned away and had his hands over his face, sobbing. Betsy tried to comfort him.

"What do you feel is the future of your relationship?" McGill said.

I was ready to kill somebody. "Are you asking me if I think such a relationship *has* a future?"

"Well . . ." said McGill.

"If I didn't think it did, do you think I'd be in it? Would I stand here and answer idiotic questions like yours for a matinee with somebody?" I could hardly breathe. "Of course it has a future. As far as we're both concerned, it's forever."

Still holding the silver bowl, Billy reached to me with his free hand and closed it comfortingly around my arm. Anguished, we looked at each other. The sadistic photographer flashed a picture of us at that moment.

"Have you got everything you want?" Billy asked McGill savagely.

"Yes, I think so. Thanks," McGill said, closing his note pad.

"In that case," said Billy, "if you don't mind, I'm going to have some tea."

I had been ready to run out of that damned bar the minute McGill was done. But suddenly it occurred to me that Billy was instinctively doing the right thing. If we all left in a big hurry, it would look like shame and fear.

Billy gave the bowl to Vince and started toward the tea urn, dignified, controlled. Silently the group shifted aside to let him pass. "You guys want anything?" he said over his shoulder at us.

In a state of mild shock, the group started to break up. "I'll help you," Betsy said to Billy and went to the tea urn with him. People were leaving, discussing what they'd heard in low voices. Shakily I sat down on a bar stool.

Vince had his hand on Jacques' shoulder. Jacques was white and silent. A number of people, runners and families, stayed, looking at us.

Billy and Betsy came slowly back, carrying four steaming cups of tea laced with honey and lemon. He slid onto a bar stool by me. Finally there were about twenty-five people left. I sensed they were sympathetic, and it made me feel a little better. If there were always these few around us, we would make it somehow.

Billy glanced at the others, sipping at his tea. "Well," he said, "you've just seen something that not many straights get to see. The gays call it coming out."

One runner said softly, "What you're doing takes a special kind of guts."

I managed to laugh a little. Billy's gay pride was buoying me. "Coming out on Christopher Street is one thing. Coming out at a cross-country meet is something else," I said.

"Somebody can have my sandwich," said Billy. For one awful moment I thought he might say that the only meat he ate was mine. But he didn't. He hauled a handful of walnuts out of his blazer pocket, gave me a couple and handed the rest around the little group of runners.

Moved, they responded to his firm attempt to put what had just happened in the context of normalcy. In a moment, everybody was dexterously cracking nuts between the palms of their hands, and talking about that subject so dear to runners' hearts: diet.

A couple of days later the *National Intelligencer* was on all the supermarket magazine racks across the country, along with *TV Guide* and *Reader's Digest.* Housewives checking out with their forty dollars' worth of groceries could see the big photograph of Billy and me frozen in that moment, looking at each other, the silver bowl in Billy's arm and that anguish in our eyes. The headline: STAR ATHLETE AND COACH ADMIT TO HOMOSEXUAL RELATIONSHIP.

The article paid due attention to Vince and Jacques, to the little gay ghetto at Prescott and even to Billy's father. But it dwelled on Billy and me, because of the shocking (to the straight) fact that I was older and Billy's teacher.

This blast of publicity had a number of very unpleasant repercussions for us.

First, Billy and I started getting letters from all over the country. About three-fourths of them were hate letters. Many were addressed to "Mr. and Mrs. Harlan Brown." I didn't let Billy read the hate letters, because I was afraid they'd upset him. But, perversely, I read them myself, and some were really frightening. They said we should be dead. For the first time it hit me that someone might try to harm either or both of us.

We also started getting threatening phone calls. They talked of bombs and kidnapping. The police investigated the calls with a curious lack of enthusiasm. We quickly had our numbers changed to unlisted ones. We gave the new numbers only to a handful of intimates, and had the college switchboard screen all our calls.

Reporters, track officials, *et al,* could reach Billy only
through me.

As Billy's coach, my duties extended to shielding him
from all this. He needed the peace and solitude to train in.
An athlete can take only so much mental pressure before
his performance suffers. Emotional stress causes the blood
lactate level to rise—the same lactate that produces fatigue
from physical stress. I had a lot of faith in Billy's toughness
and in his ability to tune things out, but I wasn't taking
any chances.

Second, to counter the bias of the *National Intelligencer*
article, Billy and I decided that an article closer to the
facts ought to get published. Bruce Cayton had been doing
his promised research on homosexuality in sports. He had
talked to a lot of people quietly, and gotten a lot of quotes,
most of them anonymous. So we offered him an exclusive
interview with photographs.

Delighted, he accepted. We sat down with him and
talked fairly frankly about our feelings and gay attitudes
and sports. We were pleased with the sensitive article he
wrote, in which this interview was the centerpiece for all
the background he'd gotten. He tried to air the subject
impartially. Was there enough homosexuality in sports to
worry about? Was it worth worrying about? He presented
both sides of the argument, but wound up implicitly
suggesting that too much fuss was being made, especially
in view of the Supreme Court decision.

But then he had a hard time selling the article.
Magazine after magazine turned it down, saying glibly,
"Timely, but not for us." Finally *Esquire* bought it. When
it appeared, it drew some of the heaviest reader mail that
Esquire had ever gotten.

Meanwhile, the AAU had been shocked out of its mind
by the *National Intelligencer* disclosure. More accurately,
certain AAU officials were shocked, including executive
director Melvin Steinbock.

Steinbock was not exactly one of the senile conservative
fanatics. He was an improvement over the previous

executive director and had changed or liberalized some AAU policies hated by athletes. But he was easily pressured by the fanatics, and his broadmindedness did not extend to homosexuality. "It's one thing to have this rumored around underground among track people," he said at a regional AAU meeting shortly afterward. "But it's something else to have it all over the front pages. It gives amateur athletics a terrible image."

Steinbock's knee-jerk reaction was to blacklist Billy, Vince and Jacques on a nationwide basis.

The blacklist is a time-honored AAU punishment. It's castration pure and simple. It's usually reserved for coaches and athletes who openly criticize AAU policies, and it cuts them out of competition. An outspoken coach, for instance, finds that his team is being kept out of meets.

In this case, Steinbock was very open about the blacklisting. Why not? It had always been done that way. He put out a memorandum saying that "action would be taken" against any meet promoters who invited any of the three boys to compete. "Action" meant that AAU funding to these meets would be cut off.

The effect within the track world was explosive.

Liberal AAU officials, long ashamed of the blacklist, protested. The angriest was Aldo Franconi, whose district the boys were in. Meet directors were unhappy because, whatever their moral views, they viewed Billy, Vince and Jacques as good box-office. The name of their game was selling tickets to track meets.

A number of track and field athletes were highly disturbed. Many of them certainly did not approve of homosexuality. On the other hand, the younger ones were inclined to be tolerant. Their attitude was, What is the fuss about? The sight of the AAU blacklisting three of them on such a naked broad-scale basis gave them all the horrors. But, with an Olympic year coming up, none of them dared to protest publicly. They were all afraid that they'd be blacklisted themselves. Several of them did write letters to Steinbock about it, and sent carbons to us.

The angriest letter was written by trackman Mike Stella, a leading activist. He scarcely knew Billy, Vince, or Jacques, so it surprised us a little to see him so vehement.

Stella wrote Steinbock: "Your action sets the athletes' rights movement back approximately five hundred years. In other words, into the Middle Ages."

But even Stella didn't protest in public.

The blacklist put the whole subject on the pages of the track and field publications for the first time. Up until now they had been delicately avoiding it, on the ground that it was irrelevant. (And they were right.) *Track & Field News* and *Runner's World* were suddenly carrying pages of editorials and letters from runners, coaches, fans, school principals, AAU officials—the whole spectrum.

None of them talked much about homosexuality *per se*. They disguised their upset by talking mostly about the political question of blacklisting. But the letters were all masterpieces of emotional writing. Some thought that the three boys and I should be awarded Purple Hearts. Others thought we should be lynched and burned.

For the moment, Jacques and Vince were not hurt by the blacklisting. They had planned not to compete hard again until the indoor season started in midwinter. But Billy had set his heart on running in the national AAU cross-country championship in Kansas City on November 15. Obviously his entry would not be accepted now.

But we were going to get a chance to strike back. The annual AAU national convention was going to be held in Lake Placid, New York, during the last week in October. So we decided to try to meet with Steinbock and the others—they would all be there. We planned some ball-crushing maneuvers to force them to lift the ban.

First, Billy, Vince and Jacques organized a zap (gay parlance for demonstration). This zap would be held on the opening day of the convention. Vince masterminded it, and did much of the work. The boys spent hours on the phone, stirring up gay activists and sympathetic student groups all over the metropolitan area. They even managed to stir up some local runners who had no Olympic ambitions.

Part of the zap would hit the Metropolitan AAU office on Park Place, since it would be hard to transport so many hundreds of demonstrators to Lake Placid, just a few miles from the Canadian border. But several busloads of angry gays would go up north and zap the convention hall in Lake Placid.

The reason the boys were able to stir up so many students was that the gay issue was becoming fashionable on many campuses. With black and women's civil rights already somewhat old hat, the gay thing was new and daring. Several rock musicians had helped out by professing bisexuality. And the front-page photograph on the *National Intelligencer* had made us the overnight sensations of this new cause.

John Sive, Aldo Franconi and I got our heads together on the legal angles.

On Sunday, October 21, the day before the convention began, the three of us drove up to Lake Placid. The magnificent drive through the Adirondacks, with the maple forests turning flame red and yellow, and the steep mountains reflected in the lakes, was oddly at variance with our grim mood.

The little winter-resort town of Lake Placid, its Olympic days decades gone, was already stirring with AAU arrivals. Cars unloaded in front of hotels, people registered for the convention, milled in and out of bars, or went out jogging on the trails around the lakes. We found everybody at a wine and cheese party at the Mont Blanc Hotel, and asked Steinbock if we could meet with him and several other officials immediately.

Steinbock was mild but firm. He had come out of the party room sipping his California burgundy, with a piece of cheese still in his hand. "I don't have anything to say to you," he said. "I'm not answerable to you."

"Well," I said, with equal mildness, "this is the boys' lawyer, and I think we'd better talk."

The word "lawyer" rattled Steinbock a little. He stood there, wearing a nylon parka and a baseball cap, looking at John, who was elegant and citified in a dark gray Bill Blass suit.

"All right," he said.

He rounded up national track and field chairman Mickey Reel, long-distance chairman Bob Flagstaad and two others who had supported his decision. Shortly we were sitting down in a stuffy smoky little meeting room in the hotel, that must have been vacated by another informal meeting a while ago. The overflowing ashtrays had not yet been emptied, and convention schedules and agendas lay around.

I introduced John to them.

"This is Billy Sive's father, John Sive," I said. "Possibly you've read about him in connection with the Supreme Court decision on sodomy. John was the architect, so to speak, of the case."

The officials shook hands with John gingerly. They sat sipping their wine.

"We want to talk to you about the blacklisting," I said. "Maybe we can work something out."

"As far as I'm concerned, the matter is closed," said Steinbock nicely, playing with his half-empty glass. "We simply can't have this kind of thing in amateur athletics, and it's my duty to discourage it. Frankly, I think you have a lot of nerve to come here."

"I'm not here as Billy's lover," I said. "I'm here as the coach of the three boys."

They all actually flushed. It amused me to see how just my talking like that put them on the defensive.

We fenced around for a while, trying to get them to see reason, to persuade them that they were meddling in an area that was none of their business. But they were more or less adamant. I could see that Flagstaad was disturbed (he wasn't a fanatic either), but he went along with Steinbock.

Finally I said pleasantly, "All right, let me put it this

way. If the ban isn't lifted immediately, then we're going to take immediate legal action."

"That's your privilege," said Steinbock. "It's a free country."

"Is it?" I said. "When you guys can crush the careers of international-class athletes who have broken no written AAU regulation, is that freedom?"

"Nobody has ever contested a blacklist legally," said Mickey Reel.

"We can fight you as long and as hard as we like," I said. "We have one of the best civil-rights lawyers in the country. We have unlimited money to fight you in court. Two wealthy gays have decided that the boys are a cause worth supporting, and they have agreed to underwrite all the legal and activist costs."

They sat drinking their wine, thinking. The AAU does not have the money to fight long expensive court cases. It barely has enough money to run its athletic programs.

"We'll also call for the Congressional committee on amateur sports to investigate the whole business," I said.

"Amateur sports are supposed to stay clean out of politics," Flagstaad said quickly. "That's the basis on which we belong to the Olympic movement."

"This isn't politics," said Aldo. "It's civil rights. If you don't think you're answerable to the civil-rights laws, then you go tell that to all the black athletes in the AAU, and all the women."

"Then," I said, "we've got that federal law behind us. Maybe you don't know about the law. John . . ."

John sat smoking a little cigar and telling them about the Supreme Court decision, and how it would apply here. "You've put your blacklisting order on paper," he said. "I have a copy of it. So there's going to be no doubt in a court's mind what is going on. They would see it as a black and white case."

They were all silent, listening, a little mesmerized by John's grim precise courtroom manner. Until just recently, AAU officials have had little to do with lawyers, because athletes did not seek legal redress—they just suffered.

"Now," John went on, "if the ban isn't lifted, the first thing we'll do is get a temporary court injunction against the blacklisting, pending a hearing. This means that you would have to let the boys run, and if you didn't, you'd be in contempt of court. Second, if we have to, we will file suit against the AAU and against all meet promoters who go along with your policy. And we will ask for big damages for the boys. Let's say, for instance, that we might ask for a million dollars each."

Again that silence, as they thought of the AAU's little bank account.

"Now obviously," said John, "you ought to check this out with your own lawyer. Have him tell you if he thinks you stand a chance in court. And bear in mind that if you lose the case, you pay all the court costs."

Flagstaad said, "Mel, the meet promoters. If just one of them gets hit with a suit, they're all going to ignore your memo."

"Then we cut off AAU money to them," said Steinbock.

"They'll find the money somewhere else," said Flagstaad. "Several of the meets are already getting funds from private industry and stuff."

"Then we won't sanction the meets," said Reel recklessly.

"What's the point of that?" said Aldo. "Do you want to hurt all the athletes?"

"There's one more thing," I said. "And that's publicity. You don't like publicity like the crap in the *National Intelligencer*. And frankly, neither do we. We're not afraid of publicity. But it's a nuisance. We're not looking for publicity at all. As far as we're concerned, it shouldn't be an issue. We're interested in peace and quiet, and business as usual, and seeing to it that the boys run."

"I agree with you there," said Steinbock. "The publicity is awful. But you were asking for it."

I shook my head. "This guy McGill comes up to us at the 15-kilo and he asks us questions about something that all the track people are talking about. Are we gonna stand there and deny it, and make fools out of ourselves? We didn't ask him to come there. There's a difference between publicity that you go looking for, and publicity you just fall into like a manhole."

"What we're trying to point out," said Aldo, "is that the more you fight the boys, the more publicity there is going to be. And there are people around who will make martyrs out of them. You guys are just going to come out as the heavies."

"*That's* true," said Steinbock painfully. "We always come out as the heavies. Nobody ever sees how overworked we are, or what good we do."

I could sense that the publicity thing was turning them in our direction.

"We can guarantee you," I said, "that if you think you're overworked now, you'll think you were on vacation if this blacklist thing stands. For instance, there's a big demonstration planned for tomorrow, in front of the AAU office in New York. The boys have been in touch with the media, and the media are very interested."

"Christ," said Steinbock.

"A bunch of people are coming up here to picket the convention," John added. "The three boys are coming up too. All the major newspapers and two of the TV networks are sending people."

The wine glasses were empty. We could see the unease growing on their faces. Pickets, demonstrations, lawsuits, all reminiscent to the AAU of the 1967 black demonstrations at Madison Square Garden against the racist policies of the New York Athletic Club.

"What kind of people are coming up to picket?" asked Reel.

"Gays," said John quietly. "Four busloads, I believe. People from the New York Mattachine Society, the Gay Activist Alliance, the Gay Youth . . ."

We watched them consider the thought of homosexuals picketing the AAU convention.

"Can it be called off?" said Reel.

"Sure," said John cheerfully.

"In other words," I said, "before we leave here, you show us a final draft of your counter-memo lifting the ban. You distribute the memo tomorrow at the convention. There won't be any demonstration. It'll be business as usual, and a minimum of publicity."

"Can you guarantee us about the publicity?" Steinbock asked.

"We don't control the press," I said. "We can't guarantee anything. But, like we said, we won't be going around looking for it."

"All right," said Mel. "I'll draft the memo right now, and we can look it over."

"In other words, if Billy sends in an entry for the national cross-country, it'll be accepted."

"Of course," said Steinbock. He pulled some sheets of paper out of his briefcase, and started writing industriously.

I had no joyful feelings as I sat there watching him write. We had won a respite. But I knew—and Steinbock knew—that now there was all the more reason to trip the boys up with some bona-fide regulation. This was why he had given in so suddenly, and so graciously. Why risk legal trouble when, if he waited, the boys might play into his hands in some other way?

In November, Billy won the national cross-country championship. And that same month, the hunters shot the first of my young birds down.

One evening Jacques and I sat alone in front of the fire in my living room, and he told me that he was quitting running for a while.

"I just can't take the abuse any more. I don't even enjoy running now, it's gotten to be an ordeal. It's politics, not sport."

I felt so sad, sitting there, looking at the firelight play on his bushy auburn hair and beard and his corduroy jacket. He was sitting stooped, his expressive Gallic eyes empty and staring into the fire.

"I have to get away from it for a while and think things through," he said. "My family have been very understanding, and after the spring semester I'm going home to stay with them for a while."

He was silent, clasping and unclasping his fingers. Then he looked slowly up at me.

"I feel very guilty at all the time and the effort and the money everyone has invested in me," he said. "Especially you. I feel that I've failed you."

I shook my head.

"But obviously I'm in no shape to think about the Olympics," he added softly.

"The Olympics aren't that important," I said. "I'd rather see you jogging two miles a day and happy."

His eyes drifted back to the fire, and his hand slid down to pat the setter, who was leaning blissfully against his leg. "And the whole thing has kinda come between me and Vince too. I'm totally confused, I don't know what I think about anything any more. I remember how simple it seemed when I first met him. That feeling is just gone. But obviously I still feel something for him, because when we have a fight, I feel like I'm going to die. I deliberately hurt him, and then when I see him bleed, all I can think of is doctoring him up. It's funny how vulnerable Vince is; he comes on as such a tough . . ."

"He's vulnerable only to people he cares for," I said.

"Maybe that's it," said Jacques.

"Well, you know I'm always here if you need me," I said. "For anything."

"Who knows," said Jacques, "I may be back for the next Olympics, with a whole new set of attitudes . . ." He smiled a little. "Actually I won't stop running completely. If I do, I'll probably gain twenty pounds. I'm just dropping competition. I'll go out for seven, eight miles a day. Maybe I can learn to enjoy it again."

I sat studying him, thinking how they had done it. They hadn't needed to hit him with the rule book. All they'd needed was psychological terrorism.

M eanwhile, winter was coming on, and Billy was really burning.

He was having another of his breakthroughs. His times were dropping spectacularly all across the two-to-six-mile range. We didn't think of him as a two-miler, but that winter he was unbeaten in that event in the U.S. He even broke 4 in the mile, running a second-place 3:57.48 at the Sunkist.

He wanted to run everywhere and run against everybody and beat everybody. I had a hard time holding him in, and chose his races carefully, wanting to keep him fresh and injury-free.

We got him over to Europe again, for a few of the great winter cross-country races. (This time the AAU gave us no trouble about travel permits.) He ran in England, Belgium, France and Spain. Of course the Europeans now knew about him. But while he was teased and taunted here and there, he was treated more tolerantly than at home.

The only country where he had trouble was Spain. We heard rumors that the Spanish government might not let him enter the country, because of their strict homosexual laws. But they changed their minds.

When Billy showed up at the big meet at Granolles, a huge crowd was there to taunt, or just gawk at, the famous young American *maricón*. Roberto Gil and the other Spanish runners were under terrible pressure not to stain the nation's honor by getting beaten. I really felt sorry for them.

It was also the kind of situation where Billy was at his most cold-blooded. The results were predictable.

The runners went off at such a hot pace I knew they'd

be stepping over dead bodies before the finish. Gil is a front-runner, and he stayed right up with Billy, and glared at him, and Billy simply ignored him. When Billy started his drive, he just dropped Gil flat, and everybody else. They came tearing down to the finish through the mud puddles looking more like sprinters, with Billy twenty-five yards in the lead. The course record was smashed to pieces. The crowd whistled Billy for winning, and whistled Gil for losing, and the police were holding them back.

During the American indoor season, between February and May 1976, Billy went on a winning binge. Now he outclassed Bob Dellinger and everyone else in his events, and no one could push him. He had the speed now, and the stamina, and a long driving finish that was as deadly as a kick. He was knocking off all the big kickers in the U.S. now.

It made his critics very uncomfortable to see him winning like that.

In Europe he could now knock off all but a few—for instance, Armas Sepponan. Every time they met that winter Armas still beat Billy—but narrowly. I was always amused to see how friendly the two of them were off the track, and how ready to kill each other they were on the track.

"You make me work harder now," Armas told Billy. "But I also get better. I think I am breaking 27:30 in Montréal."

"Twenty-seven thirty!" Billy told me later, despairingly.

"He's just trying to psych you," I told him.

The gays were keeping their promise to go to track meets. We saw them mostly in the big cities, where they felt safe enough to come out in numbers. Sometimes they exchanged insulting remarks with the old-guard track buffs.

In addition, a few runners—only a few, fortunately—were very public about their intense dislike of Billy and Vince, and took it out on them in races.

So the atmosphere often crackled with lightning tension at those indoor meets that winter.

Bob Dellinger, now twenty-five, had his eye on the same 5,000-10,000 berth to Montréal that Billy did, and he was probably the most outspoken enemy. It wasn't merely that he was, as he put it, "anti-weirdo." It was a whole question of lifestyles—Dellinger belonged to Young Americans for Freedom and Athletes in Action, and Billy's whole carefree attitude revolted him.

The promoters of the big indoor invitational meets, however much they might personally disapprove of Billy and Vince, saw them for what they were: good box-office. All that winter, the Matti-Sive-Dellinger thing packed the crowds in. Dellinger had once been able to beat Billy at any distance between two and six miles, but now he couldn't any longer. "Losing is bad enough," he said, "but losing to a queer . . ." It was a double loss of masculinity, a public castration. But he could still beat Vince in the two-mile, so he kept slamming away at the two of them.

The most explosive encounter the three had was in the gilt-edge Millrose Games at Madison Square Garden in February 1976.

That night, hundreds of gays showed up at the Garden. The gay organizations had put out the word that this was a night to show support. Here and there, as I looked through the smoky air at that huge crowd, I could see the male creatures of the night—TV's in silk turbans and feathers. There were big groups of leather-jacketed gays. There were signs reading OUR BILLY, GO VINCE, LOVE FROM THE GANG IN NEW JERSEY, BEAUTIFUL THINGS, etc.

In the seats behind me, I could hear a couple of crusty old right-wing track nuts muttering that they were sickened by all this. In other areas of the crowd, I saw other enthusiastic supporters of ours. One group had a sign reading BE KIND TO "THE ANIMAL." They were young radical and liberal heterosexuals, mostly students, who were taking up the gay cause the way they had black civil rights. The publicity that Billy had gotten, and his appealing ways, were rapidly making him something of a gay guru with these young people.

When we arrived at the Garden that night, we had to fight our way through a crowd of them. It was good to feel loved for once. We were crushed, hugged, kissed, jostled, wished well and touched. Billy was fighting off a dozen screaming girls and scrawling autographs and laughing. Some of them were wearing T-shirts that said GO BILLY.

"Can you believe it?" he said when we got in. "We have a few more friends."

When the athletes started coming out onto the track and warming up, they were no less colorful than the gays. Lately track and field athletes had been blossoming out in mod attire for the indoor meets. Vaulter Marion Wheeler was there in his patchwork warmup pants. Shotputter Al Diefenbaker was wearing his flowered T-shirt. Black sprinter Ted Fields had on a bizarre embroidered vest.

Bob Dellinger was out there warming up too, wearing his regular UCLA warmups.

But when Billy and Vince shucked their warmups, the crowd gasped a little, and a wave of whoops and wolf-whistles went up from the gays. The two of them were wearing tracksuits that glittered in the bright lights. Billy's was a little more subdued, a gold jersey. But Vince's was a blatant silver and it set off his wild black hair and beard and his hirsute body admirably.

Billy and Vince had done it as a joke. "All those other runners are gonna be in indoor drag," said Vince. "We have to show them that there's no doing things halfway."

But from Dellinger's look of disgust I knew Billy and Vince were in for a rough night.

When the two-mile started, there was pushing and shoving such as I'd seldom seen. It looked more like the women's roller derby than a men's track event.

Billy went out at a suicide pace. Dellinger and three others went with him, sitting on his back. Vince lay back, waiting to kick. Lap after lap, everybody elbowing and spiking. The crowd was screaming for blood. The gays yelling, "Burn 'em, Billy!" The old guard howling, "Smoke 'em, Bob!" The liberal students shrieking as if they were at a rock concert.

Billy and Vince were beautiful to look at in their now sweaty silver and gold. I could feel every eye in the place mesmerized by them.

With a lap and a half to go, Vince moved up for the kill, hurtling along, his white teeth showing through his beard with delight. Billy and Dellinger were running shoulder even. Dellinger shoved Billy. Billy ignored him, so Dellinger leaned on him again. This time Billy scored a solid hit on Dellinger. The man behind Billy, running boxed in, reached forward and shoved Billy right in the middle of the back, but Billy kept his balance and shot forward, starting his drive.

Vince came up beside Dellinger, and Dellinger elbowed him in the ribs. Vince bared his teeth and hit him right back. The crowd was on its feet, howling. Dellinger was leaning on Vince again. Billy's drive was burning Vince off, and he pulled ahead, leaving Vince to deal with Bob.

The next thing everybody knew, Vince had thrown a miler's flying body-check on Dellinger. The two of them staggered and stumbled aside. I jumped up, panicked, with visions of falls and injuries in Vince's invalid legs. Then, as the rest of the field raced on by, the two runners had recovered, and they were punching each other.

The crowd roared as if it was a heavyweight championship, taking sides.

The officials raced out and shoved the two of them off the track before the field came around again. In the infield, the two runners started slugging each other again. By then I was there myself, trying to pry Vince off Dellinger. Vince had a bloody nose and red spots were dripped down the front of his sweat-soaked silver. Dellinger had a swelling eye.

"You whore," snarled Dellinger.

"You straight pig," said Vince, "you keep your fucking fascist elbows to yourself next time."

Billy, aware of what was happening, poured on his strong new finish and hit the tape for a new American indoor record in the two-mile.

Then, hardly missing a stride across the infield, he headed for Dellinger himself. I blocked his way. Billy was convulsed with a cold fury—he kept trying to climb past me. We were a group of squabbling officials, coaches and runners as about two dozen of us tried to quiet them down. The whole meet came to a stop for about ten minutes.

"Dellinger hit them both first," I said.

"They're nothing but trouble," said one of the officials.

"It's other people make the trouble," I said.

"You stay outta my way next time," Billy said to Dellinger. "If I have to stop and break your neck right in the middle of the Olympic trials, I'll do that." Buddhist nonviolence was out the window.

Finally the runners walked off the track, and the meet went on.

Vince threw his arm protectively across Billy's shoulders. Several students and gays jumped down and surrounded them. Up in the crowd, Delphine de Sevigny stood up and heaved a bouquet of long-stemmed American beauties down at Billy. They had probably cost her a week's groceries. Billy caught them neatly and threw her a kiss. John Sive was sitting by Delphine, grinning with pride.

The old guard sat glumly, wishing for the good old days. I knew just how they felt. I had known the good old days myself.

We didn't know it then, but the Millrose was the glittering peak of Vince's career. From then on, it was downhill into the dark.

That weekend he had won the Wanamaker Mile for the third time. His rivals had pushed him to a 3:51.59 mile, which now put him second on the all-time list. But his fist-fight with Dellinger stirred up a storm of criticism. People conceded that Dellinger had started it, and that was all. *New York Times* sports columnist Andy Meagan suggested that Vince take up ice hockey and play for Philadelphia, a team noted for brawling.

The anti-gay element in track hated Vince more than Billy, because of his impudence and his studhorse parading. After the Millrose, everybody must have decided that Vince had to go.

At any rate, about two weeks later, Vince was barred from all further amateur competition by the AAU, who had just conveniently discovered that he had taken several under-the-table payments from promoters in the season before he came to me. They had the canceled checks.

Vince was furious, then crushed.

"Everybody was taking them," he said. "I know who, and how much. If I go, they all go with me." And he was planning on talking to the press. I shared to the full his heartbreak at this injustice. But I finally managed to talk him out of naming other names, pointing out that it didn't make things any better to have a hundred athletes suffer instead of one.

Vince's tragedy stirred up once again the controversy about the sham basis on which amateur sports are conducted in the U.S. But all the soul-searching didn't help Vince. His Olympic hopes were dead. He cried bitterly, and there was nothing Billy or I could do to comfort him.

A week later he had picked himself up and signed a pro contract with the International Track Association, for $70,000, and would be going on his first tour when school was over. But the sorrow stayed, turning into bitterness.

Now they had shot two of my three young birds out of the sky.

I worried about Billy more than ever. It had gotten so I was a chronic worrier. At the very least I was going to come out of this with a nervous breakdown, I joked to myself. At the most, I was going to have a gold-medal runner and a breakdown.

TWELVE

E arly in April, Billy took a good two-week rest. It would be the last rest he'd get till after the Olympics—if he made the team. I cut him down to a couple miles' gentle running every day, and encouraged him to eat a lot and gain a few pounds.

This rest would be the cornerstone of his Olympic buildup. By the Trials in mid-July, he would be sharp enough to make the team. The six weeks following the Trials would have him peaking by the Games. Billy could stay at a peak for about four weeks, racing flat out every three or four days, so I was hoping that, after Montréal, we could fly to Europe for some post-Olympic meets.

By now, I had more or less taught Billy how to rest. He muttered a little, but did his daily two miles obediently.

We both quailed at the thought of the summer ahead. If he made the team, officially he would not be my runner any more, till after the Games. He would be taken away to the Olympic training camp. From mid-July till after the Games, we would be seeing little of each other.

We were still in our impasse about how to live. I saw our lives being frittered away, day by day.

One weekend during that April rest, we managed to have one of our few times alone together. My memories of that weekend are powerful and poignant, and not totally happy.

Steve Goodnight had a house out on Fire Island. Not

in one of the famous little gay communities, as one would expect, like Cherry Grove. He had settled in Ocean Ridge, a little town farther east along the shore. "I couldn't ever get any writing done in the Grove," he had told me. "People drop in. Sexual distractions. The hell with it."

That weekend he invited Billy and me, Jacques and Vince, and John and Delphine out to the house. He and a strange new friend of his met us on the dock in Patchogue on Friday evening, and we took the last ferry across to the island. This early in the season we were the only people on it.

We sat on the upper deck, letting the cool wind blow our hair, watching the sun set over the Great South Bay.

"I haven't been out here since my hustling days," I said.

"You're not missing much," said Steve. "It's getting to be like Coney Island."

Billy was smiling at me. "I'll bet you've been to some parties out here."

I grinned. "I've seen some things, all right." I put my arm across Billy's shoulders, since our group was alone on the deck.

It was always good to see Steve. He hadn't changed much, though he was forty-three now. His straight brown hair was thinning rapidly, and his good English face looked a little worn. He was working on a new novel and also on some gay pornography because, he said, he needed money.

The ferry docked. We loaded the suitcases and the boxes of groceries and the cat-carrier containing Steve's cat onto a couple of the rusted red kiddy-wagons that are Fire Island's only private transportation, and started off along the boardwalk.

We felt uncommonly conspicuous. Since it was early in the year, most houses were still closed up. Only a few windows showed the warm gaslights. We had a few strained laughs about being a little advance unit in this straight town.

Steve's house was a rambling shingled affair with a look-out tower and a lot of windows and a sundeck all around it. It sat right up on the dunes overlooking the ocean, with the beach grass blowing all around it. I figured the house must have cost Steve $70,000.

It was a warm clear spring night. Steve let the cat out. We turned on the gaslights, unpacked the groceries, cooked a fast dinner and went straight to bed. Each couple had their own bedroom.

Ours was airy, with a double pine bed and grass rugs and big windows. Billy and I undressed by candlelight, and the soft flame made a flickering tender light over our bodies. We slipped into the clean sheets and made love. The window was open to the sea, and we lay listening to the surf.

"We're insane," I said softly, "not to live like this all the time."

"Yeah, two days is really going to spoil us."

The next day we all got up late. Billy and I ran our two miles. Jacques ran his slow seven. Vince ran a hard ten. After breakfast we lay around on the sundeck tentatively taking the spring sunshine on our pale skins. Billy spread a blanket on the deck and did his yoga and breathing exercises, tying his supple body into contortions. We played some volleyball over a weathered drooping net down on the beach. Steve's huge black tomcat stalked through the dune grass, and we had a few jokes about whether he was a straight cat or a gay cat.

But the atmosphere among the others was strangely subdued and unhappy. Billy and I found it affecting our contentment.

To begin with, we were all disturbed by Steve's new friend.

He was a sixteen-year-old boy, mute, withdrawn, zombie-like. He had a tangled mane of pale, flaxen curls that hung clear to his shoulderblades. His thin waxen face had an unearthly beauty. His sapphire-blue eyes were expressionless. He followed Steve around like a dog.

As we sat on the sundeck, Steve told us his story. "Here I wrote that book about the Angel Gabriel, and then I met him. I don't even know his name. All I know is, he was a runaway, and he was a chicken ever since he was twelve. The pimp specialized in the S/M trade. Whenever he didn't have the kid out on tricks, he kept him tied up in his apartment. I heard about him from a friend. He was at this party, and they had the kid there, and they were gang-raping him and whipping him and burning him with cigarettes. I couldn't get this out of my mind. So I contacted the pimp and pretended to arrange for a trick. When I got the kid in my house, I wouldn't give him back. I told the pimp if he didn't get off my neck, I'd turn him in. The pimp had Mafia connections, and next thing I know, they're threatening to shotgun me. So I had to buy the boy from him. They said he was getting too old anyway. I paid them $10,000, which was almost the entire advance from the new novel."

Steve told this story right in front of the boy. He was sitting there on the blanket beside Steve in his swimming trunks, sniffling and staring vacantly, the wind playing with his hair. It was obvious that he was in another world.

We looked at him, horrified. He might have had a good body, but it was very emaciated. He was covered with whip and burn scars.

Steve had a hairbrush, and he was brushing the boy's hair gently. He teased out the tangles until the whole beautiful mass spread silkily across his thin back. But if he caressed the hair too much, the boy would absent-mindedly pull his head away.

"He won't let me make love to him," said Steve mournfully. "He just gets hysterical. And he's a junkie on top of it. I tried to get him onto methadone, but no way. When he's down, he remembers everything, and he just cries and gets hysterical. I finally realized that smack is the humane thing for him. So I get it for him. I just have to be careful that he doesn't OD."

Billy's eyes were fixed on the boy, and he shook his

head slowly. His eyes glassed over with tears, and he looked down. Experienced as he was, Billy had had little taste of the brutal side of gay life.

"My great dream," said Steve softly, "is that he'll speak to me. I'm reduced to that."

Sure enough, as we sat talking of the Olympics and track politics, the Angel Gabriel got restless and shaky. Finally he was laying face down on the blanket, crying soundlessly, his buttocks squeezed tightly together as if trying to defend himself. We all fell silent, too depressed for words.

Steve went in the house and came back out with a cut of heroin and the works. The Angel Gabriel sat up shakily, his eyes fixed on the white powder as Steve expertly melted it down in the metal spoon over the flame and filled the hypodermic.

"You use shit, Steve?" Billy asked hoarsely.

"No," said Steve. "I'll stick to speed."

Gently as a nurse, he gave the hypo to the boy. The Angel's eyes were intent as an animal's now. Very businesslike, he hunted for a usable vein in his thin thigh, working the needle around in his flesh. Shortly he had his rush coming. He lay back down, relaxed, smiling a little at the sky. The sky was clouding over, and Steve threw another blanket over him.

The sight of the Angel Gabriel made us all think of our own problems, and of that emotional death that always threatened us.

John Sive talked to me for hours that weekend, pouring out his heart about the anxieties of gay old age. Delphine was after him to marry him, but John was past even temporary relationships. "What I need," he said, "is something to make me forget about sex entirely, for good, or I'm going to end up making a fool out of myself."

Delphine spent much of his time that weekend sitting by the window looking out at the sea, and talking to himself in French.

Vince talked to us a lot that weekend too. I had become

deeply fond of Vince, and it alarmed me to see how bitter and sad he'd become. Pro track was not working out for him. He said that running an exhibition mile alone against the pacing lights just wasn't the same. The promoters were using him as a sideshow. Step right in, folks, see the real live homo miler with the tattoos.

For obvious reasons, he wasn't getting the fat product endorsements that the other top pro runners got. "And I've got this film offer," he said. "But I've seen the script, and my god, it's just one of these slick stereotype Hollywood jobs about gays. And I'm not starving, so I said no. I don't need being exploited any more than necessary . . ."

And now, on top of this, it looked like Vince and Jacques were breaking up. I had always assumed that Vince would be the cruel one when the end came.

But the first night, Billy and I heard him arguing with Jacques in the next bedroom, through the thin paneled wall.

"You seduced me," said Jacques. "You were in such a big hurry. If you'd just let me find my way, maybe I wouldn't be paying a psychiatrist seventy-five dollars a week."

"Seduced you!" Vince's voice was breaking, incredulous. "You were moping around Eugene just dying for me to feel you up."

"What you did was, you played on all my insecurities," said Jacques. "You're a really insidious person. You do that with everybody. You're just an operator."

They went on and on, Jacques cutting and Vince bleeding. Finally we heard Vince crying. Billy and I looked at each other in the dark, and closed our eyes in sorrow and shame at having overheard.

How long would Billy and I last? We had already had several quarrels. Each time, we were never sure we would make up until we'd actually done it.

We tried hard to have a good time that weekend. I remember the tapping of Steve's typewriter echoing down the winding ladder stairway from the tower. I remember all of us cooking dinner together, and the drinking members of the party getting a little wrecked on Scotch and wine. We roasted a standing rib roast and Idaho potatoes. Billy made a bizarre salad.

That Saturday night, a huge spring storm was blowing in, and the house shuddered as the wind hit it. The noise of the surf deepened to a bellow. After the dishes were washed, Billy and I pulled on our jackets and went out for a walk on the dark beach.

We walked slowly along the sand, arms around each other, barefoot. The wind whipped Billy's bellbottoms around his ankles. His hair blew wildly and stung my cheek. In the dark, all we could see was the white rumbling surf, and the few lonely lights of the other houses.

"I can't get Stevie's friend out of my mind," said Billy. "He messes up my dharma."

"Mine too," I said.

"You whipped people."

"I whipped grown men who paid me $200 to do it," I said. "I never tortured any children."

"Just looking at him, I think—I feel almost afraid, being happy with you. It could be taken away from us tomorrow."

I stopped and turned him to face me. "What would you do if I died?" I asked.

We were standing close together. I reached up gently and held the lapels on his leather jacket, and he clasped my wrists. I searched his face with my eyes. He looked so fine and so strange there in the dark, with the wind blowing his hair half across his face.

"Jesus, I don't know," he said in a low voice. "I haven't wanted to think about that."

"I hope we're lucky enough to die together," I said. "Like in an airplane crash or something."

"If you die first, do you want me to kill myself?" he asked.

I shook my head. "Suicide is a sin against God."

"I'll kill myself if you want me to," he said.

A black shock went through me. I could see him cutting his wrists or putting a pistol barrel in his mouth. I kept shaking my head, and found that I was trembling.

"Look, let's face it," he said. "Someday we're both going to die. Probably separately, probably you first. We have to have peace in our minds about that. That's what Buddha taught. There's just no way you're not going to lose the thing you love most. Peace is what sets you free from death."

"Do you feel you have that peace? I certainly don't."

He shook his head now. "I have a very big dread about that. Do you—" He hesitated. "Do you ever think that something might happen to one of us soon?"

"What do you mean?" My heart was beating wildly.

"People hate you more because you're the older one. They see you as having corrupted me. I'm always scared to death that someone might try to get you. Send you a bomb in the mail or something. Please be careful."

"But you're the one out there in plain sight. You're the one running."

He smiled a little. "We're both out there in front. And they always try to kill the front-runner."

We had to stop this depressing conversation. We walked on.

"Actually, we're going to be reborn," said Billy, "so why are we stewing? I wonder where our karmas will take us next. Are we going to be straight? *Women?*"

I was relieved at the opportunity to smile. "You mean you want to be reborn as a gay?" I shook him a little.

He laughed, putting his arms around me. "Sure. As long as it's not as Steve's friend. Maybe I'll be reborn as your coach next time. Boy, have I got plans for you, Mr. Brown. You're gonna run 57-second quarters on your hands and knees."

The first raindrops were wetting our faces. He kissed me the way he had that first time in *Song of the Loon.*

I lost count of the times we made love that weekend. We were laying up treasures for the lonely months ahead.

That night we slept with the wind shaking the house and rain lashing the windows. Spending an entire night together was still such a luxury. We went to sleep pressed tightly together, lying on our sides, Billy fitted into the curve of my body, his back against my chest, my arms around him. He was certainly not passive in our relationship, but I definitely had a fierce protectivist feeling. Even in sleep I had to shield him from the fury.

The next morning, we woke before the others. It was still storming heavily, but the rain and wind were heady and warm. We pulled on T-shirts and bathing trunks, and went out.

The long beach was deserted, all footprints washed away by the rain. A lot of drift lumber and seaweed was washed in. Huge breakers were rumbling in from far out. When they broke, they made incredible geyser-bursts of foam.

We ran east along the shore, our bodies streaming with the sweet rain. Patches of fog drifted over us. We were half-blinded by the rain blowing in our faces. Sometimes the wind hit us so hard that we staggered. But we kept pushing along, laughing.

Finally we were two miles up the shore. There were no houses here. All along the lonely dunes, the grass blew flat in the wind, and glittered in the rain.

We stopped there and Billy circled back to me. His curls were plastered to his head and neck, and his wet glasses blurred his eyes. He was laughing, and the rain was running down his thighs. I could see every bone and muscle in his torso through his wet T-shirt. He caught me by the shoulder, and I grasped his hips and drew him against me.

"You're the sexiest drowned rat I ever saw," I said.

We kissed with the clean rain lashing us, and our mouths tasted like rain. I peeled his trunks down around his thighs. Billy started laughing. "Do you think there are photographers skulking around behind the dunes over there?"

"Listen," I said, "even if they get pictures in all this rain, where are they going to sell them? *Ladies Home Journal?*"

We put our clothes on the wet sand and lay on them, so we wouldn't get too gritty. His supple body was bent double under me, and after the cool rain, the heat of his entrails was a shock. On my hands and knees I cradled him under me. He was impaled, but safe there—I took the slashing rain on my back. Pressed hard into the curls between his buttocks, I looked down into his face. His eyes were shut against the rain. The tendons in his neck stood up whitely, and sand stuck to his hair as he rolled his head back and forth in a puddle. I wanted him to feel that hot gush clear up under his heart. The noise of the waves deafened us—I couldn't hear him moaning.

Then he had me on my back and took his sweet revenge. Straddling my torso, smiling pridefully a little, he jerked himself off over my face. That image of him stays burned in my memory: He was kneeling with knees spread, the rain streaming down him, his hair full of sand; and behind him the white boiling bursting waves. The roaring deafened us. I scarcely felt the warm spurts on my face—the rain sluiced it off right away.

We'd scarcely finished when a monster wave sent a flood of swirling foam extra far up the beach. It caught us cold, and in a second we were drenched, foamed, freezing, stung with sand. It nearly swept us back down the beach into the surf. We grabbed our clothes frantically and got up laughing so much we could hardly speak.

"Talk about boys in the sand," said Billy.

Endless gay films feature love scenes on the beach—he was alluding to this.

"The boys in the sand are a mess," I said. "They get clamshells up their ass."

We threw our clothes farther back on the beach, and Billy left his glasses there. Then he waded a little way into the icy surf. It wasn't very romantic swimming. The enormous waves were crumpling down with terrifying force, and every time the sweeping foam came up, it all but sucked us off our feet. Billy, with typical recklessness, started out to dive under the waves, but I held him back. So we just waded around thigh deep in the foam, watching each other dive and come up, the foam draining down over our genitals.

Billy waded over to me and embraced me. Then he shoved me, so that we both went over in the water. We wrestled there at the edge of the surf, laughing, rolling over and over, being really rough with each other. Another big wave went over us and we nearly drowned.

We crawled out plastered with seaweed and sand, still laughing, and lay gasping safely away from the surf.

"We have to be out of our minds," said Billy.

"Do you think they have enough pictures?" I said.

"Am I behaving like a Virgo?" said Billy. "Seriously. Is a Virgo supposed to let himself get balled on the beach in broad daylight in the middle of a hurricane?"

"Only by a Leo," I said.

We lay around choking with laughter, making various silly remarks like this. Finally we got up and went over to our clothes. The first thing Billy put on was his glasses.

"Men never make passes at boys who wear glasses," I said.

That broke us up again.

We stood around for a minute letting the rain wash the salt and sand off us.

Finally we put on our sticky sandy clothes and started walking back. We had sand in our crotches, and it itched.

We walked with our arms around each other. The rain was finally stopping.

"Sometimes I think back on how afraid I was to love you," he said. "It makes me laugh now."

"Afraid?"

"I was always afraid of loving someone as strong as myself."

Those words moved me even more than when he'd

said he loved me. I couldn't have stood anything effeminate in him.

Vince passed us with a sad little wave, going out for his own run alone. Then we passed a woman in a sou'wester, going out to walk her dog. She threw us an odd glance. We knew she was thinking that the fairies were moving in from Cherry Grove. It was a good thing she hadn't come along half an hour earlier.

Back in the house, the others were getting up with their sorrows and fixing their breakfasts, but we managed to stay happy. The hot shower was good, and dry clothes. We sat at the big redwood table by the window. I had eggs and toast and hot tea. Billy drank milk and ate some ripe pears, rubbing the juice off his chin. But then Steve and the Angel sat down, and Steve was trying to make him eat, and we both found it hard to keep laughing.

All that day Billy and I tried to shake off the sorrow. We inflicted the sight of our affection on the others. It was cold and dank in the house, so we built a fire in the Franklin stove. Billy and I sat wrapped up in a blanket together on the plaid couch. John Sive watched us with a sad little smile and shook his head enviously.

"Oo la la," said Delphine.

The Angel Gabriel watched us curiously too. Possibly it was the first time that he had ever seen anything but sadism between two men. We put on a little show for him, kissing each other tenderly. The Angel watched with a grave stoned expression.

By afternoon the rain had stopped. The gale was still blowing, but it had shifted and was now blowing out to sea. The sky was a dark ominous blue. The ocean was a weird green. The huge waves were still rolling in, but now the wind was blowing their tops off. As each wave curled over, a cloud of snowy spume blew back from it like a comet's tail.

It was an awesome spectacle, and we all went out on the beach to look at it.

Then we walked over onto the National Seashore. The

whole area was deserted. We might have been the last people left on Earth after some terrible natural disaster, and we would, of course, not be able to repopulate it.

We wandered barefoot along the boardwalk that winds through the park. All around us, nature was giving life. In the marshes, the cinnamon ferns were pushing up their great silky heads. On the dunes, the bayberry was coming into bloom. We bent to sniff the masses of little waxen white flowers, but the wind blew the fragrance away before it could reach our nostrils. I thought how incredible it was that a drop of my semen on Billy's skin, or of his on mine, would not root into life somehow. Nothing of our feeling would survive our deaths.

I broke off a spray of bayberry and brushed it on his lips, so that they were yellow with pollen. He looked at me, possibly understanding what was bothering me, and kissed me so that both our mouths were dusted yellow.

We were six threatened men. Only Billy and I walked holding hands. Each of the others ambled along alone with his thoughts. Vince was hunched, diffident, hands in pockets. Jacques was tight-faced, staring. Delphine played distractedly with his fluttering chiffon scarf. John Sive strolled heavily, hands clasped behind his back European style. Steve kept looking anxiously at the Angel, whose hair was a tangled mess in the wind. Finally, gently, he took the boy's hand, but the Angel pulled his hand sway.

We walked down along the tide ponds on the bay side of the island. There the wind ruffled the flat water.

"Look," said Jacques softly, "a snowy egret."

We stood still. Across the nearest pond, near the inlet, the tall bird stood in the shallow water. It was startlingly white and pure against the desolate stretch of salt grass beyond. It waded along slowly, bending its slender neck down, looking at us suspiciously. Then Vince moved, walking on, and the bird flapped up. It was frighteningly white against the stormy sky.

For a moment the gale blew the bird cruelly. I felt a lump in my throat as I watched it. It planed sharply to one side, fighting with its wings. Then it was gliding safely downwind, away over the tide flats and dunes.

I saw Billy's eyes follow it too. The last of my young birds.

The ferry left the island at seven p.m. Steve and the Angel were staying on, but they walked down to the pier to see us off.

As the ferry pulled away, the six of us were all leaning on the rail on the top deck, the wind blowing our hair, our collars turned up. We waved at Steve, who was standing on the pier. He waved back. The Angel Gabriel didn't wave.

Then we sat down amid the jumble of suitcases, cat-carriers, dogs on leashes, children, and casually dressed straight parents. I felt defiant. Why should I take my arm off Billy's shoulders just because we were going back into straight country? I kept holding him. Sleepy from all the fresh air and lovemaking, he yawned, slid down a little in the seat and put his head on my shoulder.

None of the others were being demonstrative, so to all appearances we were the only gays on the ferry.

Billy gave a soft chortling laugh. "You're getting there," he said. "We're gonna live together any day now."

"Life is too short," I said.

Finally a man in a heavy Irish sweater got up and came over to us, swaying, carrying a half-full glass in his hand. He was one of those Fire Island lushes who walk onto the ferry with a martini.

"Would you mind," he said, "not doing that in front of my wife and children?"

I looked up at him with macho insolence. "Would you mind not drinking in front of us?" I said.

THIRTEEN

It was incredible that right after the Fire Island weekend Billy and I had our worst fight.

With all the hassles and pressures, my fear of losing him had been troubling me more and more. I tried hard to hide the fear from Billy, but he sensed it. He was hurt more and more by what he saw as my lack of trust. He was quiet, less tender and retreated into his training, his teaching and his yoga.

On Friday morning, April 23, he mentioned casually that he had sat up late in the dorm talking with Tom Harrigan. "Consciousness-raising," he said.

I was tired and edgy, and my imagination jumped to conclusions. I questioned Billy sharply. He insisted that they had only talked, about something troubling Tom. I scolded him for breaking a training rule. At that, he just walked away from me.

All that day, he didn't speak to me much. That evening he didn't come over to my house.

The next morning, Saturday, he put in a hard workout. Around noon, I realized that he had disappeared from the campus.

I was panic-stricken and asked Vince if he knew where he'd gone.

"He went to New York," said Vince. "He hitched a ride down with Mousey, Janice and a couple of others," naming four heterosexual students. "I just thought he was going to meet his father."

A gay kid loose in New York City on a Saturday night could do almost anything. Or almost anything could be done to him. Horrors flooded my mind.

I could see him being cruised or cruising on the street. The neon lights bathed his hair and shoulders in harsh color. I could see him agreeing, walking away with the other man. This was ludicrous, because Billy had never been fond of cruising. But I could see it.

I could also see other, more possible things. He could be kidnapped and held for ransom by someone who recognized him. He could be beaten up, and his body wrecked, with the Trials just weeks away. He could be spirited away somewhere, drugged, gang-raped, whipped. I was sure that someone, somewhere, wanted to get their hands on the body of *my* Angel Gabriel.

Recently a big murder scare had hit the Manhattan gays. In three weeks, five gays—two of them known activists—had been murdered. Two were fished out of the East River. The other three were found in tenement basements. All had been tortured, mutilated and killed by multiple stabs. The killer, who seemed to be a straight Jack the Ripper with a vendetta against homosexuals, had not been caught. The gays were convinced the police weren't working very hard at it. The wildest rumors were going around, and everyone was being careful.

I could visualize Billy falling into the hands of this maniac. I could see the police photographing his nude body as it lay on the dirty cement floor, stuck in a pool of black, dried-up blood.

My first impulse was to go to the city and look for him. But where?

I hurried to my office and dialed his father's California number.

John sounded sleepy—I must have awakened him. But when I told him, he was instantly alert. Hearing his deep, warm, precise voice reassured me a little.

"I've tried hard to explain to Billy," he said, "what it

means to be a man your age, and to go through what you did. He keeps saying he understands, but I don't think he really does, yet. But I don't think he would be unfaithful. The other times, he stayed with it to the end, and the end was always hard on him. It was always the other guy who walked out."

"He told me those other affairs weren't serious."

"Serious, not serious . . . you can't pigeonhole feelings. They were intense, but they were kid stuff. The feeling he has for you is very different. One thing above all, Harlan, you have to trust him. He panics when someone he loves doesn't trust him. I learned that the hard way. I gave him a very bad time about drugs, and it was the only time he ever ran away from home. He was in love with a kid who was using drugs, and I was just terrified he'd start. But when I quit nagging him and told him he was on his honor, the trouble stopped. And I don't think that, outside of smoking a joint now and then, that he ever went near drugs. And of course when he got serious about running, he quit smoking."

"Where am I going to look for him?"

"Look, try the movie theaters. That's where he always goes when he's really down. That time, he was gone a week and I found him in a theater. You got a paper there? Tell me what's playing, and maybe I can give you a lead."

I fished the new *Village Voice* out of my pile of mail. (Ten years ago, I wouldn't have been caught dead reading the *Voice*.)

"Is *Song of the Loon* playing, by any chance?" John asked.

"No."

"Too bad. That'd be a sure bet."

"There's Warhohl's new film. There's a whole festival of Peter de Rome. *The Experiment*. That looks about it."

John was silent a minute. "Try *The Experiment* first, then the others."

"*Experiment's* at the Bedford on East 69th. Uptown. We're coming up in the world, John."

"Slumming," said John.

"The first show he can see is the two o'clock. If I leave right now, and he's there, I can catch him before he leaves."

"Call me the minute you find him. And call me if you don't."

I jumped into my Vega and drove like a madman down to Manhattan. It was a fine warm spring day, and I drove with the window open. The smell of the woods along the parkway reminded me painfully of that day, just thirteen months ago, when we'd begun our relationship.

In Manhattan I drove around for half an hour swearing out loud, trying to find a parking place in the crowded upper East Side streets. Finally I squeezed into one in front of an antique shop, and I ran, not walked, the six blocks to the theater. It was a plush new one, with a gleaming glass box office.

The time was twenty-five minutes to four. I asked the cashier, then the ushers, if they recalled seeing a young man of Billy's description. They didn't remember, which wasn't surprising, since I didn't even know what he was wearing.

So I went into the lounge and sat down on the jazzy red sofa of real leather to wait. About fifteen people were waiting there for the next show. They were drinking coffee from the expresso bar.

I waited those twenty-five minutes in anguish. I was remembering seeing *Loon* with him, and touching him for the first time. I was sure I wouldn't survive losing him. If he ever leaves me, I thought, I'll kill him, and then I'll kill myself—even if it's before Montréal. I would put a single bullet hole into his perfect body, destroying it as effectively as the murderer I was still worrying about.

Across from me, two well-dressed gays were sitting on another red sofa, sipping at their little white cups and talking in low voices. One was handsome, about six feet, with a build that even I would have called athletic. Not a runner—a swimmer, maybe. He had long, unbelievable, auburn curls. I looked at him hatefully, seeing him not as a possible lover but a possible rival.

Finally the people started coming out. I sat watching them pass the lounge door, shaking with nervousness. Then I saw Billy.

He came walking slowly through the lobby, alone, hands in pockets, wearing an abstracted air. He was wearing his most tattered jeans, a washed-out purple jersey, his eternal worn-out Tigers, and $150 jacket of brown split-suede that his father had given him for his last birthday. As a concession to anonymity, he had on dark gasses. With an aimless air, he stopped in front of the billboard announcing the coming attraction, a revival of *Last Tango in Paris*. Gravely he studied Marlon Brando as the actor grappled with his teenage daemon. He did not see me.

My muscles started to slump with relief. I was just getting up when I overheard the two strange gays talking excitedly.

"Look, that's Billy Sive," said the swimmer.

"Darling, I can't believe it."

"It's him. I saw him close up at the Garden."

"And he's alone, darling. He must have broken up with what's his name, the coach."

"God, he's beautiful," said the swimmer softly.

He got up, his eyes fixed on Billy. I knew he was going to cruise him. My first impulse was to walk over there and break his thoroughbred neck. Then a base thought entered my mind. I would try to watch what happened, and stay out of sight, and see if Billy would let himself be picked up.

Billy turned away from the billboard and pushed out through the glass doors. The swimmer followed, while his friend stayed sipping coffee. As casually as I could, I went out on the street. I could see their two heads among the people milling outside. My hands were clammy with the sweat of fear.

Billy was already halfway down the block, ambling

sadly along, not looking at anything, his uncombed hair blowing in the spring sunshine. The swimmer came up by him, walked at his side, spoke to him. Billy didn't look at him, just hunched his shoulders, and kept going. The swimmer laid his hand on Billy's arm. Billy shook it off.

They reached the corner. The swimmer was still talking and put his hand on Billy's arm again. This time Billy turned swiftly on the swimmer, his fists clenched, and even from thirty feet sway I could see the hostile expression in his eyes. The swimmer shrugged and turned back toward the theater, passing me.

Billy stepped off the curb and started across the street. He hadn't noticed that the light was red. A battered yellow cab was speeding along the crosstown street toward him. He didn't see it.

I sprang forward, yelling, "Billy!" I could see him laying terribly injured on the street, legs shattered. I could see an ambulance screaming with blinking red lights.

The cab screeched to a halt just four feet from Billy's uninsured million-dollar injury-free legs. It skidded a little sideways, the smoking tires leaving black skid marks on the street. Billy started a little and jumped sideways.

The cabbie leaned out the window. "Mutha-fuckin cocksucka! Why doncha watch where ya goin?"

Billy raised his middle finger at the cabbie, and ambled on across the street.

"Billy!" I yelled again, now on the corner. He heard me and turned. I ran across the street while the light was still red, narrowly missing getting hit myself.

He was waiting for me by a florist on the corner. We stood looking at each other. Hot sweat poured down my body under my clothes at the thought of how the cab might have hit him. I felt so ashamed that I had thought he would walk off with that swimmer. I tried to put my hand on his arm. But his eyes were somber and reproachful, and he shook it off.

We walked along the avenue in the sunshine, jostled by shoppers.

"Look," said Billy, "we can't go on if you're going to treat me like this. You're afraid of losing me, but you're creating a situation where you might."

"Don't threaten me," I said.

"It's not a threat. It's a fact. If you don't believe in me, how can we love each other?"

He stopped and faced me amid the afternoon strollers. We were speaking in low voices, but if we'd shouted, no one would have paid any attention. Stranger things happen on Manhattan streets than two gay men having a domestic quarrel.

"Look," he said, "if I could show you all the thoughts in my head, you wouldn't see anything there that would make you jealous."

I was feeling more and more ashamed.

We were walking again, toward Fifth Avenue.

"What can I do to make you more sure?" he said. "Whatever works, I'll do it. I don't care what it is. I just don't want to have these fights with you."

We went along Fifth Avenue, under the budding trees. Then we turned into Central Park and walked along the paths. Cyclists and strollers walking dogs passed us. We walked apart, under the newly green trees, over the worn lawns scattered with rubbish.

We sat on a park bench. Near us, a bum slept on the lawn in a stained overcoat, a newspaper over his face.

"Look," said Billy, "if the bourgeois rituals mean that much to you, then let's get married. What the hell. Whatever keeps things peaceful. Would that help?"

I took his hand and held it hard, wanting to kiss it.

"Let's come out," I said. "All the way. Why should they tell us how to live?"

Billy smiled a little. "The USOC will burn us at the stake."

"Let them try," I said.

We didn't have any great making-up embraces. First of all, we were in Central Park, and second, the quarrel had shaken us both very much. We roamed around the park just touching each other, full of a strange new hurting tenderness. We drifted through the Children's Zoo and petted the ponies and looked at the pigs and chickens. We wandered across the Sheep Meadow and fell into a game of tossing frisbees with some students. At the pond, we watched the children sail little boats, and helped one small boy rescue his capsized schooner. We went out on the lake in a rowboat for a while. For the first time, I didn't care if we were recognized or not.

We wound up in front of the big carousel. It was turning, bright with lights and laden with children. The little organ was playing "After the Ball Is Over," and the horses were going up and down.

"I want to ride on the merry-go-round," said Billy.

I remembered how he'd said he wanted to skate just to get me pissed. "At least you won't sprain your ankle," I said.

I bought two tickets. When the merry-go-round stopped, we climbed onto what we agreed were the two fiercest-looking horses. Nobody paid much attention—grownups lose their minds and ride this carousel all the time.

The wheezy organ started to play "Daisy, Daisy," and the merry-go-round started to turn. We went up and down in a dream. Billy leaned his head against the pole, and just looked at me. Finally he reached out and held my hand, and squeezed it so hard that my fingers crackled.

"Are you trying to blackmail me into buying you some popcorn?" I said.

When we got off, a woman was standing there with two children and she said, "Filthy queers."

"Speaking of popcorn, I'm starved," said Billy. "I haven't eaten since yesterday."

We drove downtown and ate at that restaurant whose name I won't mention. We talked about the marriage.

"Do you want to try getting a marriage license?" I asked.

"I couldn't care less about being legal," said Billy, buttering his baked potato.

Now and then two desperate gays would apply for a marriage license. They were always turned down. I decided we would forget about the license—we had enough hassles as it was.

"We can go over to the Beloved Disciple, and Father Moore would marry us tonight," said Billy.

I thought about this, then shook my head. A quickie ceremony in the gay church, like two teenagers at the justice of the peace, was all wrong.

"Let's not rush," I said. "We want to do it the right way. We ought to invite a few people, the ones that matter. Your dad would be hurt if he wasn't included."

"Whacha have in mind, man?" Billy teased. "Five hundred people at St. Patrick's Cathedral, and a reception at the Waldorf?"

We laughed. "No," I said, "we want something small and intimate."

After dinner, we went to the Saturday night dance at the Unitarian church hall for a little while. The two-dollar admission covered free beer and soda. A bunch of gays were dancing to a record player, mostly slow dances. Billy and I danced a few of the slow ones, pressed together, our arms tight around each other. People recognized us, but left us alone. Billy felt feverish— emotional stress can drive up the temperature, and I worried what effect this blowup would have on his training. Now and then we looked at each other, with that look that acknowledged how close we'd come to the edge.

We sat in the dimly lit church for a little while, and I prayed and Billy meditated. Finally we felt peaceful. Then we drove back to the college.

The next day, I told Joe Prescott about our plans.

"It may mean more pressure on the school," I said. "If you want me to, I'll resign."

Joe thought about it and shook his head. "Marian and I would be happy to have your wedding here at our house, and you can invite your friends."

Billy and I were married on Sunday, May 8.

Few straights can comprehend the gay's hunger for dignity and stability. I can't begin to explain what that little ceremony meant to us both. The first time I got married, it was because I had to, in a daze, to something I wasn't fitted for. For Billy, it was one of those dreamed-of moments when he was going to be out front, running free, attempting to lead a normal life.

Our concept of a marriage ceremony in no way resembled the straight concept, although we did borrow a couple of features and brazenly put them to our own uses. After we did a lot of talking and analyzing, Billy realized that I did not see marriage as a ritual, a sacrament, any more than he did. This was why he was finally able to give in wholeheartedly.

We saw it simply as a formal public declaration of our love for each other, of our belief in the beauty and worth of this love, of our intention to live together openly, of our rejections of heterosexuality. Neither of us was a blushing bride led to the altar. Neither of us was bound to obey, or to be the property of the other. We were two men, male in every sense of the word, and free. Yet in that very freedom we bound ourselves to each other in an equality of giving.

Our dual decision was that we didn't want even a gay minister, or a service identifiable with any church. We ourselves would be, not the ministers, but the makers of the declaration. So we ended up writing our own service.

It was a fine warm afternoon. The campus was silent, most of the students and faculty gone for the weekend. We had not announced on campus that the wedding would take place, because we wanted to keep the affair quiet and small.

Sentimentalist that I am, it seemed fitting that all nature was bursting into bloom that afternoon. All over the big lawn around the Prescotts' house, there were masses of pink, red and white azaleas. We assembled behind the house, by a border of late daffodils, near where several ancient apple trees were clouds of bloom.

Everyone we cared for was there: John Sive, Delphine, Vince and Jacques, several friends from the GAA and Mattachine, Steve Goodnight and the Angel Gabriel, Aldo Franconi, Bruce Cayton, Betsy Heden, the team, a few other faculty, runners and students who were favorites— about thirty people in all.

Aldo's eyes popped out when he saw Delphine, who was wearing a long flowing chiffon dress with green flowers on it, and a large straw hat. He looked like he was going to the Queen of England's lawn party. "When do we throw the rice?" Aldo asked. But he gallantly stuck it out.

We all sat on the grass, under one of the apple trees. They sat in a big circle around the two of us. Billy was wearing his brown velvet suit and ruffled shirt open at the neck, but he got hot so he took off the jacket. Jacques played some haunting medieval airs on his recorder.

Then Billy and I, sitting side by side, read our little service. It consisted simply of quotes, each of us alternating. In his soft voice, Billy read from the teachings of Buddha. "There is only one law," he said, "and that is love. Only love can conquer death." Then I read from the Bible, mostly the *Song of Songs*.

Our voices alternated in the silence, as the group sat unmoving, intent on us. We could feel their support and their caring.

Then I put a heavy gold ring on Billy's finger. Looking at me steadily, he said the formal declaration.

"I, William Sive, take you, Harlan Brown, as my man and my friend in body and soul. I will love and honor you for better and for worse, in sickness and health, for richer or poorer, until death parts us."

The magic of those old words (as amended by us) settled over the sitting circle. The only sound you could hear was a cardinal singing off in the woods. Billy put another gold ring on my finger, and I repeated the same words he had just said.

Then we put our arms around each other, and kissed each other on the mouth. We held each other tightly for a few moments. It was the first time we'd ever dared do that in public.

To my surprise, I heard a few muffled sobs break out around us. We drew apart, and saw tears on a number of faces. Aldo was shaking his head, as if he couldn't believe his eyes, but I could tell that he was moved and a little shaken.

To break the tension, I said, "Don't tell me they cry at gay weddings too!"

Everybody laughed. The weepers blew their noses. Vince sprang up in the apple tree and shook apple-blossom petals down all over the guests. Delphine dabbed his eyes with a lace hanky and said, "God bless you both, *chéris.*" Everybody started getting up, all smiles.

Betsy rushed over and hugged us both, red-eyed. "You're both beautiful. There's no bride to kiss, so I'm gonna kiss the two grooms."

Billy grabbed her and threw her over his shoulder. Betsy shrieked. "Harlan," he said, his eyes sparkling wickedly, "am I allowed to have a girlfriend?"

"Sure," I said. "Have ten girlfriends."

Billy paraded around the lawn with Betsy laughing and screaming on his shoulder. Nearly everybody there knew about Betsy, and the laughter was uproarious. Aldo didn't know, and his eyes bulged out again—he couldn't figure out what was going on.

Then everybody, still with petals in their hair, had wine and champagne and cheese and other delicate snacks that Marian had put on a buffet table by the flower bed. Jacques played his recorder some more. Billy and I both tasted from a glass of champagne. "I guess Buddha will forgive me this once," said Billy.

We all talked and laughed and were merry all afternoon.

"You've really done it now," said Aldo before he left.

"We know," I said.

"Do me a favor," he said. "Don't announce it on the society page of the *Times*."

"We haven't announced it to anybody," I said, "except the people here. But I guess the *Times* will find out fast enough."

That night Billy moved out of his room in the faculty dorm and into my house.

The team had done a job on my car and on Billy's bicycle. They decorated them with crepe streamers, tied on a lot of tin cans and old shoes, and a sign saying JUST MARRIED. This was their idea of a joke.

John Sive looked happier than he had in a long time. "I really have good feelings about this," he said. "I think it's going to last."

"It has to," I said. "If it doesn't, it's the end of us."

FOURTEEN

The alarm would go off at 5:30 a.m.

As I sat up sleepily to turn it off, Billy would stir in bed beside me. Every morning he was there, and the morning after and the next. He would stretch and yawn, his feet disturbing the Irish setter who slept at the foot of the bed.

"Rise and shine, meathead," I would say. "Hut, hut, hut."

The setter would jump down on the floor and shake himself.

Billy groaned. "I hate getting up at this hour." But he got up and went in the bathroom to take a leak. "You wanna know what my dream is for after the Olympics? My really big fantasy?"

"What?" I said, making the bed.

"Sleeping until nine every morning for a month."

Our routine, during those pre-Trials weeks, was simple and nearly always the same.

In the living room, we would do calisthenics and yoga to get our blood moving. This careful stretching and warming up was one of the things that was keeping Billy injury-free. Then we would pull on our shoes and shorts.

Just as the sun was reddening above the trees, we would set off on our workout. Billy would run whatever distance at whatever pace I had scheduled for the day. I would run my usual eight or nine miles at a 6:30- or 7-minute pace. Since Billy burned through his workout at nearly race pace, I couldn't stay up with him, so I let him drop me and watched him disappear among the trees ahead. I was thankful for those sheltered private trails— if Billy were training on the roads, some hostile person might try to run him down.

Our different paces worked out fine. By the time I got back, he had finished and was showered and shaved and out of the bathroom.

We fixed breakfast and ate it sitting at the pine table in the kitchen, with the sun coming through the windows. I ate my bacon and eggs, and Billy ate his fruit and sour milk. If it was his morning to make breakfast, he fried my bacon for me. Love is when you fry the other person's bacon even if you're a vegetarian.

The feminists would have been touched to see how we dealt with housekeeping. Neither of us was going to be the woman, but neither of us liked living in a pigpen either. So we divided the chores fifty-fifty down the middle. One day I cooked and made the bed, and the next day he did. Once a week we managed to get a mop and dust cloth around the house. We paid Marian's housekeeper to do our laundry and ironing.

Every other week it was Billy who rode his bicycle into Sayville, the village near the campus, to buy groceries. He was adjusting to living on a smaller bank account than his father's, and was very clever at helping me work out our budget. He could carry a heavy sack into the kitchen and announce proudly, "Hey, I got you some sirloin on sale at $1.95 a pound."

One day, though, he came back and announced that a strange car had tried to crowd his bike down into the ditch. After that I made him go shopping in the car.

While marriage had brought his $10,000 salary into the house, we lived leanly. I was still supporting my children. Traveling to meets cost us money every time we turned around. We had everything budgeted right down to the last pair of running shoes for Billy—and he went through a pair every two weeks.

Every day, after breakfast, we worked on our school programs for the coming academic year. Billy was full of ideas for expanding the gay studies program. By 12:30 we were usually fixing lunch. I might eat some soup or a sandwich or whatever else was handy. Billy's lunch never varied. He always ate a special whole-grain cereal—oats, barley, millet, etc.—that he ground just before cooking. I had long ago stopped asking him if he didn't get bored with it.

When he worked out on the Tartan track, Vince often joined us. In July, Vince was going to Europe with the pro tour, and was resting now. Sometimes reporters and track people dropped by to watch them.

The press had found out about our marriage almost immediately. When questioned, we didn't deny it. It was all over the papers. Bruce Cayton sold his photographs and his story to *Harper's Bazaar*. But track people were still in a state of shock about it, and when they came around, they tried not to mention it.

In the afternoons, with study and workouts over, we sometimes went over to visit Joe and Marian. Everybody lay around their pool and swam. Friends dropped in. The sun poured down on us, and we chatted and laughed. I got bronzed, and Billy got as speckled as a quail's egg. In the evenings, we usually retreated to the house. We liked just doing nothing together, and didn't permit anybody to break in on this. We sometimes cooked dinner outside—Billy's potatoes and my steak roasted a decent distance apart over the charcoal. He dexterously grated raw carrots and beets over the potatoes. With a salad and nuts and more sour milk, that was what he ate.

After dinner we studied some more, watched films of races to study Billy's Montréal opponents, analyzed his performance, read, took care of mail. Even if he wasn't in the room with me, some gentle sound told me he was in the house. His transistor radio playing rock softly out of respect for my eardrums. Or a cup clinking in the kitchen, or the sound of his bare feet across the old board floor.

Occasionally, if John Sive was in town, we all went down in the middle of the afternoon to Manhattan for dinner and a movie, getting back about 9:30 p.m. We also accepted a few of the many invitations to speak before gay groups in the city, doing it free for fear the AAU might slap Billy with a trumped-up money-accepting charge.

Before going to sleep, we often lay propped in bed, reading. Billy was reading Steve Goodnight's *Rape*, I remember. I often read the Bible, letting its comfort and truth sink into me. Jesus had said that the last would be first. Society said that we were the last. It could be Jesus had meant the gays.

The bedroom window would be wide open into the summer night. We could hear the warm wind soughing in the cedars and spruces. If it rained, we could hear the eaves dripping softly, and smell the wet earth. We made love and went to sleep with our bodies touching under the sheet.

On weekends we worked in the yard. It gave me a good feeling to hear the lawnmower from the back of the house. I had gotten rid of the power mower and hunted up an old-fashioned manual one because I was always afraid Billy might cut some toes off.

Joe's ox-head gardener had left a fine planting of perennials about the house, and we tried to tidy up the neglected beds a little. We had day lilies, iris, poppies, delphinium, even a few scraggly roses. I can still see Billy down on his hands and knees sniffing a few petered-out hyacinths.

"Did you know these are the Virgo flower?" he said.

I got down and sniffed them. They were headily fragrant. "How come you don't smell like that when you run?" I teased him.

"We ought to plant some more this fall," he said. He pointed at the poppies. "Your poppies look fine, though."

Behind the house, there was an overgrown plot where the gardener had had his kitchen garden. "Next spring we'll get an early start," said Billy, "and dig it all up and have vegetables. How about that? Fresh lettuce and stuff."

For now, he just spaded up a small area, working industriously with his shirt off. He put in some tomato plants that he had bought on sale at the Sayville supermarket, and staked them with some old bamboo poles that he found in the garage.

He *was* like a fragrance in my life, if you can say that stainless steel smells like hyacinths. I had craved nothing more than a lover, but I also got a friend. He was casual and practical, yet unfailingly gentle and considerate. He carried out my training program meticulously now, not because he had any more common sense (he didn't) but simply because he loved me.

When I came down with a bad flu early in June, there wasn't anything that he didn't do to take care of me. He fed me aspirin, made me herb tea, bicycled to the drugstore to get my antibiotics. I was terrified he'd get my flu, but he was fit and taking Vitamin C, so he stayed immune.

Slowly I learned how fully I could trust him. Sexual he was—he could seduce me with one steady look from his clear eyes. But he was chaste. Never once did I see his eye rove to rate another man's body. Devoted as I was to him, I was sometimes guilty of this—it was mostly habit, I'd been doing it so long. He always noticed it and scolded me possessively, but he always forgave me.

His love burned with a steady, white heat, slowly melting the last hoarfrost of years off my bones. I sheltered him, raging against the world, yet he was always the stronger one, still and steely when I was ready to crack. His faults—his cold-bloodedness, his pitilessness—were now turned only against those who threatened us. From the day of our marriage, we had no more quarrels.

This peace, this daily sharing, this accumulative tenderness, was all that any human being asks from life. Yet this was precisely what a number of people wanted to take away from us. We built each day consciously, and in implacable self-defense.

When the press reported our marriage, we started hearing from long-absent relatives. I got a call from my uncle in Philadelphia, who told me that my mother had had a nervous breakdown as a result of the publicity. She was in a hospital. "Isn't it enough that you've brought such shame on the family?" he shouted in my ear. "Do you have to kill your mother too?"

"I'm not trying to kill her," I said. "She's killing herself."

"You must be a communist," said my uncle. "You're trying to destroy the American family."

And then he had the nerve to tell me that, if my mother didn't now have Medicare, they would have insisted I help with the hospital expenses.

But the most painful encounter was with Billy's mother.

Both John and I had wondered if she would show up someday. Children who become famous have a way of luring missing parents out of hiding. About a week after the wedding, Billy received an innocent-sounding letter from Leida. She said she was living in San Diego now, and had been thinking of him all these years. Could she possibly see Billy?

Billy was mildly disturbed, but he said, "I guess I ought to see her."

One rainy afternoon in the third week of June, Leida came up to Prescott. She sat nervously in our living room, looking at the training schedule posted by the kitchen, and at our two pairs of muddy running shoes by the front door. Through the side window, she could see our shorts, jock straps and T-shirts hanging soaked on the clothesline where Billy had forgotten them.

Leida was a slender agitated woman not much older than I. She sat clutching her handbag, with spots of feverish color in her pale cheeks. She was dressed as if she was going to church: pink linen suit, a white straw hat and white gloves. She had Billy's blue-gray eyes and cheekbones, and his curly, light brown hair. But on her the cheekbones looked strained, and the eyes hid things.

Billy greeted her politely and cooly. He shook hands with her. "Hi, Leida," he said.

She looked us up and down. I think she was irritated that we hadn't dressed up more to receive her. We had just come back from the Prescotts'. We both had on old T-shirts, shorts and rubber sandals.

We had some strained chitchat. How was her trip? And so on.

Finally Leida said, "All these years I have felt very guilty. I had you when I was very young, just 18. I . . ." Her eyes were wide, almost terrified. ". . . wasn't ready for a baby. I had a terrible postpartum depression. Then I left your father when I found out what . . . what he was like. So when I divorced him, I gave him custody of you, because I wasn't ready . . ."

Billy was sitting cross-legged on the Afghan rug, shaggy head a little bent, not looking at her. "You don't have to apologize," he said. "Everything worked out fine."

"But it was monstrous of me to abandon you," she said.

Billy raised his clear terrible eyes to hers. "Why?"

"Well . . . well, because . . ." The words hung unspoken. She was sure that, if she'd taken Billy with her, he would have grown up straight.

"How did your father . . . manage?" Leida asked.

"Oh, he and Frances managed fine," said Billy.

"Frances? Did he marry again?"

Billy's eyes were expressionless, implacable. "He married a transvestite." Thus, brutally, did he give Leida her first lesson in gay sociology. "They raised me."

Leida sucked in her breath.

"You don't know how much I regret it," she said to Billy. "If I could do things over again . . ."

"Look," said Billy, getting a little irritated, "I'm happy, so, like . . . there's nothing to regret. Don't make yourself unhappy over nothing."

There was a silence.

"I thought of you many times," said Leida. "I thought

. . . 'oh, he's grown up by now, maybe he's married to some lovely girl already.' Finally I tried to get in touch with you, but John had moved. I didn't know your whereabouts until I saw the newspapers—"

She paused. Suddenly she burst out, "But Billy, it's so absurd! You'll never have any children of your own this way. Don't you want a family, children? Every man wants to see his family line go on."

I was sitting on the edge of one of the wing chairs, looking down at my rubber sandals, my fists clenched. I was vowing that I would not get involved in this discussion, that Billy was perfectly capable of handling it.

Billy smiled a little. "There are too many children anyway," he said. "We're helping the world toward zero population growth."

His joke simply offended her. She said, "Billy, I'm your mother, I only want what's best for you."

Suddenly Billy was on his feet, shaking. He was so white that he looked bled. "You're not my mother. Do you understand that?"

Leida's hands flew to her mouth. They were pale nerveless hands, fine-boned like Billy's but without his strength.

Billy went on. "Maybe you thought of yourself as my mother. But I was nine months old when you left. As far as I'm concerned, you're a name on my birth certificate and that's all. I'm not sure I have a mother. Maybe I grew in the cabbage patch. If I ever had a mother, it was Frances."

I knew Billy was not being deliberately cruel, but his truth was as cruel as intention.

"Frances changed my diapers," said Billy. "He taught me to walk. He picked me up after school. When I skinned my knee, he put a bandaid on it."

Leida put her shaking hands over her eyes and started to sob.

"Billy, isn't that enough?" I said in a low voice. I felt a little sorry for Leida.

"It isn't enough," he said. His eyes never left her. "The whole world is trying to break up Harlan and me. And you come out of the woodwork and help them. You may be a very nice lady, and I don't want to hurt you. But you stay away from me with your big guilt. Don't lay your straight imperialism on me."

"Billy," I said. I got up and went to him, and put my hand on his shoulder. I had never seen him so agitated.

My touching his shoulder kindled Leida. She stood up. "I've tried to reason with you," she said to Billy. "Obviously you're brainwashed. You're just a child."

"He was twenty-two when we met," I said. "He was a man, and no virgin, and capable of deciding how he wants to live."

"Billy," said Leida, "I'm going to take you home. I think it would be best for you."

Billy started to laugh hysterically. "Home? This is my home."

"Billy," said Leida firmly, "there are laws—"

"Listen," said Billy, furious now, his voice breaking strangely, the way he had been when I slapped him that time, "don't give me any crap about the law. My father is a lawyer. I know what the law is. Don't you read the papers? The Supreme Court did away with all those laws."

"The police—" said Leida.

"You try it." Billy was the animal now, trying to stay in front. "You don't have a leg to stand on. I'm not a minor, and I wasn't a minor when I met Harlan. You officially gave custody of me to my father. All those years you didn't use your visiting privileges. You showed no interest in my morals. So don't come crying around now. The police and the courts won't give you the time of day."

"Parents have a legal right to kidnap their children, if it's for their own good," said Leida. She must have been reading about parents who kidnap their kids back from the Jesus freaks.

"You try it," said Billy. "I'll file assault charges against you."

"God will punish you both," cried Leida.

Billy took two strides to the door and opened it. Outside it was drizzling sweetly. "Get out," he said.

Silently Leida picked up her handbag and gloves, and walked out without looking at Billy.

Leida must have checked into Billy's legal observations, because we heard no more from her. But she had struck into our lives, and left her pain.

There were many other pains like that.

Joe and Marian had a married daughter who lived in Chicago. The last two weeks in June, she sent her three small children to visit the Prescotts. They were two boys and a girl, ranging from five to eight—the sweetest liveliest little things you could imagine, all of them with blond ringlets.

They all latched onto Billy, with good reason. He had his childish moments, and knew how to play with them. They were shyer with me, but still friendly. The sunny afternoons at the Prescotts' pool were full of shrieks, splashes and laughter as we all played with inner tubes and big plastic animal floats. I can still see Billy trying to get up on the big duck, and pretending he couldn't, and falling back into the water, while the three children screamed with laughter.

Joe and Marian would sit in deck chairs, grinning, benevolent.

When we were at the track, the three of them came running across the field to watch. The other summer-faculty children often came to watch too, so sometimes there were ten or fifteen kids there. They all knew they weren't supposed to yell too much, or get in Billy's and Vince's way. But they had their own little meet, running dashes up and down on the outside. The little girl, Julie, would run madly, her little legs pumping, her curls glinting in the sunlight, trying to keep up with Billy as he scorched past at a 4-minute pace. It took about ten of her strides to fill one of his.

When the workout was over and the boys were warmed

down, the three would run up to them, screaming, "Billeeee! Billeeeee!" I can still hear their clear, high voices, like birds in the woods. One by one, he and Vince would grab them and toss them in the air. They would scream hysterically with delight, and beg the boys to do it again and again. Billy would prance around with the little girl on his shoulders, like a horse, and she would hang onto his hair. Then we'd all troop home across the meadow, the smell of hot sweet grass in our nostrils.

"Don't ask me why," said Billy, "but I love that little girl."

"Sure you know why," I said.

"Let's steal her," he said.

But when Joe's daughter came to join the children, she was scandalized that her parents had allowed the children to hang around us. She was not nearly as liberal as her parents. Joe and Marian tried to reason with her, but she was firm. "It's best for the children," she said.

After that, whenever she saw us, she would gather the children and shoo them out of sight. The three little ones didn't understand, and they cried.

"We sometimes forget," said Vince bitterly, "that we're lepers."

During those sunny weeks, Leida's words often haunted me. She was right. I had children, but Billy's superior genes would be lost. As it turned out, they had haunted Billy too, and we ended up discussing gay paternity. The subject was brought up when we received an anonymous phone call that was more vicious than usual.

To calm ourselves down, we went for a walk up along the trail where we always ran. It was a cloudy afternoon, with thunder rumbling softly in the distance and a feel of rain coming. We walked slowly along. The marks of our spikes were still plain in the earth from that morning.

"It's something that bothers me a lot," I said. "When

we die, there will be nothing left. When other couples die, there are children left. Even an inheritance. Even a name that is passed down. Even just a marriage certificate on file somewhere. For us, nothing."

"I'll make a will," said Billy, "and I'll leave you my brown velvet suit and all my old track shoes." He wasn't joking, though.

We kept walking. The woods were almost obscenely green. A fine mist was beginning to come down, and it cooled our faces and skins.

"Maybe you're going to laugh at this," I said, "but I wish we both had children."

"I've been thinking about that," said Billy. "I'm not laughing."

"Having kids was the least unpleasant part of being married," I said. "Of course they could be a pain in the ass, but it had its rewards too. You come home at night, and they run to you and say Daddy, Daddy."

We came to a little stream that was rushing, foaming full. It boiled around the rocks past us. We jumped over it and kept on.

"I always used to think that living in your children was an illusion," said Billy. "But I changed my mind. Like with little Julie. Supposing she was yours. If something happened to you, that would be all I'd have left of you. It'd be something. I wouldn't be alone, I could do things for her. And if she were mine, you could feel that way . . . It isn't you that lives on, it's the other person."

We were both trying to contain ourselves, not looking at each other much. We weren't even holding hands or anything. Billy sauntered along, hands in pockets, kicking at small stones, reaching up to pull leaves from the trees.

"I don't suppose an adoption agency would give us the time of day," I said.

"Not a chance. Dad handled two lesbian cases and one case of a gay. All three of them wanted to adopt. The agencies said no and the courts said no. The idea is that you have a right to be brought up straight."

"Anyway," I said, "it would be better to have our own."

"Sure," said Billy. "But if there was some little gay kid out there somewhere, abandoned like me, and they would give him to me, I'd take him. And I'd have my own too, if I could."

"Look, are you serious?" I said.

"Of course I'm serious," he said. "I have a very positive image about being a father. I really think I'd like it. You and I would both be good fathers."

"Well, I've been looking into it a little," I said. "That gloomy conversation we had out on Fire Island started me thinking. We can, for instance, buy a child on the black market."

"Darling, what would we buy him with?" said Billy, grinning. "We'd have to hock all my trophies, and I'd lose my amateur status."

I smiled too. I had a lump in my throat, so it was hard.

"Then there's something that some couples do who have infertility problems," I said. "Like, say the wife is sterile or something. They find a female donor, and the husband impregnates her, and then she agrees to turn the child over to them."

Billy stopped and looked at me. "That's not a bad idea. One hitch, though," he said.

"What?" I said.

"I'm not getting into bed with any foxes. Not even to have children."

"Artificial insemination," I said.

Billy smiled slowly. His hair was iridescent with the fine mist coming down. "Weird," he said. "Sooner or later you end up making deals with women. It's an injustice, really." We walked on. "But . . . what're you going to do?" He kicked another rock. "How do we find one of these brood mares?"

"How do I know? Run some kind of blind ad in the papers, maybe. Screen the applicants. Pick some broad who is typey and intelligent. Make her sign the papers before she's inseminated, so she can't walk off with the baby."

"That sounds complicated. She'll want money."

"Yeah, we'd have to pay all her hospital expenses too." Billy ran his fingers through his hair and shook his head. "It sounds like the kind of thing we can't do until after the Olympics. Assuming I get there."

"Something else too. Supposing we find out, after it's too late, that babies need mothers too?"

Billy shook his head. We were coming to another little stream, and stepped across on some broad flat rocks. Billy slipped and got one shoe wet. He walked on with his shoe squishing. We were coming toward the fork where the side trail branched off, the one we had taken on that first spring morning a year ago.

"That doesn't worry me too much," he said. "Dad and I talked a lot about that. His theory is that the important thing is a lot of attention and cuddling and touching. He doesn't think it much matters who does it. When my mother left, he was stuck with looking after me and he said he was afraid even to pick me up. He had a babysitter during the day, but she wasn't paying much attention to me. He said that I got kind of funny for a while there. I didn't notice things, and I was like a little retarded. I didn't walk till late. Finally he got over being nervous, and he started paying a lot of attention to me. He'd get up early in the morning, and spend all evening with me if he could. He said finally I snapped out of it. Then when Frances came everything was fine. He was convinced it was just the loving. Maybe that's why love and being touched means so much to me, because of those few months when I didn't get any . . ."

"You like being touched, huh?" I ran my hand up his arm.

He smiled. "That first time we kissed, and when you started caressing me, that was unbelievable."

The thunder was rumbling softly nearby. It was a soft, fertile summer storm, and if it hadn't been for the phone call in the afternoon, we could have been peaceful. We walked along the side trail. It was hard to follow now that all the ground plants had sprung up.

Billy was serious again. "You know, I wish we could do it now—start this baby. Maybe I'm being paranoid. But after what happened this afternoon, you know—something could happen to one of us tomorrow."

We came to the top of the hill, and looked down the slope that we'd gone down that morning. The mountain laurel was all in bloom. The pink and white bell-like blossoms hung heavy, and the green foliage glistened in the mist. We walked down through it slowly, our shirts getting wet from brushing on the leaves. Finally we were in the little open spot where we had lain on the leaves. It was all grown up now with ferns and wild asters.

I stood looking at the little waterfall, feeling sad and frightened, and Billy walked around slowly kicking gently at the ferns.

"Why do we always end up talking about death?" he said. He bent and smelled the mountain laurel blossoms.

"Look," I said, "why don't we do the following. Let's have some semen samples stored in a semen bank. They freeze it. You can thaw it out and use it anytime."

He walked back toward me, smiling suddenly. "No kidding."

"Sure," I said. "That way it'll be there."

"All right, let's do it," he said. "Like, let's do it tomorrow. That way we'll both be less anxious about it."

He put his arms around me and we just stood there holding each other, our bodies feeling very warm and good through our wet shirts.

We got in touch with a very discreet and liberal gynecologist and told him what we wanted to do. He thought it was picturesque, and agreed to help. We made numerous trips to the clinic and masturbated assiduously until we each had a dozen samples in the freezer.

As if in ironic comment on this, the last weekend in June I got a hate letter from my elder son, Kevin. The letter was the only personal communication I'd had from my family since the divorce.

He wrote: "We've had to move away because everybody knew who we were. The kids in school all knew my father is a fag. I hope you get what's coming to you."

On July 2, Vince left us to go to Europe with the pro tour. We were both very worried about him. He and Jacques had broken off completely. He was alone, and morose, and inclined more and more to brood about injustices done to gays in general and himself personally.

Since our wedding, the track world had been pretty quiet about Billy. No one mentioned the subject much. The athletes themselves continued to be either supportive or indifferent to the issue, with just a few of them showing hostility.

We suspected that the reason for this silence was that the AAU and the USOC were saving their ammunition to use on Billy in the Olympic Trials.

This suspicion, it turned out, was right.

FIFTEEN

With the Olympic Trials, Billy and I said good-bye to our quiet home life at Prescott. The next two months, with its disruptions and its forced separations, we would just have to live through.

"After the Games," Billy said, "you and I are going to get in bed and stay there for a week."

With the Olympic Trials, the great hassle moved into fourth gear.

The Trials are a messy, spectacular mini-Olympics. They are the finest track meet held in the U.S., and are organized by the USOC to select the Olympic teams in each track and field event.

They are also a slaughter. Any sociologist looking for choice research material on male aggressiveness will find it at the Trials. The aim is to be among the first three finishers in your event. If you're fourth, you're out, no matter how good you'd been all that season. Novices and veterans alike are thrown into the meat grinder. Runners shove and spike each other on the track. A fall, an injury, a foul, running wide, a tenth of a second, a cramp, a hot day, a sleepless night—just one of these little things can rob a runner of four years' sweat, pain and financial sacrifice.

The U.S. is the only major track power that selects its

Olympic team in this brutal way. All the others handpick their teams on the basis of that season's overall performance. Track people argue about which is the better way. Either way, there is a lot of behind-the-scenes politics that can get just as bloody as the spiking out on the track.

So, when Billy and I flew out to Los Angeles for the Trials in the first week of July, we knew that people were saying openly that Billy would not make it. The handful of powerful officials and coaches who control U.S. athletics can exert all kinds of subtle pressures.

"They'll louse him up somehow," one friendly official told me.

"And besides," everybody was gleefully saying, "Billy just got married, so . . ." Myth still hath it that sex is not good for a runner, especially before a big meet.

Another thing to worry about was that Bob Dellinger had been working hard. His own 5,000 and 10,000 meter times had improved to the point where he was within shot of Billy's best times. Like Billy he had been playing it smart. He had not been racing himself to death all season, as so many others do, only to arrive at the Trials past their peak. Like Billy, Dellinger had even passed up the AAU national championships in June.

It would have been cheaper to drive to Los Angeles. But several days' sitting on his hamstrings in the car might have made Billy stiff, so we shot the money on airline tickets. In Los Angeles, we checked into the Costa Clara Hotel near the stadium, where a lot of other runners were staying. We tried hard to keep the press at arm's length. Billy had gotten tired of answering the same questions over and over, so he mimeographed a one-page résumé of his nine years in track and silently handed it out.

The afternoon that we drove to the stadium for the 10,000 heat, it was Billy's first public appearance since our marriage, and we got a shock. A big crowd was waiting there at the entrance. When we got out of the car, we were mobbed and the police had to pry us through.

Shrieking worshipful girls and quieter worshipful gays begged Billy for autographs, and crowded him so hard he could hardly move a pencil to sign them. Dozens of admirers, both gay and straight, were wearing T-shirts that said GO BILLY and BE KIND TO THE ANIMAL. They all wanted to touch him and hug him. Some of them even wanted *my* autograph.

But in the same crowd, there were also people who screamed curses and obscenities at us. Their eyes were blazing with hate, and their faces were twisted. As we struggled through, my face and Billy's were spat in several times. Someone pitched a ripe tomato at Billy and it made a red spatter on his blue warm-ups.

Inside, Billy turned to look back at the crowd. I was shaken, wondering if it had spoiled his psych for the race. He looked thoughtful, but still calm, and wiped the spit off his face with his sleeve.

"Well," he said, "now we know how the little black kids felt the first day they walked into the white school."

Activist distanceman Mike Stella, who had also been caught in the crush and nearly lost his athletic bag, stood there appalled. He was the one who had privately spoken up on Billy's behalf.

"Christ," said Stella, "you guys ought to have a couple of bodyguards."

At the nearest water cooler, he helped us wash the tomato stain off Billy's warmups with cold water.

But the experience seemed to provoke Billy's cold stubbornness, and he ran a good tactical race that day, qualifying for the final. Stella, who also had his eye on the 10,000-5,000 double, qualified too.

The final was run on July 5. This time we avoided the crowd by sneaking into the stadium through a back entrance. But the shrieking admirers and detractors were all through the stands. Outside, a Gay Youth group and a couple of straight youth groups were hawking the GO BILLY T-shirts, and hundreds were wearing them now. A YAF group and the Jesus freaks were selling T-shirts that said STOP BILLY.

Billy posed for photographers wearing a STOP BILLY T-shirt. "They'll need more than a rag to stop me," he said.

But I knew he was just a little nervous, and barely keeping his dharma balanced. From what quarter would come the political ploy that would try to keep him off the team?

As he went to the starting line with the rest of the field, my stomach was tied in knots.

The tactical problems of this race were complex for Billy, and he was not a genius at flexible tactics. Theoretically he didn't have to run an all-out race—all he had to do was finish third or better. But he had to run fast enough, and smart enough, to stay clear of the others, particularly Dellinger. If they forced the pace and stayed up with him in a group, and if he found himself in this group, he might panic and foul somebody, and be disqualified. If Dellinger fouled him out of the race, the USOC just might not call the foul. Some pretty strange disqualifications take place at the Trials sometimes, but the runners usually accept them. For once I was thankful that Billy was a front-runner—back in the pack, waiting to kick, he would be more exposed to bumping.

As the runners toed the marks, there were boos and cheers. Through a pair of glasses, I studied Billy's face. It was alert, but expressionless.

At the gun, the runners surged down the track, and the ten thousand people in the stands sent up a roar that made my hair stand on end. Roman circus. The survival of the fittest. A runner's blood on the track—that was what they wanted.

I found that my hands were shaking a little as I followed Billy with the glasses. My whole life seemed to hang on those next twenty-seven and a half minutes and twenty-four laps that the race would take.

Dellinger made his strategy clear almost from the gun. He set a fast opening pace, obviously hoping to burn off Billy's finishing strength. Billy coolly accepted the challenge. The two of them bombed through the first mile in 4:23.7, which was near world-record pace. They pulled rapidly away from Stella and the rest. Billy was running a couple of yards in front, as if teasing Dellinger on. Dellinger pushed him grimly. The rest settled into their own pace, sure that the crazy two would kill themselves before long.

Dellinger's strategy had me a little worried. Billy always ran a better race when he could set the pace himself and pick it up later on.

The crowd deafened me, shouting blessings and curses at that distant slender figure. Through the glasses, I could see him close up—his curls lifting, his lips opened, the muscles playing rhythmically in his shoulders and arms, the blue letters PRESCOTT on his white jersey. He looked so human, so vulnerable. My lover, out there alone where everybody could stare at him. In my mind, mocking voices whispered, "They're *married*. What do they *do?* Do you think they . . .? Of course, and they also . . ."

It was a hot day, and shortly both Dellinger and Billy were shiny with sweat. Neither of them was a great hot-weather runner, so that made them even. By lap 14, they were nearly an entire lap ahead of the rest. Then, as I kept noting the lap times, their pace started easing sharply. Billy was still a couple yards ahead, but they both looked as though they were suffering with the heat. I agonized— it was a bad sign to see Billy tiring so soon (later, though, he told me that he had simply felt Dellinger letting go, so he eased up to save himself).

Far back, the pack saw them easing up, and began chasing them. Something in the way Billy moved told me that he was feeling liver cramps. It's a common affliction in thin distance-runners, and they usually bothered him most in the 10,000.

Going into lap 23, Billy and Dellinger were still together, with Billy still implacably ahead. But a group of five, led by Mike Stella, was now closing the distance between themselves and the two leaders. They were sixty yards behind, then fifty, then forty. The noise from the stands grew as the gap narrowed.

"Come on, Bob!" "Hang in there, Billy!" "Go, Mike!"

Both Dellinger and Billy looked very tired now. I would have to hope that we didn't get such a hot day in Montréal.

Halfway along the backstretch in lap 23, Billy and Dellinger came up on the runner in last place. As they shifted outside to lap him, Dellinger tried a trick that Billy should have been ready for but wasn't. He threw a burst, cut to the inside and tried to pass Billy there. They bumped and tangled feet. And Billy went down.

The crowd screamed. A jolt went through me—I could feel in every nerve how Billy hit the Tartan track hard, on his hip. Roman circus. My runner laying there in lane 1. I couldn't even go out and help him.

Amid the general hysteria, Dellinger ran on alone. Billy lay stunned for a moment, then scrambled up. Dazedly he started to run again. He was limping. I put my hand over my eyes for a moment, then took it away again and looked through the glasses again. It was so pitiful to see him. His glasses had fallen off. He had lost one shoe— Dellinger must have stepped on his foot. His rhythm and his psych were shattered like thin glass. He was moving along jerking, drunkenly. He was flapping along like a bird with a broken wing.

All around me, his admirers were groaning and crying. "He's limping!" "I can't look, it's too awful." "That's the end of him." Dellinger's fans were rejoicing, pounding each other on the backs. "Bob's got it sewed up."

Billy was pulling himself together now. But Mike Stella passed him. Then Fred Martinson passed him. He was running with one foot bare, running blind—he could see the edge of the track only fuzzily, I knew. He had stopped limping and was running evenly. But Wilt Boggs passed him. Now Billy was fifth.

But coming out of the turn, Billy seemed to realize his situation. He collected himself, and suddenly he was running like a beast. It was one of those moments when I got the cold chills, watching him wring out of his body the last flicker of response. As the five of them tore into the final lap, the entire stadium was on its feet.

Slowly Billy hauled Boggs down, and in the backstretch he managed to pass him. Then he was madly chasing down Martinson. Meanwhile, up front, Dellinger was totally exhausted and unable to protect his lead. Stella, then Martinson swept past him in the turn. With Dellinger now third, it was him that Billy had to get in front of.

As they raced down the straight, Billy was just coming up on Dellinger's shoulder. But the fall had taken too much out of him, and he didn't make it. He crossed the line fourth.

The screaming of the crowd died off. Stella, Martinson and Dellinger came jogging back. Billy stood beyond the finish line, bent over with the heaves. Then he came walking dejectedly back to where I was, limping again. His calf and the top of his foot were bleeding where Dellinger had spiked him. He pulled up the leg of his shorts and displayed an ugly bruise coming on his hip where he'd hit.

He looked sick with shock and the heat, and I wiped his face and shoulders with a cold rag. His eyes were wet, but he wasn't crying.

"Well," he said "they better disqualify Dellinger. He bumped me."

Announcer Curt Steinem was reeling off the results to the crowd. "First, ladies and gentlemen, is Mike Stella, who records a 28:03.9 . . ." Stella, Martinson and Dellinger were announced as the 10,000 team.

Then, incredibly, Steinem was saying, "Billy Sive is disqualified for fouling."

Billy's fans erupted with boos.

Billy looked at me. "I didn't touch him," he burst out. "He bumped me." An official brought him his shoe, and his glasses, which had been stepped on and broken. He took them without looking.

"Are you sure?" I asked. I felt crushed. Billy still had a shot left at the 5,000, but who knew if he'd make it, especially now that he was injured? The 10,000 was his best race. And he'd set his heart on the double.

Mike Stella came over and put his hand on Billy's shoulder. "I'm really sorry, man."

"That fucking sexual racist bumped me," said Billy.

My dejection started turning to anger.

As the afternoon went on, John Sive and I visited the ABC-TV crew. They showed us a playback of the videotape, in slow motion. It was quite clear. Dellinger bumped Billy as he cut to the inside. They tangled feet, Dellinger stepping on Billy's shoe, and Billy fell.

I was livid. I went to the officials and invited them to view the videotape. They were not accustomed to having their decisions questioned, and they refused. "Billy ran into Dellinger," they said.

The day's events ended, and the press's attention switched to the growing controversy. All the reporters at the meet looked at the videotape. Aldo, Stella and a number of other curious athletes looked at it. They all saw Dellinger fouling Billy.

"This is incredible," said Stella. "It's the crookedest thing I've ever seen."

Billy and I made a statement to the press calling for a reversal of the decision and disqualification of Dellinger. This would automatically move Billy onto the team. John Sive and I then informed the meet officials that if they didn't act before the end of the meet, we would get a court order that would make them act.

"I can promise you," John said, "when a judge sees that film . . ."

USOC official Frank Appleby responded with some remarks about John being a "goddamn meddling parent."

That night, Stella and his fiancée Sue MacIntosh had dinner with us. Billy was sore and disgusted, but Stella finally cheered him up and had him laughing. With his musketeer's mustache and his long, black hair in a ponytail and his dancing hard-boiled eyes, Stella was picturesque. He was a tough, casual, raspy-voiced individualist. He could be brusque and sarcastic, but also gentle. The other athletes had learned to respect his integrity, and the AAU to fear his clout.

"I told you, you gotta have a bodyguard," said Stella.

Having him on our side was a real coup.

The next day, the meet officials were still sticking to their decision. It, and our threat, were aired on the sports pages and TV news nationwide. Never before had an athlete threatened court action to get a Trials decision reversed. Aldo told us that the USOC had a lawyer checking into their position.

Meanwhile, the Trials ground on. An overflow of athletes was camping on locker-room floors, living on hamburgers.

Billy had a very sore foot and hip, but he wasn't badly injured. He ran his 5,000 heat conservatively, and placed third, qualifying for the final. No one tried to bump him— possibly the guys were worried about all the talk of courts and lawyers.

All this time, I was being the behind-the-scenes paranoid.

Every angle had to be thought of. The dope tests, for instance. After every event the officials took a urine sample from each athlete. Supposing they alleged that they found traces of amphetamines in Billy's urine? Billy's trancelike look in races had always brought comments that he must dope. Some runners do take bennies. Billy scorned them. (The dope tests were partly ineffectual anyway, because the blood doping and a new caffeine-derived drug that was around both left no traces.)

So I contacted a respected athletic physician in Los Angeles, George Hofhaus, and he made a show of collecting extra specimens from Billy. The USOC must have gotten the message. While two other athletes were disqualified for doping, Billy was not bothered on this score.

All during the Trials, I was the shield that everybody else was bouncing their bullets off. I worked with John on the legalities, and made myself just a little unpopular with the press by restricting their access to Billy. Behind that shield, he had the peace to compete, work out, rest and think only of running.

At night we consolidated that peace in bed. We had carried it away from Prescott with us, and we sheltered it avidly. I felt anger as I looked at his bruised hip, his torn foot. How could anyone dare to hurt him?

Stella and his girlfriend were around a lot. A few of the other runners were dropping around too, and they would sit around on the beds in our room and gab about running. Mike worked out with Billy, and was busy showing everybody that he didn't give a goddamn what they thought.

"You're a weirdo-lover," said Dellinger to Mike.

Mike looked him right in the eye. "I'd rather be a weirdo-lover than get on the team the way you did."

For the first time, we began to feel that we weren't alone against the world.

On July 12, the last day of the Trials, the 5,000 final was run. The stands were jam-packed again, and scalpers outside were selling tickets for fifty dollars. Billy's people were chanting:

> Billy, Billy
> He's our man
> Catch him, Bobby,
> If you can.

Once again, Dellinger chose to force the pace. He knew that Billy's injuries were still hurting him, and he counted on the pain to erode at Billy's ability to hold the pace. But he hadn't counted on Billy's ability to block out pain.

So it was the two of them again, a front-runner's race, slugging it out far ahead of the rest. Stubborn, furious, Billy staved in the lead. This time he made no mistakes.

He burned Dellinger off, and won by twenty yards, for a 13:22.8. Stella came forging up for third place.

It seemed like half the stands went wild at Billy's victory. A lot of young people spilled down onto the track. Billy took a grinning victory lap, jogging in their midst while they jumped up and down and pounded him on the back.

So the 5,000 team would be Billy, Dellinger and Stella.

Then the announcer said, "We also have a special announcement. At a meeting of the officials, it has been decided to reverse a decision in the 10,000 meter event. On viewing the videotape, they found that the foul was caused by Bob Dellinger, not Billy Sive . . ."

There were screams of joy from the stands. John Sive's face split into a grin. I felt myself going slowly limp. You could hardly hear the announcer still talking.

" . . . So it's a no harm for Sive . . . Dellinger is disqualified . . . Billy Sive is now on the 10,000 meter team with Martinson and Stella . . ."

Billy was so drained from the race, and from all the tension of that week, that he didn't dance for joy. He simply sat down on a bench, with his sweat jacket over his shoulders. He put his head down on his knees and cried helplessly.

The great Roman circus was over. The stands and the parking lots emptied for the last time. The area was littered with programs and paper cups. Media crews were checking out of hotels. Athletes were driving home with broken dreams. We took a plane back to New York.

We had begun to feel—we thought—a subtle shift in people's sympathies. Stella made a blunt statement to the press, and said: "I've gotten a little sick of watching Sive being harassed and laughed at. How much does an athlete have to do before he is respected and let alone? Since when is an athlete's private life any of their business? Who are these people, anyway, who are playing God and setting themselves up as the moral guardians of track? I think this whole thing is setting a very dangerous precedent."

The bellwether of opinion, Mike focused the issue for many other athletes. Several other activists made noises at the USOC that enough was enough.

The sports press was more sympathetic too, now. They had been moved by the sight of Billy running blind, shoeless, bleeding and balls-out in the 10,000. The Los Angeles *Times* trackwriter wrote: "This is a pansy? I don't know what Billy Sive is. But he ain't no flower."

But many other Americans were very unhappy at the fact that the U.S. was going to be represented in Montréal by an admitted homosexual. There were still six weeks before the Games, and a lot of trouble could be made.

The brand-new Olympic team possibly was anticipating this trouble when they got together for some important business, shortly after the Trials. They looked thoughtfully at Billy, and pondered his struggle to get where he had. And then by a majority (though not unanimous) vote, they exercised their USOC-granted democratic right to elect the flagbearer who would carry the Stars and Stripes in the opening ceremonies in Montréal.

The new flagbearer was Billy Sive.

The AAU and the USOC were furious, and demanded they elect another.

The athletes said no.

SIXTEEN

"**M**e, the flagbearer," Billy chortled softly.

We were laying in bed in the cheap motel room that I had taken a few miles from the Olympic training camp in Alamosa, Colorado. John and Vince were sharing a room in the same motel. The mountain air was cool, so we were not sprawling around nude—we had the blanket over us. The afternoon sun had no way of coming through the small dingy window at the back of the room. All you could see was a patch of blue sky and the tops of some tall spruce trees.

I had sworn that Billy and I would never make love in this kind of place, and here we were.

The antiquated black-and-white TV was shut off. The room smelled of cigarette mustiness no matter how much I kept the windows open. The thin chenille bedspread had seen better days, and the sheets had been darned with machine stitching. On the wall by the bathroom hung a calendar from the previous year with a Frederick Remington painting of Indians on it. Our clothes were flung over the only chair in the room. My suitcase lay open on the floor.

This was already the third motel that I'd been in. Two others had thrown me out when they realized who I was. "Corrupting that innocent boy," said one elderly lady owner. "I don't want your tainted money." Western puritanism seemed to differ little from Eastern, except that out here they called us "'sheepherders."

Billy stretched luxuriously beside me. I ran my hand along him. He was as thin as he had ever been, even while overtraining, and I hoped he wouldn't get much thinner. Now he was suffering sometimes from the liver cramps that afflict thin distance runners, brought on by the glycogen deficiency that comes toward the end of a long, hard run. But he was bursting with energy and glowing with health. He moved restlessly, pleasurefully under my stroking hand, hard and smooth as living, stainless steel, trying to kiss me. I remembered my despair that first day watching him work out back at Prescott, wanting to run my hand along his smooth, young, sun-speckled skin as I was doing now, and being sure I would never do it.

"Are you going to dip the flag?" I asked.

At every Olympic Games, the burning question was whether the U.S. flag would dip like all the others, or whether it would stay loftily, conspicuously high. So far it had never been dipped.

Billy was nuzzling in my chest hair. "No," he said. "I'm going to keep the flag up, as a symbol of gay erection."

I put my hands over my eyes and laughed. "No political gestures at all? No upraised fists or shuffling around on the victory stand?"

"Mr. Brown, I am a walking political gesture. I don't have to do anything, just be there." Billy sat up. "Anyway, you'd say that dipping the flag was an irrelevant provocation."

"Right," I said.

Billy reached over me and looked at my watch, which was laying on the bedside table. He sighed. "Well, this has been great, darling. But I better get back to the camp before the housemother comes looking for me."

The "housemother" was head Olympic track coach Gus Lindquist, whose status as Oregon track coach had dictated that he be assigned to Montréal. Lindquist lived in a state of perpetual unhappiness these days because he had one of the Sodom and Gomorrah three back on his "skvad." He was also a little piqued that the stone he had rejected had been made by me into the cornerstone of such an impressive building.

Reacting to criticisms in 1972 that the Munich men's and women's track teams had been lax in discipline, the USOC was trying to clamp down this time. They had set up celibate men's and women's training camps with military-type dormitories, visiting hours and early curfews.

Husbands, wives, girlfriends, boyfriends and I were being forced to room outside the camp, in hotels, motels, apartments, campgrounds or wherever we could find room. Every day, athletes made a mass exodus from the camps for purposes of sex and companionship.

The athletes were furious at this girls' finishing-school treatment. They were breaking rules right and left, and making life as miserable for Lindquist and the USOC as possible. When Lindquist suspended two rebellious trackmen from the team for violating the curfew, about thirty other athletes violated the curfew out of sheer spite. It then dawned on Lindquist and the USOC that if they kept suspending people, they weren't going to have a team. After a week's squabbling and politicking, the two men were reinstated.

Billy, following our rule of "no irrelevant provocations," was being more obedient than most. Nevertheless, Lindquist was livid every afternoon when Billy left the men's camp to visit me. But since the other athletes were being allowed to visit their sex-mates outside, and since there was nothing about sex in the obedience agreement the athletes had to sign, there really wasn't much he could do about it. Lindquist took his revenge cheaply by denying me entry to the camp, so that I couldn't see Billy work out on the track. This deprivation was mostly emotional, because Billy was carrying out his program meticulously and was coming up fine, so he didn't really need me hanging over him. But I did get to see him during his longer runs—he had to do them out on the road, and John, Vince, and I met him at the gate and went with him in the car to protect him.

Lindquist derided me as a camp-follower. That didn't bother me—by now I'd been called worse names than that.

Outside the motel, we could hear gravel crunching on tires as a car pulled up before our unit. The horn tooted. "Break it up in there, you horny bastards," said Mike's voice. "Time to get back to the convent."

Billy got out of bed and went to the window, pulling back the faded curtain a little. Mike Stella and Sue MacIntosh were sitting out there in Sue's convertible. Windblown, grinning, they had been somewhere and had some fun of their own. They were quite open about living together, and no one knew when or if they ever intended to get married.

"You're early," said Billy. "Go have a beer with Dad and Vince. I'll be right out."

"Okay," said Mike, and shut off the engine. We heard them getting out of the car.

Billy went into the bathroom. Standing in front of the washbasin, he assiduously soaped his genitals. I got up too, and followed him in. He looked at himself in the mirror. He was starting a beard, and looked poignantly like the busted overtrained youth who had landed on the Prescott campus that winter day a year and a half ago. I put my arms around him and stood pressed behind him, feeling how hard his buttocks were.

"I feel like I'm turning into two people," he said. "One Billy Sive is very excited about going to Montréal. The other one wishes he was back at Prescott mowing the lawn." He was rinsing himself off carefully.

"Yeah," I said. "Oh, well, just a few more weeks." I was pressing against him very tenderly.

He moved his rear end a little. "'Oh, you're such a sexy old man," he moaned. "If you make Mike wait, he'll leave and I'll have to walk back."

"He won't leave," I said. "He's a friend."

"That's a fact." Billy moved aside and let me get up to the washbowl myself.

We pulled on our clothes. We felt very relaxed. We went out into the winey air and down the row of units to where John and Vince were staying. The door was open, and they were all in there sitting around on the beds with cans of beer.

Mike grinned at us lasciviously. "The big advantage you guys have," he said, "is that you don't have to spend five dollars a month on the pill."

Sue giggled and colored.

Vince was sitting stooped, wearing a laced leather jerkin that left his arms bare. He had came back from Europe with more money, more tattoos, a few bizarre adventures in the gay undergrounds of London and Amsterdam, and a load of depression that none of us could lift from him, not even Billy. He had come straight out and moved into the motel with us. He was delighted that Billy had made the team, and was living vicariously in it.

"Oh," said Mike, pulling something out of his jacket pocket, "I've got something for you. Saw it on the newsstand in town." He threw it across the bed to Billy.

It was *Time* with Billy's and my faces on the cover. I was behind, with my Marine crewcut and poker-face. Billy was in front, slightly lower down, smiling and hairy. The artist had rendered his curls as carefully as Botticelli (I had learned about Botticelli from Steve Goodnight). The hand across the cover said THE GAY PHENOMENON.

"So they finally ran it, huh?" said Billy, leafing through it to find the cover story. There were three pages of color photographs giving the straight reader glimpses into the gay world. Gays sunning themselves on the grass in Central Park. Gays touch dancing in a downtown Manhattan bar. A religious service in a gay church, conducted by a gay priest. There were several photos of Billy and me, taken by Bruce Cayton. The two of us sitting on the grass at our wedding, kissing on the mouth. The two of us at the track, me timing and Billy hurtling past, blurred.

Time senior editor Ben Maddox and a girl researcher had come up to interview us in June. We had told them that we couldn't cooperate with them unless they signed something saying they would not use Billy's name in any advertising, as this would jeopardize his amateur status.

They had agreed. They had done a big research job, and we were impressed with their effort to make some sense of the emerging gay community.

"Isn't there something about being jinxed if you've been on the cover of *Time?*" said Mike.

"Buddhists aren't supposed to be superstitious," said Billy. He looked at me and grinned. "Neither are Christians."

The magazine went from hand to hand. "Lindquist is not gonna like this," said Vince. "Neither is the USOC."

"What're they going to do?" said Billy. "We talked to *Time* before the Trials. The hell with the USOC."

In the obedience agreement that Billy had had to sign, there was a clause saying that the athlete would not have dealings with the media unless the USOC gave permission. Billy had actually been happy about that clause, because he was sick of talking with reporters about being gay. He was even sick of discussing running with them. He just wanted to be left alone. The USOC were mystified at his docility about this, and relieved that Billy was going to be out of sight for a while. They weren't letting any reporters near him.

Mike swallowed the last of his beer and stood up. "Well, folks, sorry to break up this gathering, but we have to get back. I promised Martinson I'd play chess with him right after dinner."

We all got up and trooped out. At the door, Billy put his arm around me and kissed me. "Bye," he said. "See you tomorrow."

Mike, Sue and Billy climbed into the convertible. A

honk, a wave, a screech of tires, and they were out on the highway, speeding away.

"'Remind me to tell Sue to drive carefully," said John a little dryly.

We all went back into John's room.

"Billy and Mike are pretty friendly, huh?" said Vince morosely.

"Don't worry, you haven't been replaced," said John.

"There's several of them that he's really solid with," I said. "He and Mike and Martinson and Sachs are going to room together in Montréal. I'm so glad he's not in there alone and being avoided."

"Right," said Vince. "I shouldn't be selfish. But I am . . ."

Mike Stella was, in fact, the only good straight friend that Billy had ever had. And, in addition to his new allies among the athletes, Billy also had a couple on the coaching staff. I had been steeling myself to continue being his shield in Montréal, which would be difficult from outside the team. I had envisioned myself making sure he got to the stadium in time to warm up for his events, feeling that Lindquist might not bother to look after him.

But the distance coach, UCLA's Ed Taplinger, had taken Billy under his wing, and sided with him in disputes with Lindquist. Like Stella, Taplinger had begun feeling that enough hassling had been done.

Lindquist pestered Billy every chance he got. While I respected the man as one of the country's leading tack coaches, I found it hard to escape the conclusion that he wanted to spoil Billy's chances. Perhaps he thought that if he poured on enough pressure, Billy would lose his Montréal psych. If so, he didn't know Billy. Billy's stubbornness increased in direct ratio to outside pressure.

A major bone of contention was Billy's program. Lindquist couldn't believe, or said he couldn't, that Billy got such results on only 100-130 miles a week. "You're not working hard enough," he told him, and pressured him to add more mileage. Billy set his jaw and wouldn't add a single yard. Taplinger infuriated Lindquist by saying that he thought I knew what I was doing.

I was amused to see Billy defending this program that sixteen months ago he had fought me so bitterly about. The Olympic track coaches, really, do very little actual coaching. Mostly they are just putting finishing touches on work that other coaches have done. They are babysitters with blazers and whistles, shepherding finished athletes to the Games.

Lindquist hassled Billy about his diet too, and made it hard for him to get the things he needed to eat. This meant that we were always smuggling nuts and fresh cereal into the camp via Mike. Luckily, the team doctor, Tay Parker, another new ally of Billy's, was fascinated by his diet and kept close check on Billy's condition. This meant that Tay, too, had sharp words with Lindquist.

"He pick at dose salads like a goddamn girl," roared Lindquist.

"I'd like to see a girl run a 27:43 10,000," snapped Tay.

Lindquist was always complaining to the USOC that Billy was a constant cause of discord between himself and his staff.

Billy got into the politics on the team with a great deal of zest. He wanted to repay the honor shown to his cause by supporting others' causes. He was involved in the politicking that got the curfew-breakers reinstated. When six black sprinters got mad at Lindquist about something, Billy and Mike were the two mediators that smoothed things over. Lindquist didn't like that either. "Dot boy, he is not only qveer, he is vun big troublemaker."

The day that the *Time* cover story hit the newsstands, USOC chairman Frank Appleby called Lindquist, who yelled at Billy, who told me and John. We called Frank back.

"Why weren't we informed about this?" asked Frank coldly.

"It was done before the Trials, so it wasn't any of your affair," I said.

"Do you realize that the IOC eligibility committee might question us on Billy's eligibility?" he asked.

"We asked them not to use Billy's name in the advertising," I said, "and they agreed, and it's all in writing. If you want, we'll send you copies of the correspondence."

"I fail to understand," he went on in the same tone of voice, "why you two are such publicity hounds."

"We didn't go to them," I said. "They came to us. And I can think of several amateurs who have been on *Time* covers and never had their eligibility questioned, so . . ."

A couple more days after the *Time* story appeared, the owner of the motel came around to us. "You're the guy in the story?" he asked. "That kid who comes is the other one?"

"Yes," I said.

"I'll give you an hour to pay and check out of here. Don't come back."

Finally we found a motel in a nearby ski area. The lady owner let us stay even after she found out who we were. She was broad-minded, having seen all kinds of goings-on with the young ski crowd in winter.

Billy and I didn't enjoy that uprooted life. We were back on a schedule eerily like the one we'd had before we married. An hour here, an hour there. He'd call me up from the camp and we'd talk affectionate nothings over the phone. "Mr. Brown," he'd say, "I want to make sure you're not feeling up any cowboys out there." "Oh," I'd say, "I can't stand the smell of horses." But we comforted ourselves via the purpose of it all.

I passed the empty hours talking gay politics with John and Vince, running, looking at TV, reading a little. We had brought along Billy's typewriter and I even did a little personal writing, putting down some of my thoughts and observations about what I'd lived through. Other athletes came and went, visiting. We always had somebody sitting around with a beer, telling us about his injuries and his hopes.

With Vince I took long runs on the mountain roads.
He was laying off until winter, just wanted to do some
easy road work, was going to the Games with us. Vince
and I talked a lot as we strode along in the silence. Those
weeks were when I really got to know him for the first
time. Vince had always been a little guarded with me,
following my rebuff his first week at Prescott, and possibly
being careful not to provoke Billy's jealousy.

At the bottom of my mind I always had that question of
whether there had ever been anything between Billy and
Vince, and I had never inquired in detail into their years
together in college. Why should it matter anyway? I asked
myself. But I recognized a deep fear of finding out something
about Billy that didn't fit into my picture of him.

For his part, Billy was mildly disturbed at the time I
was spending with Vince, but I reassured him.

The rootless days passed. Every day Billy came, seeking
that peace that kept him moving. Our bodies were cool
and dry in the mountain air. In my old age, I was at last
being permitted to make the discovery that lovemaking
gets better and better with time, if it's with someone you
care for.

His body seemed to be changing before my eyes, harder,
more fined down, the veins more pronounced. My
imagination was an X-ray—it could see into him, see all
the physiological changes that training forces. In the high
altitude, his blood was spawning millions of new red
corpuscles—he and the others would go to Montréal with
that extra oxygen-carrying capacity. He was doing the
second workout now, and the added distance was making
his capillaries branch and spread still more finely. Every
ounce of weight lost was a better power-weight ratio. The
Vitamin E he was taking was building heart strength for
those last minutes of the race when he would be committing
near-suicide to stay ahead. His lungs were growing their
last cubic millimeters of oxygen capacity. To feed this
system he had a huge blood volume, with a far greater
proportion of plasma than the unconditioned person.

He was in another of his breakthrough periods, and every day he was faster. The team traveled to two meets for some last sharpening, and Billy broke 27:40 in the 10,000 for the first time, recording a 27:38.2. Over in Europe, Armas Sepponan was equally hot—he came very close to breaking the world mark in the 10,000, which meant that he was still six seconds ahead of Billy. Everybody was conceding that, barring an act of God, the 10,000 and the 5,000 would be a balls-out duel between the two of them. The riskiest kind of front-running against the most explosive kind of kicking, with each of them having to calculate his pace down to the last split second. I was thirsting to see it myself.

But some Americans were less than eager to see this duel.

After Billy made the team and the *Time* story appeared, the anti-gay activist groups who had opposed the Supreme Court decision started making noises again. They showed their political shrewdness by putting heavy pressure on legislators—the U.S. Olympic movement was financed largely by Congressional appropriation. They demanded that Billy be removed from the team. One group was composed mostly of teachers and educators who had the horrors about homosexuality taking over the schools. Another called itself MAMA (Mothers Active for a Moral America). None of them seemed to have faced the fact that gays were not sexual omnivores who went around seducing everybody in sight.

In reply, John Sive and Billy let it be known that they would instantly file a discrimination lawsuit if he was dropped from the team. The USOC, caught in the middle, just agonized. Lindquist kept complaining that Billy was a source of disruption, to the point where it was affecting the team's training and morale.

This "disruption" consisted almost entirely of the fact that a number of the younger, wilder members of the team liked to run around with Billy, Mike and Sue outside of the camp, after they'd put in their work for the day.

I can still see that convertible of Sue's bombing along the road from the ski area, and turning into the parking lot by the motel with a juicy screech of tires. It was full of athletes shrieking with laughter and very windblown. They were serious about running, vaulting, high hurdles or whatever, but they were also serious about living. The car radio was blaring country music. Almost before the car had stopped, Billy had jumped over the side and hugged me.

"If you pull a muscle doing that," I said, "you're going to get a two-hundred-dollar whipping."

Mike got out and pushed Sue up to me. "Harlan, we gotta show you something." He was unbuttoning the sleeve of his paisley shirt and rolling it up. On his right shoulder he had a brand-new tattoo—a Capricorn.

I shook my head. But Mike was still grinning. He pulled up the sleeve of Sue's striped short-sleeved jersey. There was a Gemini.

I couldn't help laughing. They were all doubled up around me with silly snorts and guffaws. Billy was leaning on the fender choking with laughter. It made me happy to see him like that. He was getting one of his first tastes of his dream: being himself, being accepted, being free.

"Just to show you gay characters that you don't have a monopoly on the zodiac," said Mike.

Meanwhile, the USOC was having a go-around with the press about the media rule. The Dick Cavett Show wanted to have Billy for an entire ninety-minute talk, as they often do with really controversial people. The USOC said nothing doing. Both the press and some of the other athletes were criticizing the rule, demanding that it be dropped. Finally the Cavett people asked if they could have several athletes on the show, with Billy as one of them, and agreed that sexual sociology would not be discussed. Grudgingly, the USOC agreed to this.

Billy's eyes sparkled. "To be on the Dick Cavett show and not talk about being gay . . . that's fantastic. Maybe we're making some progress."

Cavett's people asked for Billy, Mike, girl swimmer Jean Turrentine, Jesse Jones and vaulter Stan English. The five of them flew to New York. I went with Billy, and sat in the green room while they were taping the show.

Cavett sat with all five of them, and they had a beautiful freewheeling conversation about athletics, young people, life, their hopes at the Games. Cavett's gags, and Mike's and Jones' witticisms, kept breaking the group and the audience up. Billy was wearing a soft brown plaid suit and had combed his hair and was being his sunny irrepressible best. On the set near me, I could see his face in living color as the millions of TV viewers would see it. Whenever he spoke, the camera panned up to him. He looked strangely young with his new beard, and responded to Cavett with the warmth and candor that I knew so well.

"How do you think you're going to do in Montréal, Billy?" Cavett asked.

"Well, I've never been better," Billy said. "A lot will depend on the opposition. Especially Armas Sepponan. But if he pushes me, and if I can stay ahead of him, I think I can run some pretty amazing times. I think I'll go under 27:30 in the 10,000, maybe under 13:05 in the 5,000. I'm still discovering how much speed I have, so who knows . . ."

"What is your strategy going to be?" Cavett had done his homework—he knew how important that was.

Billy grinned. "I'm not saying. But everybody knows I always run in front. I have the privilege of making everybody else wonder if I'll try to run away or set a slower pace."

I had a lump in my throat when the show was over. All those millions of TV viewers who avidly tuned in to hear a verbal sexual circus had gone away disappointed. But they had seen him sitting there with the rest, looking so natural and so harmless, and maybe some of them had realized he was not a monster after all.

After the show, Cavett told me, "I hope we can get

him back after the Olympics, and talk turkey. He's a beautiful interview."

"I'm sure he'll agree," I said. "He's not afraid to talk about it."

As August ground on and the Olympics were only a scant two weeks away, the rumors that there'd be an attempt to drop Billy from the team grew more insistent. Finally one night Aldo Franconi called me.

"Be ready," he said.

"But they know we'll file suit," I said.

"The buck is being passed up to the IOC," he said. "They're going to question Billy's eligibility."

My heart sank a little. Being an international body made up of members from all the Olympic countries, the International Olympic Committee was beyond the clout of the Supreme Court decision.

"But we're clean on eligibility," I said. "We've been so careful. I've killed myself thinking of everything."

"Well, there's one thing you might have missed," said Aldo. "His job at Prescott."

"His job? That's ridiculous. He isn't even remotely connected with the athletics department. He teaches sociology."

"That's just it," said Aldo. "They're going to say that he uses his running as a podium for homosexual politics, and his job is ditto, and therefore his job is cashing in on this."

"That's the most Machiavellian thing I ever heard."

"Well, be ready," said Aldo. "Because that's what they're going to ask him."

Seething inside, I hung up the phone. The Olympic movement allowed competition by Soviet and European athletes who openly received financial support from their governments. Armas Sepponan himself received annual stipends from the Finnish government. Yet, out of sexual hysteria, they would question Billy's modest little teaching post.

Two days later, the accuracy of Aldo's intelligence was proven. The IOC eligibility committee mildly inquired about the propriety of Billy's job. They requested that he appear before an emergency meeting at their headquarters in Lausanne, Switzerland. He and one other athlete would please explain themselves.

Billy's first reaction was cold fury.

"I'll be damned if I'll go in front of them humbly and plead," he said. "I'll call a press conference and tell them off in public."

Most of the Olympic team reacted angrily too. Only the handful who really disliked Billy were pleased. Mike Stella and the other activists went around raising the athletes' consciousness. They all saw it as just another hassle—if it could happen to Billy, it could happen to them. Mike on the men's team, and sprinter Vera Larris on the women's team, circulated a petition to collect protesting signatures. About seventy-five percent of the track team members signed it. Mike, and a number of others, said that if the IOC declared Billy ineligible, they would not go to the Games.

"I have no intention of participating in an affair where this kind of thing can be done to a person," said Mike to the press.

The USOC was a little rattled by the team's reaction. Clearly they had not expected this. They saw themselves going to Montréal denuded of a number of medal prospects, and with a skeleton team.

Angrier still were the gays. The activist front in New York City organized a huge protest demonstration in front of Olympic House on Park Avenue. Finally even the Canadian government spoke up—homosexuality had been open and legal in Canada for many years.

But when Billy calmed down, he was ready to go to Lausanne. He, Vince, John, Aldo and I climbed on a jet and we went.

When we arrived at the modern glass-walled building in Lausanne where the IOC had its headquarters, John and I had already decided we would not actually go into the meeting. It would look too threatening to have the lawyer father and the angry lover stalking in there. A little bit of last-minute diplomacy still might swing things our way. The only one who would go in with Billy would be Aldo.

We were shown to a reception room. The meeting was already underway, and British miler David Walker was already in there being interrogated. And then, from one of the sofas in the reception room rose a man whom we had not expected to see there at all. It was Armas Sepponan.

He came toward us with his light, quick step, dressed in a plain baggy black suit and white shirt, looking like the village fireman that he was. He shook hands with all of us.

"I am reading the news about it in the newspapers," he said. "I am deeply distressed."

"Well," said Billy, "if they won't let me run, I guess I can't run. I'll be joining Vince on the pro tour, maybe." He looked at Vince and smiled a little.

We sat down.

"I am distressed for selfish reasons," said Armas. "I am being very honest with you. I am now twenty-eight. It is my second Olympics. I shall probably not go to a third. If you are not in the 5,000 and 10,000, my performance will have no value."

We sat silent. Billy and Armas sat with their eyes fixed on each other.

"There is no other man who is testing me as you test me," said Armas. "You understand." Billy nodded. "And I think that you would feel the same way. Or no?"

"That's right, I would," said Billy.

Armas smiled. "You and I, we are not running for medals. We are not running for glory. We could run the same race some other place. Or no?"

"I don't follow you," said Billy.

Armas kept smiling his crinkled, simple, village smile. "These gentlemen make politics. But you and I make better politics. I think that after they consider, they are letting you run."

"What do you want to do?"

"It is only if you say yes."

Billy nodded.

"So . . . I am walking in there with you. I am saying that I also am ineligible. My government is giving me stipends. Therefore neither of us are running. Then I am saying that you and I are going to some other place, Helsinki, New York, wherever we decide. There we are having our own world championship in these events. It can be in the week after the Games, when we are still . . . how you say . . . peaking. I think we are having no problem while finding a promoter who will hold such a meet. It can be invitational, we are bringing together all the best men. You understand? I am sorry my English is being so bad . . ."

We all sat there flabbergasted.

Billy laughed his slow, chortling laugh, as he always did when some new idea beguiled him. "Sure," he said. "But, my God, you might be giving up a lot."

Armas shook his head. "I am generous, a little, but not so generous. I think I give up nothing. These men are not letting us have our little championship. If they do—" he spread his hands in one of those piquant European gestures "—they lose very much face. Or no?"

Now we were all beguiled. John grinned. Vince leaned back and laughed out loud. Aldo cackled and slapped his knee.

"It's a gamble," I said.

"I like the gamble," said Armas. "In Montréal, Billy and I are gambling also."

Billy's eyes sparkled wickedly. "All right. We'll do it just as you say."

"In the meeting already is my IOC delegate," said Armas. "The Olympic committee in my country is maybe not supporting me. But they are respecting me in this thing. They cannot force me to run. So . . . let us go in then."

We watched Billy, Aldo and Armas walk off toward the meeting room.

John was rocking with laughter and shaking his head. "Armas should have been a lawyer," he said, "instead of a fireman."

Later Billy and Aldo would describe the meeting to me.

All but one of the eligibility committee were present. They looked a little taken aback when Sepponan walked in with Billy. None of them, of course, knew why he was there, but they were obviously uneasy. Sepponan sat down by his IOC delegate and didn't say a word.

Billy stood, with his hands casually in his pockets. He was wearing the brown plaid suit that he'd worn on the Dick Cavett Show. He had himself very much under control. He was pleasant and precise, and his voice was soft.

"I think I can set your minds at rest about my amateur status," he said.

He paused a moment, looking around at all of them. "I was a gay before I was a runner. Do all of you who aren't American understand the word gay? It's our word for homosexual."

A few heads nodded, a few grunts of assent.

"Okay," said Billy. "I was invited to help develop a gay studies course at Prescott because I was gay, and because I majored in political science. I was not invited to do it because I was a runner. We had two other gay athletes at Prescott. One of them, Vince Matti, was also hired to help with the course. He was a sociology major. The third gay, Jacques LaFont, was not invited to help via the course. He was a biology major specializing in birds. So . . ."

He paused to let the point sink in.

"The gay studies program is not an athletic program. Athletes have come to our counseling service, but so have many nonathletes. I am not connected with the college athletic program in any official way. Sure the college pays me for my teaching work. They pay all their professors. But they're paying me to teach, not to run. I'm sure you gentlemen wouldn't expect me to teach for free, after my father plowed about $40,000 into my education so that I could someday earn my own living."

The committeemen sat stone silent, Aldo said later, looking fixedly at Billy as he stood there making his sexual avowal, talking about being gay as casually as if he were talking about the weather.

"My salary as an untenured professor at Prescott is $10,000 a year," said Billy. He had a sheaf of mimeographs and handed them to the nearest committeeman, making a motion to indicate that they should be distributed around the table. "I have listed all my expenses here for the single year I've been teaching. You can look at the trivia yourselves. All I'll say is that by the time I have paid my taxes and living expenses and all the expenses of being an amateur athlete, traveling to meets and stuff, right down to the last pair of shoes and $3.50 for my AAU card, I am about $535 into the hole."

He paused and the room was silent. "You gentlemen have accused me of making unethical profits from my sport. So . . . I want to know, what profits are you talking about?"

They were all studying the sheets. The room was filled with the gentle sound of rustling.

"Unlike many athletes in my country, I have never taken under-the-table payments or free equipment from manufacturers, because I knew damn well that somebody would use that against me before all this was over. The figures on this sheet are the stark truth about my financial situation. You can take them or leave them."

He paused again, looking down for a few moments as if thinking, and then raised his head again. Aldo said later that everyone in the room was as if immobilized by the touch of those clear eyes of his.

"Then there's your charge that I have used my running as a podium for gay politics. All I can say is, if I am on a podium, it is because people like you have put me there against my will."

"Mr. Sive . . ." said the chairman.

"I'm not finished." Billy's voice cut like a whip. "Let

me finish, and then you can say whatever you want. Let's go clear back to when this all started, to when I was on the team at Oregon U. I never once, in all this time, stood up and said, Look, everybody, I'm gay. Gus Lindquist found out about it and he kicked me off the team, and I didn't say a word. Then word got around to everybody in track, and behind my back they were saying, Hey, the kid's a queer, and I didn't say a word. Finally a reporter asks me, Oh, hey, Billy, are you really a homosexual, and I said I was, because he asked me a question and I believe in answering questions."

His voice seared them like acid. It was shaking a little now.

"Then all the uproar started, and not once did I say I was gay. People spat in my face and stabbed me in the back and reporters came around wanting to interview me. When the man I live with and I decided to, like, formalize our relationship, we didn't announce it to the press. It was everybody else who made the fuss. Every single step of the way, I've been on the defensive and saying as little as possible. It's everybody else who's having hysterics. All I want is to run and be left alone, and I'd be happy if the word gay weren't even mentioned. But as long as people like you keep fussing, then the issue is going to be there. Besides, if you think running can be a podium, then you must not know much about athletics. Being on a podium takes a lot of energy. Running the way I do takes a lot of energy. You can't do both, it's impossible, you'd go insane."

He stopped, breathing a little more quickly. Then he shrugged a little and said softly, "If you want me off that podium, then you take me off it yourselves. The burden of this whole thing is yours, not mine."

He turned away, and sat down by Aldo Franconi.

"Gentlemen . . ."

It was Armas' voice. Armas stood up.

The head of the committee, Feit Oster of Germany, said, "Mr. Sepponan, this is not your affair."

"It is very much my affair, yes," said Armas. "I think

that you will listen to me. If you do not listen here, then you will be reading my words in the papers." His voice was even, but the threat was there.

They listened. Armas said what he had to say. Subtle looks of consternation went around the table. When he had finished, Armas said, "Billy and I will await your decision. We are hoping that you are not forcing us to be so . . . how you say . . . so dramatic."

He and Billy walked out of the room together.

We had dinner with Sepponan, and then he caught his plane back to Helsinki. "I think I am seeing you in Montréal," he said to us, smiling his small, northern smile.

Two days later, the IOC eligibility committee announced mildly that it was satisfied with Billy's explanation about his job, and cleared him for Montréal.

We were all a little limp.

All but Billy. He was peaking, and he was breathing fire. He could hardly wait to get to Montréal. He wanted to burn up the whole world.

SEVENTEEN

The huge stadium was packed with its 70,000 crowd. The place was overflowing with flags and band music and tension. Scattered clouds blew over—the place darkened and brightened as the sun came and went. It was windy— the flags unfurled smartly.

It was the opening ceremonies of the Games.

The whole group of us were in our seats down close to the track, opposite the stretch of straight that led to the finish line. John Sive, Delphine, Vince, Steve and the Angel, Betsy Heden, the Prescotts, a number of gay activists and celebrities. The only one missing was Jacques—he was off in the field immersed in research, but he had sent Billy a good-luck telegram.

Everyone in the group was excited at all the color except me—I had been to the Games before. But I had to admit that the Canadians were putting on the most magnificent show ever.

All that Canadian love of pageantry was pouring onto the track. Mounties in scarlet, regiments of kilted Scots, the Parliament Guards from Ottawa in their bearskin hats. Then all the minorities of Canada were marching past: Indians and Eskimos, French Canadians, Germans, Ukrainians, all in costume.

I sat there bemused, exhausted from the weeks of struggle, shaky with nervous exhilaration. The band music and the skirl of bagpipes dizzied me.

Only one lone marcher was going to mean anything to me. And soon he came.

The teams started pouring onto the track. Each with its flagbearer in the lead. In my old age, I had come to disapprove of the Games as a vehicle of senseless nationalistic politics. And yet, when the American team stepped onto the track, and I caught the first glimpse of the Stars and Stripes waving over the massed heads of the athletes, I got an incredible case of the chills.

I clutched John's arm. "There they are," I said.

Slowly the U.S. team came striding—the team that so nearly was torn to pieces by Billy's persecution. They marched in two solid blocks—the 226 men and the 83 women. They were all in their smart red blazers, the men in white trousers and the women in white skirts. The men wore blue ties and the women had blue silk scarves fluttering at their necks.

In front of them, alone, walked Billy. He was proud, graceful, almost military, bearing the heavy flag slanting a little against the breeze. His glasses glinted in the sunlight and his curls ruffled. He had a happy grin on his face.

As he paced slowly down the center of the red tartan track, the sections of crowd opposite him burst into cheers and warm applause. The applause followed him along like a slow wave.

Few athletes had ever come to the Games trailing as much publicity as Billy had. His fight to get there had finally turned much of the hostility to warmth or at least well-wishing. Most people in the stadium now seemed to feel, "All right, he's here, let's be kind to the Animal and see how he runs."

He was opposite us now. He knew our seats were up there somewhere, and he dared to loose one hand from the flagstaff and toss a little wave at us. I threw one arm around John and the other around Vince and hugged them both hard. I had a lump in my throat. John had tears running down his cheeks. Vince was nodding a little, grinning sadly at his own bad luck.

"Look at him," I said. "He would have made a damn fine Marine."

Delphine was sobbing joyously. "He's so *fresh,*" he kept saying.

Steve had his arm around the Angel, who seemed to recognize his gentle acquaintance down there and was smiling a little, his blond mane blowing back against the knees of a stout middle-aged lady. Betsy was bouncing up and down in her seat, clutching Vince's arm. The Prescotts, sitting in front of us, turned around with huge grins. Joe slapped me happily on the knee, and Marian squeezed my hand.

"We made it," said Joe. "It just hits me now."

The loudest applause for Billy was from the gays scattered through the stadium. Hundreds had come from the States, scraping together money for tickets and camping in the city parks. The richer gays had flocked to the Cartier Hotel, where John and Steve were staying. They had come from all the Canadian cities. They had even come flocking from Europe. Two rows in front of us, we could see a couple of handsome young Canadian guys in faded levis, yelling Billy's name and hugging each other.

The American team was past now. All we could see was Billy's mop of curls above the others' heads, and the flag snapping. They neared the reviewing stand, and there was the usual moment of suspense. Would the flag dip, or wouldn't it? All the other flags were dipping, one by one, as they passed the Prime Minister of Canada.

Old Glory was coming up to the reviewing stand now.

I leaned over to John and Vince. "He's not going to dip it," I said, and I told them Billy's joke about the flag as a symbol of gay erection. John and Vince broke into helpless laughter.

That flag passed proudly by the reviewing stand, straight up. American arrogance and honor had been upheld once again, by a youth that America had disdained.

I was laughing myself. That lump just stayed in my throat, and wouldn't go away.

B ut the tension in the stadium was real and gripping, and we could feel it that very first afternoon. Every person who was at the Games remembers it as the Games of rumors and threatened violence. The rumors kept coming and going like the sunlight on that first day.

The ghosts of Munich and Mexico marched in that opening parade, carrying their black flags. So many extremist groups had threatened to bomb the Montréal Games that everyone there sort of *assumed* that there'd be some kind of massacre. Everyone hoped that the bullets wouldn't fly while they were watching their favorite event. It was a sad proof of how accustomed we all were to violence.

Rumors said that the French-Canadian separatists were going to bomb the Games. Black protesters were going to bomb the Games. The Canadian Indians and Eskimos were going to bomb the Games to protest racial discrimination. Jewish radicals were going to bomb the Games to avenge the massacre in Munich. A few telephoned threats to the Olympic officials had even informed them that the Games would be bombed if they permitted Billy Sive to compete.

So the Canadian government had reacted by throwing a massive cordon of troops around the Olympic area.

When we had arrived at the stadium that first day, we had been amazed at the elaborate security precautions. Every single ticket-holder had to walk past one of those metal-detectors used in airports. If he showed metal, he was frisked. The Olympic Village, where the 1,700 athletes spent all their time save for those moments when they appeared on the field, was under such tight guard that athletes could not sneak in girlfriends and wives as they had done even at Munich. The athletes could leave the Village to visit downtown Montréal, but they were warned that they did so at their own risk.

The threats against Billy had upset us all. But the Canadian government assured us that they were taking every precaution. They were treating Billy with great courtesy, no doubt hoping to pick up a few points with their own gay population.

Billy was staying with Mike, Martinson and Sachs in an apartment on the second floor of the U.S. dormitory in the athletes' Village. The apartment was under guard at all times, even when the boys were out. In addition, the Canadians had provided two big armed bodyguards who went with Billy everywhere, and one who went with me. The bodyguards could be trusted to do their duty fervently—they were gay.

Now and then I had nightmare thoughts about Billy being blown up by a bomb, but I tried to relax. You're really getting paranoid, I told myself.

The clank of troops had put a damper on the Games. I could feel it right there in the stadium. The crowd was trying desperately to have a good time, but all around I could hear people talking about their adventures at the frisking point.

"What's the point of having the Games," Mike Stella had told me the night before, "if they can't be open and carefree?"

Everyone—spectators, the press, athletes—kept looking around hungrily for something to give warmth and positive focus to the whole chilly affair. And that something was turning out to be Billy.

He had walked into the athletes' Village with his sun-lit smile, his crop of curls, his glasses, his brown suede jacket and his spikes slung over his shoulder, and he had said "Hi" to everybody. In about twenty-four hours, his Pied Piper charm had disarmed most of the athletes. They were all young too—sixteen to thirty-five. Many were nonconformists in their own right, and they responded to Billy as someone whose struggle and hard work they could appreciate.

They talked to him and found that the notorious, young,

bearded gay was just a human being like themselves. They found that while he'd discuss homosexuality if they pressed him, he really preferred to talk about sport, chess, yoga, rock music, politics, the weather, life and other things. Suddenly the little group of devoted friends around him had swollen to hundreds, of both sexes.

The media were already getting bored with all the rumors of bombings, and they sought out Billy for a little bright copy. The athletes' and the media's warm feeling spread to the spectators. Shortly he was the most popular, most talked-about athlete at the Games.

As I watched it happening, it seemed like a miracle to me. After all the brutality we'd been through, it seemed like everyone's hearts were suddenly being touched with grace.

Billy went wild in the Olympic Village, and I let him. He was living as he'd always dreamed of doing. He had overcome the fury by nonviolence and compassion. He was out front, running free. He was accepted for what he was.

He was even valued now, as someone who might speak for a whole universe of human feeling that had been denied. It was so ironic that, after all the efforts to keep him away from the Games, he should become their central figure.

He was everywhere at once. He was playing chess with Armas Sepponan. He was in the Village record shop buying records. He was in the shoe shops trying on new track shoes (and refusing gift pairs). He was walking through the Village holding hands with the black African runners (who hold hands with everybody because that's their custom). He was working out on the track with athlete friends jokingly yelling "Go Beelee" from the sidelines. He was holed up in the dorm having serious human discussions with people.

He spent a lot of time in the discotheque, and danced so much that Gus Lindquist complained. The British and European girl athletes were crazy about him, and fought to dance with him. It was that phenomenon of the straight female finding the unavailable macho gay so irresistible.

British girl miler Rita Hedley told the press that she was hopelessly in love with him. "He's the sexiest man I've ever met," she said, "and the closest I can get is dancing."

Billy was very nice to Rita, very gentle, and danced with her to her heart's content. One evening when I was able to visit the Village, I got to see them.

The discotheque was jam-packed, and most of the dancers on the floor had drawn aside to watch Billy and Rita going at it. Rita had on a midi-length red jersey dress that showed off her litheness. Billy was wearing faded bellbottoms, and an ancient T-shirt that said KEEP ON TRUCKIN', and he was irresponsibly, gloriously barefoot.

Both their bodies were grinding, snapping, whipping, twitching. It was sexual, but also—somehow—pure and joyous. There was that gulf between them. She was dancing at Billy, but without hope. He was dancing at himself and me.

Vince and I stood there watching, as the crush of young athletes around the sidelines stomped, clapped, whistled and demonstrated their enthusiasm. Several of the other dancers were imitating Billy's style.

Vince was shaking his head. "The whole goddamn place is doing the boogie," he said. "Do you think they know what kind of a dance that is?"

"He's started a fad," I said.

We stood there being very amused.

Billy saw us there and threw us a theatrical wink. The crowd roared with laughter.

"Move it, Billy!" Vince called. "Shake it!"

"Aren't you jealous, Harlan?" asked a Canadian hammer thrower.

"Jealous?" I said. "What for?"

When the music stopped, Billy and Rita came walking over. Rita gave an ironic little bow in my direction, as if to say that she was returning Billy unharmed to my custody.

Vince went wild at the Games too, but it was a different wildness.

The press, and the gays in Montréal, were aware of his presence there. He was becoming a kind of antihero—the one who had been cut down so unjustly. He followed the track and field events, and Billy's performances, with melancholy avidness. Training little now, he put in a couple of token miles around the area daily, and that was it.

In the evenings, when I was talking on the phone to Billy, Vince would plunge off into the night life of Montréal. He had blossomed out in a black leather cap with a gold chain on it and seemed bent on tricking with every gay in central Canada.

What worried me most, though, was that he was drinking. I reminded him as diplomatically as possible of what hard liquor can do to an athlete's blood vessels. "Oh," he said carelessly, "I'm just a little depressed and blowing off steam. I'm not drinking much. When we go home, I'll quit and start training again."

Not having drunk hard liquor before, Vince had no tolerance. In the wee small hours of the morning he'd crawl back to the press village totally smashed. He slept at odd hours, started popping bennies to stay awake, and didn't eat much. It was amazing how unhealthy and dissipated he started to look in a few days.

Billy tried to reason with him too. He was actually curt with Billy and said, "Just leave me alone."

Billy and I didn't see much of each other during the Games. For his own safety's sake I wanted him to stay shut up in that security-ringed Village. The U.S. dormitory was so heavily guarded that, even when I did get into the Village, there was no sneaking inside to Billy's room to make love. And I didn't want to make a fool of myself climbing up to his balcony like a lovesick Romeo.

So we did without sex for a whole week. The only

thing that made it bearable was the endeavor that we were both caught up in.

Since the USOC considered me *persona non grata,* they had not brought me to Montréal attached semiofficially to the team as they had several other coaches. To get myself in, I had wangled an assignment from *Sports Illustrated* to write an exclusive report on the Games. This got me in as a media person. Vince came with me as my research assistant. The two of us shared an apartment in one of the buildings in the press village.

So, with my press pass, I could get into the Olympic Village to interview athletes and, of course, to see Billy. The military had no qualms about letting me in, because they figured I wasn't going to bomb anybody.

Whenever I came to the Village, Billy was always waiting at the main gate. The minute the troops let me through, he threw his arms around me. He stayed with me and Vince all through our interviews with other athletes. With work done, we could stroll over the lawns or sit in one of the outdoor cafés drinking milk or mineral water. We held hands, or had our arms around each other. Everybody seemed to get used to the sight.

When we were apart, we fell back on the telephone.

We'd be on our beds in our separate rooms miles apart, and talk about how much we missed each other.

"I won't last the whole Games," he said. "It'll make me too tense. Maybe one night I'll come out. We can spend the night in Dad's hotel room."

Or we talked about the experiences he was having.

"What a gas," he told me. "All these kids. Some of them are unbelievable. That's what the Games is, isn't it? It's like Woodstock in sweatsuits. It's just a bunch of kids getting together. All the adults with their politics and their rules are just not . . . not the Games at all. And it's so strange to be treated like a human being for a change. I'm going to get a swelled head."

"Are there any other gay people in there?" I wanted to know.

"Listen," he said, "you wouldn't believe. Not many, but some."

And he told me of several young people, two of them women, who had come out to him in private, and told him their gay griefs. He had spent some time with them, trying to help them sort out their feelings about themselves. "After they leave, I always cry," he said. "What can I do for them?"

"Any cruising in there?" I said.

"Well," he said, "like, yesterday, this decathlete wanted to talk to me. Turned out he didn't want any gay counseling. He wanted my body. I told him to get off."

But despite all the excitement and the human distractions, Billy didn't forget for a moment why he was there.

Some of the other athletes were partying too much, going to bed late, eating crazy things. But Billy went to bed every night at the exact hour he was supposed to. He worked out scrupulously, and was following his pre-meet diet down to the last spoonful, for packing glycogen into the muscles. Distance coach Taplinger was taking good care of him, shepherding him through the red tape.

Under every grin, every twitch of his body in the discotheque, Billy was aware of the red track waiting for him there in the center of the monster stadium.

When the 10,000 meter was run on the first Sunday of the Games, I went to my stadium seat with a strange mixture of peace and nervousness. We had done everything we could. All Billy had to do now was run.

What can I say about his victory in the 10,000 meter? It isn't the 10,000 but the 5,000 a week later that I have to write the most about.

In the 10,000 he ran a perfect tactical race. It was his race from the gun. He took command, set a suicide pace, and ran away. Armas Sepponan was forced to set a faster early pace than he preferred, to stay within striking distance of Billy. In the last two laps, Billy eased off the pace, and Armas moved up strongly. But Billy had burned his kick to a cinder, and had just enough strength left to protect his lead.

They came balls-out down the final straight with Billy three yards in the lead, and the 70,000 spectators going berserk. Both of them were staggering. Billy was white with the pain of his liver camps.

He hit the tape with both arms flung up in dizzy exultation. Sepponan crossed the line a half-second later. I sat there so weak with relief that I could hardly react.

The times were up on the big scoreboard, but I already knew from my stopwatch. For the first time in history, the 27:30 barrier had been not merely broken, but smashed. Both of them had done it.

BILLY SIVE U.S. 27:28.9. ARMAS SEPPONAN FINLAND 27:29.4. JOHN FELTS AUSTRALIA 27:35.6

. . .

Vince had shouted himself hoarse during the race, but neither John nor I had made a sound. Now Vince and John were both crying. They hugged me, and I was so stunned with joy that I hugged them back automatically. Betsy kissed me on the cheek, and I gave her a peck back.

The entire stadium was on its feet applauding, which always happens when a popular favorite wins.

Down on the track, Billy was going berserk with joy. Striding back to the finish line, his face alight, he jumped up and down and blew kisses at the crowd. Obviously the pain of the liver cramps was forgotten. Mike Stella had come in sixth with a respectable 28:01.2, and the two of them hugged. Then Billy and Armas hugged each other. The two of them walked drunkenly around, sweaty and disheveled, their arms across each other's shoulders.

Then Billy started his victory lap. He tugged Armas with him, and motioned the other exhausted runners to join them. Shortly most of the field were jogging with him around the track. Billy and Mike and Armas went along hand in hand. The ovation went on and on. The cold chills just kept going up and down my body as I listened to that mass of humanity pay its tribute. He had repaid their warmth and support by showing them something new of what a man was capable of.

"Come on," I said to Vince and John.

We scrambled down to the trackside gate where family were allowed to join with the athletes when they came off the track.

Billy was just finishing the victory lap. He saw us waiting there and came jogging over. His face was wet with tears. In another moment he was in my arms, smelling of wet hair and wet cloth and good sweat. He held me so hard that he hurt me. Everyone was staring, but we didn't give a damn. His whole body was shaking as he cried with happiness.

I tousled his damp hair and said, "Hey, Mr. Sive, you were pretty good out there."

Then Billy hugged his father and Vince. He wiped his eyes on the tail of his singlet and pulled on his sweats, and then he cried some more. He hugged Taplinger and Tay Parker.

Even Gus Lindquist thawed to the point where he said grudgingly, "Dot vas nice running, Billy."

An hour later, showered and somewhat combed, wearing the U.S. team's fancy blue warmups, he was on the victory stand. The gold medal was glinting on his chest. He pulled Armas and John Felts up on the top step with him. The three stood straight and unmoving while the American flag went up and the anthem played. Billy was seen to shift his feet a little—he had bad blisters. He had himself under control now. He looked, simply, very happy and a little tired.

He had felt a lifetime's release. I envied him that release. It would have been nice to cry a little. But tears were not in my education. However deep my happiness and pride, my eyes stayed dry.

Not long after that Billy, Armas and I were in the ABC-TV quarters. We were interviewed live for the edification and information of the folks back home. The three of us sat with commentator Frank Hayes holding the mike to our faces. We had one of those beautiful banal post-mortems on a race, and homosexuality was not mentioned once.

HAYES (to Armas): Do you feel that you made any mistakes?

ARMAS (shaking his head): No. I am running smart race. I am starting my kick at just right time. But Billy is the more strong this time. That is all.

HAYES: Are you disappointed, Armas?

ARMAS (shaking his head again, with his elfin smile): In 1972 I am winning the golds in this double. Now Billy is winning them. It is fair. You must understand, I am not caring about the medals. I am running always against clock. My goal in this race is breaking the 27:30. So I am having the new personal record, and I am pleased. If Billy is not being in the race, maybe I am not running so good. Another time, possibly, I am being the more strong.

HAYES (grinning): Do you feel that maybe that time is coming in the 5,000 next Sunday?

Billy and Arms looked at each other, grinning savagely.

ARMAS: Billy is knowing that the 5,000 is my race.

BILLY (to Armas): Trying to psych me, huh?

We all laughed.

HAYES: Well, let's hope that we can look forward to some more brilliant competition between you two.

BILLY: We're an ideal combination, really. The way we work at breaking each other, who knows how far we'll knock those 10,000 and 5,000 times down.

HAYES: You don't feel that you've reached your ultimate?

BILLY: No. And I don't think Armas feels that way either.

HAYES: How do you feel about owning a world record, Billy?

BILLY (with Virgo candidness): Good.

HAYES: You feeling the pressure of owning a record?

BILLY: Oh yeah, already. The race is over just a couple of hours, and already the pressure about the 5,000 is incredible. But I don't really put that pressure on myself.

HAYES: What are your plans for after the Games, both of you?

ARMAS: I am competing in Europe. I am peaking maybe two, three weeks more, maybe I am breaking Billy's record. (He grinned at Billy). Then I am going home and being fireman.

BILLY: This guy is trying to do a psych job on me here.

We all laughed.

BILLY: I'm gonna go home to New York and teach. (He looked at me.) We both are. We have to earn a living. I plan to take a nice, long rest, an easy cross-country season, have some fun. Then hit the boards.

HAYES: How about you, Harlan? You were an Olympic prospect in your day. Are you maybe living in this a little vicariously?

ME: Well, if somebody had given me the choice of winning a medal myself back in '56 or '60, or of helping Billy win it today, the choice would be pretty clear. This medal means so much more.

BILLY: A lot of people don't realize how much Harlan's coaching did for me. When I came to Prescott, I was doing nearly everything wrong. If Harlan hadn't twisted my arm so that I'd train in a way that was right for me, I'd still be messing around there over 28 minutes. Maybe I'd be off the track altogether with injuries . . .

HAYES: Twisted your arm?

BILLY (laughing): I'm very stubborn.

HAYES: Armas, what about you? Are you feeling the pressure about the 5,000?

ARMAS: From my countrymen, yes. (He was alluding delicately to the fact that straight Finnish track fans felt that the national masculinity was at stake. But he then slid over his own allusion by adding diplomatically): You see, my countrymen are feeling that the 10,000 and the 5,000 are Finnish property, and our country it is very small, so . . .

We all laughed. I sat there feeling very smug that the folks back home were being forced to watch this on their tubes.

BILLY (drawling): You mean that I'm an American colonial imperialist who is taking over Finnish territory . . .

We all laughed harder.

That night, Billy and his bodyguards left the Olympic Village for about three hours. They came to the Cartier Hotel in downtown Montréal for a celebration. A group of about thirty-five of us had dinner, hosted by Billy's very proud father.

After dinner, Steve Goodnight threw a huge party in the hotel bar, the Petite Fleur. This bar, as it happened, was one of the leading gay bars in Montréal. All the others must have been empty that night—it seemed like every gay in town was crowding in there. Champagne, wine, whiskey and beer flowed like the river Jordan. A great number of straights, athletic people and sundry celebrities mingled with the gays, but finally they became a little intimidated by the heavy gay pride in the air. Only the Prescotts and Mike and Sue stuck it out, and finally the Prescotts got tired and went to their own hotel.

Billy, looking a little exhausted by now, was lionized, worshipped, cruised, felt up, kissed and hugged. Finally he couldn't take it any longer, and he hopped up and sat on the grand piano to be above the crowd. He sat there smiling wearily, answering questions, sipping his mineral water. He was wearing a casual beige silk suit, another that his father had bought him a couple years ago, that everyone said was straight out of F. Scott Fitzgerald. Looking at him, I pondered on how this situation could drive me wild with jealousy if I didn't see the Virgo in him firmly refusing all advances.

Steve got up on a barstool and made an incredible fifteen-minute speech full of raunchy gay puns, that didn't mention Billy at all. He was so drunk that he could hardly stay on the stool. Everybody roared with laughter. The sharp smell of amyl nitrite got stronger and stronger in the air. Vince was wandering around, somewhat drunk also, with his arm around a wild depraved-looking young French Canadian of about eighteen. Vince was wearing his leather cap tipped rakishly over one eye, and a black leather jerkin that left his arms and chest bare and displayed his tattoos. The jukebox blared endlessly.

The crowd begged Billy to get up on the bar and do the boogie.

He refused. "I did my boogie on the track," he said.

Finally I was trying to fight my way through the crush to Billy with another glass of mineral water for him, and somebody's hand started to unzip my fly. I put my free hand down there, and pushed the hand away, and zipped my fly back up. Leo is not next to Virgo in the zodiac for nothing.

Billy was looking a little gray. "Harlan, let's go back to the Village," he said. "I've had enough of this, and I'm falling apart."

We tried to find Vince, but he had disappeared with his friend, so we caught a cab to the Village alone.

The next morning late, Vince returned, hung-over and subdued. He must have purged some of the poison building up inside of him, because for the next few days he stayed right with us.

"I don't know what came over me," he said. "Last night I made a spectacle of myself. I don't understand myself any more."

Billy showed great concern for him, and he responded, and it seemed a little like old times. Every day the three of us sat in the stands with the rest of the group, and watched the track and field events of our choice. Billy and Vince yelled for their friends on the team.

Rita Hedley bombed out in the semifinals of the women's 1,500, and Billy said, "I hope it wasn't because I danced the legs off her."

Down in the States, Billy's victory was all over the media. Telegrams of congratulation poured in to him. One was from Jacques, sent from the small Michigan town near where he was doing his field work. It said: THANK GOD FOR TV, IT WAS BEAUTIFUL, YOU MAKE ME WANT TO START RUNNING AGAIN, GOOD LUCK IN THE 5,000, LOVE, JACQUES.

As the Games ground on, I began to see a subtle change in Billy. His euphoria was wearing off, and he (like me) was beginning to find being a celebrity very wearing: the demands on his time and emotional energy, the loss of privacy, the feeling of being looked at by 100 million TV viewers via satellite every day.

"Are we going to live like this from now on?" he asked me.

"I hope not," I said.

"You know," he said, "I'm dying for that race on Sunday, but I'm also dying to go home."

Right there at the Games, he received two lucrative film offers. One was from M-G-M, to do a feature film about an athlete. The other was from European director Luigi Servi, to do a feature film about gays. The M-G-M offer he turned down immediately—he couldn't do it and stay an amateur. Two book publishers wanted to bid for his memoirs. He put all these people off, saying he needed time to think about it. And he and Armas Sepponan received a $100,000 offer each from the International Track Association to join the pro tour. Both he and Armas said flatly, "No."

In the 5,000-meter heats, Billy and Armas qualified easily for the final. Bob Dellinger made the final too, but Mike Stella missed.

All around us, you could hear people talking up the 5,000 final on Sunday like no other event. Even the glamour of the 1,500 event was being eclipsed.

Some incredible bets were being made. Steve Goodnight had recklessly bet a rich conservative American track buff $10,000 that Billy would win the 10,000 meter. "Good thing I won," he told me, "because I didn't have $10,000." Now they were renewing the bet—$5,000 for the 5,000 meter.

O n Saturday, when I saw Billy, he was oddly subdued and tense. "I'm going to come out tonight," he said, "and we'll spend the night together. I really need you. I didn't sleep good last night. Another night like that and Armas will blast me off the track tomorrow. Everything is getting to be too much."

Early that evening, John cleared out of his room and I waited for Billy there. The bodyguards and Vince brought Billy to the hotel, and we all searched the room for bombs, and then the bodyguards left and camped in the corridor outside.

We locked the door and were alone for the first time in more than a week.

Billy was curiously quiet and keyed-up. He slipped off his brown split-suede jacket and prowled around the room, stopping to look out the big window. Evening was just coming. The sky was rose-red and the city lights and smog of Montréal spread out to the horizon.

I just watched him, waiting for him to unwind. He was dressed up a little for once. He had on a soft blue silk shirt, unbuttoned at the neck, and gray knit slacks with flared cuffs that showed off his long legs and small rear end to perfection.

It struck me how much he had matured in the twenty-one months we'd known each other. Love, struggle and hard work had burned all the last traces of coltishness out of him. A certain blurred youthfulness was gone from his face, leaving it defined, burnished, expressive. He was twenty-four now, or would be on September ninth. He was very much a man, very much my peer.

As he moved around the room, I couldn't take my eyes off him, loving his quietness, his hardness, his seriousness.

"Foxes," he said. "Rubbing up my thigh all week."

I laughed a little. "Has that got you bothered?"

"It makes me remember what I really like."

We stood by the window a little, looking out at the lights. He pulled the gold medal out of his pocket and put it in my hand. "It's yours," he said. "Keep it."

I laid it on the dresser.

"I keep trying not to think about tomorrow," he said. "I have to do it again, and I don't know if I can. When I came out of the last turn in the 10,000, I was dead. I reached down and there was nothing. Good thing he was dead too."

"You've got one up on him," I said. "He's thinking about how you beat him once, and how you might do it again."

We talked for a while about the race, and slowly his apprehension eased. We decided that he wouldn't try to run away this time. He'd set a slower pace at first, but fast enough to drain Armas steadily. Then starting at 3,000 meters he'd stage a long drive to burn off Armas' kick in the last half-mile.

Finally, wordlessly, he kissed me on the mouth. Then he moved away from the window, unbuttoning his shirt slowly. Shrugging it off, he threw it over a chair. In the soft lamplight, he was a living anatomy lesson.

"You're in a heavy mood," I said, taking off my tie.

"I've got a real load on," he said. He smiled a little, with that seductive ruttish look in his eyes. "If we don't get it off me, I'm gonna be like with five pounds of lead in my jock strap tomorrow."

He stripped off his slacks and his snug, white cotton briefs. Jerking the bedcovers all the way off the bed, he lay down on the sheet. To tease him a little, I took my time taking off my own trousers and underpants. He lay there propped on one elbow, twitching pleasantly with impatience, running his free hand up and down his flank.

"Come on," he said. His eyes were level and hot as two blue-gray flames of pure oxygen.

"Coming," I said, trying not to smile.

He kept caressing himself, rolling his head back and forth, and his body flexed and writhed a little on the sheet.

I stood naked at the foot of the bed, lifted one of his bare feet and inspected his sole. "How are those blisters? Hm, they look pretty good. Parker takes good care of you."

He laughed with exasperation and jerked his foot away from me. Rolling over on his stomach, he rubbed and worked himself into the sheet. Then, with a lithe, slow twist, he was over on his back again, his whole body wringing with need and life. He seethed with that effervescent peak that would last maybe two weeks more before going flat, like a living champagne. I just stood there admiring him, making him admire me, playing with myself to tease him more.

"They mixed up your birth certificate," I said. "You're a flaming Scorpio."

"Astrology is a lot of crap," he said.

I lay slowly down by him, and we embraced with an exhalation of relief, rolling slowly this way and that, our thighs tangled and gripping. We made love with slow, deliberate, obscene tenderness. There was the sureness of the thousandth time we had done these things. There was even something of the sharpness of that first time eighteen years ago, in the theater with the youth in the red jacket. Slowly we doubled and twined and kneeled and slid on the bed. We didn't speak except to whisper some request. My whole life was in every touch of his mouth or hands on my body. Just his warm hair brushing my thighs made me shake all over. At first our bodies were dry, but shortly an iridescent sweat came out on us. We kept looking at each other. His face was grave, absorbed, alight.

Finally, when we'd prolonged it till we hurt, we let

ourselves get frantic. We lost control then. I remember, with a terrible clarity, the heat of his driving body on my back, and the low gasping animal cries that he gave as he came, and his weight on me for a long time after, lips against my neck, hair falling forward on both our heads.

Finally he drew a sigh. "That was worth waiting a week and running a world record for."

We took a shower together and horsed around a little, laughing. Then we pulled bathrobes on, and I phoned down to order our dinner sent up.

Billy ate hungrily, going heavy on potatoes and other carbohydrates to finish the glycogen-packing. He was now his usual relaxed self. We talked as if we were home, about the plans we had for the gay studies program, about how we'd defend our privacy, about things we'd like to do.

"Steve wants us to come out to Fire Island before the season ends," I said. "You've never seen it in the fall. It's beautiful."

"I'll bet," he said, his eyes sparkling. "Are there big storms in the fall too?"

He took off his robe and slipped the chain of the gold medal over his head. It looked indecently beautiful on his bare chest. He walked around a little with macho seductiveness.

"I never knew you were so perverse," I said.

He laughed. "Neither did I." He took the medal off.

We went back to bed and had another mild one. Then we lay together talking, the blanket over us. He was deeply relaxed now, his eyes soft and vague. Our conversation turned to the direction his next few years of running would take.

"I'd like to try the marathon again," he said. "I ran a 2:22 that summer with Vince, in the Golden Gate. With the speed I've got now, I ought to be able to do a 2:12 right off."

The vaguest unease crossed my mind. It was one of the rare occasions when he mentioned those years with

Vince. As always, I asked myself if they'd been lovers, and then asked myself what difference it made—except that Vince was still around and could conceivably someday take him away from me. His friendship with Vince had outlasted any of his loves, including (so far) his for me.

Out loud, I agreed about the marathon. It's axiomatic in running that the outstanding 10,000 man is often outstanding as a marathoner, because the same type of training works for both.

I teased him a little. "You just want to run marathons because it's more miles."

He laughed, warm against me. "You should have seen Vince and me. We were a couple of nuts. Vince had never run farther than fifteen miles. The most I'd done was about twenty. But we were very sure of ourselves. We went out at a 9-minute pace and we were just having a ball. We were in second place, running together. Then along about sixteen miles, Vince's knees started hurting. I think his knee troubles date from that race. Anyway, he couldn't hold the pace and he told me to go on. So I did, and I thought, this is a snap. I was on for about a 2:16. Then the guy in the lead, Gerry Moore, eased up a little and I passed him. Gee wow, I thought, I'm gonna win this thing. And then about the 22-mile mark, I just fell apart."

We were both laughing, in each other's arms.

"That man with the hammer really knocked me on the head," said Billy. "So of course I had to ease off, and Moore passed me, and a couple other guys passed me. I came in fourth with a 2:22.35, and I felt so bad after the race that I couldn't eat. Poor Vince walked in, I think he got a 2:50. That was his last marathon. He says the marathon is too goddamn far."

"Well," I said, "you've been a good boy, so I'll let you run a marathon or two, and we'll see how you do."

"Maybe you could run them with me. You could run unofficially. I'd like that."

"I couldn't stay up with you. I could do a 2:45, maybe."

He was gazing softly, getting sleepy. "We have to start

thinking about 1980. We could double in the 10,000 and the marathon that time."

"You're going to be a busy father by then," I said.

"Yeah," he said. "We have to start fox-hunting when we get back."

I gave him a massage. He kept saying it felt so good.

"Poor Vince," he said softly, his eyes closed. "He ought to find somebody. He's so alone."

Suddenly he was asleep, breathing slowly and shallowly like a child. It was about quarter of ten. Quietly I turned out the bedside light, and lay down by him carefully so that he didn't wake up. Sleepy and relaxed myself, I drifted straight off.

How many more times would I have embraced him that night, how many more times would I have kissed him, if I had known the name of that stranger lover who was already in Montréal, who had already bought his stadium ticket from a scalper for the 5,000 tomorrow?

That implacable lover who was going to turn Billy's eyes away from me forever.

EIGHTEEN

It was just a few minutes before the 5,000 final began.

Those minutes, plus the thirteen-odd minutes that the race would last, and another day, and we could all go home.

The twelve runners were jogging up and down the track, keeping warm and loose until the moment the officials told them to go to the line. In the infield, the high-jump finals were going on. The marathon was out being run on its 26.2-mile course through Montréal, and would finish up here later. Right after the 5,000 the 1,500 final would be run—the race that Vince should have been in, and wasn't.

The murmur of the stadium spilled down onto the track. Nobody was watching the high jumpers. They were all watching the two slender runners jogging around, Billy and Armas Sepponan. I knew that the eye of the TV cameras would be fixed on them. Via satellite, their image would be flashed to millions of viewers in dozens of countries. It was safe to say that the entire civilized world was looking at Billy at that moment.

He was unaware, inward, alert, as he jogged along the straight, then wheeled gently and came back. His number 928 was pinned to his breast. Dellinger passed him jogging the other way, but they didn't look at each other.

Vince was by me, wearing his sleeveless jerkin. Next

to him was Mike Stella, who had bombed out in the 5,000 heats.

Vince looked at me. "Harlan, right now he's not even thinking about you." He smiled a little.

"'I hope not," I said.

The crowd's murmur grew. The officials were motioning the runners to the line. They stood there in a ragged little row, loose, doing their final psychs, hands on hips, looking around a little. Then their line straightened, crisp, military, each man bent and toeing the mark.

We scarcely heard the starter's pistol as the crowd yelled them off.

I sat there keeping track of Billy's laps. This time around, I was a bit more relaxed. Possibly, as I looked back on it, it was the months of fatigue setting in. Even if he loses, I was thinking, he'll still have the gold from the 10,000. Very likely he'll get a silver or a bronze here. It won't be a great tragedy, really. He will have made his point.

With his usual cheerful willingness to be the guinea pig, Billy had put his body up front. He was clipping along at a near-world record pace. He wasn't running away this time, just teasing them on at that punishing tempo. The field went with him, Sepponan running in next-to-last place. They were nicely bunched. Billy pulled them through the first 3,000 meters, averaging 62 seconds a lap.

At 3,000 Billy shook up the field by accelerating sharply. They started stringing out behind him. The next lap he gave them was a 58.1. Doggedly, Bob Dellinger had moved into the No. 2 slot, and Sepponan was forced to start moving up.

"Here we go," said Vince. "The show's on."

In the next lap, Billy raised the ante to 57.3. With the runners well into the last half of the race, the crowd noise was swelling. So intense was their concentration that you didn't feel the usual "dead space" that the crowd sometimes feels in these long-distance races on the track.

The field, a little shaken by his display of confidence,

was really stringing out now, and Sepponan moving up on the outside. Billy led by thirty yards. Dellinger struggled gamely to stay ahead of Armas, then let go, and Armas was in the clear.

The crowd had surged to its feet and the yell had risen to its Olympic shriek—that massed yell of humanity that you hear only at the Games, high-pitched, deafening as the keening of a hurricane wind.

They went into the next-to-last lap. Now it was Billy's and Armas' race, with the rest trailing and shattered. Armas was kicking, rapidly closing the gap between himself and Billy. Vince had his hand clenched on my arm so tightly that it might have hurt had I been more aware.

Through my glasses, I watched that distant pale figure, stretched out in full flight, with his long hanging slow stride. His sweaty face was as calm as if he were swinging along a trail in the woods. Mike was yelling hoarsely and jumping half out of his seat. Betsy was shrieking on the other side of me.

They came streaking down the straight and into the final lap. The bell clanged. Their long legs were devouring the track. Armas was now fifteen yards behind Billy. Billy had forced him to start his kick early, but still . . . I started wondering. It was possible that we had gambled wrong, and that Billy should have tried a runaway after all. He possibly was going to kill himself with this last blazing lap, and fade near the finish, letting Armas gun him down.

Billy turned his head quickly and saw Armas hauling him down. Incredibly he accelerated again. Everyone around us seemed to be going berserk.

Vince and Mike weren't yelling any more, just sitting and staring.

"This last lap," said Vince, "is going to be murder. They're *sprinting.*"

"Yeah," I said numbly, "it looks like it's going to be under 50 seconds. The last mile is going to be under 4."

I thought distractedly of the rare occasions when a

last lap like this was run. Juha Vaatainen in the Helsinki Games 10,000 meter in 1971. Marty Liquori and Jim Ryun in the Martin Luther King Games.

The two of them swept into the first turn of the last lap. In the infield, the high jumpers had knocked off because they couldn't concentrate. For a few moments, all I could see through my glasses were the two men's sweat-soaked backs. Armas' hair flopped wetly, and ahead, Billy's curls lifted moistly.

Then, as they rounded the turn, their profiles came into view. They were both hurting now, and both blocking that hurt. Armas' face was twisted into a grimace. Billy's face was still smooth, but the pain was in his eyes, in his open mouth with the teeth showing slightly, in the slight rhythmic jerk of his head.

They stormed into the backstraight, Armas now five yards behind.

I felt that deep prickling rise of my hackles, as always on the few occasions when Billy really awed me. Actually, they both awed me. We were watching some elemental force of nature, a storm at sea, a volcano erupting, an earthquake.

So much history, so many lives, went into each of their strides. From centuries of genes and family affairs to the last red corpuscle crammed in at high altitude. In Billy's case, I knew the factors more intimately: the clash about his training, the hills on the Prescott trails, the kiss in the movie theater, my efforts to shield his peace of mind, right down to the tender loving and the massage last night. Even the people who'd hassled him had helped forge his stubborness. It was all being put together now.

As his great strides gulped up the backstraight, I could see him again on the Prescott track that first morning, reeling out those beautiful 60-second quarters. I could hear him saying, "I'm thinking of the Olympics," and myself saying, "That's a big order."

As they went into the last turn, I stood dead silent, with chills running up and down me. They were both splendid as the sun, terrible as an army with banners. There was no doubt in the mind of anybody in that stadium that this was going to be one of the great runs, and a record at the end of it that would stand for a long time.

As they peeled out of the last turn, Armas had pulled up to Billy's shoulder. They both looked sick now, both deeply in oxygen debt, both dizzy and calling on the last bit of glycogen. They were both running like animals.

Armas hung at Billy's shoulder for about ten strides. And then, almost in mid-stride, he cracked. Billy had broken him. With whatever his final fatal edge was, gay desperation or maybe just Vitamin E pills, he had broken the iron Finn.

Still in control, though dying himself, Billy pulled away. He was a yard ahead, then two yards, as Armas came apart at the seams.

I felt my muscles go limp with relief. Vince grabbed my arm and shook me with silent joyous delirium.

The two were halfway down the straight to the finish line, with those two yards between them and Armas staggering, when it happened.

Later on, in the videotape, I would see it in slow motion. Billy seemed to falter a little, and his head snapped a little to the left. Then his legs gave way under him, just as if somebody had flicked the switch powering his legs to "off." Still burning forward, yet falling at the same time, he slumped slowly, gracefully to the track.

As he hit the red Tartan, the jolt snapped through his body. He slid a little on his left side, his right leg sliding forward as if to take one last stride. His head struck heavily against the low board rim on the inside of the track.

Actually, it happened so fast that the crowd didn't burst its lungs with a huge scream until it was over.

On the videotape, you could see Armas, dazed, glancing down at Billy as he passed him. "I thought it was luck,"

Armas would say later. Then he gathered himself and ran
heavily on, easing the pace sharply because he didn't have
to worry about anybody catching him. When he hit the
tape, he was staggering.

Back up the straight, Billy lay sprawled by the board,
in lane 1. He didn't move. The other runners were skirting
him, looking at him, running on.

I was worried, not even thinking of the lost medal.
What could have happened? All kinds of crazy possibilities
ran through my mind. At the least, a terrible muscle pull.
A concussion as his head hit the board. A massive leg
cramp. A heart attack.

Beyond the finish line, Armas was on his hands and
knees, looking more like a spent decathlete. Officials were
running toward Billy. I also saw the U.S. team doctor and
distance coach Taplinger running toward him. The stadium
was a sea of babbling and comment. Many people were
applauding Armas' victory, but just as many were standing,
their eyes fixed on Billy.

He did not move.

I was already scrambling down to the track, pushing
and shoving blindly. Vince and Mike were behind me.

We were on the track. Several officials tried to stop
us. I shouldered one out of the way. Vince punched one.
Three of them caught Mike and held him.

Vince and I ran up the track.

A number of people were already bending around Billy.
Tay Parker was kneeling by his head, and motioning them
back. "Give him air," he said. "Get away."

Billy lay on his left side, with his left arm flung forward
on the track, the gold ring glinting on it. His face was
turned down and his hair fell forward, hiding it. He had
fallen with such force that his glasses had been jolted off.
They lay just ahead of him, shattered. The only motion in
him was the sweat trickling earthward on his limbs. It
seemed incredible that this body, which seconds ago had
been moving as fast as a distance-running man is capable,
could be so still.

"He may have hit his head on the board there," Tay Parker was saying.

Then we saw a little pool of blood spreading from under his hair. It was the darkish blood of a runner deep in oxygen debt. I told myself that I didn't see it.

"Christ," said Parker. "He couldn't have hit himself that hard."

The officials, bug-eyed, were crowding around. Parker motioned them away again. Vince was kneeling by Billy's feet.

Gently Parker turned Billy over. Then we saw what his hair had hid. The whole left temple and part of his forehead was gone. In their place was a pink and white bleeding crater. Bits of bone, blood and brain had exploded down his face and into his hair. Pieces of bone, with hair attached, came away in Parker's hands.

I told myself that I did not see this.

Parker was shaking his head, dazed. He was feeling in Billy's hair on the other side of his head.

"I can't believe this," he said. "It's a bullet wound."

"A bullet wound?" I repeated stupidly.

"I was a medic in Nam, I've seen plenty of them," said Parker. "Look, here's where it went in." He showed us the small, dark red hole, parting Billy's hair so that the sunlight hit it.

I was kneeling there clutching Billy's warm limp hand as he lay there with his head on Parker's knees. It was beginning to occur to me that his hand would never squeeze mine again.

I looked dumbly up at all their faces. They were all silent, stunned, not reacting yet. Gus Lindquist had just come up and shouldered through the group, and was getting his first look at Billy's bloody head. Our eyes met. At that minute, I think, Lindquist began to understand the tragedy that he had participated in.

It was Vince who cried the unutterable cry for me. He bent down over Billy's feet, his head almost touching them, and he gave a sound like an animal being crushed to death in a press. He stayed there like that, holding Billy's spiked feet, and sobbing in that suffocated way, as if there were no air in his lungs.

Slowly I let Billy's hand go. I picked up his broken glasses and my fingers closed around them so hard that the glass crackled. On the track where he had lain, there was a wet imprint of sweat from his limbs. It was already drying.

I looked at his eyes. They were half-open, gazing softly, so clear, so empty now. The left eye had a film of blood over it.

Some of the runners had come jogging back up the track to see what the trouble was. Armas, somewhat recovered now, was with them. He bent beside me, looked at Billy, muttered something in Finnish, and put one hand over his eyes. His shoulders started to shake. Someone pulled him to his feet and led him away.

Someone put his arms across my shoulders. I looked blankly up, into Mike Stella's face. He was dead white, and the tears had run clear down to his jaws. Tay Parker was kneeling there with Billy's head on his knees, crying. More and more people were coming across the infield. A photographer shouldered his way through the group and flashed a picture. Then another one.

It began to occur to me that it was strange—all these tears, but none in my own eyes. I was clenching the broken glasses so hard that my hand was cut.

Suddenly the voice of the announcer cut through everything.

"Ladies and gentlemen, Billy Sive is badly hurt . . . the information reaching us from the track is garbled . . . a correction . . . we regret to announce..." The announcer's voice was breaking. "We regret . . . Billy Sive is dead . . ."

A wave of gasps and screams went through that huge place. Even in my benumbed state I felt it.

". . . Dead . . . apparently shot from the stands . . ."

Screams of panic at the thought of a gunman loose in the crowd.

". . . Ladies and gentlemen, please, no panic . . . the police have arrested the gunman as . . . trying to leave the stadium . . ."

The voice was cutting through my head.

"Billy Sive is dead . . ." The announcer himself breaking up, trying to control his voice.

The high jumpers and officials beginning to run across the infield, abandoning their event.

Somebody was prying my hand open, taking away from me the broken glasses, mopping my hand with a handkerchief. I was helping Tay to carry Billy. He was so warm and limp, and his shattered head rolled against my breast. They had killed him, right there on the track where we'd thought he was safest.

" . . . Dead . . . shocking . . . tragic . . . keep calm . . . the athletes are . . ."

In the first-aid room, Tay was picking the glass out of my hand and taking a few stitches. Billy was on a stretcher, covered with a sheet. Someone was jabbing a sedative shot into Vince's shoulder to quiet him down.

My eyes were dry. They were almost unblinking.

The times were still up there on the huge scoreboard.

ARMAS SEPPONAN   FINLAND 13.04.5
FRANCOIS GEFFROY   FRANCE 13:10.1
JOHN FELTS   AUSTRALIA 13:10.9
VITALIY KOSTENKO   USSR 13:11.4
BOB DELLINGER   USA 13:11.6

It was not until later that I was able to reflect on the irony. Only death could force my front-runner to give away a world record, like the one he gave to Armas.

It was not until later that I was able to reflect on it as history. At Munich and Mexico City they had slaughtered the innocents out of sight, behind the scenes. Here they had slaughtered the innocent in full sight of the crowd, at the peak of his life.

NINETEEN

S lowly, in the next couple of days, as Canadian police questioned Billy's killer, the story came out.

How he became increasingly disturbed at our existence, how his latent, repressed homosexuality made him fear love, and hate Billy. How he became obsessed with the idea of killing Billy on the track, how he finally decided there was no better place to do it than the Olympics.

How Richard Mech traveled to Canada weeks before the games. How he posed as a workman, smuggled his weapon into the stadium and concealed it, foreseeing that security would be tight because of all the rumors. How he was not able to carry out his plan during the 10,000 meter, and had to wait till the following Sunday. How he stood in one of the exits off the stands, holding the rifle under his coat. How he snatched it out quickly as Billy and Armas rounded the last turn and no one paid any attention because they were screaming and yelling. How he held his fire because he didn't want to hit Armas by mistake. How he fired as Billy pulled away in his finishing sprint.

Like me, Mech was a military man and a marksman. Like me, he loved the Bible. But in his fear he saw himself as God's avenging angel, sent to wipe Billy from the earth with the ardor of his own personal fire and brimstone. Insane though he was, I understood him.

That was the terrible thing. In spite of my grief, I

understood just what had gone on in Mech's mind. He and
I had branched from the same American root.

We took Billy's body back to New York on a special
jet supplied by the Canadian government. The whole
group was still together. John had collapsed in the stands
when he saw it happen, but he was able to walk off the
plane unaided at Kennedy, white and unspeaking. Even
the Angel had seemed to understand that his
nonthreatening acquaintance had been killed, and he cried
against Steve's shoulder.

I was still experiencing things without reacting to them.
It seemed to me that I had become a camera, that recorded
images in a mechanical way.

In New York, I recall being in a large room somewhere
with a lot of reporters and a mike in front of me, and
making some remarks about how if I could have every
person who had hassled Billy, from people who wrote him
hate letters to officials who wanted him off the track,
charged in court with first-degree murder, I would do so.
But I added that unfortunately there were not enough
courts and lawyers in the country to process the case.

The world was in its usual state of futile guilt. We
have all become so accustomed to violence that the hand-
wringing was now just a social ritual. There were editorials
about how such things shouldn't happen. I read some of
them. Unbelievably, there were also people who said that
Billy deserved to die.

The gays had occupied buildings in New York and
Washington, demanding a Congressional investigation into
the continuing persecution of gay people, demanding the
death penalty for Richard Mech. Thousands of shocked
straights flocked to these demonstrations, most of them
young. Like an automaton, I put in an appearance at one
of the big zaps in New York, and said a few words to the
massed men and women, and was overwhelmed by their
grief and sympathy, which I did not know how to react to.

The athletes, now home in their countries, were saying that unless their lives could be unconditionally guaranteed at the next Olympics, they would not go. They had struck and walked off the field Sunday after Billy was killed. The Montréal games had ended with the running of the 5,000 meter. Armas Sepponan and the other two finishers had refused their medals. The victory stand stood empty. The anthem was not played. The closing ceremonies had turned into a gigantic memorial service for Billy, with festivities canceled. The Olympic flame was dimmed out with the stands packed and everybody weeping but me.

It looked as if Billy's death might have broken the back of the Olympic movement.

But the only thing now real to me was Billy's body in the expensive ornate black coffin hastily supplied in Montréal.

There was the decision of what kind of arrangements to make.

"The decision is yours," said John.

"A big messy funeral," I said, "so the gays can cry over him. Then cremate him."

The funeral at the Church of the Beloved Disciple on Fourteenth Street was bigger and messier than even I'd anticipated. It was a hot muggy day, and gays were fainting in their feathers, sweltering in their leather. The streets around the church were packed. It was another of those gay social affairs overrun by straights and celebrities and tourists. The police had a hard time maintaining order. The separatist gays tried to beat up some straights and chase them off, saying, "This is our funeral." Finally I had to go out and talk to them. In the name of Billy's nonviolence, I asked them to let everyone come that wanted to.

The hot church was packed with hard, gay faces. The smell of sweat, leather and flowers was overpowering— the only smell that was missing was amyl nitrite.

I sat in the front pew with the group, staring at the casket.

It had stood open there for a day and a half, almost—

you could say—in state. Thousands of people, mostly gays and young people, had filed past it. Billy had belonged to the young, and he had been openly, coldly assassinated, like a Kennedy, a King. They looked at him and cried and piled flowers around the coffin and spoke yet again of how American society was insensible to human subtleties.

Billy lay there wearing his brown velvet suit. Behind his glasses, his eyes were closed. The gold medal lay on the ruffled breast of his shirt. His left hand, laid over his right, wore the gold wedding ring. The Montréal undertaker had washed the blood out of his hair, combed it carefully, and had done a passable job on his head. But no, he didn't look like he was sleeping.

The angel of death had cruised him. Death, that hustler, that last lover.

Delphine had put a huge bouquet of white lilies on his body. He had tried hard to find hyacinths, but found to his surprise that hyacinths don't bloom in September. So he had settled for two weeks' groceries' worth of lilies, and their fragrance seemed to fill the church.

The Prescott pro musica played some slow mournful Renaissance songs. Jacques had come, and blew into his recorder waveringly, sometimes breaking off.

Father Moore stood up in the pulpit. The church was very quiet as he spoke.

"Harlan Brown has asked me not to deliver a eulogy," he said. "And he's right. Billy's eulogy is written in thousands of hearts. Anything we could add would be superfluous. Instead, Harlan has asked me to read some passages from the Bible and from the teachings of Buddha that he and Billy read at their wedding."

We all sat with sweat rolling down our bodies. Not a sound disturbed the silence of the church, except an occasional muffled sob from somebody. In his gentle, deep voice, the gay priest read those immortal words:

"'Let us live without hate among those who hate . . .'

"'Set me as a seal upon your heart, as a seal upon your arm, for love is strong as death . . .'"

Surely I'm going to cry now, I thought. Oh God, help me to cry. I don't even want to be comforted.

But my eyes stayed dry and burning. With all its strength, my body denied his death. Yet in my mind, his death was so present that I couldn't even remember him. As the priest read those passages, I tried to recall how Billy had looked sitting on the grass in that brown velvet suit, with the spring sunshine bright on his hair. But the image was gone.

The gay priest was saying, ". . . And I'll close this brief service with a contribution of my own. It's fitting, I think. It's A.E. Housman's poem 'To an Athlete Dying Young.'"

As he read it, I tried to remember how Billy had looked running on the track in Montréal, just—it seemed—scant hours ago. But the image was gone.

"'. . . And find unwithered on his curls/ That garland briefer than a girl's,'" Father Moore read, finishing the poem.

Beside me, Vince bent over his knees, choking out loud. John sat very straight and silent with the tears running down his cheeks. A wave of sobs went through the church.

Even Father Moore was crying. He looked down at the coffin and said in a stifled voice, "Good-bye, Billy. One of the joys of paradise will be seeing your blithe spirit again. Good-bye."

After the funeral, we took him to a Manhattan funeral home. The director, a gay man, had offered his services free of charge. We watched the casket rolled away to the crematorium.

A few of us stayed and waited. His death was before me. I had X-ray eyes and could see through the thick walls of the crematorium. I could hear the roar of the retort and feel the heat. The flaming coffin burst open, and the fire ravished that perfect body. It cramped into rictus. the curls ablaze, the velvet smoldering, the brain seething in the shattered forehead. Molten glass dripped from his eyes, and molten gold ran off his breast.

He would not burn like other men. No fat there, only bone to char and muscle protein to carbonize. The lactate would still be in his blood from that last effort.

Several hours later, the funeral-home director put in my hands a heavy tin canister, labeled with Billy's name and the date, containing his ashes.

The next day I departed from the group, and drove back up to Prescott alone. I had told everyone to stay strictly away from me for the next 48 hours, and they did.

The house was just as we'd left it. The Irish setter ran to meet me—one of the campus maintenance men had been feeding him. He jumped and barked. Billy's bicycle stood on the porch. In the border, a few lilies, asters and phlox were in bloom. Behind the house, the tomato plants were wilting a little from lack of water, but they had ripe tomatoes on them.

Moving like an automaton, I put the sprinkler by them and turned the water on.

In the house, a pair of his old Tigers, the ones he wore for everyday, lay dusty by the door. His typewriter on the table by the window, and the folders full of plans for the gay-studies program. In the kitchen, nuts and cereals on the shelf, and a few much-sprouted potatoes in the refrigerator. His belts and old jeans hanging in the closet. The burled-walnut bed, with dust on the bedspread.

I locked the door and sat alone in the house the rest of the day, not eating, hardly moving. The canister of ashes sat on the bedside table. It was hard to remember that he'd existed. Yet there were those ashes, and those things in the house, and a dozen semen samples in a clinic deep-freeze, and one Olympic world record, and all the headlines, and all the memories of him in other people's minds.

Night came. I had asked the campus switchboard to take all calls, and nothing disturbed the silence of the house. I lay down on the bed fully clothed, with all the lights out. Through the window came the soft soughing of the breeze in the spruce boughs. Then, as the hours passed, I could hear a dripping from the eaves. It was raining, a gentle warm autumn rain. The canister sat on the bedside table.

Exhausted, I must have dozed off. Suddenly I woke up with a terrible start. A sound. I lay on my elbow, listening. In the silence of the house, it came again. A clear musical clink in the kitchen, like a teacup.

I began to shake all over violently, and a hot prickling sweat sprang out on me. In that moment, possibly, I was close to insanity. I got quickly out of bed and went into the living room. The sound came again, making me shudder with a terrible joy. My legs trembling, I went toward the kitchen. What did I expect to see there?

A dark shape moved in the kitchen, came toward me.

It was the dog. He had been nosing in his china feed bowl, and his metal ID tag had struck musically against it. He was hungry, and sad, and came whining to me, pushing his nose into my hand.

Sinking into a kitchen chair, I sat there a while and managed to stop shaking. Then I turned on the light, opened a can of dog food and fed him.

The gray light came at the windows, later now that the season was advancing. Did I expect to hear the joyous abandoned bird songs? But it was fall, and few birds sang now.

I got up and put my shoes on. It was just past five a.m. Without putting on a raincoat, I took the canister in the crook of my arm, left the dog shut in the house, and went out alone.

First I went over to the old cinder track, and scattered a couple of handfuls of his ashes there, to sweeten the spikes of my freshmen. I felt no horror at handling them. In fact, I felt nothing at all.

Then, with the mist cool in my face, I took the long three-mile walk up into the woods. No one had used the main trail since Billy and I had last run there, back in

July. The marks of our spikes had long ago been washed away by the rain.

Turning off onto the side trail, I made my way along, detouring around poison ivy and getting my pants caught in brambles. Finally I came down the slope through the mountain laurel. The seed pods hung on the laurel like clusters of tiny green grapes. The clearing was all grown up with ferns, which were now yellowing and dying down. The leaves on the giant beeches were browning a little. The waterfall over the mossy ledge had dried up to a tiny trickle.

I scattered the rest of his ashes there. I scraped a hole in the loam and buried the canister. Then I washed the ashes and dirt from my fingers in the trickle dripping from the ledge.

The Buddhists would have said that he'd been returned to the round of life.

Two weeks later, school opened and I went back to coaching. Joe Prescott had offered to give me a semester off, with my assistants taking over, so that I could go off somewhere and rest. But I didn't see how that would help me.

A week after the flood of students arrived, I gave the usual campus-wide talk with color slides, to get the kids to turn out for track. The talk wasn't up to its usual par— I didn't crack any jokes—in fact, it was more low-key than usual. But 115 freshmen boys and girls signed up immediately. It was the largest number I'd ever had.

In addition, we had another influx of quality runners from other colleges and universities. For the first time, we were going to have a big-time team in terms of depth, rather than in terms of a couple of superstars like Billy and Vince. The boys came to me with their eyes blazing with ambition, and with sympathy because of Billy. Several wanted to talk about the 1980 Olympics.

Two more gay runners came to me, a pair of

marathoners from UCLA. I had to shelter them. Who else would, if I didn't? Billy would have died in vain if I had turned them away because of my personal grief.

"But you're coached by me at your own risk," I told them. "Make sure you understand that."

In the warm autumn sunshine, I was out at the track-side every day, with the Harper Split in my hand and runners hurtling by, their spikes gnashing in the cinders. For the first time in my life, I saw those runners stripped of sexual myth. They were moving objects, oxygen capacity of lungs, glycogen breakdown, nothing more.

I tried hard to remember Billy running on that track, standing by the bleachers toweling himself, his shoulders and thighs steaming in the winter sunlight. But his living memory had been obliterated. As I looked at the track, all I could see was his body laying in lane 1 with the broken glasses by it.

In the locker room, I could see his body on the bench, one leg fallen aside, the spiked shoe resting on the cement floor. The blood was dripping slowly from his head onto the floor.

At every spot on campus where a memory of him might have been evoked, I saw instead his death. It was stuck in my mind like a color slide stuck in a projector. In our living room, he had fallen forward in his chair with his head on his typewriter, and the blood had run onto the disordered papers. Out in the yard, he lay dead in the unmown grass, by the last asters in bloom in the border.

It was the same in New York City, when John and I sometimes went down on business. We passed Central Park and I could glimpse the carousel off through the trees—he was slumped on the gilded horse, his head leaning on the pole, and blood ran down the pole as the carousel turned slowly, playing "After the Ball Is Over." We passed the theaters where the all-male films play, and I could see him laying in the seat with his head fallen back, his shirt open. In the light from the screen, the blood glistened on his face.

For the first time in my life, I cursed the control I had—that control that had deprived me of five months of his love. I prayed to God, "You're helping me too much, God. You've made me too strong. Lay off a little. Let me come apart at the seams, let me cry, let me grieve, let me go a little berserk and howl and beat my head against a wall."

I ran ten miles every day, prepared the cross-country team for the upcoming Eastern meets, and fended off necrophiliac reporters.

With both Vince and Billy gone, the gay-studies program was drifting rudderless. Joe quickly brought in a young New York activist, Jan Van Deusen, to take over, and he, the psychotherapist and several students pulled it together. It wasn't easy, because Billy's compassion and personality had been its heart. But Van Deusen agreed with me and with Joe Prescott that such a program had to have a value independent of that of the people running it. Shortly the gay-crisis switchboard was in operation again, to take those sporadic but desperate calls from other campuses, some of them from miserable athletes.

That fall I saw little of Vince. After Billy's death, he had seemed to go completely haywire. In a way, I envied his enormous capacity for experiencing grief.

He announced that he didn't want to run any more, and quit the pro tour, and hung up his spikes. Settling in New York, he shortly was involved in the heaviest kind of gay activism. His status as Billy's best friend, his own status, his raging grief and his physical impressiveness moved him immediately into the front ranks of the radical gay leaders. Shortly he wore the charisma of a revolutionary.

When Vince did come up to Prescott to see me, or when I ran into him in New York, he always talked about Billy so much that I was glad when he left. He was the only one in my circle of acquaintances who hadn't learned that I couldn't bear even to have Billy's name mentioned in my hearing.

With the cross-country season under way, I had to face up to the "fox-hunting," as Billy called it in Montréal. I wondered emotionlessly if maybe, with his child around, I would finally be able to feel human again. It was a painful business, and I might have procrastinated, except that the doctor warned me that the frozen semen was good for only about two and one-half years. If we found a suitable woman soon, we might be able to get two children out of those samples.

One afternoon in late October, Betsy Heden came to talk to me in my office in the athletic building. She was wearing a long tightly belted green raincoat, carrying her briefcase, and her hair was damp.

She sat down in the oak armchair by my desk, and we talked about her running. She was having some problems doing the amount of training for the level I thought she could be running at.

"The trouble with me is, I'm not very competitive," she said. "I think deep down I just do it to feel good and have a nice figure. I'm not really motivated."

"Motivation is important," I said.

"Like Billy," she said. "He was motivated."

I looked down at the desk. After a moment, she said softly, "I'm sorry, Harlan."

"It's my fault," I said. "I just haven't adjusted."

She sat there looking down at her briefcase on her lap, very slender and contained. She had taken Billy's death as hard as anybody among his friends, and it had left her quieter, less of a soapbox orator. She had been burying herself in her senior-year studies, and had not been attending the team open house.

"Harlan," she said, "you've got to forgive me, but there's something I have to talk to you about."

A class was trooping past in the corridor, and I got up

and hung the COACH IN CONFERENCE sign on the door and closed it.

"I heard that you're looking for a woman to . . . to . . ."

"Who told you that?" I barked. I'd been very anxious that this wouldn't get bandied around.

"Vince did. Don't worry. He didn't tell anybody else, and I didn't."

"Vince always did talk too much," I said bitterly.

"Don't be mad at him. He just wanted to help. Anyway, what I wanted to say was . . ." She sat playing with the handle on her briefcase. ". . . Billy was the sweetest friend I ever had. He was the only man I never felt threatened with. I really hated men up until then. Men always seemed so egotistical and out to satisfy themselves. Billy showed me that they could be gentle, and that they can be an awfully good kind of a friend."

I sat straight and immobile, staring straight ahead at the piles of papers on my desk, schedules, entries for meets, track magazines.

"Anyway," said Betsy, "I've been thinking. I've always wanted to have a baby. But, like, I couldn't stand to let myself be screwed by some guy, even for that. But . . ."

She was blushing just a little now. "If it's artificial insemination you're going to do . . . I think if there's one guy whose baby I'd have, it would be Billy's. You understand what I mean? Just because he was a friend. I'd do that for him."

I found that I had both hands over my face. In that moment, I found out how great my capacity for feeling pain still was.

She was sitting right there in the chair where Billy had sat on the day we'd met. I tried hard to remember how he had looked in his battered Mao jacket how he had fixed me with those clear eyes of his and said, "We're gay."

But I couldn't even remember it. In that moment, even the images of his death were obliterated. He had never existed. He was just a fantasy, one of those fantasies from the gay films where the lovers are always young and horny and beautiful and there is no death.

"Oh Harlan," she said, "I'm so sorry I made you cry," and she put her head down on a pile of papers on the side of my desk and started to sob.

"I'm not crying," I said.

But she kept on sobbing. I sat there unmoving— comforting weeping females had never been a specialty of mine. Finally she quieted down, sat up and fished in her Mexican over-the-shoulder bag, presumably for Kleenex. Silently I hauled out my own handkerchief and gave it to her.

"It isn't clean," I apologized.

"That's all right," she said, and blew her nose in it and wiped her eyes.

I was trembling just a little.

"Well," she said, "I don't know what you're looking for in a . . . a woman. Maybe I don't meet the requirements. Would you consider me?"

I looked at her. We had never, for some reason, considered the idea of a lesbian, and I wasn't so sure. On the other hand, we knew Betsy far better than some stranger we'd be screening. And Billy had cared for her. That made it more personal, more fitting somehow.

"Well, here's the deal," I said, and explained what would be required of her.

"Look," she said, "it's okay if you pay the medical expenses, but I don't want to be paid extra. But the problem is, I want a baby to take away and keep for myself."

"Who says we have to stop at one baby?" I said. "He left a dozen specimens. If you give me one, you can have another one for yourself."

She nodded. "That sounds reasonable."

"And we have to have the doctor check you out first," I said. "I don't want anybody with hereditary diseases. And we have to make sure you're functioning right before we start. We can't waste even one of those specimens. You understand, don't you?"

"I hate doctors."

"This is a gay doctor," I said. "I think he'll be all right."

"Actually," she said, "it's not as if I'm going to take the baby away to the North Pole. I'll be around here, probably. We'll see each other, the children can get together. Maybe we can live in the same neighborhood or something. I think you'd feel sad if I took one of Billy's children far away somewhere. Wouldn't you?"

The doctor found her to be a healthy female with a clean medical history. He ran some tests, ensured that she was ovulating and determined the exact day for her insemination. One day in November, we were in his examination room. I had requested to be there, because every cell of my body cried out that I should be there, and Betsy, after some vacillation, had agreed.

She lay draped modestly on the table, her knees up and her bare feet on the sides of the table. She had refused to put her feet in the metal stirrups. Her cheeks were afire.

"Now don't you look at me, Harlan," she said.

"Why the hell would I want to look at you?" I said.

The doctor was very gentle with her, but she winced anyway when he inserted the speculum. Then, as he had explained, he inverted a small cup containing the precious thawed semen over the cervix.

"Now just lay there for twenty minutes," said the doctor.

We were alone in the room, the door closed, hearing the nurses bustle gently in the corridor outside, smelling the medical smells. Betsy lay looking up at the ceiling, her knees flat now, completely covered by the stiff white drape.

Suddenly she smiled.

"What?" I said.

"Oh, I was just thinking," she said. "It's a front-runner's race going on in there."

I found myself smiling. "How do you know there aren't any kickers in there?"

I found myself taking her slender hand and patting it. "You're one of the few women I've ever known," I said, "that's worth a damn."

Nothing happened that month, and we both got very worried. I was keeping track of the days on an old training schedule, and I think I was more nervous than she was.

But the next time around, in early January, Betsy said gloatingly, "I've missed my period."

She finished her senior year getting bigger and bigger. "Betsy, have you gone straight?" the students asked her incredulously. She smiled mysteriously. Only she, I, Vince and John Sive knew that it was Billy's child.

Betsy became very involved in her pregnancy. She took scrupulous care of herself, exercised moderately, jogged clear into her sixth month, and talked about natural childbirth to anybody who would listen.

The baby was born on September 2, 1977, three weeks early, at Lenox Hill Hospital in New York. I would have liked to be in the delivery room, but under the circumstances that was hardly possible. And it was probably just as well—Betsy had a difficult delivery because of her narrow hips.

John and I went through the waiting-room agonies. If I'd been a smoker, I'd have filled a couple of ashtrays at least.

Finally the doctor came in, smiling. "It's a boy. He's a small baby, only five pounds, eight ounces. But they're both fine."

"Billy was small when he was born too," said John.

Later, when we went into her room, Betsy was propped up on the pillows in a pink lace peignoir. She looked exhausted, out cold like a runner after a hard race. She was very pale. She had the peignoir open, and was giving the baby what she had impressed on us as being the important first breast-feeding.

She colored when she saw us, but she smiled a little, weakly, and didn't cover her breast. Her eyes were almost defiant. We sat down by the bed and watched. "I'm a *little* disappointed," said Betsy. "I wanted a girl. But it doesn't matter, he's a lovely baby."

When the baby finished nursing, she put him in my arms and opened the wrap so we could see him. He was a quiet little thing, so small and slender that I worried. He had the fine bones and fair skin of both his parents. But he kicked his tiny feet against me with surprising strength. He had a few wisps of pale brown hair, and his squinty blue eyes looked up at me unseeingly.

I sat riven with pain, thinking of the body that had sired this mite of life.

That pain never seemed to diminish. I would go along for days, surviving, managing to be businesslike and cheerful and concerned about other people's lives, and suddenly the ground would give way under my feet and I'd fall 10,000 meters into pain. In New York, we might pass the Continental Baths, or the Bedford Theater, or the restaurant where we always ate, and it would hit me like a blow.

I had sat in the doctor's waiting room one day while the doctor gave Betsy the periodic examination, and I was fishing through the old magazines looking for something to read, and there was the year-old issue of *Time* with our faces on the cover. Billy must have existed—there was his face. Driven by a kind of fatalism, I turned to the cover story and the two pages of photographs. There we were, sitting on the green grass, side by side, our arms around each other, kissing. There we were at the track, I standing there with the Harper Split in my hand, shouting the split time at him as he blurred past. The photographer had caught his long floating stride at its greatest stretch.

John and I had visited Steve and the Angel out on Fire Island that spring, and we had all walked along the beach barefoot. It was a cloudy windy day and the surf was a little rough. Our numbers were fewer—Vince,

Jacques and Delphine were gone. Only the four of us were left.

We walked up the shore until only the lonely dunes were by us, their grasses blowing in the wind. We came to, and passed, the spot where Billy and I had made love. But the only image in my memory was his body being carried in by the white foam and left laying on the sand. His hair was full of sand and seaweed, and he did not move. As the foam came up again and again, it simply moved his limp legs a little.

Was it possible that we had known each other for only twenty-one months? We had met on December 8, 1974, and he was killed on September 9, 1976. It seemed to me that I had lived through several lifetimes of suffering before I met him, and several lifetimes of love in those twenty-one months. I would not be able to love anyone like that again.

I sat cradling his child. He had said he would be reborn. But it was an illusion, perhaps the only one he had permitted himself. We would never again know each other as we had. There is no marriage in heaven, not even for gays.

Two weeks later, with Betsy recovered, we took the baby to the Church of the Beloved Disciple, and Father Moore christened him John William. Just a few people were there, and Steve Goodnight teased me a lot about being so middle-class as to want to christen the baby.

And still I could not cry.

TWENTY

At Thanksgiving, John Sive and Vince Matti came up to spend the holiday at Prescott with us. It was snowing heavily, a surprise early storm. When I saw John's car pull up the drive, I went out. Vince got out into the swirling snow, the first flakes of it sticking to his hair. He was wilder looking and hairier than ever. I had expected to see him heavier because of his not running, but he was as thin as ever from all the frantic activism and running around. His eyes met mine a little guardedly, but he squeezed my arm.

"Good to see you, Harlan," he said.

"Yes," I said. "We've lost touch."

Betsy was waiting at the door wearing a flowing red crepe pantsuit. Vince kissed her on the cheek and laughed a little. "How's my favorite Amazon?"

In the house, we sank into chairs by the fire and Vince looked around. "Been a while since I was here," he said. "You've changed some things." A little of the old teasing note entered his voice. "You've been decorating, Harlan. What's come over you?"

"That's Betsy's doing," I said. "She likes to mess around in the house. I've got a little money now, so she can do what she wants."

"When we drove up, I noticed the addition you built on," said Vince.

"Yeah, we needed a couple of extra rooms," I said.

"One for Betsy, one for the baby. What can I get you guys to drink?"

"The first thing I want is to see Billy's child," said Vince.

Just hearing his name wounded me.

"No sooner said than done," said Betsy.

She was bringing the baby out of the nursery. Little John was three months old by then, and wearing his pale blue sleeping outfit. Betsy kneeled down on the old Afghan rug by Vince's chair and put the baby on Vince's lap. Vince held up the baby tenderly so that John stood braced with his tiny feet on Vince's thighs.

"He's growing," said Vince. "That's Billy, all right. The brown hair and the eyes. God, Virgo eyes. Did you guys plan that?"

Everybody laughed but me. They laughed a little nervously, because they knew how I must be hurting. "No," said Betsy. "It just happened that way. The first time they tried to inseminate me, he would have been a Virgo, but it didn't take. The next month it did, and that would have made him a Libra. But then he was born three weeks premature, so that made him a Virgo." Her eyes were fixed on the baby, and she patted his diapered rear end.

I was beginning to realize that this was going to be a painful Thanksgiving. Vince's willingness to talk about Billy was going to pick all the scabs off the wounds.

John was dandling the baby now, his face alight. He was definitely the dotty grandfather.

He had asked for something to make him forget about sex, and he got it. Billy's death had shoved him into an angry, celibate and activist old age. He had moved to New York and started a law firm with three other gay lawyers. Burton, Cohen, Manolson & Sive was taking only discrimination cases against gay men and women, and John told me that the complaints were flooding in, the way they had from straight women after the women's lib movement began. John seemed bent on single-handedly winning enforcement of the Supreme Court decision in American life.

A poignant sign of his commitment was that he stopped tinting his hair—it was now streaked silver and natural. Just looking at John, that night, made me think of Billy.

"Well, what can I offer you guys to drink?" I said, getting up.

"Scotch on the rocks," said Vince. He was lighting a cigarette, drawing on it hungrily, inhaling deeply. I brought the drinks, and some 7-Up for myself. Betsy was just finishing peeling potatoes, and she took off her apron and came in with a glass of white wine. We sat talking about the things that mattered, and invariably the conversation touched on Billy.

For instance, Delphine's name was mentioned, and everyone fell silent a moment with pain. Finally Vince said softly, "Sleeping pills . . . just like a real woman."

John sighed heavily. "Poor Delphine. I never knew whether he was putting on, or psychotic. I couldn't have lived with him."

"He didn't kill himself because of that," said Vince. "He did it because of Billy. He was wild about him."

My hand tightened on my bottle of 7-Up.

A little later, Vince said, "Steve still in California?"

"Yes," I said, "or I would have had him up here tonight."

Vince laughed a little. "I still can't believe they're filming *Rape*. If they'd come around to me with that script two years ago, I would have said yes."

"You would have made a helluva virgin," I said, trying hard to fall back into our old-time teasing.

"Billy could have played that role, though," said Vince.

My hand was about to break the 7-Up bottle.

John tried to rescue me. "Steve still hasn't laid the Angel, you know. But he's getting there."

"Oh yeah?" said Vince, not really diverted from the subject of Billy.

"The kid doesn't talk," said John, "but he will now let Steve hold his hand and kiss him. Steve has him on methadone now, and he's hoping to get him off the habit entirely. The Angel is growing up too, and he's indecently beautiful."

"Billy was indecently beautiful," said Vince. He was already a little smashed.

The baby was wiggling in Betsy's lap with amazing strength. "That kid's going to be a sprinter," said Vince. "You sure you know about coaching sprinters, Harlan?"

I picked up the baby and jounced him on my knee hobby-horse until he smiled and grinned. "Well, I wouldn't object if he turned out to be an athlete," I said. "What I want most for him is to be free. Free to choose how he wants to live, and free to do it no matter what."

Vince was gazing sadly at the fire, one foot up on the brass fender, the smoke from his cigarette rising pale in the rosy light. "Do you ever hear from Jacques?" he said.

"Did you know he got married?" I asked.

"No." Vince turned pained eyes to me, then looked back at the fire.

"He's teaching biology at Illinois. He's got a grant to do field research on wild birds. He married a student of his, a girl named Eileen Meriwether, and she's helping him with his work. She seems like a nice enough girl. They're expecting their first child."

"So he's finally happy," said Vince, with a soft tone of bitterness.

"He seems peaceful. He's running again, you know."

Vince seemed suddenly depressed. "Well, I guess that was predictable. Track?"

"No. Long distance, road races. I think he likes to lose himself in those big fields. He's doing very well, just turned in a new personal best in the marathon, a 2:27. I'm still coaching him. The important thing is, he's enjoying it again. He's even got Eileen running a little."

"People hassling him?" In his sorrow, Vince was still protective.

"No. Not much. The road races, you know, that's a very liberal scene. But even in track . . . I think that's one

thing that did change. The guilt that everybody felt . . ."
It was going to be impossible to avoid talking about Billy.
I could feel a terrible strangling non-feeling building up
inside of me. "Anyway, we've got four new gay runners out
in the open now, and a few of the old men are muttering,
but mostly everybody is kind of leaving them alone."

A sad, heavy silence hung in the room.

John tried to break it. "Harlan's being modest. He's
not telling you about his running."

Vince grinned sadly. "You mean, *competing?*"

I laughed a little. I was playing with the baby,
pretending to be fierce and growling a little, and he
was grinning and loving it. "The AAU's got a new rule
now. Pros like me can compete with amateurs in the
masters events. You're looking at a very hot over-40
trackman."

Vince threw back his head with a sad little laugh.

"Don't laugh," I said. "I've got a 4:05 mile. In college
I only ran a 4:04. It's really amazing, the speed that some
of us old guys have got."

Vince leaned forward suddenly and put his hands over
his face, but then took them away again and stared into
the fire.

"The whole thing was my fault," he said.

"What do you mean?" I asked.

"I was a horny idiot back at Oregon, and took off
Jacques' belt in the locker room. If I hadn't done that, the
three of us would probably have drifted apart, and
Billy would be alive, and you'd be here living your peaceful
life."

I stood up. "Vince, would you stop talking about it!"

"I killed Billy," he said. "Christ, I would have stopped
that bullet with my own head, so that the two of you could
still be together."

I was starting to come apart myself. "A lot of people
are guilty. But are we going to call it guilt? I'm guilty. But
is it guilt? If I'd just stuck to my rule about not laying
athletes, Billy might still be alive. But at the time, the

choice seemed very simple. The choice was, was I going to live out the rest of my life without ever having loved a single human being. Is that guilt?"

I stood staring into the fire. The big blackened log lay on the bed of glowing coals, flames rising softly all around it. Suddenly it looked like a human torso to me—Billy's torso in the furnace. I turned away.

Vince got up and came to me, gripping my arm wordlessly. Finally he said, "I'm sorry. I'll shut up."

Betsy was standing in the kitchen door, wiping her wet hands on her apron, her eyes wide and sad. She had overheard us. John was holding the baby, looking down, with little John's hot silky head resting against his tie.

The scene was mercifully ended by the doorbell ringing. Joe and Marian were outside, cheerful and covered with snow. "Whew," said Joe, "six inches already." I could tell from their faces that they sensed we'd probably been having a painful discussion.

But we all managed to start being social and superficial. Betsy put the baby to bed, and we brought the food to the table. Betsy lit the candles. I said the blessing and we sat down. John carved the turkey with skillful grace. We loaded our plates with mashed potatoes, cranberry sauce, asparagus, stuffing. We must have looked like a scene straight out of Norman Rockwell. It was one of those family holidays, and I was alone again.

We stayed up late, talking softly so the baby wouldn't wake. Finally, about one, Joe, Marian and John got up. John was going to spend the night at their house. I had told Vince he could stay with us, so I couldn't very well suggest he go with them now, even if he'd made me sad.

Betsy yawned. "I'm going to bed," she said. "You two talk as long as you want to." She kissed Vince on the cheek, and went to her bedroom.

Vince sat drinking yet another whiskey. He was close to being stoned out. I threw another log on the fire, and sat down in the other wing chair.

"You have separate bedrooms, huh?" he said.

"You didn't really think we're sleeping together," I said, a little offended.

"Sorry," he said. "I keep putting my foot in it. I just can't get over seeing the two of you living together."

"It was a hard decision to make. Billy and I"— impossible to avoid mentioning his name—"planned that insemination thing without thinking through all the human angles. I guess it was pretty naive of us. After the baby came, Betsy was so in love with him, and being such a good mother, that I realized John might be damaged emotionally if I made her give him up. And I was living alone—how was I going to look after him during the day? I didn't want him to grow up with babysitters."

"What you needed was a Frances," said Vince, grinning drunkenly.

"Well, I'm not into queens, as you ought to know," I said, again a little offended. "And Betsy and I had gotten along pretty cooperatively. So we decided it would be best for the baby if she just moved in with me."

Vince was laughing with the soft raunchy laugh I remembered. "The eyebrows went up all over New York. Harlan Brown going *straight*, man . . ."

"Listen, I wouldn't touch her. And she'd probably shoot me if I tried. This place is sexless as a monastery. I worry about that too. John and Frances had a warm and loving sexual relationship that Billy probably sensed even as a baby. I keep thinking . . . I could never love anyone again like I loved Billy, but I ought to have someone around here that I care for in some way . . ."

"Aren't you sleeping with anybody?"

"Oh, when I get horny, I go down to the city for a quickie, like I always did."

"What does Betsy do when she gets horny?"

"Well, I don't know. At the moment she doesn't seem very interested in sex. But she may grow past that, and bring a lover into the house too."

"That'll be something new," said Vince. "A whole new kind of family."

"It's funny," I said, "how I've come full circle. Betsy has taught me a lot of things about the way women can care and give. Her offering to have the child simply floored me. But their caring and giving, and ours, are just two different worlds. Theirs begins where ours leaves off."

Vince was leaning forward, hands clasped between his knees, gazing at the log blazing on the bed of coals. "After Billy died, I suddenly found I wasn't a bisexual any longer. I don't know, maybe it was the hatred and resentment at anything connected with the straight world. Maybe it was a desire to identify myself more with Billy. But I can't respond to women any more. I'm in that three percent hard core now."

"Look," I said, "you have to realize, it's very hard for me to talk about all that."

Vince shook his head, closing his eyes. "You and I are going to talk about Billy. We're going to have it out."

I stood up and was about to walk off, but Vince stood up and grabbed my arm. "You always wondered if I slept with him, didn't you?"

I stood still and stricken. Finally I said, "Vince, please!" My hoarse whisper cracked in the still room.

Vince was gripping my arm painfully. He looked straight into my eyes. "I loved him too. I loved both of you. Deep down, I always had this thing for you, and I wondered if you and Billy might break up someday. And I always knew you had a thing for me too, because you weren't pure like Billy."

I closed my eyes.

"We'd better talk about it," said Vince. "I have to tell you about Billy and me. I know he never told you much because he was so afraid of your jealousy."

I sat back down in the wing chair, numb and trembling a little. Vince sat down on the rug before the fire, one knee drawn up, with his arms clasping it, his coal-black mane falling over his shoulders, the firelight playing in his splendid eyes.

Finally he said, "When I met Billy back in 1970, I'd

been so alone. I was competing with that awful secret inside of me, thinking I was the only gay in track. And then I met this gutty beautiful individual at this high-school invitational, and he wiped me out, and after the race we were talking, and I think he's gay. I just sense it.

"So I invited him to have dinner with me, so I can get him alone. And in the car I just managed to drop my amyl nitrite on the floor. I figure if he isn't gay he won't know what it is. And sure enough, he picks the popper up and gives it back to me, with this little smile on his face that gives him away.

"Well, I just couldn't believe it. And I thought, Wow, man, we're gonna be lovers, there's going to be two of us running at that level of competition, it's going to be an incredible joke on the athletic establishment. So we had dinner and talked the whole night. I was so amazed to meet somebody who was peaceful about the things that were tearing me up inside. So I played up to him, and I said, Billy, I really like you, you're a dream, how about it? And Billy said, Gee, Vince, I like you too, but the thing is, I've got a lover right now, I'm really serious about him. And I said, How's he gonna know, and anyway, we owe it to each other, we're these two track brothers, and a lot of other crap . . ."

Vince suddenly turned his head and looked up at me. "And do you know what he told me?" He put his head on his drawn-up knee, half laughing, half sobbing. "He told me, *I go to bed only with people I love.*"

The house was silent. All I could hear was the sighing of the fire and the ticking of snow against the window-panes. I felt something beginning to crack inside of me. What came out first was laughter. I could just see Vince the great firebreathing Scorpio stud running smack up against Billy's Virgo firmness, and it struck me as funny. Vince had Billy's way of phrasing things just right.

And suddenly Billy was there in front of me, alive and real.

Vince had looked back at the fire. "So I decided—you

know me, Harlan—as far as I'm concerned, lovers are a dime a dozen. A friend like Billy was worth a hundred lovers. The main thing was, I didn't feel alone any more. After the meet, I went and visited him and his dad in San Francisco. And one night we lost our minds and went into a tattoo parlor and had our sun signs put on. We'd decided that we'd face our destinies bravely . . ."

I had my hands over my face. I was making strange animal-like noises. Was this what crying was like? Yes, definitely, there were hot tears running out of my eyes.

Vince got up on his knees, put his arms around me and held me silently. I cried on his shoulder, both my hands clenched in his jacket. He kissed and fondled my bursting head, and pressed me against his chest. My body was so racked with spasms that the muscles felt ready to tear loose from the bones. If this was crying, I was grateful to have been spared other crying bouts back through the years.

After a while I felt Vince's body begin to shake, and realized that he was crying too. Vince was a silent crier— I couldn't hear anything. But I felt his face, and it was as wet as mine. When we'd both quieted down, Vince told me everything about Billy's life, from his senior year in high school through his meeting me. That whole lost era of Billy's life, that I'd been so afraid to know in detail, opened up to my eyes. I saw him in a thousand anecdotes, and not once did Vince tell me anything that was not consistent with the picture I already had of him. Slowly the image of Billy laying dead on the track in Montréal began to fade, and I could see him warm and living again, running with his long soft stride, his hair lifting in the sunshine.

The dawn light was showing at the windows. First an aching gray, then a tender red light. The snow had stopped. Outside the landscape was smothered in white, the tree limbs hanging heavy, the bushes bent over. I made Vince some coffee, to help him sober up, and myself a cup of tea. Betsy came into the kitchen to give the baby his early morning feeding, and said, "Are you guys still up?" We all sat around the kitchen table. The cups clinked on the saucers, and the baby sucked greedily at Betsy's breast.

"Harlan, where did you scatter his ashes?" Vince asked.

"Up there in the woods."

"If you don't mind, I'd like to go up there."

So we put on warm clothes and overshoes and went out. As we started up the main trail, the trees and bushes were bent into a pure tracery. They were sheltered against the spring, their buds waiting. The ferns and wildflowers had already made their new growth, and were waiting under the snow. The sun was already so bright that we squinted—we should have worn dark glasses. We crossed the track of a rabbit that had come out from his warm hole under the snow and was off somewhere. The birds were stirring too—we could hear the soft winter whistles of the titmice and the song sparrows as they looked for food.

A deep peace was coming over me, and a sweet release. On that path I could remember Billy without pain, remember him loping along hardly leaving a spikemark on the earth, looking over his shoulder to say, "Seven minutes."

When we turned off onto the side trail, we had to push our way through the snowy brambles, snagging our pants. The brush seemed to have grown thicker here, as if to discourage anyone from coming this way again.

Finally we reached the top of the slope, and looked down.

The little clearing was virgin white. All around it, the mountain laurel was bent under the snow. The laurel had dropped its seeds, and the dried-up clusters of seed cases had withered away. I couldn't see walking on down there, knocking the snow from those stately bushes and leaving our tracks everywhere, so I made a sign to Vince that we would go no further. Even from where we were, we could hear the little stream noising as it fell from the ledge into its small pool.

We stood silent, looking down the slope. I leaned

against a tulip tree, and Vince walked around a little unsteadily, smoking a cigarette. Now and then our eyes met, with a direct open look—that look that acknowledges the imminence of a sexual relationship, and, in our case, that look that finally acknowledged the deep affection we had always felt for each other.

Billy lived again in that look.

EPILOGUE

I am out on the track under the smoky lights, and I feel the noise of the crowd, and all the eyes on me.

It is February 11, 1978. The event is the mile final in the AAU masters championship at Madison Square Garden in New York. I have had to put my body out here on the track again—to feel what Billy felt, to honor his memory with my own pain and sweat.

There are eleven of us warming up, already stripped to shorts and singlets. We are all over forty, all wiry mature men with varying degrees of baldness and gray hair. But, in contrast to our faces, our hard glistening bodies look strangely young. We are among the finest-looking old men in the world, no doubt about it. We have found the fountain of youth. I feel young as I jog around. I am even a little shaggy, with just a few gray hairs in my longish hair and my new beard.

In these last minutes before the race, we are all completing our psych job on ourselves and on each other. Each is making out that he is cool and confident, though he might secretly be sick to his stomach with nerves. I am full of nervous energy, but not upset. This is because I know that I am psyching them. They are more worried about getting beaten by me than I am worried at getting beaten by them.

The promoters have packed the Garden to the last seat. I am aware that I am the box-office attraction this evening, the prime bait of a little genteel Roman circus. Twenty thousand people are going to watch ten straight middle-aged Christians try to eat one gay middle-aged lion.

"Kill 'em, Harlan!"

"Go, Gary, burn that queer bastard!"

Through my concentration I hear the voices. I am still thinking about tactics. I have drawn Lane 1, which is a bad place to be. Everything will depend on the pace. If they go out slow, and I don't get boxed in, I might try to run away. But I have a feeling that they will go out very fast, and that there might be blood all over the track, and a new American record.

I can feel a certain hostility, from the crowd and from a few of the other runners. But I also feel a lot of support. This is a big advantage I have over the others: New York is my home territory, and the gays have flooded into the arena to back me. My entire team is up there in the stands, plus a couple busloads of Prescott students and faculty. John Sive is there with Steve Goodnight and the Angel. Jacques and his wife are there. Betsy is there with the baby, sitting by John. Vince is there.

I pause for a moment to retie my shoe.

One of the runners who is friendly, forty-one-year-old Mike Branch, jogs by and claps me on my tattoo. "The old lion finally grew a mane," he said.

"Yeah," I said, clapping him back. "About time."

I have been pointing toward this meet all winter. Because of my coaching and teaching obligations, I could get to only a few meets, so I was reduced to sharpening myself mostly in workouts. I know so much more about training now than when I was in college. And I learned so much from Billy. He taught me as much as I did him. To my delight I found myself able to recapture the promise that got wasted by circumstances when I was young. The lifetime of taking care of my body finally paid off.

And I have a mental edge that I have been nourishing for weeks. It is a peace, and no one will ever rob me of this peace again. It is Billy, his living memory inside of me. His psych was yoga, and mine is him. He runs inside of me, with that effortlessness and that total fearlessness of pain. In each race, I recreate that image of him in my mind, and it works.

To kill him now, they will have to kill me.

As we jog to the line, I am dimly aware of the rising crescendo of cheers and boos from the crowd.

We are bent at the line. My tattooed shoulder brushes the arm of the man in Lane 2. The old lion is fulfilling his destiny. These days I constantly have a feeling of coming full circle. God has been good. For every bitter cup He gave me to drink, He has later given me a sweeter one.

The gun fires, and we roll off the line.

As we sprint down the straight, everybody nips to the inside. Just as I feared, I am neatly boxed in. They'll keep me in this box, impotent, as long as they can. And it's a scorching pace. The others seem to feel that this is a 60-yard dash.

Now if I were Billy, I'd be going out of my mind in this box. But I'm a kicker, and I like running in the pack till my moment comes. I'm not afraid of their elbows and spikes, and I know how to use my own.

With the box and the crazy pace, I make my final decision on tactics. I decide to gamble. If I lose the gamble, it won't be a public loss of masculinity, because my enemies are sure I don't have any anyway and my friends will still love me.

I decide to stay there in the box and let them carry the pace and carry me along. If I try to maneuver out of the box, dropping back or cutting through, I might lose time and/or foul somebody. I know they can't hold this pace, and sometime in the third quarter they'll start dying and dropping off. The field will open up, and I'll be out of the box the easy way.

So we go through the first quarter like it is the Kentucky Derby and I am walled up in fourth place, just concentrating on staying loose and not getting my spikes tangled with anybody else's. But I am hooked onto the front-runners and they feel it. I am pushing them, making them set themselves up for my kill.

In the turn the man next to me leans on me, and I barely miss putting my foot off the track and breaking stride. It's a nervous moment, but I throw him off. We hit the 440 at 61.2 seconds, which is not bad for a bunch of invalids. The Garden is a well of noise—focused as I am on the race, I can feel it. There's that mass of people out there yelling for me.

As we whip through the second quarter, I am running easily, teeth gritted. I am into Billy's controlled motion, with that grim joy pushing me, that sweet angry peace. I am five pounds lighter than I ever was, around 150, and feel so light.

One man has moved up on the outside, putting me into fifth place, but we are still tightly bunched at the front. I'm not worried. Any time now that pace is going to start tearing the field apart. We are jostling and bumping shoulders, and somebody elbows me, and I hold him off. Somebody's going to get disqualified for sure. Maybe me. Oh well. Worse things have happened to me.

At the half-mile, we are at 2:02. This pace is insanity. We've all lost our heads. One of the four ahead of me is already letting go. Slowly he drifts back past me and the man beside me, and I am fourth again. Back behind me, there are two big kickers. I know the pace must be getting to them too, because I am now feeling it myself. Sometime in the next minute, all three of us are going to make our move, and it'll be a question of who is deader than who.

Death is setting in now. The third quarter is going to be a shade slower. We're dragging a little, paying the price. I'm feeling just a little heavy, but I tell myself that I'm feeling light and effortless.

As we're coming toward the three-quarter mark, the man beside me lets go and drops back, opening up my right side. Immediately I shift out in the clear. I'm dangerous. As we go into the last quarter, the old lion is opening up into his killing sprint.

The race breaks wide open. The other two kickers are blasting toward the front too. But I'm in front of them. Through the effort and the final rush of adrenaline, I can feel the hysteria of the crowd. They're screaming for everybody to kill everybody else. But the only voices I hear are "Smoke 'em Harlan!" "Hang in there, Harlan!"

I am an animal now, Billy the animal. I am running all out, the way Billy taught me can be done. I am not afraid to hang out my soul and my blood and my veins and my lungs and my balls. I kill off the third man, then the second.

Then I surge past the first man, and I'm out in front. I'm free.

About a hundred yards to go. We are practically sprinting. I can hear the other two kickers hauling me down. I have control enough that I don't turn my head to look, but I feel them hooked on me. I'm in oxygen debt. I'm hurting. My shoulders are heavy. My body and soul hurt. I am putting out everything, Billy Sive in Montréal in the last seconds of the 5,000. If you have to die, it's a good moment, when you're at that blazing peak of existence.

One kicker is tightening up and he lets go. The other is at my shoulder. We peel out of the last turn. The Garden is going wild. The tape is dimly visible off down the straight. I am dead. I have reached bottom. But the other kicker is dead too. He stays on my shoulder and can't pass me. I am dead but alive. Nobody is going to kill me.

My fainting body manages to continue hurtling down the straight. My legs are still making giant strides, but I have the feeling that they're folding under me. The roaring in my ears is both the crowd and the dizziness. I am tightening up and sick. My eyes are blurring. The two of us are plunging at the tape, diving into it as if it were water.

With a last effort—I don't know from where I bring it up—I lean forward, flinging up my arms. The tape breaks across my breast.

It takes a minute to recover. That last quarter was 59.3 seconds. The time is 4:03, just off the record of 4:02.5.

I walk around in circles and gag a little, and finally I feel human again. My students are jumping up and down. A few gays and a few of my team have jumped down onto the track. A strange gay hugs me and gets my sweat stained on his expensive suede. I wonder if they will disqualify me. Miracle of miracles, they disqualify one of the other guys.

With some of my team jogging around me, I take a victory lap, waving at the crowd with both hands. Maybe it's my imagination, but the whole place seems to be applauding. There's a lump in my throat. It all comes so many years late, but it's good anyway.

Finally I'm back in my warmups, off the track, surrounded by people. Jacques pounds me happily on the back. Vince makes his way through the crowd and embraces me. He and Jacques look at each other and smile for the past.

I still have this lump in my throat.

The CBS-TV sports interviewer shoves his microphone at me. The camera crews are there. "How does it feel to come so close to an American record at your age, Harlan?"

"It feels good," I say. "I have to thank the others. They nearly handed it to me with that early pace. Maybe next time I'll break it."

"Do you think there's going to be a sub-four-minute masters mile one of these days?"

"I think so. I don't know who, but somebody will go under. The kids, meanwhile, are going to be breaking 3:50, so . . ."

"You think you can break 4?"

"Who knows? Anyway, I can only compete and train as much as my obligations to my own team permit. We'll see. Let's say that I'm back on the track with a lot of motivation, and that I plan to stay around as long as my legs are in one piece."

With the interview over, Betsy comes up quietly and puts the baby in my arms. He wiggles against my chest, a mite of life but amazingly strong, now five months old. With his small fists clenched, he gazes around at the athletes, the bright lights, the smoky arena, with his wise, dopey Virgo eyes. He is unafraid, dignified.

As I look down at him, I think that he already knows what kind of race he's in. He knows that it is going to take everything he has to stay up in front, to run free.

About This Book

*T*he *Front Runner's* 20th anniversary edition was created "hands on" with computer print technology. The text of the original Morrow hardcover was run through a scanner using an OCR program, then cleaned up and completely redesigned on the Mac IIx of Barbara Brown Desktop Publishing, using Aldus PageMaker.

Fonts: Century Schoolbook and Radiant. Schoolbook was chosen because its lean, traditional look seemed well-suited to carry the "voice" of narrator Harlan Brown.

Jacket art and halftone illustrations were created by Laguna Beach artist Jay Fraley, on a Macintosh 8500. He used the Photoshop program to manipulate his photograph of the broken glasses mentioned in the book.

P.N.W.

ALSO IN PRINT FROM WILDCAT PRESS

The Front Runner — **20th Anniversary Limited Edition**
By Patricia Nell Warren
Collectors will be glad to hear that this classic, first published in 1974, is available in a beautiful 20th-anniversary leatherbound limited edition, signed and numbered by the author.
ISBN 0-9641099-1-3 .... $155.00 net

The Fancy Dancer — (Trade Paperback - Fiction)
By Patricia Nell Warren
This 1976 bestseller was one of the first novels to portray with unflinching honesty a Catholic priest's struggle with homosexuality. The story, set in a small conservative Western town, has stayed a steady backlist seller with Bantam and Plume. We are proud to bring it out in our own quality tradeback.
ISBN 0-9641099-7-2 .... $14.95

Direct Mail

We welcome business from individuals who want to buy books direct. At your request, any book will be custom autographed . . . just tell us exactly what you want written. Call us for information on prices, postage and handling.

Bookstores

Buy from us direct and get discounts as well as the kind of small-press customer service that you'll appreciate. We are dedicated to the survival of the independent bookstore. And we also appreciate the chains who know that books about gay life sell well in the mainstream. Our books have proven strong in steady sales and backlist, with low returns. We offer customized PR support on developing book-signing events.

Wildcat Press
8306 Wilshire Blvd., Box 8306
Beverly Hills, CA 90211
323-966-2466 • E-Mail: wildcatpress@aol.com
Web page: http://www.wildcatpress.com